FLASHPOINT

FLASHPOINT

AN FBI THRILLER

CATHERINE COULTER

WM

WILLIAM MORROW
An Imprint of HarperCollinsPublishers

FLASHPOINT. Copyright © 2024 by Catherine Coulter. All rights reserved. Printed in the United States of America. No part of this book may be used or reproduced in any manner whatsoever without written permission except in the case of brief quotations embodied in critical articles and reviews. For information, address HarperCollins Publishers, 195 Broadway, New York, NY 10007.

HarperCollins books may be purchased for educational, business, or sales promotional use. For information, please email the Special Markets Department at SPsales@harpercollins.com.

FIRST EDITION

Designed by Michele Cameron

Library of Congress Cataloging-in-Publication Data has been applied for.

ISBN 978-0-06-328309-1

24 25 26 27 28 LBC 5 4 3 2 1

TO THE MAN, THE EDITOR, THE LEGEND—THANK YOU, ANTON

—CATHERINE

FLASHPOINT

Chapter One

London
Eaton Square, Belgravia
MONDAY

The rain came on suddenly. In an instant, heavy rain clouds darkened the afternoon sky to a dingy gray. Like every Londoner, Elizabeth carried a brolly with her, just as she always carried her current novel and lipstick. She pressed the release with one hand without dislodging her grocer's bag with its cargo of frozen cheese pizza, crisps, hummus, and the carrots she'd bought to still her mother's voice in her head. And a bundle of yellow tulips, her favorite. She didn't fumble, too much practice.

She was alone in the street. She looked over at Eaton Square Park just opposite and saw a young couple, oblivious to the rain, their heads together, holding hands, a single large black brolly over their heads. Elizabeth loved the park, the trees still late-winter bare, but in another three months, the leaves would be unfurled in all their glory. She loved her home on Eaton Square—well, really, her family's London home for five generations. Her father had told her once he wanted it to be hers and her younger brother Tommy's equally, but for now it was hers alone since, justifiably, her father had finally given up on his son.

Elizabeth had already started putting her stamp on it, her first purchase a lesser-known impressionist painting by Pissarro.

She'd hung it in a place of honor over the neoclassical fireplace in the sitting room.

She quickened her steps. She had to change clothes for her dinner with the Honorable Giles Beresford Arlington, second son of the Earl of Clode, an old friend and a man with a mission. He was leaving tomorrow on his long-planned voyage to Greenland, sailing a ship he'd replicated, flying a huge red-and-white-striped sail. Except for the video cameras on board to record his passage, it was in all respects like a Viking ship from a thousand years ago. He and his crew would sail as the Vikings did, eat only what they ate. She'd teased him about whether his furs would have zippers. Should she dress like a Viking woman, ask for a slab of raw codfish at dinner? Giles would be amused, maybe.

She heard a car engine, loud, louder, saw a black Aston Martin barrel around the corner going too fast. At the last minute, it jumped the curb, aimed right at her. Elizabeth leaped backward and landed in a yew bush in front of the Todd-Smithsons' doorway. The Aston Martin roared past her so close, she felt the heat of the engine on her face. It clipped one of the Todd-Smithsons' decorative pillars, veered back onto the road, and sped off, barely missing a rubbish bin. The couple in the park yelled and came running.

The boy covered Elizabeth with his brolly as the girl helped her up. She was young, all English peaches and cream, a delicate ring in her nose and another at the corner of her left eyebrow. "That idiot! Are you all right? Do you want to go to casualty?"

Elizabeth's heart was kettledrumming, nausea rising in her throat. She swallowed bile and managed to whisper, "No, I don't need to go to hospital. I'm fine, he didn't hit me."

"That guy was a nutter or stoned out of his mind," the boy said, craning his neck to see if the Aston Martin was still in sight, but of course it wasn't. He was tall and good looking, his hair in short dreads dyed a fire-hot red. He handed the girl the brolly and gathered up Elizabeth's groceries. He started to give her the grocer's bag when he saw how wobbly she was and settled it on his arm. He said, "Maybe the asswipe was stoned, but it seemed to me like he wanted to hit you, I mean he headed right for you. I know that Aston Martin model, it's a couple of years old, but sorry, I didn't get the number plate. I think you should call the police."

She nodded numbly. "Could you give me your names and mobile numbers? Maybe the police will find them." Was he right, was it on purpose? No, that was impossible, it didn't make sense someone would want to run her down with an Aston Martin in the middle of the day. She hadn't pissed off anyone she could think of, certainly not enough to warrant a death run. *Not true, not true. You nearly died last year with hundreds more at St. Paul's, all because of Samir Basara.* But it couldn't be him: Samir was dead, long dead.

Her hands were shaking so badly she couldn't enter their information on her mobile, so the girl, Mandy, did it for her. They walked her to her home, only six doors away, the last house on the crescent, three stories of stately blazing white. Elizabeth assured them again she was fine, thanked them again for being there to help her, slipped inside, and slid the dead bolt home. She leaned back against the door, her heart still pounding so hard she wondered it didn't burst out of her chest. She felt lightheaded, closed her eyes.

She took deep, slow breaths to get hold of herself. She repeated over and over, *I'm alive, I'm alive.* Finally, her heart slowed and she felt calm enough to think. Even the boy, Thomas Dauber, had agreed whoever was driving the Aston Martin could have been drunk or taking drugs. It was common enough. She'd seen her younger brother, Tommy, flying high on cocaine and driving like a maniac, didn't matter if there was anyone around him, in a car or walking.

Elizabeth realized she'd gotten a glimpse of the driver, but only for a second, long enough to see his dark glasses, a black watch cap pulled down low, and yes—there'd been another man next to him she'd barely seen. The driver had seemed young, maybe about Tommy's age, and just as out of control, convinced he was immortal.

Elizabeth carried her grocery bag into her newly remodeled kitchen—a present from her mother—pleased she wasn't weaving around any longer. She eyed the crushed pizza box. Who cared? She shoved it into the freezer. The tulips were only a bit bunged up. Slowly, with great concentration, she put them in a Waterford vase that had belonged to her great-grandmother Maude and added water.

Suddenly her hands were shaking again so hard she nearly dropped the vase. She set it carefully on her kitchen table, closed her eyes. *You're fine. Breathe. Maybe the men in the Aston Martin were on drugs, maybe they were mad, maybe they tried to hit you for a lark. So many explanations to choose from.*

Yet again, she wondered if there was anyone who could possibly hate her enough to try to kill her. Yet again, no face came to mind. She thought of Tommy's drug dealer, Carlos— yes, she knew his name, knew he hailed from a small town in Spain—but that didn't make sense; she was the one who always made good on whatever her brother owed when he couldn't pay. No reason Carlos would want to kill his golden goose. Half of what she'd earned from her last sale of a painting went to Carlos. She sighed. No, she wouldn't think yet again about how to stop being Tommy's enabler, not now.

Elizabeth took two aspirin, carried a bottle of chardonnay to the sitting room, and stretched out on the eighteenth-century brocade sofa, next on her list to be re-covered. She was calmer, in control now, but aches and pains in her back and shoulders started to broadcast. She drank two glasses of chardonnay and sank back against the sofa pillows. The wine helped a bit, until what came crashing back into her mind full blown wasn't the Aston Martin coming straight at her, it was the horror of her near death a year ago at St. Paul's, the man dressed like an old woman who'd hidden packets of C-4 throughout the church. She'd never forget his name as long as she lived—Bahar Zain. He was a terrorist, taking orders from Dr. Samir Basara, a handsome, smart, and don't forget charming Algerian and a renowned professor at the London School of Economics. And she'd slept with Samir, flaunted him in front of her appalled father. In the end she'd realized the face he showed to both her and the world was only a front. He'd used her, sent her to her death. Her father hadn't said a word when it was over, even when the newspapers had hounded her and her family for weeks about her affair with him, a man who'd been perfectly willing to murder her in St. Paul's along with hundreds of others. Her mother hadn't chided her either, ah, but she couldn't hide the tears or avoid the looks. As for Tommy, bless his heart, he'd hugged her and laughed and whispered in her ear, "Obviously only outdoor weddings for you from now on."

She'd had nightmares, still did occasionally, of the famous St. Paul's dome crashing down on her, her friends, her family, and she'd jerk awake, heaving, sweat soaked, the stark terror still as vivid as that day. No one would have survived. No one. If Officer John Eiserly of MI5 hadn't seen what Bahar had done on the security cameras, there wouldn't have been any night-mares, she'd be dead. Of course, Samir had been safe in his penthouse flat, waiting to see the smoke rise from St. Paul's in the distance above London.

Did Samir know you cashed out his expensive gifts to you to pay Tommy's drug dealer, Carlos? Yes, Samir had to know, it probably amused him. Ah, but the cachet it earned him to squire around a blond English aristocrat, everyone knowing they were sleeping together and she reveling in the knowledge that her stiff-necked father, the Earl of Camden, was appalled. She remembered clearly one night Samir had laid his hand on her belly and remarked in a lazy voice, "How perfectly white you are, Elizabeth, inside and out." He'd kissed her belly, caressed her, and she'd forgotten to ask him what he'd meant.

Whenever that day invaded her mind with soul-deadening horror, she still felt a mixture of terror and shame she couldn't shake, even after nearly a year. Who it was exactly Samir Basara had targeted to assassinate that day in St. Paul's was never discovered.

The only good thing to come out of that horror was Ellie Colstrap, the bride, had decided not to marry Johnny Bridgeton, as addicted to gambling as her own brother was to drugs. When Johnny was told what nearly happened that day, he'd blamed Ellie's father for insisting the wedding take place at St. Paul's. At least it was good riddance to that arse.

What should she do? Call the police after all? No, they'd agree the guy was probably drunk, and how would they even prove that, if they found him?

She dialed Tommy, asked him if he'd done anything to piss someone off, owed anyone money he hadn't told her about. He was flying high on cocaine and, happy as usual, claimed his dealer was always happy to see him, so what was the problem, sis? He remembered to ask her for money.

He was all of twenty-eight years old and would be living in a ditch if not for her, their father having finally disowned him nearly a year ago. But he was her little brother. She'd protected him all her life. What could she do to keep him safe, since he refused treatment? Keep rescuing him until he overdosed? Until his body simply gave out? She drank a third glass of wine and fell asleep on ancestor Maude's rock-hard sofa.

She jerked awake at the loud hammering of the lion's-head knocker on her front door. She started to open the door, thought of the Aston Martin swerving toward her, and looked through the peephole. She'd expected to see Viking-lover Giles, but she saw no one. She called out, "Tell me who's there or I'll call the police." She waited, heard nothing, and pulled the entry hall drapery aside to look outside. The night was perfectly black, no stars to see through the still-pounding rain. She heard a car rev and drive away. She called Giles on her mobile and apologized, claimed a migraine, and wished him luck on his sail to Greenland dressed in bearskins. She wondered if he'd take a toothbrush.

Chapter Two

The next morning, Elizabeth woke up stiff from sleeping on Maude's horsehair-stuffed sofa. Her back and shoulders ached from her crash into the yew bush, but her brain was sharp and clear. She showered and dressed, ate scrambled eggs, and drank two cups of coffee.

Why hadn't the git who'd almost hit her at least cared enough to stop, make sure she was all right, apologize, maybe? If the git had lost control of his car.

Put it aside, lock it away. Today she was going to work.

Elizabeth took a third cup of coffee to the sprawling second-floor office on the west side of her house she'd turned into her studio. She'd picked that room because the floor-to-ceiling bow windows flooded the room with natural light after the heavy rain that had fallen throughout the night. She lifted the white sheet off the nearly finished portrait of her mother, to be her birthday present in August. She stood back, studied brush-strokes, light and shadows, her mother's beautiful face, and sighed. Her mother rarely smiled anymore because of Tommy and because of her husband's endless infidelities.

Elizabeth was painting the portrait from a photo of her mother taken soon after she'd married her father, the newly minted tenth Earl of Camden, before he'd dried up her smile, her joy in her new life. In the photo, twenty-four-year-old Lady Millicent Palmer was running down the long, graveled drive toward her new home, Darlington Hall, just to the east of Brighton, set high on a grassy hill looking out to the Channel. She was laughing wildly, her blond hair streaming out behind her, shining beneath a bright sun. She looked ethereal, a fairy queen come to life. Was she running to meet her new husband, Elizabeth's father?

Maybe the portrait would make a difference, remind her mother of the happiness she'd felt when they were first married. Just maybe she'd speak to her husband about those early years. Elizabeth sighed. She loved her father, commiserated and argued with him about the never-ending problems with Tommy. She wondered if he'd ever stop taking on mistresses and working all hours at his precious bank long enough to recognize he had a wife who needed him. Elizabeth knew he loved her, cared about her, but—there was always a *but* with her father. How would her father react to her painting of his bride? Would it possibly make a difference to him?

It was nine o'clock, the sun in and out of dark clouds. The rain had stopped, always a blessed event in England, but it was still cold. Alas, the central heating system had the hiccups, roasting her one minute, freezing her the next. At least she'd finally gotten a repairman to agree to come that afternoon.

Her workroom grew uncomfortably cold, so she lit the fire in the seventeenth-century Carrara marble fireplace. She managed a minuscule flame, nursed it until the flames sprang up. She got to her feet, rubbed her hands on her jeans. She shoved a chair close to the fireplace, pulled a blanket around herself, and snuggled in. She'd get back to work as soon as the repairman performed his magic. If he showed up, another of life's uncertainties. Elizabeth thought how nice it would be to fly out of Heathrow and park her bikinied butt on a beach in Majorca, a rum punch in her hand, the bright Mediterranean sun on her face.

The lion's-head knocker sounded.

She checked her watch, frowned. It couldn't be the repairman, it was far too early.

The knocker sounded again, twice, louder this time.

Her heart picked up. Was it the man who'd nearly hit her yesterday? Had he found out where she lived?

It couldn't be Giles; he'd texted her he was nearly ready to leave for Ireland, where he'd get prepped to row down the River Liffey and raise his sails in the Irish Sea and into the Atlantic for his voyage to Greenland with his two best mates. All of them were nutters in her opinion.

Was it one of her friends? No, her friends worked, and they'd have called her first, not showed up unannounced at her door. Tommy, come to get money? Yes, it could be Tommy, but he'd just unlock the front door with his key. She walked slowly to the thick black-lacquered mahogany front door, original to the house. She looked through the peephole her mother had insisted on installing when Elizabeth moved in. Oddly, she saw a black brolly, even though it wasn't raining.

"Who is it?"

A man's voice called out, "A delivery for Elizabeth Palmer."

Did he have a slight accent? "Leave it next to the front door, please."

"Madame, I need a signature."

Yes, there was an accent, but not unusual given it was London. Still, no way was she going to open the door. "Sorry, I'm not dressed. You'll have to come back."

The door knocker sounded again.

"Please open the door. I cannot leave the package without your signature."

"Raise the package so I can see it."

She heard the low voices of two men, and a noise, like someone bumping against her flower urn beside the front door. She pressed her face to the door. Were they whispering or was it the rising wind?

Two loud shots rang out. The door shook from the impact of the bullets, but they didn't penetrate the thick old door. Elizabeth slammed the dead bolt home and backed away. She pulled her mobile out of her jeans pocket, dialed 999 as she ran from the door to her kitchen, and jerked her prized butcher knife from its block.

She heard another bullet hit the door lock. How long before it gave?

"What is your emergency?"

"My name is Elizabeth Palmer. Two men are at my house, shooting at the lock on my front door." She managed to get out her address. "The dead bolt's holding, but I don't know for how long."

"Hide, NOW. Police are on the way."

Hide where? Behind a sofa? In a closet? The house was large, but they'd find her eventually, and then what could she do? They had guns, she had a knife. She heard the rain suddenly start up again, falling so hard she could barely make out the gate in her backyard that led to her small Ford Fiesta and the rubbish bins.

Elizabeth saw movement through the whipping rain outside the rear door. She ran to the door, flipped the dead bolt. But this door was new and not nearly as sturdy. A man's gloved hand broke the narrow window high up on the door and reached for the dead bolt, but he couldn't reach it, the window was too far up. She didn't wait, she stabbed the knife deep into the back of his hand, jerked it out. He yelled out, quickly pulled his gloved hand back.

She felt giddy and sick to her stomach as she bent low and ran back toward the front door. Her heart nearly stopped— booted feet were kicking the door right below the knocker, and it shuddered. Would the dead bolt hold? How long would the door itself hold before it sheared away from its hinges? Elizabeth raced up the stairs, ran down the hall into her bedroom.

She slammed the door, locked it. Not enough, not enough. She dragged a heavy armchair in front of the door and ran to the side window. She pulled the thick drapery aside, unlatched the window, and squeezed through it onto a skinny balcony. She reached in, jerked the drapery closed, praying it would buy her time. A full-leafed ancient live oak snuggled up against the side of the house, there only because, thankfully, her house was the last in the colonnaded crescent.

She drew a deep breath and jumped onto the closest branch thick enough to hold her. The rain was so heavy now it sheeted through the thick leaves, soaking her in an instant. She swiped her hair out of her face, slowly pulled herself along the branch until she was plastered against the trunk. She began a slow descent, one branch at a time. Even if they realized she'd gone out the window, she hoped the thick foliage would cover her enough that they wouldn't see her. She hugged the last branch, nearly six feet from the ground, and waited. In the next minute, she heard a police siren and jumped to the ground. She slipped forward along the side of her house and saw three police officers already banging on her front door. She saw no sign of the men who'd shot and kicked at her door. They must have run when they heard the police siren.

She raced out toward them. A woman officer caught her, and Elizabeth clutched her, gulping in huge breaths. "Two men tried to break in and kill me." She fell against the woman's shoulder.

"It's over now, you're all right," the woman said. "Let's go inside out of this cursed rain. We need to search the house. Then you can tell us what happened."

Elizabeth fetched her key from beneath an azalea bush and opened both locks on the battered door. The woman officer walked her to the kitchen and sat her at the table. Soon Elizabeth had a cup of hot tea in front of her. "I'm Officer Beresford.

Come on now, Ms. Palmer, take a sip." Elizabeth did, and it felt wonderful.

The two male officers came back into the kitchen, shook their heads at Officer Beresford.

Beresford, who was evidently in charge, said to Elizabeth, "Now, talk to me, Ms. Palmer. Do you know who these men are who came to your house? Why do you think they wanted to kill you?"

Over her second cup of tea, Elizabeth finished telling them what had happened yesterday. She told them about Basara and St. Paul's.

Officer Beresford said, "So you were at St. Paul's last year?"

"Yes."

Beresford looked thoughtful, then she said, "You're cold. You need to change. Then we're taking you to see our inspector at Scotland Yard."

When Officer Beresford mentioned Basara's name to Inspector Dobbs, the game changed.

Chapter Three

Deputy Director John Eiserly of the Joint Terrorism Analysis Centre pushed a thumb drive into his computer and read through his embedded officer's encrypted reports on the new imam at the South London Mosque, Ali Ahmad Said. His officer, Khaled Aziz, was a perfect choice to go undercover. He and the new imam were both young, both Syrian, Khaled from Aleppo and Ali Ahmad Said from Ar Raqqah. While Khaled's family were traditional middle-class Muslims living in York, the young imam's family were wealthy and Westernized, and lived in Knightsbridge. The differences in their backgrounds fed nicely into Khaled's legend. John read: *The new imam, Ali Ahmad Said, is twenty-eight, educated at Cambridge. Father owns Closys International Bank, two high-end car dealerships in Berkeley Square and Piccadilly, and two successful restaurants, one in Notting Hill, the other near Covent Garden. His sister, Adara, is twenty-four, a graduate of Oxford, reading Middle Eastern Studies. All are English citizens. The young imam is vastly different from the former imam, Hädi ibn Mirza, both in temperament and background.*

John paused a moment, thought about the old firebrand imam who'd actively recruited young men to radical Islam and worked hand in glove with Samir Basara, the man who'd tried to bomb St. Paul's. The old imam was jailed in Belmarsh, or Hellmarsh as it was called by its inmates, the high-security prison in southeast London. John had arranged for him to spend the rest of his life there. He wanted to keep the old imam close enough to monitor his visitors.

He continued reading Khaled's report: *I have attended the imam's services, met with him privately on two occasions. He presents himself as devout and kind, quotes the Koran fluently to make a point. He is soft spoken, logical and pragmatic, his Arabic as fluent as his English. I have heard no hate speech from him, no calls to jihad. I've heard rumblings of terrorist sympathizers but seen no such activity within the mosque since the old imam went to prison. But I would not trust this polished hypocrite to buy me a cinema ticket.*

John sat back in his chair, closed his eyes, and reflected. Khaled had great instincts, a sharp mind. John had already known the background of the new imam and knew it was rumored the old imam had had a hand in picking him.

John read his encrypted reply to him and their exchanges: *No sightings of any of the jihadists who worked with the old imam or with Samir Basara?*

None yet. Getting closer to the inner circle, waiting for the imam to ask me in.

Do not take unnecessary risks.

John ejected the thumb drive and slid it into a folder on his desk. He looked at the photos of his wife, Mary Ann, and of his daughter, Cici, who was walking now and banging her tiny fists if her spaghetti didn't magically appear. He'd studied

Khaled's reports again because Lady Elizabeth Palmer was due to see him any minute, sent to him by Superintendent Hillary Morgan of Scotland Yard. He remembered that day at St. Paul's with perfect clarity, knew he'd never forget it, imagined occasionally picturing it on his deathbed. It was only by chance he'd seen his wife and baby at St. Paul's on a security camera, sitting next to a man disguised as an old woman, the man who'd planted the bombs, Samir Basara's henchman, Bahar Zain. He shuddered, thanked God. He'd almost lost them both that day.

His junior associate, Jenny Snow, knocked lightly on his open door. "Deputy Director, Lady Elizabeth Palmer is here." She paused a moment, then, "She looks wrung out."

John had been waiting for her after the phone call from Superintendent Morgan. Morgan had told him only that Lady Elizabeth had nearly been killed by two unknown men. He wanted John to hear Lady Elizabeth out without any preconceived ideas. Of course, the new imam sprang immediately to mind, but why would he want her killed? She'd nearly been a victim herself, hadn't done anything against them. He'd hardly spoken with Lady Elizabeth since the day he'd told her himself it was her lover, Basara, who'd orchestrated the near destruction of St. Paul's. He'd liked her, found her intelligent and helpful once she'd calmed. She'd helped him and his team dissect Samir Basara's life.

"Mrs. Snow, please ask her to come in."

John rose as Lady Elizabeth walked into his office. He'd forgotten how beautiful she was. Tall and slender, her blond hair worn down and longer now, held off her face with two gold clips, all curls and waves. Small diamond studs gleamed in her ears. Her eyes were a sort of hazel and framed by lashes darker than her hair. She was dressed in black pants, low-heeled black boots, a white silk blouse, and a boxy dark green jacket. She looked, to his mind, like the aristocrat she was. He studied her face. Jenny was right, she looked wrung out.

He came around his desk, shook her hand. "Lady Elizabeth, I am pleased to see you."

"Deputy Director Eiserly," she said in her marvelous clipped accent, worthy of the BBC. "Believe me, I'm pleased to see you as well. I believe Superintendent Morgan was relieved he could foist me off on you."

John smiled because it was quite true and pulled out a chair for her. "Please sit down and tell me what has happened."

Haunted eyes stared at him as she sat down in front of his desk. She said simply, "Two men tried to run me down yesterday and tried to kill me again this morning at my house." Elizabeth had repeated what happened so many times she was able to keep her voice calm, her recounting fluid. "A young couple walking in the park at Eaton Square saw it all." She paused, dug deep. "I really wanted to convince myself the driver was drunk or on drugs, but then last night someone knocked on my door, but I didn't open it. Then this morning, two men came to my house and tried again to get me to open my front door." She told him about the gunshots, the second man trying to break into her kitchen, swallowed. "I grabbed a butcher knife and stabbed it into his hand. Then I ran upstairs to my bedroom, jumped into the live oak near the window, and made my way down through the branches. It was raining really hard."

John marveled at her ingenuity. "Stabbed him through the back of his hand. That's good to know. He'll need attention." He made a note. "Continue."

"The man at the front door spoke English well but with a nearly undetectable accent most people wouldn't notice, or would ignore since we have so many nationalities represented now here in London. But his accent was close to Samir Basara's, so I picked up on it immediately. Samir liked to brag that he had no accent, but of course he did. He also believed himself more intelligent than the rest of us, but you already know that from our conversations after St. Paul's."

John sat back and tapped his Tibaldi pen on the desktop, supposedly a birthday present from his year-old daughter. "Superintendent Morgan sent you to me because it's obvious the two attacks on you may be related to Samir Basara and his plot to blow up St. Paul's and murder the hundreds of people there at your friend's wedding. Let's consider someone holds you responsible for Basara's death. Why would they have waited so long? Were they out of the country and only just returned? If this is to make any sense, these people must believe that since you knew Basara intimately, knew details of his life, you must have betrayed him to us."

Elizabeth said, "That sounds possible if you were speaking of someone other than Samir. The fact is anyone who knew him well would never believe he'd tell his English lover, namely me, much of anything if it could possibly be dangerous to him, and certainly not that he was a jihadist and assassin for hire. I myself wouldn't have believed it until you told me exactly who and what he was that day at St. Paul's.

"I honestly believed he was only a professor at the London School of Economics and, of course, a popular public speaker and frequent guest on Al Jazeera." She sat forward. "But maybe it's not about Samir. Maybe someone believes I'm responsible for your arresting that dreadful old imam, even though I never met him."

John said, "I strongly doubt that. Hädi ibn Mirza will reside in Belmarsh prison for the rest of his life. One of my officers reviews the list of his visitors and their photos each week, looks into them if their names are unknown. I have reports on his activities every week. He suffers from toothaches, but he won't allow the dentist to see to him." John grinned. "He's afraid."

Elizabeth said, "Alas, many Brits would agree with him." She sighed. "So there have been no visitors who concern you?"

"Lady Elizabeth, this may be unpleasant for you to consider, but could these attacks be related to your brother, the Honorable Thomas Broderick Palmer? We're quite aware of his financial situation and cocaine addiction. Does he owe enough money to his cocaine dealer to make it worthwhile for them to come after you, take you perhaps, to frighten your father enough to pay his debts?"

Elizabeth wasn't surprised he knew about Tommy's life choices. Tommy the Earl's Son had starred in the tabloids often enough. "Here's the truth. Tommy's cocaine dealer would never consider hurting me because I'm always spot-on with his payments when Tommy's allowance runs short, which it always does. If you didn't know, Tommy also gambles, but he's sworn to me he'd cut back and owed his bookmaker only a couple of quid, which to me translates into no more than a hundred pounds or so. He left it unsaid, but he prefers to spend what money I give him on cocaine." She paused. "All right, he was high when I called him, so I can't be certain of anything that came out of his mouth, but I do believe him."

Elizabeth stared down at her clasped hands. She had a ragged thumbnail. She tucked it into a fist. "Deputy Director, I've wracked my brain for other explanations, but I've had no murderous ex-boyfriends, no boyfriends at all, really." She forced a laugh. "To be honest, I suppose I've rather shut down since St. Paul's, kept to myself and worked, and frankly, all my friends are too busy with their lives to be concerned with my problems." She drew a deep breath. "I personally don't understand why anyone might blame me for Samir's death, since Samir died a continent away, killed by that FBI agent. As I told you, no one who knew him or did his dirty work for him would ever believe he'd trust me with his secrets. But these two men with their accents must have some connection to Samir—can you think of another explanation?" Elizabeth heard her voice rise, pulled back, breathed slowly, and tried to relax, but it was hard. Fear crawled through her, making her heart pound, her knuckles whiten. She clearly saw herself scrambling through her bedroom window clutching the butcher knife, thinking she was going to die.

Chapter Four

John saw she was distressed and distracted her. He said easily, "My wife will be pleased to hear we've met again. She's an admirer of your art, particularly enjoys your impressionist landscapes. As for myself, I prefer your portraits, like the one of the bent old man selling melons at Les Halles in Paris."

She blinked, drew a deep breath. He saw her shoulders relax, watched her come back. Elizabeth searched his face, gave him a twisted smile. "Thank you, that was well done." She paused a moment, smoothed out a crease in her black trousers, and met his gaze directly. "Do you know, I would have gladly killed Samir myself if I'd only had the opportunity. Then at least I'd have honestly earned getting attacked for it."

I would have killed him too, in an instant, John thought, but he didn't say it aloud. He said, "Think back, please, to yesterday afternoon. In the second you saw the Aston Martin swerve at you, what exactly did you see?"

"I saw two men in the car. I couldn't tell how old they were, they both wore black watch caps and dark glasses. I do remember the driver wasn't wearing gloves. I saw the flash of a ring of some sort on his hand—yes, it was a young hand, not as white as mine, darker, strong."

"Excellent. Now close your eyes and picture the ring. Was it gold? Silver? Plain? A stone set in it?"

Elizabeth closed her eyes and concentrated. "It was silver,

heavy, with some sort of stone—that was the flash I saw. Yes it was definitely a stone—" She shook her head. "I'm sorry, that's it. It all happened so fast."

"Did you see a watch on his wrist?"

"Yes, yes, it was a black watch, big, with a round face." She opened her eyes. "But how can that help? A watch and a ring. That could be most every male Londoner."

He said patiently, "Lady Elizabeth, when we find the driver you'll recognize the ring and the watch."

"Please, just Elizabeth."

John smiled. There were endless formalities at MI5. Even after six years together, his assistant Jenny was always Mrs. Snow and she always called him Deputy Director. He said, "It would be my pleasure. Please call me John. Now, there are always leaks, from your neighbors if no one else, which means what happened to you is going to hit the tabloids and social media. You remember the media frenzy after St. Paul's, and here you are again, the irresistible story—the beautiful aristocrat attacked in her own home. They will give no quarter. Warn your parents they'll be hounded about their son, about St. Paul's. Needless to say, you should all refuse interviews, answer only with no comment, no matter how brazen the questions. You cannot react, that would only encourage them. Your friends too will be harassed, just as they were after St. Paul's."

Elizabeth said, "Perhaps if I gave a statement saying I knew nothing about Basara's hidden life?"

"Elizabeth, the people who want to kill you won't believe a word out of your mouth. Once you're recognized as an enemy, they're like guided missiles." He saw she realized he was right, saw the helplessness in her eyes. He rose. "Excuse me a moment."

John left his office to tell Jenny—Mrs. Snow—to bring a pot of fresh tea. He also asked her to schedule an immediate appointment with Director Sir James Hanson regarding the two attempts on Lady Elizabeth Palmer's life.

He walked back into his office and sat down, followed soon by Jenny carrying a tea tray. She poured them tea and left. John added lemon, Elizabeth a dollop of cream. She sipped the tea, felt her heart slow, felt her world settling back into place. "Thank you, John."

He smiled. "I wanted the tea more than you. Did Samir Basara mention anything about his family that might help?"

"As I told you, Samir loved to talk, but never about his family. I knew only what everyone else did—he was Algerian, attended the Sorbonne, then Berkeley in the United States. He did tell me once he fit right in with the students at Berkeley. They were evidently of like mind. And that's a scary thought." She took another sip of tea, laughed. "The reason he was interested in me is that I was his entrée into a society that otherwise would have excluded him despite his being something of a celebrity. I realized, of course, that I was forbidden fruit. He gloried in enraging my father, stirring up gossip. But you must know more about his family than I do."

John said, "He had two married sisters living the high life in Paris. His father and mother still live in Algeria, third-generation owners of a successful vineyard. His father has been an invalid for several years now, and his mother runs the winery. No other close living relatives. As you know, one of his primary operatives here in Britain, one of his most trusted, was Bahar Zain."

"Yes, the man disguised as the old matron who planted the C-4 packets in St. Paul's."

"That's right. Zain now resides in Wakefield prison in West Yorkshire and will remain there for the remainder of his life, in the high-security unit. He will not have an easy time. As to visitors, I'm told they are few and far between."

"I've heard Wakefield is called Monster Mansion."

"That refers to the inmates and is well deserved, as Zain has doubtless discovered. I brought him up because, unlike Basara, Bahar Zain has a large family, most of them still living in Syria.

We know he has two younger siblings, but we've had no reason to search them out, until now. Zain's mother lives in the West End, owns a chemist shop not far from the South London Mosque."

Elizabeth sipped her tea and carefully set the lovely cup back onto the tray. She looked at him squarely. "What should I do?"

John rose, came around his desk, and took her hand as she stood up. "You're going to return to your home, paint, and keep your head down while we investigate. I imagine we've already collected whatever evidence they left behind. I'm assigning an officer to protect you. Both your front and back doors are again functional, and they've finished with forensics. By the way, there are no cameras aimed directly at the crescent in Eaton Square, but in other cameras nearby, they spotted a black Ford with its license marker covered. Did you see it?"

Elizabeth said, "No, I was never outside until I climbed down the oak tree. I imagine there are a great many black Fords in London."

John said, "Yes, quite a few." He picked up his mobile, punched in a number, spoke quietly, and punched off.

In a moment Elizabeth turned to see a dark-eyed, stork-thin older man, his face the color of polished mahogany and with only a fringe of black hair around his head, saunter into John's office like an American film cowboy. John said, "Officer Bentworth Bewley, this is Lady Elizabeth Palmer. She will give you background and bring you up to date on what's happened, though I assume you already know the highlights. You are to protect her. Retrieve a weapon from the armory."

Officer Bewley nodded. He said to Elizabeth with a smile that showed a crooked eyetooth, "Bentworth is a mouthful, so please call me Benny, Lady Elizabeth, everyone does." He saw the hesitancy in her eyes and added, "Trust me. No one is going to harm you on my watch. Let's go get me armed."

When they left, John sat down, finished his tea, and leaned his head against the soft leather headrest of his chair. The two men in an Aston Martin, both wearing black watch caps and dark sunglasses, had followed her, waiting for their chance to kill her? Trying to run her down on the sidewalk with a car was hardly a plan, it must have been a spur-of-the moment decision. What they'd done today, breaking into her house in the middle of the morning, opening fire when she refused to open the door, wasn't any smarter, hardly professional. It didn't make sense to him.

There was urgency at work here, or ungoverned rage. Family, he thought, or someone else very close to Bahar Zain or Samir Basara. Bahar Zain's younger brothers? Had someone fed them lies about her, spurred them on? Zain's mother? The new imam at the South London Mosque, Ali Ahmad Said?

John pushed the thumb drive back into his computer and wrote another text to Khaled: *Have Bahar Zain's siblings ever attended South London Mosque? Has their mother? I will send you a file on Lady Elizabeth Palmer. Acknowledge receipt and give me your thoughts.*

John pressed send and poured himself another cup of tea. It was up to him now to find whoever was trying to kill Lady Elizabeth Palmer. And to keep her alive.

Chapter Five

Elizabeth stared at her darkened ceiling, still wide awake in her lovely sleigh bed at 2:00 A.M. Even though Officer Bewley was sleeping down the hall and had assured her the locks were secure, it wasn't enough to make her heart stop racing, listening for every sound that shouldn't be there. She looked back toward the bedroom window, saw herself escaping that morning. But she'd done it, she'd saved herself, she should never forget that. She nearly screamed when she heard a footstep on the creaky seventh stair, then nothing. Could it be Benny, making rounds? No, she'd pointed out the stair to Benny, so he knew it creaked, and besides, why would he step on it and then stop?

It was someone else, not Benny Bewley. Whoever it was realized he'd made a noise and froze, waiting to see if he'd awakened them. Was it the two of them again? The two in the Aston Martin, the two who'd broken into her house that morning? No, no, her brain was making it up out of whole cloth. No one was here in her house, no one was climbing her stairs. Still, Elizabeth slid quietly out of bed, picked up a poker from the bin beside the fireplace, tiptoed to the door, carefully opened it a couple of inches, and listened.

She heard nothing.

She started to call out Benny's name but stopped herself. She kept listening, not moving, barely breathing. It had to be nothing, had to be, but still she was so scared she couldn't get spit in her mouth. Suddenly the bedroom door slammed open against her, knocking her backward against her bed. She yelled, "Benny, help!"

Two men in dark clothes were on her, masks covering their faces. One grabbed her hair and jerked her up. She slammed the poker at his head, but he pulled away in time and the poker struck his shoulder. She heard a gasp, then a curse in sharp clear English. The other man grabbed her leg to upend her, but she jumped away from him, yelled out again, "Benny!"

"Bitch! Shut up!" A fist slammed into her face, knocked her down on her back. The man she'd struck with the poker stood over her, a knife in his hand, the silver blade gleaming in the moonlight coming through the window, long and sharp. Was he going to kill her with it? She slashed upward with the poker, striking him in the leg, and the man screamed. "Get that bloody poker away from her and hold the bitch down! I'm going to cut up that pretty face."

Elizabeth didn't think, she fought with all her strength. She couldn't die; who would take care of Tommy? She saw her mom's face, her father's face. She struck out with the poker again, but she had no leverage. The knife came down at her and she twisted away from it. She felt a sharp, icy-cold pain as it sliced into her arm.

Knife man jerked the poker out of her hand, came down on his knees over her, and raised the knife again.

Benny's voice came from the doorway. "Get off her now or you're both dead!"

Knife man jerked around and hurled the knife at Benny in a move so fast it was a blur at the same time Benny fired. Knife man fell to his side, gasping for breath, cursing, this time not in English, but in Arabic, a curse she'd heard Samir say. She didn't think, kicked him off her, grabbed the poker, and struck out at him again. He backed away from her.

She looked over at Benny, who'd fallen to the floor, grasping his chest. The second man grabbed his partner, heaved him up over his shoulder, and ran out of the room. She heard his footsteps in the wide hallway and down the stairs, heard the front door slam.

Elizabeth raced to the wall and flipped on the light switch. "Benny? No!"

She fell to her knees over him, stared down in horror at the knife sticking out of his chest. She felt panic bubble up, tried to keep it at bay. "Benny, what should I do?"

Benny's voice was calm as a judge's. "Leave the knife in me, otherwise I'll bleed to death. Ring 333, it's the emergency number for MI5."

She dialed quickly, hearing his labored breathing as she spoke to a woman and told her to hurry.

"It's all right, Elizabeth, I'll live. At least they didn't kill me before they came for you, why I don't know. They knocked me on the head and left me. It took me some moments to get myself back together again. They must have cut the alarm and come in through the kitchen, it's not as sturdy as the front door." He fell silent, lips seamed, breath labored. His pain had to be unspeakable, but he said, "Your arm. You're hurt."

She hiccupped a laugh. He was worried about her? In that moment, she admired Benny Bewley more than he'd ever know. She swallowed down the tears, prayed, and for the first time Elizabeth looked at her arm, saw the blood dripping onto her carpet. It was like a thousand needles were digging into her flesh, burning-hot needles.

Again, Benny's calm, steady voice. "Press your hand hard against the wound, and keep it there. You have to get the bleeding stopped."

They waited together, Benny with a knife in his chest, Elizabeth with blood running down the arm of her white pajamas as she pressed as hard as she could against her wound.

Two days later Lady Elizabeth Palmer was released from hospital surrounded by private security guards her father had insisted on hiring. She ignored the cameras and the reporters screaming questions at her.

Two days after that, she disappeared.

Chapter Six

Something bad was coming, something really bad, not today, maybe not tomorrow, but it was coming and there was nothing he could do about it. Tash knew it was coming because he was trapped in suffocating blackness that pulsed around him like a living thing, like one of those snakes that squeeze the life out of you. He couldn't see, there was no light at all, only the throbbing blackness. Terror clutched his chest and he couldn't breathe. He heard vague noises, like voices whispering, then a distant sigh that sounded like his father's voice, like he was dying. He wanted to scream, but his voice was trapped in his throat.

Tash Navarro jerked awake, heaving for breath, the covers wrapped around him like one of those shrouds for dead people in the Bible. He wanted to run to his father, like he did the first time he'd had the dream, but he couldn't. His father was with his new wife now, Sasha, and Tash knew they'd be all scrunched together. She wouldn't want him there, wouldn't want to make room for him.

He forced himself to breathe slowly until he felt his chest ease. It was the third time he'd had the dream. He thought it was a warning. He'd tried to tell his dad after the first dream, but he couldn't anymore. Sasha would give him that look, whisper in his dad's ear that Tash was making it all up, tell his dad he should find a shrink for him. That's what he'd heard her say the last time, a shrink. He knew his dad was already worried about him. Tash would look up sometimes and see his dad staring at him, confusion and uncertainty in his eyes.

Tash knew one thing for sure, knew it in his bones. It wasn't just a dream. Something bad was coming. Would his dad ever believe him? Would it even make a difference? Tash felt cold and alone. If only his mama hadn't died. She'd have believed him.

Chapter Seven

Titus Hitch Wilderness
Titusville, Virginia
MID-JUNE

"Autumn, stop!"

Autumn Merriweather was on the point of jumping from a pile of large rocks that crossed over a narrow bend of the Sweet Onion River to the other side. She stopped and turned to Tash Navarro, who stood a few feet behind her, holding his hands out to grab her.

"Come on, Tash, it's easy. Watch me. It's just a little jump and you'll clear the water." He didn't move, just stared at her, shaking his head. Something was wrong with him. She no longer felt the same impatience with him she'd felt when her mother had first asked her to take him under her wing four days before. When she'd first seen the pasty-faced little private-school boy, she'd known, just known, he'd ruin her very fine summer. But no choice, he would be her summer job, spend five days a week with him, teach him how to hike and swim and whatever else he couldn't do. She was also supposed to give him more confidence in himself, and how did one do that? Autumn had planned to spend the summer with her friends and helping her mother with her outdoor adventure business—Titus Hitch Adventures—hiking, white water rafting, camping, having all sorts of fun and making sure big-city folk didn't drown. At least spending time with Tash was a well-paid gig, and 90 percent of what the kid's dad was paying her would go into her college fund. The other 10 percent would buy them all Christmas presents, her dad had told her, with a wink to her mom. She'd heard her dad's dispatcher, Faydeen, say Tash's dad owned a big-time investment fund in Philadelphia, and wasn't that something. Mr. Navarro had seemed nice enough when she'd met him, a big man, handsome and fit, older than her stepfather, Ethan, with dashes of gray at his temples. His wife, Sasha, was much younger, with lots of thick, wavy blond hair. Her toenails were painted sky blue, a color Autumn wanted to try, and she'd showed off her body in tight white capris and a crop top. Autumn wondered how long it had taken her to fix her hair and makeup. Archer Navarro smiled down at Autumn and shook her hand like she was a grown-up. "My brother, Rebel, tells me you're the best, Autumn, you know every square inch of the Titus Hitch Wilderness, like your parents do. I'm pleased you'll be spending the summer with Tash. I'm sure you'll do well with him. As you know, he's staying with Rebel for the summer."

Autumn had turned to the little boy grudgingly. He hadn't smiled or met her eyes, just stared down at his painfully new sneakers. She wondered how she would ever be able to teach this thin, wimpy little kid how to fish, pitch a tent, make a fire, or cook on a Coleman stove. He looked pathetic in his stiff jeans and ironed T-shirt, and who ironed a T-shirt? Five days a week with him—full days—until the end of August. She'd shaken his limp white hand and finally he'd looked her full in the face. She'd seen a sort of dull acceptance on his face, and something she didn't expect—loneliness. In that moment Autumn knew to her adolescent shame that she'd been wrong to dismiss him as a dweeb impinging on her precious time.

She'd said his name and smiled and he'd smiled back, at least a try at a smile. She'd leaned down and whispered, "We're going to have a blast, Tash."

Autumn had turned twelve years old the previous week and celebrated with a red velvet cake and a birthday party with kids from her class at school. As was her habit for the past six years, even on her birthday, she'd spent a few minutes before going to bed thinking about a particular something that had happened during the year, something good or bad, didn't matter. Her mama had taught her to do that, to use this private time to look back at herself and weigh what she'd done, what she'd experienced, and plan what to do the next time something like that happened. That night she'd thought about how her friends at school would never really know her, never know what she could do with her mind—only her mama, her stepfather, and her special friend, Dillon Savich, and that led her to think about her father, who'd died. She felt a sort of distant sadness at his memory because she knew she'd loved him, she remembered that. Her mom had told her it was okay and not to feel guilty, he'd always be in Autumn's heart as he was in hers. And that made her think of Ethan, the sheriff of Titusville, her dad for a long time now. She loved him, admired him, trusted him. She also knew her mom was crazy about him. She'd seen her mom pressed against the wall, her stepdad kissing her all over her face, the two of them laughing. She'd realized she no longer had nightmares about her birth dad's insane family in Bricker's Bowl, her mad old grandmother, Shepherd Backman, and her crazy uncles, Grace and Blessed, all of them monsters. Her uncle Blessed could control most people with his mind, make them do whatever he wanted them to do, horrible things if he felt like it. *Most people, but not her.* Her father, Martin, hadn't been like his brothers, and he'd escaped them. He never used his gift for his own gain. He'd been a good man, he'd loved her, she knew that, and he'd passed his gift on to her.

No, she wasn't as scared anymore when she remembered them all, they were long dead and gone.

Things were good now, and she'd smile as she slid into bed.

But how could things be good when she had to be responsible for Tash Navarro all summer? But then Autumn quickly learned Tash wasn't a coward; he tried his best to do everything she asked him to do, and if he failed, he just kept trying. At first he rarely smiled or spoke unless spoken to. But after nearly a week with her he didn't seem as sad or lonely, didn't act like his life was rotten. It became clear as day—Tash Navarro was happy.

Still poised to jump from the rock, Autumn cocked her head at Tash and realized he was scared. For her. But why? Did he think she couldn't make that easy jump, and fall into the creek?

"Tash, I've jumped the creek from these rocks a thousand times and so can you, I promise. You just push off. Watch me, okay?"

He shook his head frantically. "No, no, Autumn, don't do that. I—well, th-the rocks don't look all that steady, and—" His voice fell off a cliff. He looked away from her, his head down. She stepped off the rocks and walked back to him, took his thin shoulders in her hands. To her shock, when she touched him, she felt fear rolling off him. "Tash, what's wrong?"

He shook his head, wouldn't meet her eyes.

Autumn kept her hands on his shoulders, focused on him, softened her voice, and spoke slowly. "Tash, come on, you know you can tell me anything. I'm like your big sister, right?"

Still, he wouldn't look up. He pointed to the stacked large rocks on an incline above the creek, her takeoff point. He whispered, "That biggest rock on top, it doesn't look very steady. Maybe it'll slip out from under you when you push off. Maybe you'll fall, maybe you'll be hurt."

Autumn walked to the rocks she'd used as a springboard for years, saw nothing unusual. She leaned down and shoved hard at the largest one. To her surprise it broke loose, tipped forward, and tumbled down the incline into the creek.

Tash had known, he'd seen what would happen, but he was afraid to admit it.

Autumn felt her heart beat faster. How did Tash know? There was no way, she'd never crossed the river with him there before. But he'd known. She looked at Tash's white face and saw he was afraid she'd be mad at him, or worse, think he was a freak. She knew very well what that was like, always being careful, always worrying about how people might react if she did something no one would understand. She had so many questions, but she didn't want to scare him. She held back. She smiled down at him as she took his shoulders in her hands again, looked at his small pinched face. "The rock didn't look loose, Tash, but you saw me falling?"

Slowly he nodded, his head still down.

She hugged him. "Thank you. You saved me from getting hurt. Is this the first time you've seen something happen that hasn't happened yet, something you could stop or avoid?"

Finally, he nodded, whispered, "Well, one time my father was about to drive through an empty intersection but I saw another car we couldn't see coming fast at us and I saw it hitting our car hard and both of us would be hurt really bad. So I yelled for him to stop. He was so surprised, he did, and then the other car raced through. He stared at me, because he knew I couldn't have seen it. He got a funny look and shook his head. He never said anything about it."

His father hadn't thanked him, hadn't questioned him, asked him how he'd known. He'd probably been really scared himself they could have died, afraid to ask about what he'd seen, afraid of what Tash would say. She said, "Have you seen other things happen?"

He swallowed. "There was my mom."

"Tell me."

Chapter Eight

When Tash spoke again, it was still in a whisper. "When my mama was dying, the hospice doctor said she really wasn't there anymore because they'd given her morphine so she wouldn't feel any pain and now she was in a deep coma. The doctor didn't say she wouldn't wake up again because I was there, but I knew what she meant. Mama was already gone in her head and it would be soon now she'd be gone for real. I took my mom's hand and I knew right away she wasn't gone, she was afraid. I didn't know what to do. I knew there was nothing I could say to the doctor or my father, so I started singing to her in my mind, an old lullaby she'd sung to me all my life. I felt her calm, her fear melting away. She opened her eyes and smiled up at me and she whispered my name and said she loved me. I leaned down and kissed her." Tash gulped, tears sheening his eyes. "And then she died. Sh-she was still smiling. I heard the hospice doctor suck in her breath as she leaned over my mother, but I knew she really was gone now. My father asked the doctor how Mom could open her eyes, smile, and speak to me."

Autumn felt tears clog her throat. "What did the doctor say?"

"She said she'd never seen it before. Then she shook her head and said miracles sometimes happened. I didn't think, I told them my mom smiled at me because I was with her and I was singing to her." He sighed. "The doctor looked at me like she thought I was crazy. My father just stood there, crying. I heard the doctor tell my father later he should think about getting me counseling."

Tash is gifted just like I am. I'm not alone.

Autumn squeezed him again, stood back. "That doctor, Tash—she didn't understand, Tash. That was a wonderful thing you did for your mama. You made her happy. Thank you for telling me." His face jerked up. Autumn saw dawning hope in his pale gray eyes, eyes the exact shade of his uncle Rebel's, Titusville's local celebrity.

He whispered, "You believe me? You don't think I'm crazy?"

"Of course you're not crazy. What you are is gifted." She paused a moment, punched his arm. "And so am I." She studied him a moment. "Do me a favor, Tash. Think about what you saw when I was about to jump." Autumn placed her hands on his shoulders and touched her mind to his. To her surprise, she saw what he was thinking, saw what would have happened if Tash hadn't warned her away from the rock. She saw herself planting her foot squarely on the big rock, ready to push off and jump the creek. The rock slipped out from under her and she stumbled, hurtled forward, fell, and threw her hands out to catch herself. She felt a sharp jolt of pain in her right arm, felt the bone snap. She yelped.

She said simply, "Tash, you saved me from a broken arm. I owe you big time."

He stared up at her, licking his lips. "What did you just do? You saw what I saw?"

She tamped down her excitement, tried to sound matter-of-fact. "Yes, I could see what you were thinking."

He studied her face as if he suspected she was making fun of him. "B-but that means you were in my mind."

"Sort of. I don't know if I could have seen exactly what happened, but you gave me a very clear picture. If I'd jumped

I would have broken my arm and the whole summer would have been a bust. You'd have had to do everything for me—carry my pack and the camping equipment all by yourself, make sandwiches for me, scratch my back if I needed it. So you saved both of us."

A rare smile broke out, a charming little-kid smile, nearly from ear to ear. "But how, Autumn? How?"

Autumn took his hands between hers, felt the calluses, the new scratches from slapping brush out of the way on their hikes. She said simply, "I'm gifted too, Tash, but my gift is different from yours. I can't see when bad things might happen, like you can."

"I don't see things very often, but this time I did and I had to tell you, but I could have been wrong—you really saw what I saw?"

"Yes, Tash, we both have an amazing gift. You and I, we're special. I know of only three of us now, and all our gifts are different from each other." Autumn gave him a big smile.

He gaped at her. "Really? You know someone else?"

She nodded. "His name is Dillon Savich and he's an FBI special agent. He lives in Washington, D.C. We can speak—ah, connect with our minds, like with you right now. The last time we connected he told me his wife, Sherlock, was pregnant. They're both so happy. He'll be excited to hear about you." She paused a moment, smiled. "Dillon told me our gifts might change and evolve, but we shouldn't be afraid, we should be grateful because our gifts will make our lives a fun ride. Like my parents, he's told me to keep my gift to myself and only those I trust completely. Same with you, Tash. Have you told anyone else?"

He shook his head. "All the kids in my school think I'm weird anyway, my dad and Sasha didn't believe me, and no one else knows."

"Good. Don't tell anyone in town about either of us, even if you trust them. Like your dad, most people wouldn't understand, and that makes them afraid and worried."

"There are three of us? Really? In the whole world?"

"Who knows? Maybe there are people in India or in Italy who can do what we do, but my mom and dad don't think there are all that many. Wouldn't it be nice, Tash, if all the gifted kids in the world could get together, sit around a campfire roasting marshmallows, and tell each other what we can do?"

Another big smile lit up his face. "That would be so cool. No one would make fun of me."

He was so happy a nimbus of bright colors seemed to be swirling around his head. He said, "When we were driving from Philadelphia to Titusville we stopped at a restaurant for a snack. When Sasha went to the bathroom my dad told me not to say anything that would make the other kids here in Titusville wonder about me." He scuffed the toe of his sneaker against the grass. "But I had to say something to you, Autumn, I couldn't let you get hurt."

"My right arm thanks you, Tash. If you ever see danger again, you warn me, okay?"

Again, Tash smiled, a blazing smile that lit up his face. "Can you see what I'm thinking now, Autumn? Like before?"

She searched with her mind, but she couldn't tell. "No, not right now, and I don't know why. But we'll practice, Tash. Who knows what we'll learn how to do?" She was as excited as he was, couldn't wait to tell her parents and Dillon.

Autumn took his hand and walked him up the creek to another crossing, another rock they could jump off. There was a meadow of knee-deep grass on the other side of the river, and they raced across it together, Autumn holding his hand.

Chapter Nine

Rebel Navarro shut down his laptop, sat back, rolled his shoulders, and worked his fingers. They were beginning to cramp from his writing marathon. He simply hadn't been able to stop, the ending yelling at him not to dawdle, to get on with it. He was nearly to the end—one final scary scene to go—but it was a jumble in his mind. He was tired, he needed a break. Maybe he could finish the book off later in the day if he could get his brain back to work again.

He looked up and gave a start when he saw his nephew, Tash, standing in the doorway of his study. He wasn't the Tash of two weeks ago who'd arrived wearing stiff new jeans, a pale, painfully proper little boy who spoke only when directly spoken to. He'd put on needed weight. He was tanned, his dark hair all over his head; his jeans were grungy; his polo shirt wasn't only dirty, one of the sleeves was ripped. Best of all, his sneakers looked like they'd been through a couple of wars. He looked like a little boy should look on a hot summer day with nothing more on his mind than having fun.

Rebel realized he'd been working so many long hours, he hadn't paid enough attention to his nephew. His brother, Archer,

Tash's father, had seemed torn about leaving his son with him, but Sasha, gorgeous young Sasha, his wife of six months, had bubbled on about the trip they'd planned for their honeymoon. He'd been surprised when his brother had asked him to keep Tash with him the whole summer. It was a long time to be without his son, but Sasha had been so excited about their honeymoon trip she'd planned, visiting all the romantic places she'd never seen, and made Archer glow and look stupid in love.

He'd said, "The thing is, Reb, Tash is undersized, he's shy, and he doesn't seem to get along with other kids. I can't keep him with me all summer, not while I'm honeymooning with Sasha. I figured being with you here would be good for him."

Rebel had gladly accepted. He'd given it some thought and told his brother he should hire a young girl named Autumn Merriweather, a really nice kid, as much an outdoors girl as her mother, who ran a local wilderness adventure business. She could take Tash under her wing and teach him about the outdoors. He remembered Archer had glanced over at his son, who was playing on his iPhone, and said, "If you think she'd toughen him up, then yes. He was being bullied at school and the principal couldn't seem to do anything about it."

His brother hadn't done anything himself about the bullying? Rebel had kept his voice measured. "I think Tash and Autumn will have a good time together. You can trust her, she's very responsible. She'll keep him safe out there." He'd paused, grinned. "You should pay her well, Archer."

And so Rebel had made a call and they'd gone over to the Merriweather house and he'd introduced his brother and wife to the Merriweathers and to Autumn. Sasha had remarked to Archer as they left, with a shudder in her voice, thinking they were out of hearing but weren't, "The little girl and her mother, Arch, both of them look like their clothes come from a dumpster. And their hair"—another shudder—"it was falling out of their ratty ponytails."

Archer had said, "I thought Joanna Merriweather and her daughter were lovely."

Sasha had smiled and shrugged, said nothing more, and turned away. Rebel, always the cynic, had thought that was well done of her. *You don't want to disagree with your meal ticket, Sasha.*

Rebel said now to the healthy little boy who stood in his doorway, "Hey, Tash, I'm done for the day, how about a beer?"

Tash grinned at him, a big-kid grin. "Honest? A real beer, Uncle Rebel?"

"Well, put root in front of it, and sure. How long have you been standing there?"

"Only a little while. Autumn and I got back from a hike along the Sweet Onion River. Her mom made us a picnic lunch. We ate in a meadow under Autumn's favorite willow tree. She calls the tree Old Cletus. There were birds all around, chirping up a storm, and Autumn knew their names, like northern cardinal and tufted titmouse. Isn't that a funny name? Gray squirrels were racing across the meadow in front of us and there was a great horned owl in a tree close to us. Autumn said she saw some scat—that's poop—so it meant a bear was roaming around and we had to be careful. Autumn said her mom made the potato salad and she made the tuna sandwiches." Tash wished he could tell his uncle how he and Autumn spent lots of time trying to communicate with their minds when they hiked, or that she was teaching him how to fish and climb a tree. He hadn't managed to speak to her with his mind yet, after that first time when she'd seen herself fall. Autumn said maybe they could communicate only when there was trouble and one of them was afraid. But she believed he could see what might happen. She'd told him it was called prescience. He was prescient. He loved the word and looked it up first thing when he got home—*knowledge of things before they happen.* They'd agreed he shouldn't say anything to his uncle about it, not yet. He probably wouldn't understand, that's what Autumn had said. He didn't want his uncle to think he was a freak or a liar, like Sasha did, or maybe get scared.

So many words at once out of his nephew's mouth. Rebel was pleased and surprised. He realized Tash was happy, having the time of his life. Rebel laced his hands over his lean middle, felt his stomach rumble. He'd forgotten to have lunch. He said slowly, "When I looked up and saw you just now, I wondered who you were. You've only been here two weeks, Tash, and you look like a different boy."

Tash smiled at him. "Autumn says I'll be strong as a horse by the end of the summer. I hit the target three times with my arrows today. Autumn kept moving me back and I hit it all the way from fifteen feet." He paused a moment, blurted out, "I don't want to go home, Uncle Rebel. I want to stay here with you and Autumn. Autumn says her school's really good. And Sasha wants to send me to a boarding school, this fancy place in Connecticut. She was showing my dad brochures and everything."

Had Archer completely lost his bearings? Was he so consumed with Sasha he'd lost sight of his son? What to say to Tash about wanting to live with him? Rebel's brain worked overtime, but all that came out of his mouth was, "Well, Tash, I don't know if you'd like being here so much in the winter. It gets really cold, tons of snow and your toes freeze if you're not real careful."

Tash shrugged, just like his father, had he known it. "Autumn says you have to take the good with the bad, that the bad only makes the good all that much better when it comes, and it always comes. Besides, Philadelphia is cold in the winter, too, and the snow's only pretty right after it falls." Tash walked over to his uncle, laid his hand on Rebel's arm. "Do you think Dad would let me live with you instead? He has Sasha, he doesn't need me so much. I could see him sometimes on weekends.

Maybe Sasha could visit her friends while I was there. I already met some kids at Autumn's house, and they like me, Uncle Rebel, and I like them. Autumn's mom and dad are cool. And everyone plays with Lula and Mackie, they're the cats, and Big Louie, he's the dog.

"We could go camping, Uncle Rebel. I can build a fire now and make stew. I could show you Autumn's cave, Locksley Manor—that's from Robin Hood—if she said it was okay. Autumn and I roasted marshmallows in the cave. She told me when she was little, she and her parents hid in the cave from her scary uncle, Blessed." Tash stopped talking, stared down at his sneakers, and said quickly, "Dad wants Sasha lots more than me—so can I live with you, Uncle Rebel? Can I?"

Autumn had a scary uncle? Blessed was his name? And what a strange name that was. What was that all about? Rebel looked closely at his nephew, at his light gray eyes, the exact same shade as his, not nearly black like his father's or light blue like Celia, his mom's. Rebel said slowly, feeling his way, "I don't think that's true about your dad, Tash. Sasha is brand-new to him, that's all, and he's, ah, all excited to be with her now, but he wants you too. You don't like the kids at your school in Philadelphia?"

Tash shook his head. "They don't like me either."

"I tell you what. I'll talk to Archer about this and we'll see." Talk about the stereotypical adult put-off. But what could he say? Rebel knew Arch loved his son, but he'd seemed standoffish with Tash while he was there. Maybe spending time with Tash gave him pain because Tash reminded him of Celia? He'd seen Sasha look at Tash like a necessary nuisance attached to her rich husband, nothing more. It was obvious his brother was existing in a sexual haze. Fact was Rebel had been relieved when his brother and Sasha had left to fly to Paris only two days after they'd arrived. Archer had called Tash from Paris, told him he loved him and missed him, and that he and Sasha were having a fine time. At least he'd remembered to ask his son if he was having fun, but he couldn't remember Autumn's name.

Rebel planned to spend more time with Tash as soon as he finished the book. He wanted to talk to him about what he liked to do. He wanted to take him on hikes in Titus Hitch, maybe to places Autumn hadn't yet taken him, and fish with him—there were great fishing holes in stretches of the Sweet Onion River, and just maybe Autumn didn't know about them. He could take both kids, see how they played together, how they dealt with each other.

He'd set his mind to it, he'd finish the damned book tomorrow. It was time for him to have some fun too.

Rebel was thirty-one years old and he'd been something of a recluse since he'd moved from Philadelphia to Titusville over three years ago. He'd been searching, exactly for what he didn't know. When he'd driven into this small picturesque town in the mountains next to open wilderness, with its straightforward, friendly people, he felt like he'd found what he was looking for. He'd found home. He'd found property, designed a house he knew was perfect for him, and had it built, in under a year. He hadn't made any close friends in the three years he'd lived in Titusville. But maybe that could change, like Tash was changing before his eyes in only two weeks. What would he be like by the end of the summer? What would Rebel be like?

He felt guilt even as he thought it, but—could he talk Archer into letting Tash stay with him, live here with him? He knew he'd have Sasha on his side. And it would be better for Tash than sending him to some private school in Connecticut. He'd develop a whole truckload of reasons why Tash was better off here.

Rebel picked Tash up and set him on his lap facing his computer. He pointed to his computer screen. "Look at this, Tash, page 487. I'm nearly done with the book, then it's off to my editor." He paused, felt his way again. "After that, you and I can have lots more time together. I know you're with Autumn during the week, but you and I can do more things in the evenings than we do now, and just you wait for the weekends. Maybe I could join you some days with Autumn, spend some time with her parents." He was ashamed he knew so little about Joanna and Ethan Merriweather, not much more than to say hello and talk about how they needed rain. He'd heard people say Ethan Merriweather was a good sheriff who played by the book, a man you could trust. And that Joanna, why, that woman could deal with a bear and take on the wildest rapids laughing her head off.

But Tash wasn't listening. He was reading Rebel's manuscript on his computer screen. He bounced up and down on Rebel's legs, pointed. "Wow, that's scary."

"Good. I'm glad you like it. Scary is what I always aim for."

"What's it about?"

"The main character, Charis Arnett, inherits an antique store from her great-aunt in Paris filled with lots of old paintings, furniture, jewelry, stuff like that. Strange things start to happen after she's there awhile, and she discovers she can call up a demon named Hilgar. She uses him to help her catch the burglar after her store is robbed. So then she starts roaming around Paris at night looking for criminals, and she calls Hilgar when she needs him. But Hilgar corrupts her—that is, he makes her bad, and she loses her way. Will she be saved or will she become as evil as the demon?"

"Imagine, calling up a demon," Tash whispered. "I wonder if Autumn can." He realized what he'd said and blurted out fast, "My dad says it's amazing you can make money writing such weird stuff."

Rebel grinned. "He's right. I'm lucky there are lots of people who like to read my weird stuff. And you know what? I'm really lucky because writing is what I was meant to do. Slogging through the writing isn't all that much fun a lot of the time, but when I finish a book and this big pile of pages is sitting square in the middle of my desk, I drink a glass of champagne and bless the powers that be for giving me enough talent to write it."

"I wish I could write weird stuff," Tash said. He touched a finger to a word on the screen. "What does this word mean?"

"Beelzebub? It's another word for the devil. Beelzebub and Hilgar are buddies."

"Please tell me Charis ends up good."

Rebel studied his little face and decided in that moment the ending he'd choose. It had been a toss-up, but no longer. "She's going to come back into the light and banish Hilgar back to hell."

"That's good. Can I have the beer now?"

Rebel stood up, took Tash's small hand in his. "Don't forget the root."

Chapter Ten

Savich was on the edge of sleep when he heard Autumn's soft voice saying his name. Slowly, she came into focus, her beautiful hair pulled back in a fat braid, her face scrubbed clean, wearing her favorite summer pink-flowered shirt and sleep shorts.

Autumn, good evening. What happened today to put that big smile on your face? Have you and Tash discovered something new you can do together?

Savich already knew about the little boy. Autumn had told him quite a bit about Tash Navarro since he'd first appeared in Titusville, about his connection with his dying mother and his saving Autumn from a fall. She was convinced his prescience was as real as the gift she'd inherited from her father. Savich wasn't completely sure yet, because the gift Tash Navarro seemed to have had to be rare, though he knew gifts like Tash's could simply appear, without any history of it in his family, as Savich's own gift had simply appeared when he'd been a teenager. And he'd been blessed because his father had believed him implicitly, unlike Tash's father.

It's amazing, Dillon. I couldn't believe it, but today Tash finally connected with me, like you and I do. I heard his voice clearly, like he was talking to me out loud, though it was only for a second. But it happened.

Savich knew they'd been trying, but this surprised him. Tash could connect with Autumn, and he was prescient? He remembered the pole-thin boy Autumn had shown him a picture of not yet two weeks ago, his shoulders slumped, his too-proper clothes hanging off him. *Autumn, show me Tash again.*

She scrolled through her photos and held up her phone. Dillon was surprised again to see a tanned little boy with light gray eyes so bright they seemed to reflect the sun. He was smiling really big and held a fishing pole in his right hand he'd obviously made himself, maybe with the help of his uncle, Rebel Navarro, or Autumn, more likely. His sneakers looked damp, his jeans and polo shirt streaked with mud. He looked healthy and eager, ready to take on the world. Autumn and the Titus Hitch had worked a miracle. Autumn set her phone down and looked back to him again, and now he saw she looked worried.

Tell me what's wrong, Autumn.

Tash doesn't want to go back to Philadelphia at the end of the summer with his father and stepmom. He wants to stay in Titusville and live with his uncle, Rebel Navarro. Rebel loves Tash, wants to spend lots of time with him now that he's almost finished his novel. Tash says he'd miss his dad, but things aren't the same now since his dad married Sasha. My dad called her a looker and Mom laughed. Tash knows Sasha has plans to send him to a private school in Connecticut in the fall. Remember I told you how he was bullied in his school in Philadelphia? It wouldn't be any different in a snooty private school, would it? He wouldn't be bullied here. The kids like him, and he's with me. So what do you think? What should we do?

Does Tash's father know his son wants to stay in Titusville?

I don't know. His dad and stepmom are in Paris. His dad calls him every day, Dillon, always has him say hello to Sasha. He says his dad thinks he and Sasha will come to love each other, but Tash doesn't think she'll ever change toward him. He said she always gives him this fake smile. He thinks she'll talk his dad into sending him away.

You told me Rebel Navarro's single, spends most of his time alone, writing or hiking in the Titus Hitch Wilderness, probably plotting his books. So what does he have to say about taking on an eight-year-old boy?

Well, he hasn't told Tash he could stay, not yet. He'll have to speak to Tash's father, see what he thinks. There's something else, Dillon, and it's really big. Tash told me he and Uncle Rebel were playing pool and Tash saw his uncle was going to make an incredible bank shot in the side pocket. He told his uncle to try it, but Rebel said it was next to impossible. Tash talked him into it. And guess what? It went in.

What did his uncle say then?

He picked Tash up and hugged him, told him he was the best because he had faith in his uncle. He didn't say anything more about it.

Autumn started humming, a sure sign she was thinking.

Dillon, I asked Tash if he could see himself staying here in Titusville. He concentrated, and then he turned pale and started shaking. He told me all he saw was a strange, scary, rolling mass of black, like a storm streaming in, and it covered everything. He said he'd had this same nightmare several times and he knew it meant bad things were coming. He didn't want to say any more about it because maybe if he did the nightmares would for sure come true. He's scared, Dillon. He said he knew it was about his dad.

Autumn believed Tash Navarro was gifted, and Savich was beginning to believe it himself. *Reassure him, Autumn. Tell him the nightmare could mean anything, okay? It doesn't necessarily have to mean his dad's in any kind of danger. And, Autumn, encourage him to tell you more about them, more detail if he can remember.*

Autumn cocked her head at him, sending her French braid over her shoulder. She gave him a solemn nod and left him.

It seemed to Savich every time he visited with Autumn he saw changes in her, saw the promise of the woman she would become. Amazing, soon she'd be a teenager, then an adult.

Sherlock said quietly, "All is well with Autumn?"

"Yes. Lots of interesting things happening in Titusville. Go back to sleep, sweetheart, I'll tell you in the morning more about Tash Navarro, the little boy she's shepherding this summer."

Sherlock said against his throat, "I would like to visit with her and Ethan and Joanna this summer, it's been too long." She kissed his cheek, her hand splayed on his chest, her fingers lightly kneading. "Can you believe Griffin and Kirra are getting married in two weeks? Griffin told me they're having two ceremonies, the first one here, the second one in Australia, and her uncle Jim will give her away at both ceremonies. They're going skiing in New Zealand for their honeymoon. What do you think we should get them?"

"How about a boomerang?"

"That's a good idea, but alas, Kirra already has one. Griffin said she's good with it, one of the team taught her. Hmm, how about a puppy? I think Astro and Mr. McPherson's Gladys are in love, and I know from personal experience what could come from that love business."

Savich laughed. "The puppy would certainly be a world traveler." He felt her answering smile, felt her bouncing curls tickle his nose. "I haven't a single doubt those two are in it for the long haul."

"I think you're right. They fit together. Sort of like we do."

They fit together? She was right, of course, she was his other half, his mate. He pulled Sherlock against him, felt the slight swell in her belly, and felt blessed. He wondered if the baby was feeling as snug and content as he did.

Chapter Eleven

Rather than a phone call, Rebel Navarro usually got texts from his brother. This text from the Ritz in Paris didn't particularly surprise him. *Sasha's in love with Les Deux Magots, Versailles, the Louvre. She wants to tour the chateaux and vineyards, wear her bikini in Cannes. Another month. All right? Hope you and Autumn Merriweather are having as wonderful a time as Tash, who'd rather hike in the Titus Hitch Wilderness than visit Paris. He's young.*

Rebel understood how a young, beautiful woman like Sasha could focus a man's brain on his honeymoon. He texted back: *No problem. Take as long as Sasha wants. Autumn, Tash, and I are having a great summer. He misses you, of course.*

Rebel looked up to see Autumn and Tash standing in the doorway of his office, Tash's hand raised to knock on the door. Rebel smiled. "Good timing, kids. Tash, I just got a text from your father. He and Sasha will be in Europe for another month. He says he's going to tell you all about the joys of Paris and he swears no more talk of museums."

Tash bloomed out a huge smile. "Another month? That's great."

Rebel said, "He said Sasha wants to go to Cannes."

Tash said, "Yes, I know. Autumn says that's on the Mediterranean."

Autumn said, "Sir, did Mr. Navarro agree to Tash living here with you forever?"

Forever? The word stretched the years out in his mind. Great years with Tash, challenging years, and oddly, Rebel thought about what he'd get Tash for Christmas this year. But he dreaded the talk with his brother. Still, if Tash was right and Sasha really didn't want him around, if she wanted Archer all to herself without his being underfoot, just maybe he could make it happen. She'd probably have kids of her own, and then how would she treat Tash? This private-school business—surely Archer wouldn't allow that. He said slowly to the expectant faces, "I haven't brought it up with Tash's father just yet. Are you sure, Tash? You and your dad love each other, and—"

"It isn't Dad, Uncle Rebel, it's her. She doesn't want me around." He gave a little shrug. "And Dad will do what she wants."

Tash was probably right. Children knew, they always knew. Rebel said, "Let me think about how to present it to him. Don't worry, I will." He could hear Archer saying no, impossible, Tash belonged with him, attending his fancy private school in Philadelphia, and if he was still bullied there, he'd go off to another fancy private school in Connecticut, Choate maybe, then Yale, of course. He could hear Archer say in a disbelieving voice, "You want him to get a half-assed education in that bumfuck little mountain town in Virginia and end up a canoe salesman?"

Rebel smiled at the pretty little girl, the image of her mother, Joanna. He'd asked her yesterday about her mean uncle with the weird name—Blessed—that Tash had mentioned, asked her who he was. She'd frozen, given him a deer-in-the-headlights look, mumbled something he couldn't understand, and was out the door the next second. He was still curious, but he didn't want to embarrass her again. Maybe Tash would tell him more.

Later that evening, their plates loaded with hot dogs, baked beans, and Tash's favorite wavy potato chips, they talked about Rebel's favorite hikes in the Titus Hitch Wilderness. The best, Rebel told him, was climbing Sod Drummer's Ridge, a jagged, toothy line of rocks that cut the wilderness in half. He asked Tash if he'd like to go with him, maybe Autumn too, have a picnic with his specialties, tuna fish sandwiches and lemonade. Tash thought that sounded great. Rebel pulled another hot dog from the long-pronged fork that had been resting near a burning log in the fireplace. It was nearly black, as he and Tash both liked them. He was amazed at how much food the kid could sock away. He watched Tash squirt mustard on the hot dog, and said easily, "Autumn's mean uncle, Blessed, tell me more about him."

The hot dog didn't make it to Tash's mouth. He stared at his uncle, who looked all unconcerned, forking down a bite of beans, as if he'd asked about an everyday thing, like if he'd washed his hands before dinner. Tash didn't know what to say. He hadn't asked Autumn if he should tell his uncle Rebel or if this uncle Blessed was a secret. He said carefully, "Autumn said her uncle was real scary—maybe even scarier than Hilgar the demon from hell in your book, but he's dead now, made her parents really happy, because Blessed hated them." He paused, then burst out, "Blessed was like Autumn and me, Uncle Rebel, only he was rotten and crazy and he could make people do anything he wanted with his mind. All they had to do was look at him. I think he was worse than Hilgar."

It was Rebel's turn to forget his hot dog. Tash thought Autumn's uncle could force people to do things with his mind, just looking at him? And Tash and Autumn were like him? Why was Autumn filling his head with nonsense?

Then Tash spurted out, "But I'm not like him exactly, Uncle Rebel. I'm prescient, that's the word Autumn told me. And I'm not nasty or mean and neither is Autumn."

Rebel was floored, hoped Tash didn't see it. *Tash thought he could see things that hadn't happened yet? He was prescient?* Rebel studied Tash's serious little face, realized he really believed it. He said slowly, "Tash, remember when you wanted me to try for that really tough bank shot when we were playing pool yesterday?"

Tash nodded, looking wary.

It was hard, but Rebel kept his voice matter-of-fact. "I made it, against all the odds. Is that what you thought you were doing, seeing what would happen, seeing me make the shot before I even tried it?"

Tash nodded. "I saw the ball go in and you laughed."

Tash really believed he'd seen it? He really believed he was prescient? Go slow, go slow. "So tell me what else you've seen before it happened."

Tash told him about how he saved his father from being T-boned by a truck speeding through an intersection. "Dad didn't ever mention it to me again. I think it scared him."

You bet it scared him spitless. Rebel kept his voice calm, matter-of-fact. "Anything else?"

Tash nodded. "My mama."

Celia? He'd been only six years old when Celia had died of cancer, and both he and Archer had been devastated. "What about your mama, Tash?"

"Dad brought me in the bedroom to say goodbye to her. The doctor said she was unconscious and I knew she meant Mama wouldn't wake up again. She was never going to wake up, she was just going to die. I knew my dad was trying really hard not to cry. But, Uncle Rebel, when I took her hand I knew she was still there and she was scared, so I sang her the lullaby she sang to me every night when I was little, in my head. Then she opened her eyes and smiled at me and said my name and told me she loved me." Tash started crying, deep wrenching sobs.

Rebel pulled him into his arms and rocked him. He'd been a little boy and he thought he'd helped his dying mother—with his mind. Rebel knew Autumn had nothing to do with this memory. Tash believed it, believed it to his soul. What to do, what to say? "Did you tell your dad about singing to your mama?"

Tash blew his nose on a paper napkin Rebel offered him, nodded, and slipped off his lap. "I heard the doctor tell him I should get counseling from a shrink—that's what Sasha calls them. But Dad never called a shrink. He never said anything about my singing to Mama either, just like after the truck that almost T-boned us."

Now that he'd opened the floodgates, Tash let more of it burst out. "Autumn's helping me, Uncle Rebel. She's gifted too. She's amazing. She told me her uncle Blessed could stymie almost everybody—that's the word her uncle used—you know, stymie people to do whatever he wanted, even kill themselves, just by looking at them. But he couldn't stymie Autumn or Dillon."

He, the writer, again didn't know what to think, what to do. He heard himself say, "Who's Dillon?"

"He's an FBI agent Autumn knows. She says he's her hero and she loves him. She told me they'd been through a lot together, but she hasn't told me about all that yet."

Rebel wanted to know how it was Autumn could have become such good friends with an FBI agent, but it wasn't Tash who could tell him. He felt like he'd wandered into an old *Twilight Zone* episode or into one of his own novels. Whether any of it was true or not, Tash believed it, and Rebel accepted that. He had to find out what it was all about.

He had to talk to Joanna Merriweather.

The next morning, just as Rebel was going to text his brother, he looked up to see Autumn standing in the doorway of his study.

"Good morning, Autumn. Where's Tash?"

"He's in the bathroom. I didn't want him to hear this about his father. He's only a little kid."

Chapter Twelve

FBI Special Agent Wilson Ballou's remains were uncovered by a Weimaraner puppy digging in a sunken plot of land next to the Calmett River near Bensonville, Virginia. Two bullet holes were found in his skull, and a safe deposit key was pressed flat into the heel of his left shoe. Wrapped around the key was a small square of paper with numbers scrawled on it. Everyone thought it was a latitude—and if so, it passed through northern Virginia.

Information moved at the speed of light in the Hoover Building. Agents in the CAU, and most outside it, soon knew the whole case history of Special Agent Wilson Ballou, who'd disappeared on June 7, 1978. It was thought his wife, Cynthia Ballou, or her assumed lover murdered and buried him somewhere, but there was no physical evidence and so she'd skated. She'd later remarried, birthed three children with him, and the son by Wilson Ballou made four, all grown now, with children of their own. When Agent Roman Foxe called Cynthia Ballou, now Hendricks, after Ballou's body was found, she repeated what she'd said many years ago—she'd told Ballou she was

divorcing him and he'd said that was her problem because he
was about to get rich. She thought he'd been involved with
criminals for some time, tried to take money from them, and
they'd killed him for it. No one had believed her at the time.
Agent Foxe told her about the safe-deposit key they'd found in
his shoe, and did she know the bank? She said she had no idea
what he was talking about.

If his wife hadn't murdered him along with a lover no one
was ever able to identify, then who had killed Ballou? What
bank's safe-deposit boxes used this key? If they found the right
bank, would the box hold the longitude? Would they then be
able to identify the exact spot where some treasure was hidden?
Uncut diamonds in a leather pouch? Maybe from Amsterdam?
There was endless speculation among the agents, techs and
secretaries, even Mrs. Milsom, who ran the Mexican food kiosk
in the cafeteria. Savich's boss, Mr. Maitland, bless him, assigned
the case to the CAU, which brought on loud cheering, and everyone wanted to be involved. All they had to do was find the right
bank that used this particular key.

Excitement remained at a peak until Shirley, the CAU secretary, pointed out that Special Agent Wilson Ballou had been
killed over forty years ago and the bank where that safe deposit
box resided would have required a yearly fee. And Ballou hadn't
been around to pay it, so whatever was in the safe deposit box
was long gone. What they should be asking was whether, if they
found the right bank, there would be records to show what had
been in the safe deposit box. The chances of this happening
were less than nil.

Sherlock was wondering about a connection to a diamond
heist in Amsterdam that year when she felt a feather-light kick.
She laid her palm against her belly and smiled. "Awake and
ready to salsa, are you? Going to be a while yet before I can
dance with you." Her pants waist was soft and stretchy, her
jeans history as of three weeks ago. She still wore her signature

white shirts, but no longer tucked in, nor was her Glock clipped to her waist. She wore a soft, lightweight shoulder holster now. She was thankful she hadn't thrown up once so far, hadn't felt a moment of nausea. Boy or girl, this one had decided not to torture its mother. Sean was all for a brother, but Marty, his next-door neighbor and best friend forever, wanted a girl so the two of them could gang up on Sean. Sean insisted his terrier, Astro, also wanted a boy.

Sherlock looked up to see a woman walk into the unit with security guard Mac Sommers. Mac spoke to Shirley, both unit secretary and commandant, filched a sugar cookie from the plate on her desk, and spoke briefly to the woman at his side. He waved at Sherlock and left the unit. As the woman headed toward Sherlock, every agent in the unit followed her progress. She was tall, in her early thirties, fit and trim, wearing black pants and boots, a pale gray silk shirt, and a dark gray leather biker jacket. Her blond hair was pulled back from her fine-boned face and clipped at her nape. She wore only a dash of coral lipstick. She was a knock-out, as doubtless every agent in the unit now watching her would agree. She looked strong, vibrant, very sure of herself, her stride long and purposeful. She looked somehow familiar, but Sherlock couldn't place her. Maybe an agent from a field office? Sherlock slowly rose, cocked her head.

The woman gave her a beautiful white-toothed smile and stuck out a long-fingered hand with short buffed nails and no rings, though there was an oversized black Apple Watch on her left wrist. Sherlock automatically took that long-fingered hand, felt calluses. The woman said in a BBC voice, all clipped and self-assured, with a whiff of arrogance, "We've never met, but you may have seen photos of me. After all the hullabaloo at St. Paul's? Last year?"

Sherlock studied her face, said slowly as she rose, "Yes, I recognize you. You're Lady Elizabeth Palmer. I'm Agent Sherlock."

"Yes, I know," she said. "You look somehow different from the photos I saw last year." *Somehow* was an understatement. The photos Sherlock had seen of Lady Elizabeth Palmer after her near-death experience at St. Paul's showed a shell-shocked, white-faced woman, her face frozen, her dark blue eyes blank, her tangled blond hair falling into her face. And no wonder. Sherlock remembered thinking she looked somehow tragic, coming to grips with the knowledge that her lover, Samir Basara, had planned for her to die.

Elizabeth was scared to her toes, but she wasn't about to show it. She looked Special Agent Sherlock dead in the eye and gave a low musical laugh. "I hope I look different. That—that was an awful time. I've tried very hard in the past three months to leave my former spineless self behind." She stopped, eyed Sherlock. "You're glowing, like my friend Mary Ann Eiserly was when she was carrying Cici."

Sherlock laughed. "Yes, I'm pregnant. Usually people hesitate to congratulate someone in case she's not pregnant at all. How embarrassing that would be. Come, let's sit down. Tell me why you came to see me."

Elizabeth sat in the comfortable chair beside Sherlock's desk, crossed her legs. She said simply, "I'm sure the story didn't travel here across the pond, but three months ago I was attacked three times in London over the course of a couple of days. I managed to survive with only a knife wound, but my parents and I did a good deal of talking and planning while I was in hospital. We agreed it would be safest for me to disappear for a time, while we gave MI5 the opportunity to investigate and, we hoped, make arrests. We decided to give them three months, and I knew my father would see to it they kept the investigation a priority." She leaned closer. "I used a doctored passport and flew to the United States on a commercial jet to make sure no one could track me here. I'd contacted a man who specializes in teaching people, mostly business executives, how to protect themselves when they have to travel to foreign climes that might be dangerous, places where there is little rule of law and someone might try to take them for ransom, such as Haiti or Venezuela. The second benefit was he's located in an isolated spot with little outside communication."

Sherlock cocked her head to the side again, sending her curly hair over her cheek. "You mean Hurley Janklov's setup near Porterville?"

Elizabeth nodded. "Yes. Hurley said you probably knew of him. I paid him to reschedule six of his clients and spend three months only with me, so no one but he would know I was there. I wanted him to make me as dangerous as the people who attacked me in London." She paused, flexed her fingers. "Hurley nearly killed me, but believe me, I was motivated to live through anything he could dish out, as you Americans say. Last week Hurley told me I shoot as well as he does, at least with a handgun. I'm still not very good at distance. Last night, Hurley made sure to remind me that even if I could face one of them down, even two attackers, it still wouldn't be enough. He said if someone wants me dead, I'll be dead sooner or later if I go back to London and show myself. Car bombs, snipers, I couldn't defend myself against any of those. He's recommended for weeks now that I bring in the FBI, not go back to John Eiserly at MI5. He gave me a grin and said we Brits were all well and good at using our brains, but if I don't want to die, if I don't want to live my life being afraid and always looking over my shoulder, my best chance was to come to you. I came to you specifically, Agent Sherlock, because it was you who shot Samir Basara down when he escaped here to Washington. Hurley agreed there was no one better." Elizabeth paused, felt her heart pound hard and fast because her life depended on what this woman said. "I came here to ask you to help me."

Sherlock felt a rush of excitement, managed a grin. "I think we can overlook your, ah, doctored passport, given what you

faced and your excellent motives. And Hurley's right if someone wants you dead, you'll be killed unless you find them and
stop them first." She paused, took Elizabeth's hand in hers,
again felt the calluses, the strength. "Yes, I'll do my very best to
help you. First off, I'll need every detail you can give me, and
everything MI5 has found. We'll contact them, ask for their
support."

Elizabeth whooshed out a breath, a boulder lifted off her.
She felt hope. "Thank you. Believe me, every single detail is
imprinted in my brain."

Sherlock waved toward Dillon's glassed-in office. "I think
you know the head of the CAU is Special Agent Dillon Savich,
who also happens to be my husband. Let me tell you, Dillon
and John Eiserly are good friends. They worked together last
year to locate Samir Basara. I don't know if John told you, but
he was the one who spotted Bahir sitting next to his own wife
and baby, Cici, in St. Paul's. I know Dillon trusts him implicitly,
thinks he's dedicated and competent. And the best thing about
John is he never gives up. I imagine John must have been frantic
when you left, wondering where you were or if you were dead
and at the bottom of the Thames. We'll contact him immediately. Then we'll need to speak to Dillon's boss, Deputy Director
James Maitland, and hope he'll clear our helping you."

Elizabeth said, "I did hear talk it was Mr. Eiserly who spotted
Bahar Zain at St. Paul's, but he never said anything about it to me.
A bit of British reticence, I suppose. I rang Mr. Eiserly on what
you Yanks call a burner phone, assured him I was all right. He
apologized, but I knew he couldn't promise there'd be no more
attempts on my life. He didn't urge me to come home. I told him
I'd come home when he saw to it the people who attacked me
were in prison or dead. I told him I wouldn't put any more of his
officers protecting me in danger. The first MI5 officer assigned
to guard me—" She paused, swallowed hard. "Two men broke
into my house, disabled the alarm. I heard a creaking stair only

a minute before they pushed into my bedroom. Benny heard me yell out and ran to me in time to help me. One of the men threw a knife into his chest." Elizabeth's voice caught. "Benny could easily have died because of me. He's still recuperating. When I called him, he was like a Greek chorus, telling me to stay hidden until they found out who was behind this."

Sherlock turned and sent a fist wave to Dillon indicating urgency. "Excuse me a moment, Elizabeth." She called Mr. Maitland, told his dragon gatekeeper Goldie she needed an immediate appointment. "No, sorry, Goldie, it's not about Wilson Ballou's safe-deposit key, it's something else entirely and much more important. Tell him Lady Elizabeth Palmer is here asking for our help."

Goldie said in her no-nonsense voice, "Oh, yes, now I remember her name, Sherlock. What is this about?"

"Right now we don't know much of anything. Can Mr. Maitland fit us in?"

"I can shuffle things around. Bring her up now, Sherlock. Goodness, I can't wait to meet a real live English aristocrat."

Sherlock punched off. "Mr. Maitland will see us now, but before we go up, does anyone else know where you are? Anyone in your family, any friends?"

"My father and I made a pact. I contact him on my burner mobile once a week so he knows I'm all right, and yes, he knows I was coming to you. The only other people outside of MI5 who know I'm no longer in England are my younger brother, Tommy, and his drug dealer, Carlos. I hired Carlos to secure the faked passport. But even he didn't know where I went." She gave a crooked smile. "Believe me, even if he knew, Carlos is the last person who would rat me out, as you Yanks say. And of course, there's Hurley. I imagine after three months of trying to kill me, he even knows where my birthmark is."

"Good. The fewer people who know where you are, the better. Where are you staying?"

"Hurley called a car service and they picked me up in Claxson and brought me here. I haven't booked a room anywhere." She smiled—a lovely smile, Sherlock thought—and added, "I'll rent a car here. Don't worry about my driving. Hurley taught me to drive on the wrong side of the road in his big F-150, so I'm not a danger, even in your awesome traffic tangles that look to be nearly as bad as London's."

Sherlock made a decision on the spot. "Then you'll bunk with us for a couple of days until we figure out the best way to proceed. I hope you'll like a five-year-old little boy who'll want you to play basketball and a terrier named Astro who snores and licks your face. Here comes Dillon. I guess we'll be late to lunch." She patted her stomach. "It's Taco Wednesday. Tacos are all I've wanted to eat for the past week, even cold in the mornings, with lots of salsa."

Savich stopped by Sherlock's desk, smiled at Elizabeth, and stuck out his hand. "It's good to see you, Lady Elizabeth. I was on the point of calling John Eiserly but decided to hear from you why you've come to see us."

Elizabeth wasn't surprised he knew who she was. "Thank you, Agent Savich. Please don't call John just yet. Please."

Savich eyed her closely and slowly nodded.

Sherlock laid her hand on Elizabeth's arm. "Dillon, Mr. Maitland's expecting us. Let's all go upstairs now and we can hear all about it."

Chapter Thirteen

Rebel was on his feet in an instant. "Autumn, what don't you want Tash to hear about his father? What's happened?"

"I was speaking to Dillon last night, and he told me Tash's father is being investigated for fraud and embezzlement from his own company and it would all come out soon. I told Mom and Dad, and he read in the *Wall Street Journal* on his laptop that money is missing from the Navarro Investment Fund and Mr. Navarro was unavailable for questions."

Rebel stared at her, his mind racing. It was ridiculous. It wasn't Archer, simply couldn't be Archer. There was simply no way he would embezzle from his own company. Rebel remembered clearly how proud he'd been when he'd gotten his investment fund up and running. How could anyone possibly think he'd take his clients' money and run off to Europe?

Rebel's cell pinged a text.

Reports about my wrongdoing are untrue. I let my COO Carla Cartwright take over management of the portfolios when Celia died, my fault. Can't come home until all is resolved. Arch

Rebel texted back: *I know you didn't do this, they're making a mistake. Where are you?*

Better you don't know. Keep Tash safe.

Rebel took Autumn's hand in his. "Autumn, you're right. We won't tell Tash about this yet, not until I can find out exactly what's going on and who's doing the investigating. Please tell your dad I'll call him. He'll know who's in charge."

"He said it was the FBI in Philadelphia and the SEC—he said that's the Securities and Exchange Commission and they police businesses." She gulped, looked frightened. "Dad looked really concerned. This is bad, sir, really bad, isn't it?"

"It might be." Rebel had two problems now—Tash and his father. He took Autumn's shoulders in his hands. "Try not to worry, I'll do enough for both of us."

He saw the two kids off to go swimming in the Sweet Onion River. He knew he'd first speak to Joanna Merriweather about Tash, and then Sheriff Ethan Merriweather to get his thoughts about Archer and what he could do. He knew from Autumn her mother would be home until one o'clock today, when she was scheduled to lead a white water rafting adventure. Rebel had met her several times, believed she had both feet firmly planted in reality, prayed it was true. She had to be the best person to talk to about why Tash believed both he and Autumn had some sort of powers. And was this Uncle Blessed even real? Did Joanna know Autumn had told Tash he could look at a person and they'd do whatever he told them to? So many questions about both Tash and Archer.

His brain skipped to his brother. What if he was found guilty of embezzlement and sent to prison? Tash had lost his mother, he simply couldn't lose his father too. Rebel didn't lock the front door, never did, and decided to walk downtown. He heard a robin sing out and turned to look back. He'd built his house on a slight rise surrounded by pines, white oaks, and hemlocks a quarter mile from downtown Titusville.

He vaguely registered the weather was glorious, not too hot, with the mountains always there, like your best friend guarding your back, and the peaks spiderwebbed now with the late-morning mist.

He reached downtown, waved at locals, and stopped occasionally to chat though he was desperate to hurry, to get some answers. He remembered his brother's grief after Celia died, how he'd drawn back from his business. The investigators weren't stupid, Archer would be cleared sooner or later, he had to be. He wondered what would happen to Tash if Archer was found guilty of embezzlement and sent to prison. He wouldn't think about it, the thought was unbearable. Tash couldn't lose both his father and mother. Rebel couldn't bear to lose his brother as he'd lost his sister-in-law, beloved by all of them.

At least he didn't have to worry about his manuscript; it was in his editor's hands now. His eleventh book, hard to imagine, and it had seemed like endless work, endless editing. Now he only had to hope his editor would like the book, as every author did—if the editor was happy with it, all would be good in the kingdom. He wondered if he'd still worry whether his editor would like his fiftieth book, if he wrote that many. He liked the title, *Death Day*, but would the marketing people think it wasn't unique enough, or that it had been used too recently?

Focus, focus. The smell of cinnamon and sugar wafted to his nose as he walked past Ms. Maude's bakery, Treat Yourself. He saw there was already a line of tourists inside, but he hadn't had breakfast yet, and he walked in. He chatted with Kelly, one of Maude's teenage summer employees, a pretty girl who had a crush on Cork Thomas, owner of the Bountiful Wine Shop. He bought a piping-hot cinnamon roll with thick, hot white frosting oozing down the sides.

The cinnamon bun was history by the time he passed Tuber Willis's nursery, Garden of Eden. Tuber, a skinny older dude who usually had black dirt under his fingernails, gave him a nod and a smile as he handed off a flat of yellow tulips to Mrs. Gray, a retired schoolteacher. He walked past Gerald's Loft, a large B and B filled to the rafters in the summer, and nodded to Tollie Tolbert, retired FBI agent, who was sitting on a rocking chair in front of Gilly's Market reading one of his endless spy novels.

When he'd walked past the small town center, he looked down Maple Street, lined with old pine and oak trees, big yards and stately old Victorian houses. He remembered he'd thought about buying the old Farmington Victorian halfway down the block, but he'd decided to build his own house instead. He'd never regretted his decision.

The Merriweathers' two-story cottage was a quarter mile west of town. He breathed in the pine-scented air and wondered if his brother was still in Paris or whether he'd run. Since Archer knew about the investigation, Sasha had to know too, no way around it. Where would they go? What countries didn't have an extradition treaty? He'd read Tunisia and Madagascar and ever-pleasant Russia. Was Archer guilty? Was that the reason he'd taken Sasha to Paris, because he thought he didn't have a choice? Why he'd brought Tash to him, because he knew what was coming? No, no, that couldn't be right. He knew Archer, knew he was still crazy in lust with his wife, so that had been his only purpose, a long honeymoon. Yes, that was why he'd left the country. But why had he given Rebel only a couple of days' warning?

Archer was years older than Rebel, smart and cagey. As a kid he could talk his way out of anything, and Rebel imagined he'd only gotten better at it. He was a charming, outgoing boy who'd talked Liz Murray out of her thong when he was fifteen and she an older woman of eighteen. Everyone admired him at school, were sure he'd be a success. He knew how to seem both charming and sincere. Rebel had to admit it—Archer was a master at manipulation, it was why he was so successful in finance. But was he a crook? Would he really strip his own company of its clients' money and disappear? Rebel told himself yet again it simply wasn't possible.

He turned into the sheriff's long, graveled driveway lined with stately old Virginia pines, its yard brilliant with summer color. He liked the Merriweathers' cottage—well, it was really more like a good-sized house. It was older, but well kept, painted a soft blue with white trim. Pots of petunias hung from the porch rafters, and rocking chairs lined the covered porch. He imagined the small tables set beside them were for iced tea, maybe guacamole and chips, on warm summer nights.

Rebel climbed the half dozen steps, knocked on the bright blue front door. In the next instant he heard Big Louie barking madly, running all out, his nails scrabbling on the hardwood floor.

He heard Joanna laughing. "Come on, Louie, back off." She opened the door and smiled at him. She was wearing jeans and a Warriors sweatshirt with Steph Curry's number thirty on the chest. Her blond hair was pulled back in a ponytail and her feet were bare, her toenails a pretty sunset color. He was looking at Autumn in twenty years. "Rebel, how are you? Come on in. If you want Ethan, he's at the office. And Autumn is with Tash."

She stopped short, searched his face.

"This isn't about my brother, Joanna. I'll be speaking to Ethan about that situation. No, this is about Tash and Autumn. Can we talk?"

Chapter Fourteen

Seeing her pale, Rebel said quickly, "Nothing's wrong, the kids are fine." He smiled. "Big Louie sounded really scary."

Joanna gave him a tentative smile back, gave a little laugh. "Don't believe a bark out of his mouth. He gave you his signature performance."

Rebel leaned down to scratch Big Louie's head and petted Lula, who had joined them and arched up into his hand. Mackie rolled over beside Big Louie, who was now on his back, and Rebel went down on his haunches and stroked both their bellies. He grinned up at Joanna. "Do they all sleep with you and Ethan?"

"They begin the night with Autumn. Once she's asleep, sooner or later they troop like little soldiers into our bedroom, Lula leading the way. They each have their own spot, and woe to the one who encroaches. Amazingly, it works. All of us sleep like logs, even though Big Louie tends to snore. Would you like some iced tea?" She looked at him closely. "Then you can tell me what the trouble is."

The critters abandoned them in the bright yellow kitchen once they realized iced tea was the only offering on the menu.

As Rebel stirred lemon into his tea, Joanna said, "Rebel, I'm very sorry about your brother's troubles. Have you spoken to Ethan yet? Or Tollie? You know, he's retired FBI and he understands how these investigations work. Ethan told me he was going to call FBI Special Agent Dillon Savich, see what exactly was happening. Do speak to him."

"I'll see Ethan next." He didn't know how to begin, what to say, but the words flew out. "Joanna, Tash told me he thinks he's prescient, that Autumn told him he was. And he told me Autumn is telepathic. I honestly didn't know what to say, and quite frankly I don't know what to do. Has Autumn told you anything about this? It occurred to me Autumn might have been playing around with him, maybe trying to boost his confidence, and he believed it."

Joanna saw the utter disbelief of the reasoning adult and understood. What should she say to him?

Rebel leaned forward. "Joanna, Autumn told Tash she had an uncle Blessed, that if someone looked Blessed in the eyes, he could make them do exactly what he told them to do. She made this Blessed sound like a freak out of a horror movie. Tash said Blessed is dead now. Please tell me if he was real, and what happened to him."

She stared at him, nonplussed. Autumn had told Tash about Blessed? And Tash had told his uncle Rebel?

Rebel said, "I know he told Autumn he wouldn't say anything about Blessed, but Tash is a little kid and it burst out. And to be frank, I had no idea what to say."

Naturally Rebel didn't want to believe it. Who would? She and Ethan had planned to tell Rebel themselves that Tash and Autumn weren't like other children when they thought the time was right. They'd planned to explain to him what he thought was kids' imagination, sheer fantasy, was real, that both Tash and Autumn were gifted. Well, Tash had jumped the gun, so there was no choice now. Rebel was Tash's uncle, and for now, his only family here. How could he accept Tash for what he was unless she was honest with him?

She said slowly, "I know this will be very difficult to believe, you might even think I'm unhinged, but Blessed Backman and what he could do were very real. He was my first husband's much older brother. There were three sons, all of them psychic. We believe Autumn inherited her gifts from her father." She saw the disbelief on his face. "I know, I know, it's very hard to accept, but there's no choice: you will have to come to grips with it, Rebel, sooner or later. My husband Martin's whole family were twisted and dangerous, drunk on their own power, insane really. Blessed was the most dangerous of them, and in addition to his gift, he was a psychopath, a monster. He didn't need a gun, he could control another person just by looking into their eyes. This is the truth, Rebel: he could make them do anything he wanted, even kill themselves. He very nearly made me kill myself. Have you met Ox and Glenis, Ethan's deputies? He took control of them once too, 'stymied' them, that's what his family called it." Joanna paused, stark images of it racing through her mind. She swallowed. "As it turned out, only Autumn could resist Blessed, and even more than that, she destroyed him." Her voice caught. "She nearly died, Rebel. Her grandfather, a vile old man and Blessed's father, shot her in the chest when he saw she was more powerful than he was and couldn't control her, couldn't get her on his side." Joanna swallowed again, willed herself not to lose it. "It was nearly six years ago, but in my nightmares it's happening right now."

She saw Rebel had become very still. He was staring at her expressionless. Well, she'd started it, so now she had to finish it. "Every day I count my blessings the lot of them are dead. Whenever I see the scar on Autumn's chest from the bullet wound I remember." She took a drink of her tea, difficult with the lump in her throat.

She cleared her throat. "Rebel, I realize this is very hard for you to accept, but Autumn wasn't playing with Tash or trying to boost his confidence. She believes he's gifted, and believe me, she would know. If you are willing to suspend your disbelief for a while, as you writers call it, accept there may be a precious few people who are gifted psychically, you'll be able to move forward with Tash, help him through everything that's happening to him and his dad. You're the only one who can. Know this for a fact—Autumn is nothing like her father's family. Even at twelve, she's responsible and sensible. She has a pure heart. She's excited about what Tash can do, what they can do together. She's the perfect friend and guide for him."

Joanna saw he was taking in everything she was telling him, but had her words made him open his mind to the possibilities? She didn't know. "You said Tash told you himself about his gift?"

Ethan took a sip of the delicious tea, looked into her beautiful blue eyes, Autumn's eyes. He felt like he'd walked into one of his novels. She was sincere, she was serious, but . . . "He didn't mean to. It just slipped out. I didn't laugh at him, nothing like that, but naturally I didn't believe him, couldn't begin to believe something so outlandish. As I said, I thought he was either very imaginative or maybe Autumn had put him up to it. But he was dead serious." He paused a moment, then told her about the accident Tash had seen happen before it happened, and his final moments with his mother. He felt his throat close when he said Celia's name, dead of breast cancer two years ago, when Tash was only six.

"What could I say? His father, my brother, Archer, hadn't told me anything about either incident. So could Tash simply have made up both? A little boy's attempt to deal with his mother's death? And only a spot of luck the car roared through the intersection at that particular moment? Look, the fact is he was left too much alone since his father remarried six months ago, and his stepmother doesn't want a little kid underfoot." He searched Joanna Merriweather's face, saw understanding and compassion. He said slowly, "You think it's all true, both you and Ethan."

Joanna nodded. "Yes, for the simple reason we both lived through what happened with Blessed and saw what Autumn was able to do with her mind. As for Tash, if Autumn believes he's gifted, I accept it. It was a wonderful thing he did for his mother, and yes, I believe without a doubt he connected with her before she died. He's a valiant little boy."

Rebel felt as if he'd wandered into an alternate universe. Autumn's mother seemed a rational adult, and she was completely serious, convinced both children were psychic. He said slowly, "How can I believe all that? I may write about supernatural beings walking the earth, but it's fiction, entertainment, and my readers know it isn't real.

"You said Autumn inherited her gift from her father's family, the Backmans. Do you think then Tash could have inherited his gift from someone in our line?"

"I don't know. It seems reasonable, but I do know of an exception—Dillon Savich. He said his gifts simply came to him when he was a teenager. No one really knows, there are so few we know about."

Rebel slowly shook his head. "I can't remember anyone in our family ever talking about prescience or telepathy or anything like that. Sure, my grandmother always seemed to know when someone was about to knock on her front door, but her hearing was very sharp and we all thought she heard us coming."

Joanna waited, saw the same look on his face she'd seen on Ox and Glenis six years before—a rational adult faced with something he couldn't comprehend.

Rebel said finally, "All right, suppose I go ahead and tell Tash I believe he's gifted until proven otherwise. Gifted—it's a nice harmless word for artists, but in this case it means something beyond reality as I know it, as almost everyone knows it." He heaved a sigh. "All right, Joanna, I'll suspend my disbelief, if you think that's what Tash needs right now. And what then? How can I help him?"

Lula jumped on Rebel's lap, followed by Mackie settling himself on Joanna's. Her fingertips had been lightly tapping the smooth oak table, but now she began to stroke Mackie until his purr was engine loud. Lula never made a sound, even though Rebel rubbed her whiskers and lightly scratched her ears.

The kitchen was otherwise silent save for the soft ticking of the clock on the wall.

Joanna knew Rebel Navarro was going to pretend he believed Tash even though his brain wouldn't allow it. She couldn't blame him. It was a lot to accept. Well, it didn't matter, if he did it well and Tash believed it. She said, "I'd counsel you to do what Ethan and I have done with Autumn. We've warned her to keep her gifts under wraps from the outside world because it would scare people, push them away, and there's no reason to do that. I told you Ox and Glenis suffered when Blessed came here and stymied them, but they don't talk about it for Autumn's sake. There were lots of rumors at the time, but I don't think most people in town believed what they heard. We've focused Autumn on the outdoors, on being a kid growing up in Titusville. She thinks of what she can do as just another skill, a fact of her life. I do know, though, that if there was danger threatening anyone, Autumn would act in an instant regardless of what the consequences might be, and that's as it should be."

"Does she ever slip up?"

"Not really. Well"—Joanna shook her head, smiled at the memory—"one time last year a boy at school was bullying a little girl, making fun of her glasses, shoving her. Autumn didn't make any kind of a scene that could make the other students wonder about her. She looked into the boy's eyes and told him he had stomach cramps. He ran away holding his belly. I was very proud of her. She was only eleven, but she was smart enough to think it through and act without causing alarm.

"Another time, we were driving home in a torrential downpour when Autumn yelled, 'Dad, there's a man coming and he's in pain, he's scared, and he's losing control of his car!' Ethan pulled over right away, flicked his lights on and off. The driver managed to skid to a stop a few yards away from us, sideways in the road, and then he passed out. He'd had a heart attack, and somehow Autumn had known. His name is Mr. Philips and he lives on a farm maybe fifteen miles away. He's fine, and he's Ethan's biggest fan. We never told him Autumn was the one who very probably saved his life. And ours too.

"Rebel, the fact is none of us know where these kids' gifts come from, or if they might change. I doubt anyone does, even Dillon Savich. He and Autumn are good friends now, they have a strong bond. Tash will be fine with Autumn."

She sat forward, took his hand. "It's an amazing twist of fate they found each other. I have no doubt they'll be close for the rest of their lives. I think it's simply impossible for Tash's father not to suspect already, given his two experiences with his son. Will he believe he is gifted? Probably, but that will have to wait until the mess he's in is cleaned up." She glanced down at her watch, hugged Mackie, and set him on the floor. "It's time for me to teach three couples from Terre Haute how not to drown while white water rafting. They're young, eager, and unafraid. My job will be to keep them safe while I scare the crap out of them."

Joanna watched Rebel set Lula on the floor, give both cats pats on the head, and stand. She touched her fingers to his arm. "My very best advice? Be yourself with Tash. If you do, he'll be fine, both of you will be fine. Tash and Autumn are on a journey of discovery together, and there'll be some hiccups for sure, but Autumn was right when she told him they'd have a blast together.

"You have your brother and his troubles to deal with now, too, and it doesn't seem there's much you can do about that except wait and see. Do ask Ethan if he's heard anything more from Dillon Savich." She smiled at him. "I'm glad you came to see me, Rebel. Remember, whatever happens, whatever you see, Tash isn't crazy and neither are you. You'll work it out."

Joanna watched him as he walked down the drive. She wondered how much of what she'd told him he'd ever believe, until Autumn or Tash made it impossible for him not to believe. Maybe he'd spend some time looking into his family tree to see if he could find a great-uncle Festus or someone else who'd spent his life in an attic. She knew he'd never understand any more than she did how a child could be a math genius or a music savant, much less have psychic gifts. She pulled her cell phone out of her pocket and called Ethan.

Chapter Fifteen

Hoover Building
Deputy Director's Office
Washington, D.C.
WEDNESDAY

Deputy Director James Maitland rose, stepped around his big mahogany desk, and shook Elizabeth's hand, surprised at her firm grip and the calluses on her fingers and palm. He'd expected a blue-blooded English aristocrat, all proper and polished, not someone who looked like a tough-as-nails special agent. He nodded to Savich and Sherlock and waved them to his conference table. He'd remembered her name from Savich's report a year ago about Samir Basara's gun battle with Sherlock, ending, thankfully, with his death on the steps of the Lincoln Memorial. He'd had time to glance through the brief biographical file Goldie had pulled up for him before they'd arrived. He studied Elizabeth Palmer—*excuse me*, Lady Elizabeth Palmer— daughter of the Earl of Camden, wealthy banker and member of the House of Lords. He'd read her younger brother, Thomas, Lord Audley and the future Earl of Camden, was a drug addict. What a disappointment that had to be for the present earl. He thanked the Lord his four sons were all straight arrows. He had a son named Tommy, too, following in his footsteps. He'd transferred to the Boston field office and was engaged to marry Juliet

Ash Calley, a concert pianist and one of the most beautiful women Maitland had ever met.

He said in his smooth baritone voice, "Sherlock, tell me how you think we might assist Lady Elizabeth."

Sherlock said, "There were three attempts on her life in London three months ago. The final attempt nearly succeeded. Perhaps the attempts were connected to her former relationship with Samir Basara. I think it's best Elizabeth tells us all about what has happened herself."

Elizabeth took them through the three attempts on her life in a precise, clipped voice that reminded Mr. Maitland of the BBC at its snootiest. When she finished, Maitland said, "Are you certain they wanted to kill you? Not take you? For possible ransom?"

Elizabeth blinked at him. "I never considered that, nor did John Eiserly. At least he didn't say anything to that effect."

"Why?"

"I felt their hatred for me, especially when they broke into my house at night that last time. I thought the knife would have gone into my heart if the MI5 agent guarding me hadn't taken the knife in his own chest instead. I thank God he survived."

Mr. Maitland said matter-of-factly, "Whoever they were, they weren't trained operatives. The first attack seems spur of the moment. There you were, run you down, hurt you, but kill you? Not certain. The second, trying to shoot through your door in the middle of London, was hardly an improvement. It showed urgency, perhaps, but little planning. The third, breaking into your house at night, now that showed some thought and planning, some brain power. You were lucky to end up with only an arm wound. They were committed, no doubt about that, but again, I ask, to what exactly?"

Sherlock said, "We haven't had a whole lot of time to process this, but if we're talking killing her, it could be revenge for Basara's death, or for the imam's and Bahar Zain's imprisonment, one or all but it doesn't make a lot of sense to me they'd wait a year. So, just maybe there's something else going on here."

Elizabeth drew a deep breath. "If it's something else entirely, Basara not in the picture, I can't think of anything. I've done nothing to draw attention to myself this past year. I've lived my life, painted, taken care of my brother, visited my mother and father, kept to myself mainly. But after that third attempt and I ended up in hospital, I knew I had to do something to protect myself. I know Mr. Eiserly was pulling his hair out trying to find out what was going on, but he was flummoxed. My father found Hurley Janklov and convinced him to hide me away and train me at his survival camp in Maryland."

Sherlock gave him a fat smile. "Imagine, sir, three months with Hurley and she's still alive to tell us about it."

Mr. Maitland laughed. He knew Hurley Janklov, retired from both the special forces and as a trainer at Quantico. "I know firsthand what Hurley can do. I've seen him toss champion fighters around and walk away whistling. Like Sherlock, Lady Elizabeth, I applaud you."

He was looking at her with a warm, reassuring smile, like her father's. She'd been studying him closely as she told her story, her stomach churning and her anxiety threatening to sink her, because she knew this man held her future in his hands. His position, she knew, was like that of John Eiserly's boss at MI5. She'd impressed him? She said, "I barely made it, sir. For the first couple of weeks, I didn't think I would survive. Whenever I curled up on the ground and prayed for death, Hurley would come down on his knees beside me and whisper in my ear, 'Come on, Liz, show me some grit.'" She shook her head. "And so I did, because there was really no choice." She paused, gave him a crooked smile. "But you know, sir, there were times I really wanted to punch him. Or shoot him."

Everyone laughed. Looking at her, Mr. Maitland thought

she'd found her grit just fine. Still, he'd call Hurley, get his opinion of her.

Elizabeth's chin went up. "Hurley did end up saying he was surprised a fancy-assed white-faced Brit would turn out to be a brick. It sounded like a compliment, but I wasn't sure."

Mr. Maitland said, "Hurley really said you were a brick? Here's the truth—that's his highest compliment. Well, except for what he called Sherlock here. Hurley called her a goddess."

Sherlock laughed. "Goddess of what, I wonder."

Mr. Maitland said, "As for you, Savich, Hurley kept threatening to get in the ring with you."

Savich grinned. "When I feel like having a couple of bones broken, I'll give him a call."

Mr. Maitland turned back to Elizabeth. "And what do you have in mind? Tell me how you think we can help you."

Elizabeth sat forward in her chair, hands fisted on the tabletop. "Since it was Sherlock who killed Basara at your Lincoln Memorial, I hoped she would help stop whoever is behind this from killing me."

There was silence for a long moment, as Mr. Maitland looked first at her, then over at Savich and Sherlock, and down at the pen he was weaving through his fingers. Elizabeth tried not to fidget, but she prayed this man would agree to help her. In what seemed like an eternity of silence, she stared at a photo on his desk of his family—four young men, his sons, she imagined, all as big as their father, and the small light-haired woman they surrounded.

She glanced over at Savich and Sherlock and felt a stab of envy. Would she ever feel as close to anyone as they appeared to be? What were they thinking? Their expressions gave nothing away. They were waiting to hear what their boss would say.

Mr. Maitland knew in his gut if he decided not to involve the FBI in this British mess, Savich and Sherlock would help her anyway. Then there was the fact he wasn't sure how his Brit counterpart, Sir James Hanson of the Joint Terrorism Analysis Centre, would take their getting involved. They'd worked closely together before, so maybe he wouldn't get bent out of shape. He wanted to shake his head at himself—of course he wanted to protect this young woman. Her only mistake had been sleeping with an assassin and living to tell about it, then he was all in. And Sherlock's taking down that assassin had gleaned great publicity for the FBI, a very nice bonus.

Still, he threw the ball in Sherlock's court. "Since Lady Elizabeth came to you specifically for help, Sherlock, what do you recommend?"

Sherlock sat forward. "Sir, as you know, Dillon and John Eiserly, now deputy director of the Joint Terrorism Analysis Centre, are good friends. They worked together to help find Basara, so I don't expect any blowback from John if we get involved. He has local resources we obviously don't have, and he has direct access to the major players who worked with Samir Basara, all of them in English prisons. I can't say how his director will react, but I think you could easily handle any concerns he might have." Was that laying it on too thick? "As I said, I don't think this is about revenge, I think it's about something else. With John's help, we can find out exactly what that is."

Mr. Maitland turned to Savich, raised a salt-and-pepper eyebrow.

Savich said without hesitation, "I agree with Sherlock. Elizabeth can stay with us for now, hopefully keep her off their radar." He looked at Elizabeth. "I'm willing to bet John Eiserly already knows where you've been. I know you tried to cover your tracks, but we can't know for sure whether anyone else has traced you, only that they didn't come after you in Maryland. Either they couldn't find you, or it no longer fit their plans."

Sherlock said, "Or they know about Hurley Janklov and knew that was a no-go."

Savich said, "That's the truth. Now, if they discover, Elizabeth, you've come to the FBI for help, their plans might change. We'll need to control what they know and when they know it. We don't want them attacking you in the middle of Dupont Circle."

Elizabeth looked at each face, said slowly, "Do you think you can use me as bait?"

Sherlock took her hand, squeezed. "Let's hope it doesn't come to that. If we can find out who they are or who they've hired, we can take them in immediately if they enter the country. Above all, we want to keep you protected. Dillon, what do you think of assigning Rome Foxe to stay with her?"

Mr. Maitland said, "Foxe? He's fairly new to the CAU, isn't he?"

Savich said, "True. Rome's still feeling his way in the unit, but he's smart and he's resourceful."

"So you want to throw him in the deep end, let him prove himself?"

"I think he'll do fine, sir." He didn't add that he wondered how well Special Agent Roman Foxe, the only son of a police captain who ran the detectives out of New York City's nineteenth precinct, would get along with an English aristocrat.

Mr. Maitland tapped his pen on the tabletop, a longtime habit, and slowly nodded. "All right." He arched an eyebrow at Sherlock as he said smoothly, "I'll call Sir James Hanson, make sure he's on board or at least willing to cooperate. Savich, it's up to you to see what John Eiserly can do for us. It is possible Eiserly will ask us to send you back to London, Lady Elizabeth."

Elizabeth rose straight up, leaned forward, and planted her palms on the conference table. "I won't go back, sir. I can't, not until this is over. I came here because of Sherlock. She's

Hurley's goddess. I want her to be my goddess too. She'll help me take care of these insane nutters." Her chin went up. "You can't kick me out, I'll claim asylum. And please, call me just plain Elizabeth. After all, we're here in the United States."

Mr. Maitland knew she was scared. He was impressed how she was trying to hide her fear behind a rather well-done rant. He smiled. "All right, Elizabeth. Savich will make your feelings clear to Eiserly, and I'll make them equally clear to Hanson." He rose, shook Elizabeth's hand. "Savich, Sherlock, get this figured out and keep me in the loop. I believe we're done here, folks."

Sherlock lightly touched her fingertips to Elizabeth's arm as they walked past Goldie, Mr. Maitland's own personal dragon. She actually smiled at Elizabeth. Sherlock said, "It's past time for lunch and the baby and I are starving for a taco. What do you say, Elizabeth? You hungry?"

Elizabeth said, "I confess I've never eaten a taco."

Savich said, "My wife claims tacos are a nutritionist's dream, all five food groups in each bite. You'll have to tell us what you think."

Chapter Sixteen

Special Agent Roman Foxe was speechless. Like every other agent in the CAU, he'd watched Savich and Sherlock speak with a young woman and leave with her, and wondered what it was about. There was lots of talk, but no one knew who she was. But no longer. Rome stared at his boss and said, his voice incredulous, "You want me to bodyguard the woman who slept with that maniac assassin Samir Basara and claimed she didn't know who and what he was? And she thinks now—a year later—maybe terrorists are trying to kill her because they think she betrayed their boss?"

Savich said, "Well put, and yes, that's what I want you to do. Keep her safe. She came to Sherlock for help because Sherlock was the one who killed Basara, really no other reason. I've forwarded the link to her files to you, and I've already been in touch with MI5, asked them to send us the details of their investigation into what happened to her in London. I'll let her tell you what she's been up to since she came to the U.S. You know the drill. Spend time with her, gain her trust, find out whatever you can from her. Get to know her well enough to predict how she will respond if something does happen.

"As I said, above all, your primary assignment is to keep her alive, Rome, and work with us to determine who's after her. We don't know whether the people who want her dead will find her and come after her again. Maybe she's right and it's payback, but their waiting a year for that doesn't make a lot of sense to me or Sherlock.

"I'm counting on you, Rome. Sherlock has finished speaking with her for now, and it's time you met her. Come, let me introduce you."

Rome didn't want to be responsible for an uppity Brit who'd clearly shown she had appallingly poor judgment. It would pull him away from tracking down the psychopath who'd murdered three retired physicians in Lincolnville, Tennessee, working with Lucy McKnight and her encyclopedic brain, an agent he liked and trusted. But Savich was in charge. He remembered how proud his father, the chief of detectives at the nineteenth precinct, had been when he'd graduated Quantico six months before, telling him he was going to work for one of the best FBI agents in the bureau. Roman suspected his father had something to do with his being assigned to Savich's unit, the CAU at the Hoover, the central nervous system of Disneyland East, as it was called in the field offices. But now everything had stopped in its tracks because of a nitwit Brit airhead who'd shown she'd had the judgment of a gnat—intimate for months with a murderer, claiming she didn't know? Didn't even suspect? It was like sleeping with Hannibal Lecter for months and claiming she had no idea he got off on eating people's brains.

Savich said as they walked out of his office together, "I've assigned Davis Sullivan to work with Lucy on the Lincolnville case. Give them all your materials, insights, and recommendations. Now you'll meet your priority—Lady Elizabeth Palmer."

Roman never changed expressions. "Do I call her Your Majesty when I meet her? Bow or drop to one knee?"

Savich laughed. Obviously, his new agent wasn't thrilled, but he knew he could trust him. Lucy spoke well of him, said he was tough, smart, and had great reaction time. Best of all, she'd said he paid attention to every detail in the field, was always aware of his surroundings. "Call her Elizabeth and shake her hand. The two of you can use the conference room. She'll tell you what happened three months ago. When you've heard her story, take her out of here, someplace she'd like, to distract her. Give her some relaxation time, some non-stress time, she deserves it. She'll be staying with me and Sherlock in the short term. Drop her off with us this evening."

Savich paused a moment, saw Rome wasn't happy. Savich laid a hand on his arm. "She saved herself in London, got a knife wound in her arm during the last attack. She escaped England and came here. She trained with Hurley Janklov for three months, one on one."

Rome's head jerked up. "What? Are you serious? She spent three months with Janklov and she's still alive and walking upright? I heard stories about Janklov at Quantico—talk about a hard-ass maniac." Rome couldn't help it, he was impressed, until he considered maybe Janklov had gone easy on her, made sure she wouldn't break a fingernail. Too, everyone knew Janklov had been a major horndog until his marriage awhile back.

Rome realized he was being an ass, but he was angry; he wanted his assignment back. He wanted to do something important, not babysit a fricking Brit. But Savich, and evidently Mr. Maitland, thought otherwise.

Savich said, "She's been through a lot, Rome, and I don't just mean Hurley. Come meet her."

Sherlock saw them and smiled, waved him and Savich over to her in the conference room. "Rome, I'd like you to meet Elizabeth Palmer. She's now in your charge. Elizabeth, this is

Special Agent Roman Foxe. As I told you, you'll be counting on him. He's mean, he's tough, he can lift a car off you while whistling Bon Jovi. Well, that's what I heard. Oh, yes, everyone calls him Rome."

When he got close, he saw Elizabeth Palmer was prime. She came up to his nose, every bit as tall as Sherlock. Her eyes were a clear hazel, her hair a natural blond, no doubt in his mind about that, and on the long side, sort of wavy and pulled back from her fine-boned face, fastened to the back of her neck with a plain silver clip. Her eyebrows and lashes were darker. She wore a slash of coral lipstick, no other makeup he could see. She was wearing tight black jeans and a gray jacket over a gray silk blouse, black low-heeled boots on her feet. She looked expensive, and something else that hit him solid— she looked hopeful.

Elizabeth stuck out a white hand and Rome shook it. Whoa, what was that? She had calluses? So Hurley had really trained her?

"How do you do, Special Agent Foxe," Her Majesty said in a cool Brit voice.

He gave her a dip of the head. "I'm fine, thank you, ma'am."

Savich said, "Elizabeth, I know you've been through this a dozen times, but it's important Rome knows everything that's happened, from your mouth. He'll be bringing you to our house this evening for dinner. And that has to stay confidential, all right?"

No way Rome could refuse, and that meant a call to Lindy James at State to break their dinner date. An emergency, but no explanation. Lindy wouldn't be happy.

The CAU conference room was good sized, with a big table and twelve chairs and a glass wall looking out into the unit. Roman pulled out a chair for her, earning him a raised eyebrow and a crisp "Thank you." Rome sat opposite her, pulled a small tablet out of his suit coat pocket. "I'd like to record this, if you don't mind. Tell me everything."

Elizabeth recited what had happened three months ago in London, fast and fluent. She even anticipated questions, since she'd answered so many, and weaved them in.

When she'd finished, she took a sip of water from the glass in front of her and sat silently, waiting. Roman set his tablet down. She'd been calm as a judge. Rome was impressed. He said, "Each time you said there were two men. Are you sure about the number? And are you sure it was the same two men all three times?"

No one had asked this before. After a moment, Elizabeth nodded. "There were definitely two in the Aston Martin because of the fact that no more than two would fit. The same two all three times? I can't be sure. I didn't see the man who tried to talk his way through my front door before the two of them tried to shoot their way in. There could have been more, I don't know, but the feeling I had was that it was just the two. As I told you, at least one of them had a hint of an Arabic accent, like Samir Basara." She sat forward, clasped her hands. "The third time, I recognized the man's voice who'd come to my front door, but I didn't see either of their faces, and they were wearing masks." She paused, looked thoughtful. "Do you know, what I remember most about them was their utter hatred of me." She swallowed, got herself together. "As I already told you, one of them was a large man, the other smaller, but both were fit, and vicious. They were young, I'd say. Benny, Officer Bewley, shot the smaller one who was on top of me ready to cut me with a knife. The fingerprints on the knife the surgeons pulled out of Benny's chest were too smeared to be of use. MI5 officers found the attacker's blood, but there was no DNA match. Deputy Director Eiserly told me that only meant the man Benny shot isn't in the system, which didn't necessarily mean he hadn't committed any crimes elsewhere. There wasn't even anyone identified as a close relative in the DNA databases."

Rome said, "Sounds like the two of them were trained outside of England, probably a terrorist camp in Syria or Iran, maybe Lebanon, lots of choices. Their being on the young side fits the bill. You said Bahar Zain had two young siblings. Now, he was the one who actually placed the packets of C-4 in St. Paul's, right?"

Elizabeth took another sip of water. "Yes. Mr. Eiserly told me he was a longtime disciple of Samir's and a devout jihadist. He worshipped Samir, did whatever Samir told him to do, thought of him as his brother-in-arms, as it were. As to Bahar Zain's siblings, there are no birth records in England, and their mother, Almira Zain, who lives near Covent Garden, wouldn't talk to MI5 officers.

"That last night, the man with the knife seemed to be in a wild, ungoverned rage, a crazed excitement, nearly out of control. We all thought they might have been Bahar Zain's brothers, but MI5 couldn't find them."

"But I don't even understand how Zain's brothers could believe I betrayed their brother. I didn't even meet their brother, didn't even know his name until after St. Paul's. The only terrorist I knew was Samir Basara, and as I've learned, he was basically a murderer for hire."

"Zain's siblings or someone else close to Basara could believe Basara told you too much in his pillow talk, maybe not enough to know exactly when and where, but enough to lead to Bahar Zain's capture or Basara's death."

She blanked all expression from her face and said in a clipped, cold voice, "Samir never talked about his business with me. Ever."

Rome nodded. "But no one else would know that, would they? All right, do you have anything else to tell me?"

Elizabeth shook her head. "No, I've told you everything I can think of. Wait. This might not be important, but I told Deputy Director Eiserly one of the two men in the Aston Martin was wearing an unusual ring—I only caught a glimpse of it. It looked heavy, silver, and I saw some kind of stone set in the crown. Maybe if we find him he'll be wearing that ring."

Rome typed this in on his tablet, then raised his head. "What did Hurley Janklov teach you in three months?"

"Defensive driving, how to analyze dangerous situations and decide the best course of action in a millisecond, how to fight, and how to shoot." She gave him a cold smile. "And most important? To accept nothing but a win."

Rome stood, slipped the tablet back into his pocket. "That's quite a list. I'll want more specifics so I can judge for myself the level of your skills in all these areas."

"Hurley said I could outshoot him, well, nearly, and that I was a brick."

That drew him up for a moment. "A brick?"

"That's right. A brick. Mr. Maitland said it's his highest compliment."

"A brick, yeah, that sure sounds like a compliment." Rome shook his head and motioned for her to follow him. He walked her back to Sherlock, who looked from him to Elizabeth and saw Elizabeth looked stiff, her face set. She was angry and trying not to show it. What had happened?

Should she kick Rome now or wait and see if the two of them would work it out between them? Dillon had told her Rome wasn't happy about this assignment. Maybe she could just whisper in his ear to suck it up. At least she could remind him to do what Dillon had already asked. She said, "Rome, it's time for you to get Elizabeth to relax now. Let her be a tourist and decompress. Show her some sights before you come to dinner tonight. Dillon has been speaking with John Eiserly, talking him out of the information he has. He might have all of it by tonight."

Rome said, "You're saying I should don my special agent's tourist director's hat? And get paid for it?"

Well, that was snarky.

Chapter Seventeen

As they walked toward the elevators down the impossibly wide empty hallways of the Hoover Building, Elizabeth knew this big man, with his perfunctory smile that didn't begin to reach his hard eyes, didn't want to be with her. And why would he? She'd been thrown at him with no warning. Of course he'd rather be hunting criminals than babysitting a Brit he didn't know who'd been stupid enough to sleep with an assassin.

They stepped onto an elevator filled with agents and staff. Rome saw everyone was looking at Elizabeth. He didn't introduce her. One of the agents asked him about Ballou's safe deposit key, but Rome said he wasn't involved any longer.

The agent didn't let it go. "You think there's a treasure map in Agent Ballou's safe-deposit box? I heard it's somewhere in Virginia. I'm thinking he and his cohorts wrapped a steel chain around an iron chest or something, sank it in a river."

Rome said without pause, "Yeah, that might be right, Gates. I did hear there was dried slime on the key."

An agent grinned at Rome on his way out. "Right. Slime. Thanks for the entertainment."

Elizabeth said, "Quite a tale Gates spun. I especially liked your slime. Do you think anyone bought it? And what, may I ask, did they buy, exactly? A magic key? What's it for? Was this about a case you were working on before Agent Savich assigned you to me?"

"Not really. I was working on the murder of three retired physicians in Tennessee. But you are my work now. Sherlock thinks you need a break from all the questions, all the accumulated stress, so I'm going to show you my favorite place in Washington."

Roman took her to the Franklin D. Roosevelt Memorial. An SUV with three wilted children hanging out the windows to catch a breeze drove out of a parking slot and Rome took the spot fast. He waited until she was out of the car before he said, "This is the famous Cherry Tree Walk. It runs all along the Tidal Basin. Over there is the National Mall."

"But where's the monument?"

"It's not really a single monument, it's a memorial and all outdoors. Come along. There are four rooms that really aren't rooms at all, they're enclosures, and each represents one of Roosevelt's presidential terms." They wove through tourists reading quotes, looking at displays, and snapping photos of each other in front of the waterfalls. In the third room the waterfall was much larger and much louder. Elizabeth stood still, staring up at the sculpture of FDR in his well-disguised wheelchair, his terrier, Fala, beside him.

Rome said, "Fala performed tricks on demand, even had his own comic strip. My folks brought me here when I was a kid and I'll never forget Dad telling me the waterfalls sometimes froze in the winter." He fanned himself. "But not now."

They saw a little boy try to reach Fala, watched his mom pull him back and stick a straw in his mouth from a bottle of water so he wouldn't whine.

Elizabeth said, "Frozen. Really? It's hard to imagine. There'd be utter silence." She paused a moment. "I can see why you like this place. My grandfather met President Roosevelt."

"What?"

"He was on Churchill's staff during World War II, even traveled with him. He didn't see any fighting, though he'd been trained at Sandhurst—that's the royal military academy and officer training center. They assigned him to the War Office in London because of his talents, and that's where Churchill spotted him."

"He wasn't picked because he was an aristocrat, like Churchill, an earl of the realm?"

If her voice had sounded royally snooty before, now it nearly froze him. "I can see why you might think that, Special Agent. Actually, Churchill was brilliant at spotting talent, but you can sneer away, if you wish. You seem to be quite good at it."

Well, that was a nice solid hit. "All right, no more sneering. Actually, I'm fascinated. What did your grandfather think of Roosevelt?"

"I do remember he said the president was valiant. That's the word he used. That's all I remember, sorry. At the time, I didn't quite know what he meant." She pointed at the statue. "Is it true everyone tried to hide the fact he was in a wheelchair?"

"Evidently it wasn't hard to hide his disability from the public since there was no social media, no TV. What Churchill said, that single word makes a perfect tribute."

"My father told me Grandfather said all the leaders he'd met agreed the war was horrendous and a tragic waste, so many lives lost, so much destruction, all because of a single megalomaniac and his mad ambitions. He wondered what the world would be like when I grew up, but he was sad to say he doubted humanity would change. There'd always be people who wanted what others had and would willingly kill to get it."

She paused. "I remember my father telling me my grandfather met Clementine, Churchill's wife. He believed without her Churchill would have continued on, but he'd be dead inside.

"He stayed on with Churchill until he married my grandmother Mary Anne in the late fifties. He was forty-one and Grandmother was twenty-eight. He died too soon, of a heart attack when he was only seventy-seven. I was seven. She died the next year, of a broken heart, my parents believe. When I was a child, many times at dinner, my parents would raise a toast to Grandfather and Grandmother. I remember Grandfather carrying me around on his back down to our lake to swim and fish. I missed him. I still miss him." She raised her chin and said in her coldest voice, "That's when my father inherited the title and became the tenth Earl of Camden. And yes, it was because he was born to it. He didn't have to earn it."

Rome looked at the colossal cascading waterfall, so loud it drowned out all tourist conversations around them. He leaned closer so she would hear him. "What did your grandfather think of Churchill's paintings?"

She'd thought Rome was a git, tough and smart mouthed, but hardly interested in Churchill's art. She looked over at him, said slowly, "Churchill painted mainly to keep what he called his black dog of depression at bay. Churchill saw that my grandfather admired a particular impressionist work painted in the South of France and gave it to him. My mom told me Grandfather was very fond of the only painting Churchill ever did of his wife, Clementine, but of course he couldn't very well ask for it. The French landscape still hangs in my father's study."

"Speaking of your parents, do they know what's happened to you and where you are?"

She said after a moment, "My dad helped me arrange my getaway from England. I doubt my mother knows all of it. I certainly didn't tell her. The last thing I wanted was to add more alarm. I text them every couple of days, reassure them. And I know Deputy Director Eiserly speaks to Dad frequently. But he's kept up the pretense he doesn't know where I am. But I didn't tell either of them the truth when I left Hurley's."

Rome was frowning at her. "Do your parents know about Samir Basara?"

Elizabeth's voice was matter-of-fact. "Of course, everyone did, it was common knowledge. My friends thought I was very cool. The two of us were very popular in my circle. As for my father, he was appalled. He tried to talk me out of seeing him, said it was making him a laughingstock, and, to be honest, I was secretly pleased to hear it. You see, I was angry at him for hurting my mother with his string of affairs. It was my way of striking back."

"Your mother knew about your dad's mistresses?"

"There was a long line, and yes, my mother knew, she knew about all of them. I suppose part of my motivation for being with Samir was to let him feel what it was like to have no power."

"Of course she has power. She doesn't have to put up with that crap. She can divorce him. That isn't against the law now in England, is it?"

Elizabeth grinned. "No, not against the law, and that was pure snark. My mom's very old-school. She was taught when you married, you signed up for life, so she's always suffered in silence. Even now, my relationship with my father is strained, though we've mended it somewhat over the past year and he did help me get away from England."

Rome said nothing more as they walked back to the parking lot, baking in the hot, heavy air, wishing he'd had the sense to bring some bottled water. Parents were herding cranky children, guzzling the water he wished he had, no longer snapping photos with their cell phones.

"I can't believe it's so hot this late in the day," Rome said, and first thing, he turned on the air conditioner in the Range Rover. They both leaned over toward the vents. He glanced at his watch. "Perfect timing. Savich knows quite a bit about World War II. You should tell him about your grandfather."

As Rome started toward Georgetown, he asked her, "Do you drink coffee?"

"Of course."

"You're in for a treat. Savich makes the best coffee on the planet."

Chapter Eighteen

Rebel and Tash sat in front of the still-orange embers in the fireplace, the remains of BBQ and potato salad from Uncle Willie's BBQ Palace on paper plates beside them.

Rebel hadn't told Tash about his father yet, and now he knew he couldn't put it off any longer. He hated to. Tash was happy on his full stomach. No choice. He took his nephew's small, scratched hand in his, gave a light squeeze.

Tash looked up, cocked his head to one side, and said, "What's for dessert, Uncle Rebel?"

Rebel would have laughed in ordinary circumstances, but not now. "I can't believe you have an ounce of room left," he said, and lightly tickled Tash's stomach. Tash laughed and tried to tickle him. Rebel let him, then he pulled Tash against him, squeezed him. He couldn't think of a way to sugarcoat it, so he just spit it out. "This is about your dad, Tash. Someone has been embezzling—stealing—a great deal money from your dad's investment fund. The FBI don't know where your dad is now and he hasn't answered my texts or calls since this morning."

Tash pulled back. "I don't understand."

"The FBI believes your dad could be involved."

Task jerked away, jumped to his feet. He was shaking. "You mean they think he stole from his own company? That's crazy! My dad wouldn't do anything like that."

"I don't think so either, Tash, but since a great deal of money is missing, and your dad is in Europe, they suspect him. It's got to be someone who works for your dad, someone he trusts, who stole the money. We're going to have to trust the FBI to find out who it is. All you and I can do right now is wait, and keep trying to get through to your dad."

"He didn't call me either."

Rebel heard the fear in his voice and didn't know what to do. "We'll keep trying, Tash."

Tash ran his tongue over his lips. "I'm scared, Uncle Rebel." He laid his small hand on his uncle's arm. "You promise you don't think Dad's a crook?"

"I promise. The FBI will discover who is. You don't need to be scared, all right? We just have to wait."

Easy words to say to a little kid he knew was scared spitless. He was an adult and he was scared spitless himself.

Tash looked ready to burst into tears. He was wringing his hands. "You don't understand, Uncle Rebel. I had dreams before we came here. They were real scary and awful and they were all the same and I knew they were about my dad. Something bad was going to happen to him. And now it has and it's my fault. If I hadn't dreamed about it—"

Rebel kept his voice calm and smooth. "Tash, a dream can't make something happen, bad or good."

But Tash wasn't buying it. He shook his head back and forth, whispered, "I think it's just starting—no, I'm sure it's just starting. It's going to get really bad and I can't stop it."

Tash thought his dreams were premonitions? No wonder he was so scared. Rebel pulled Tash onto his lap, cradled him in his arms. "Try to forget the dreams, Tash. That's all they are, just bad dreams. You and I—we're going to stay together until your dad can come home."

Tash laid his face against Rebel's shoulder. "Does everyone in town know about Dad?"

"Yes, very probably. News like this gets around really fast."

"Do Autumn and her mom and dad know?"

"Yes, they do, and Ethan's going to help however he can. And so will FBI agent Dillon Savich."

Tash suddenly straightened, his small hands now fists. "If the FBI knew my dad they'd never think he could be a crook. He wouldn't."

"I agree. Listen, Tash, the FBI has a division that looks into financial crimes like this. They'll find out the truth and your dad will come home."

Tash fell silent and Rebel continued to cradle him close. To his surprise, Tash said against his shoulder, "After Mama died Dad changed. He used to be really happy and then she got sick and died. He'd hold me and he'd cry. He didn't smile much at all, and then he met Sasha." He gave a sigh.

Rebel stared at Tash's small serious face, his eyes so like Rebel's, nearly the exact same light gray. He felt something he'd never felt before in his life—overwhelming love and the soul-deep desire to protect this little boy with his life. He squeezed Tash closer. "Maybe when this investigation is over and your dad comes back, he'll agree to let you live with me at least part of the time. What do you think?"

Joy clashed with Tash's awful fear. He bounced up. "Yes, yes, that'd be great!" Then he stopped cold. "I hope my dad doesn't forget me now he has Sasha."

Rebel ruffled his head, pulled out a grin. "Fat chance. I'll have to beg your father, maybe crawl, so he'll let you spend time with me."

Tash was quiet, then he said in a hopeful little voice, "Do you really think so? You don't think Sasha will tell him she doesn't want me around at all?"

"Sasha has nothing to say about this, Tash. Will you believe me?"

Slowly, Tash nodded. Rebel held his nephew against his chest and kissed his forehead. Tash drew back. "Could I call Autumn to tell her? It's not too late."

"No, it's not too late, you can call her before you go to bed." Rebel hated to say it, but he had to. "Tash, regardless of what happens, it's got to be your dad's decision how much time you live with me, you know that, right?"

Before he could answer him, the doorbell rang, startling both of them. "Stay here, Tash. I'll see who it is." Rebel stood, set Tash on his feet. "Really, stay here."

A man and a woman stood on his front doorstep. They raised their badges in concert. "Mr. Rebel Navarro? I'm Special Agent Loretta Morales and this is Special Agent Louis Briggs. We're from the Philadelphia FBI field office. We'd like to speak to you about your brother."

Rebel eyed the small woman in her thirties, solidly built with short brown hair and dark liquid eyes, wearing black pants and a black blazer. No one offered to shake hands. He said slowly, "I certainly wasn't expecting this. Why are you here in Titusville, at my house, so late?"

Morales said, "There was an accident about ten miles east of here and we were held up. May we come in, Mr. Navarro?"

Rebel didn't move. "I know nothing at all about my brother's business. I have no idea where he is, if he isn't still in Paris. I just heard the news about the missing funds like everyone else."

Special Agent Briggs stepped around her. He was older, in his mid- to late forties, tall and beefy, with a fringe of salt-and-pepper hair circling his head. He looked Rebel up and down and said, his voice deep and aggressive, "As Agent Morales said, we are here to speak to you about your brother, Mr. Navarro. We'd like to know where he is. May we come in?"

It wasn't a question. Rebel stepped back, waved them into the entrance hall, and closed the front door. "My nephew is in the living room. Please wait here until I take him to his room and put him to bed." Rebel turned back toward the living room.

Briggs said, voice sharp, "Your nephew, Tasher? Your brother's son? We didn't know he was staying with you, but I suppose that makes sense. You're not going to run, are you, Mr. Navarro?"

Rebel jerked around. "Run? Is that some sort of FBI humor? Why would I do that? This is my home. My brother left his son with me for the summer."

Special Agent Morales put her hand on Briggs's arm. "Go take care of your nephew. We'll wait."

Tash said from behind him, "Uncle Rebel, I don't understand. Why did they come here?"

Rebel went down on his knees, eye level with Tash. "They want to ask me some questions about your dad. Now, let's get you upstairs. You had a shower when you got home from your canoe trip with Autumn, so let's get your teeth brushed and—"

Special Agent Briggs said, impatience shimmering in the air around him, "He's a big boy, he can brush his own teeth—"

Morales cut him off. She smiled down at Tash, stuck out her hand. "I like your name, Tash. My name's Loretta."

Tash gingerly took her hand. "My mama named me Tasher after her papa, but I'm Tash."

"It's a great name. You look like your uncle."

Tash beamed at her. "Yes, I do, and my dad too. I want to come and live with him part of the time once you prove my dad didn't do anything wrong."

Morales smiled at Rebel. "Do what you need to do, Mr. Navarro. It was a pleasure to meet you, Tash." Morales and Briggs watched Rebel Navarro take the little boy's hand, walk with him up the stairs, and disappear down a hallway to the right of the landing.

Morales said to Briggs, who towered over her, "You know I've got a kid about his age. They need care, okay? I get it—we're both tired and hungry. I know it's a stretch for you, Lou, but he's a child, make nice."

Agent Lou Briggs said, "It took us forever to find this god-forsaken place, Loretta, and we still need to get home tonight. This guy probably knows exactly where Archer Navarro is. He left his kid with him until the two of them could hook up again." He waved his hand around him. "You know he's involved, how else could he afford this place?"

Loretta smacked his arm. She was small, but she was stronger than you'd expect, and he flinched. "I know what you think, but we came late to this case. Didn't you read the brief about the Navarro family?"

"I know enough to do my job, like this guy writes scary stories, but look around you, Loretta, no way does he make enough for this mansion. He had to get the bucks from somewhere. It only makes sense they dreamed up this scam together."

Chapter Nineteen

Morales rolled her eyes. "Since you mostly read about sports and fencing, Lou, it's obvious you don't know Rebel Navarro is famous for his bestselling horror thrillers. He's probably the richest guy in town, and he's made lots of money for a good while now. He can afford this house, trust me."

"Okay, who cares? But you know as well as I do some people always want more, nothing's ever enough for them." Briggs started pacing the beautiful wide-planked oak floor, with geometric rugs tossed here and there. He loved the oak, wished he had it in his own house.

Rebel had heard Briggs as he came down the stairs and managed to quash his anger. He called out, "Maybe you'd enjoy reading one of my scary little stories, Agent Briggs. I could let you have one. I could even autograph it for you."

"I don't have time for punk-ass novels," Briggs said, and he walked away toward the living room.

"Do make yourself comfortable," Rebel called after him.

The aroma of BBQ and potato salad lingered in the air. Morales said to Rebel, "We're hungry, no time to stop for dinner. Are those wonderful smells coming from your kitchen or from a local spot?"

Rebel eased a bit, as, of course, she wanted him to, and he told her about Uncle Willie's BBQ Palace. "It's in town, maybe ten minutes from here. It'll be on your GPS. Best place in town."

Briggs sat forward on the long burgundy-leather sofa, clasped his big hands between his legs. "You've been wasting our time, Mr. Navarro. Tell us where your brother is and tell us now."

Rebel arched a brow. "Or what, Agent Briggs?"

"Or I'll arrest you for obstruction and take you to Philadelphia to our fine jail." He added, voice hard, "We'd have social services deal with your nephew."

It was clear to Rebel the minute Briggs opened his mouth he was playing bad cop, and Morales was his perfect foil, but then again, maybe not. Briggs was very likely playing himself. Rebel sat down in his favorite chair facing the sofa. He eyed the two of them. "I know you'd like me to spit out my brother's address and burner phone number, and maybe his numbered bank account in Switzerland, but again, as I've already told you, I have no idea where he is or what he's doing. I do know he would never in this lifetime steal from his own company. He's out of the country on his honeymoon, nothing more suspicious than that."

Morales said, "He's been married six months, a little late for a honeymoon."

"He told me there was so much to get done before he and Sasha could leave for a while. They did take a long weekend after their wedding. They were both very excited. Would you like some potato chips? There are still some in the bag by the fireplace."

Briggs jerked up his chin, looked Rebel dead in the eye. "Yeah, I'll bet he had a lot to get done, like stealing his clients' money. You know lying to us is a federal offense, don't you? Listen, you tell us the truth and our boss will cut a deal for you with the federal prosecutor. If you don't, you'll be in this as deep as your brother."

Morales cut him off again, her voice polite. If this was a routine, they were very good at it. "When did you last communicate with your brother, Mr. Navarro?"

"Archer and his wife left Tash here with me in mid-June and flew to Paris, on a delayed honeymoon, as I already told you. He said they'd be staying at the Ritz."

Briggs said, "Yeah, yeah, we knew that, but surprise, they're not there now. That's enough, Mr. Navarro—"

Rebel pulled out his cell phone, scrolled down, and handed it to Morales. She read aloud, "*Sasha's in love with Versailles, wants to tour the chateaux and vineyards, wear her bikini in Cannes. Another month. All right?*"

Morales continued, "And you texted back, *Take as long as Sasha wants. Autumn and I are enjoying Tash and he's having a great summer. Misses you, of course.*"

Morales looked up, frowning. "Isn't your brother worried about Tash? Has he stayed in touch with him?"

"He calls and texts him. They both enjoy that," Rebel said. "Tash is happy here and having a great time. Scroll down some more, Agent Morales, there's one last text from my brother, from this morning."

She read aloud, "*Reports about my wrongdoing are untrue. Someone else has to be responsible. Although I hate it, I have to consider my COO Carla Cartwright. I let her take over management of the portfolios when Celia died, my fault. Can't come home until all is resolved. Arch.*"

"And you, Mr. Navarro, texted back, *Where are you?*"

Rebel said, "You'll see he didn't answer me. He texted Tash that he loved him and missed him. Again, when Tash texted back, he got no answer from his father."

Briggs shrugged, sounded bored. "Convenient, don't you think? If all he claims is true, then why doesn't he come back and prove it?"

Rebel wanted to leap on Briggs, but he held steady. "I'll bet he's doing his best to exonerate himself, but obviously he's afraid to come back until you can find out the truth. But you know what? Sounds to me like you people want to railroad him, you've already made up your minds he's guilty. What about everybody else at the firm? Have you considered Carla Cartwright?"

Morales said, "Mr. Navarro, we're interviewing the employees at your brother's investment fund right now. Our forensic accountants are examining their books. If what your brother texted is true, they should find a trail. We already know large sums were gradually funneled into an offshore investment account that existed in name only. We have to be realistic, Mr. Navarro—your brother has disappeared as well."

Briggs said, "Seems rather obvious your brother is the mastermind here, don't you think? You know what? We don't think your brother pulled this all off alone."

Rebel looked at each of them. Could the feds be right? Had Archer lost his way so much after Celia died that he'd started siphoning off his clients' money? No, not possible, Archer wasn't wired that way. "You know the reason he's not here, and it has nothing to do with his stealing from his own company. He isn't guilty. It sounds to me like these interviews you're conducting are for form only. As I said, you've already made up your minds, haven't you?"

Briggs brushed off his words. "Are you planning to join him, Mr. Navarro? After all, a writer can write his little stories anywhere, right, all's needed is a laptop."

Rebel said, "My brother is a very smart man, very intuitive, Agents, a genius with people, and that's why he's so successful." Rebel leaned forward in his chair. "Listen to me. There was no reason for him to destroy what he'd built with years of hard work. If he believes this Cartwright woman or someone else is responsible, my money's on them. Why are you in such a hurry to convict my brother?"

"Because he's guilty as sin," Briggs said. "He was in charge, he made all the important decisions. He cleaned out his company over a matter of months, then he ran. It can't get much clearer than that."

Morales realized Rebel looked ready to leap on Briggs. She said quickly, "Tell us about Mrs. Navarro, Sasha is her name?"

Of course they knew her name, they probably thought she was as guilty as his brother, as guilty as they thought Rebel was. He said, "My brother was devastated by his wife Celia's death from cancer two years ago. He was lonely and vulnerable. Sasha worked at his firm as an assistant to Carla Cartwright. Let me speak plainly here. I think of Sasha as my brother's trophy wife. She's twenty-seven to his thirty-eight and very beautiful. She smothered him with her concern and sympathy, her admiration for him. She was smart enough, sexy enough, to attach herself to my brother.

"To be honest, though it rankles, in the short time they were here, it seemed to me Sasha really cares for my brother. On the other hand, she doesn't want to be bothered with her new stepson. She pretty much ignores him. Personally, I have no problem with her myself, but like her? Let me say she's nothing like my brother's first wife, Celia. She was an incredible woman."

Morales's voice was sympathetic. "Where do you think Mr. Navarro might go if he and Sasha left France?"

"You mean if he's guilty and knows he has to run and hide?"

Briggs said, "Of course that's what she means."

Rebel kept himself in check. He said calmly, "I can't see Sasha content to be isolated on some South Seas atoll. I'd say wherever they'd decide to go together would be more cosmopolitan. Beyond that I can't say. You saw his texts and mine." Rebel splayed his hands in front of him. "As much as you don't want to hear this, Agents, that's all I have for you."

Morales rose and smoothed out her black jacket, forcing Briggs to follow suit. "If he contacts you again, you're obliged to let us know, Mr. Navarro. You have to think about yourself, and, of course, about Tash."

Rebel said nothing more until he opened the front door and ushered them out. "Why not consider for a moment that my brother is telling the truth, Agents, that someone else did this, like Carla Cartwright? My brother never was a techno whiz, he hired people for that. Have you interviewed them? Have you interviewed Cartwright as—vigorously—as you did me?"

"Vigorously—now there's a stupid writer's word." Briggs grunted a laugh. "We know how to do our jobs, you can count on that." He looked Rebel up and down. "We'll be seeing you again, count on it." He strode after Morales down the flagstone steps.

"I'll look forward to that pleasure," Rebel said. "Do let me know what you think of Uncle Willie's BBQ Palace."

Briggs turned back, pointed a big thick finger with a heavy college ring on it. "Don't even consider running. If you try it, I will make it my mission to find you and haul your butt back here."

Morales looked pained. She smiled up at Rebel. "I know this situation will be hard for you, and for Tash. He's lucky to have you. He seems like a sweet little boy, very bright."

Rebel said, "You have no idea."

Chapter Twenty

Savich's cell phone belted out Post Malone's "Sunflower," his song from *Spider-Man: Into the Spider-Verse*, as he was handing a covered basket of garlic bread to Roman. He listened, said only, "Well done. Keep me posted. Don't do anything that crazy, Coop, or I'll assign you to clean the bathrooms at the Washington field office." He punched off and said to the table at large, "Cooper's located the Brewster County murder suspects in Texas. He was ready to go in after them before the local police arrived."

Sherlock grinned. "That threat should be enough to hold him in check, but knowing Coop, he needed to hear it from you, the idiot." She added with a smile to Elizabeth, "Special Agent Cooper McKnight's the idiot, not Dillon. Coop's really smart but a bit of a cowboy. We're counting on Rome being better behaved."

"He's behaved quite acceptably so far, Sherlock," Elizabeth said.

Savich said, "Rome told me he took you to the Roosevelt memorial. What did you think?"

"It was completely unexpected the way the four outdoor

areas were fashioned. Spectacular, in fact. I loved the water-falls. It was very moving."

"She told me her grandfather was in Churchill's government and traveled with him," Rome said. "So it was a good choice."

Elizabeth nodded. She pictured her single carry-on sitting unpacked on the bed in the upstairs guest bedroom, a charming room with front-facing windows and a painting of a landscape by Savich's grandmother Sarah Eliot adorning one cream-colored wall. She'd seen her first Sarah Eliot painting when she was ten years old, at a gallery in London. "Rome thought you'd be quite interested to chat with me about him." She smiled from Savich to Sherlock. "Let me thank both of you again for welcoming me into your home. You're both very kind."

"You're welcome," Savich said. "Now to business. I'm sure you'd both like to know what John Eiserly had to say when he heard you were with us. He was relieved and a bit upset when you sent him your two-sentence note telling him you'd left and that he wouldn't know where you were any longer, with a thank-you to Officer Bewley. Then he laughed, said he'd decided you were probably right to run, and he wasn't worried about you any longer after he tracked you here to the United States. He was impressed to hear you'd spent three months with a trainer retired from Quantico. He sent us all the details of their investigation since you've been gone, three months of it. I made copies for both of you to look over."

She didn't want to believe her perfect escape, known only to her parents, had ended up being common knowledge—well, MI5 knowledge. She felt stupid. "Carlos—no, he wouldn't have said a word, and besides, I didn't tell him anything specific."

Savich said, "John spoke to your brother, who was both high and worried about you. John convinced him you could still be in danger and that he needed to cooperate if he wanted to stay out of jail. Your brother folded, admitted you'd hooked up with his drug dealer, Carlos, and Carlos had arranged your doctored passport. As for Carlos, he knew when to fold to avoid arrest—he gave up the name on the passport, Margaret Courter.

"Despite your disguise that day at the airport, the cameras caught you when you momentarily put back on your dark sunglasses coming out of the women's restroom. He tracked down the car you hired at Dulles and used the onboard GPS to track you to Hurley. He decided to leave you alone there, keep an eye on you from afar."

Elizabeth very deliberately placed her fork next to her eggplant parmesan. She snapped her fingers. "That fast and I was so pleased with myself. Of course there are cameras everywhere in London, so I was really well disguised—red wig, colored contacts, sunglasses. I flew coach. I thought I was disappearing off the face of the earth. Coming out of the women's room— only a moment of not paying attention and I really screwed up, as you Yanks say. And Tommy—I said so little to him, but it didn't matter. All I managed to do was prove I'm incompetent." She picked up a slice of garlic toast and crunched down. When she swallowed, she looked at their faces, sighed. "I thought I was being so careful. I'd be a wanker of a crook."

Rome lightly punched her arm. "Truth be told, Palmer, most people would. Don't beat yourself up."

Savich said, "Rome's right. You actually did quite well, given the situation. Your decision to leave may have saved your life."

Her hand fisted around her fork. She remembered the knife sticking obscenely out of Benny's chest and sitting in the surgery waiting room with the officers from MI5, John Eiserly and Sir James Hanson, promising the Lord good works if he survived.

Sherlock said, "Elizabeth, John wants you to consider coming home, working with him. He's evidently at a standstill. Lots of suspects and possible scenarios, but still nothing solid."

Elizabeth said slowly, "I see. So I'm to be bait? Otherwise, I don't see how I can help him. And to be honest, I'd rather be bait here with you watching out for me."

Savich said matter-of-factly, "John knows we'll protect you, but you know there could well be danger for you as well. It's up to you."

Elizabeth ate a bite of eggplant, looked inward. "If I did decide to go back to London, given what's happened so far, at least I'll be prepared to be in a cock-up."

Rome said, "Cock-up? Who talks like that? Yes, it's up to you, but I think it's too soon for you to consider going back to London."

Elizabeth studied the man sitting next to her. She'd only met him today, and he was making fun of how she spoke and telling her what to do? Should she smack him in the jaw or laugh? Instead, she said, "I can understand John wanting to take me back and try to draw these people out again. I think too that after what happened last time, if I went back, I'd have so much protection I couldn't go to the ladies' by myself, which would make them hide rather than try for me again. The difference now is I'm no longer helpless, I can take care of myself."

"I agree with your assessment," Savich said, nothing more. "Again, Elizabeth, it's up to you what to do."

She ate another bite of eggplant parmesan. "This is so delicious. Oh, yes, Hurley advised me it would be a bad idea for me to come to the Hoover Building with a gun, so he refused to give me one. He told me to trust you guys. But, really, I'd feel safer if I had one."

Sherlock and Savich looked at each other. Savich said, "Rome will be with you, and he's licensed to carry a weapon. Our supplying you with one would be illegal."

"Ah, yes, the legalities. I can see you're in a quandary. Hurley said as much. All right, I've made up my mind. I'll call John in the morning, tell him I'll be staying in the States for now. And, Special Agent Foxe, cock-up is a perfectly good word."

They heard a popping sound. Elizabeth jumped.

Savich laughed, rose. "It's all right. I believe that's the sound of a demon in Sean's new video game biting the dust. Sherlock, stay put, I'll shut him down for the night."

Sherlock studied Elizabeth's set face. She said in a calm, matter-of-fact voice, "I'm pleased with your decision, Elizabeth, and you're welcome to stay with us as long as you like."

Savich reappeared in the dining room doorway with Sean at his side holding his hand, wearing Spider-Man pajamas. Astro stood tall next to Sean, his tail wagging. He was on alert, eyeing the strangers. "Sean wanted to say good night to our guests, Rome and Elizabeth. As for Astro, pet him and he won't think you're an enemy."

Sean eyed her and said in great seriousness, "Papa said he was protecting you, Elizabeth, because bad men might be after you. He'll keep you safe. If you have a nightmare tonight, I'll wake you up and Astro and I will come and sleep with you."

"That's very kind of you, Sean. Does Astro like to spoon?"

He beamed at her. "I've never tried to spoon with him, but he loves to cuddle, sticks his nose right under your arm. Hi, Uncle Rome. Maybe if I don't have to go back to bed, we can play."

Sherlock said, "Sorry, champ, but you have to be ready for all sorts of adventures tomorrow."

Rome marveled at the little boy, so like his father. He was tall for his age, with his father's black hair and olive complexion and dark eyes. Rome had met him at a barbeque the week he joined the unit, at Special Agent Ollie Hamish's house. He knew very well what he was expected to say, so he said, "We'll do that next time, Sean, but prepare to be destroyed."

Sean gave him a big-kid grin. As for Astro, he was unmoving, staring at Elizabeth. She patted her leg, and to everyone's surprise, he yipped and ran to her and leaped up in her lap. He stood on his back legs and licked every bit of skin he could reach. Elizabeth laughed, hugged him close. "Sweet boy, if you get tired of Sean's snoring, come sleep with me."

Sean gave her an approving look. "Astro likes you." He walked to his mother and lightly laid his palm on her stomach. "Mama, I really want a brother, so please make one."

Elizabeth, still hugging Astro against her chest, said seriously, "Sean, a sister could kill demons right alongside you too."

It was obvious Sean didn't agree, but she was an adult and Astro liked her, so he didn't argue.

Savich said. "It's late, Sean, time to send the demons back to their crypts for the night. You and Astro need to refuel."

Sean told them all good night, and Astro, after a final lick at Elizabeth's chin, jumped down from her lap and ran over to Sean. They heard Sean talking a mile a minute about Elizabeth as he walked beside his father up the stairs.

Sherlock rose. "You ready for some apple pie and ice cream? Sean already had a slice. He gave part of it to Astro when he thought I wasn't looking."

Two hours later, Elizabeth lay in the very comfortable bed, but she couldn't sleep. She was tired, but so much had happened, it was hard to turn off her brain. Hurley had told her Sherlock and Savich wouldn't give her a gun. She went round and round in circles about if she should try to buy one on the sly, when, suddenly, everything was crystal clear.

She had a plan.

Chapter Twenty-one

Autumn knew things were bad for Tash's father. She'd eaves-dropped and overheard her dad tell her mom Rebel Navarro called to tell him two FBI agents from Philadelphia had come to his house and grilled him, and one of the agents had treated him like a criminal. She crept back to her room and got into bed and called Tash on his iPhone. He told her about the two agents who believed his uncle Rebel was guilty. "I'm scared, Autumn."

She knew exactly what to do. She calmed Tash down, said there was absolutely no evidence and not to worry. Then she focused on the soft night mountain air in the breeze coming through her bedroom window to clear her mind, and pictured Dillon Savich's face. He'd make things right, he always did.

And there he was with her, smiling at her.

You're worried about something, Autumn. Is this about Archer Navarro? He waited.

Tash can't reach his dad, and everyone thinks Archer Navarro stole millions of dollars from his own company and he's hiding in Europe or in one of those countries that don't send criminals back to us. If he did steal the money, maybe he'll never come back, never see Tash again.

Does Tash know?

He told me about the two FBI agents who drove from Philadelphia to see Rebel tonight. He didn't stay in bed, he snuck back downstairs and listened. He told me the man agent was mean and accused Rebel of plotting with Tash's dad, accused him of knowing where his dad was hiding. I told him you'd take care of things. Can you, Dillon?

Savich was surprised two agents would drive over three hours to Titusville from Philadelphia to conduct a simple interview. It indeed sounded like an interrogation.

Autumn, here's what I know. I spoke to the FBI forensic accountants in the Philadelphia field office who are investigating what happened at the Navarro Investment Fund. They say Archer Navarro's fingerprints are on everything they've uncovered so far, and only Archer's.

Autumn: Mr. Navarro texted it wasn't, and he believed it could be his COO, Carla Cartwright. Tash is really scared, Dillon. So are Mom and Dad even though they don't say it aloud.

I understand. Now listen, Autumn. You keep Tash as far away from this as you can. And try not to worry, leave that to me. I'll speak to the Philadelphia SAC, ask her about those agents coming tonight to speak to Rebel. I'll make sure to take a close look at everyone, particularly this Carla Cartwright.

Thank you, Dillon. Oh, yes, I wanted to tell you too Rebel visited with my mom today, not about Mr. Navarro but about Tash and me. She had to tell him all about the Backmans, and about everything. She said he didn't want to accept it, but he knows all of us do. Mom thinks it'll take him a while to realize how special Tash is, and accept it so there'll be no more secrets.

Autumn sat back, leaned against her pillows. Savich smiled at her. *I like your jammies. I think they'll look cute on our little girl in about ten years.*

That's funny, Dillon. If Sherlock has a little girl. What will you name her?

I'm thinking of another season. Since you're Autumn, how about Summer?

She laughed, though it was hard. *Summer Savich? Dillon, can you imagine how kids at school would torture her? What do you think of Felicity? Felicity Savich.*

He looked thoughtful, decided Felicity was a beautiful name. *Sherlock's convinced she's going to have another boy, so Felicity will be a big surprise. Hang in there, sweetheart. But you know, I have this feeling there'll be a boy in the future. What do you think of Beauregard?*

You're laughing. But you know, Dillon, Beau is really cool.

Indeed it is. Go to sleep now. Good night and thank you for Felicity.

Savich felt Sherlock's curly hair tickle his nose, smoothed it away.

"How's Autumn?"

She always knew, she'd told him, because he got very still, and she could almost see his brain working. "She's really worried, mainly for Tash. It's not looking good. Two FBI agents visited Rebel Navarro tonight. Autumn said the male agent treated Rebel like a criminal. I'm thinking they had a reason, Sherlock, but I have no clue what it could be since I don't believe Rebel Navarro is involved with his brother. I'll check with Claire Gregson, the SAC at the Philadelphia field office, see what's going on. How do you feel?"

"Grand. Maybe Beau will go to sleep real soon and stop practicing his field goal kicks."

Had she really said that name? But how was that possible? Savich said carefully, "Beau? When did you think of that name?"

"It just came to me. Not Beauregard, that's too old-fashioned, but Beau. Beau Savich. I really like it. What do you think?"

"It's a fine name for a boy, but how about a girl?"

Sherlock didn't answer. She was asleep.

Savich felt a feather kick against his side. *So you're still awake, are you? Do you like the name Felicity?*

He felt another kick. *I'll take that as a yes.* He kissed Sherlock's ear through her curls, felt her cheek against his shoulder, and slept.

Chapter Twenty-two

Roman Foxe's house
Wilton Place
Washington, D.C.
THURSDAY MORNING

Elizabeth supposed she'd expected Rome's home would be an ultramodern, all-glass condo in a hip section of Washington, fit for a young, single Neanderthal with a macho job. She'd pictured dirty underwear in a pile in the bathroom, maybe a couple of empty pizza boxes on the living room coffee table. Or, like Giles, the neo-Viking, a discarded bearskin hanging over the back of a chair. She hadn't expected Rome to turn into the driveway of a house on Wilton Place, a tree-lined street of well-tended, older houses set back from the street, all of them surrounded with greenery and beautiful blooming flowers. The house was two stories, painted white with bright blue trim, flower boxes set along the upper balcony overflowing with petunias, her favorite. More flowers displayed themselves in hanging baskets suspended from the roof-covered deep front porch. There was only a slight breeze, but enough to make the baskets sway gracefully. The porch held a rocking swing and four rattan chairs surrounding a round table. The double garage sat at the end of the smooth asphalt driveway and connected to the house. It all looked lovingly tended, homey, and welcoming. Roman switched off his Land Rover and turned to her.

Elizabeth smiled, waved her hand. "This is amazing."

"Thank you. I'll accept amazing. Do you want to wait here while I get my cell? I still can't believe I left it on the charger."

"If you don't mind, I'd like to see inside. Your house is hardly what I expected."

Rome realized he'd been nervous when she'd stared silently at his house. Had she expected him to live in an apartment surrounded with drum-playing cokeheads? He said slowly, "I know it's not what you're used to. There aren't any Wedgwood bowls in a front entrance hall where you can toss your car keys before you waltz into your four-hundred-year-old drawing room and ring for tea." He knew that sounded moronic, and grinned.

She said matter-of-factly, "What I'm used to, Agent Foxe, is plumbing that desperately needs to be updated and furniture I can't stretch out on in sweaty clothes without worrying about ruining some fabric selected by my great-great-grandparents. How old is the house?"

"Not six hundred years old with a pedigree and a freaking name."

She punched his arm. "Don't be a snob. My house in London doesn't come with a name." She paused, added, "Well, my father's country house—the family seat—does have a name, Darlington Hall, bestowed on it by the first Earl of Camden, in the late sixteenth century. Now I've told you my secrets, so tell me yours. Come on, how old is your house?"

"My grandparents built it in the late sixties. They lived here their entire married life until they were both killed skiing at Aspen six years ago, well into their eighties. Have you heard of Aspen?"

"Oh, yes, but I've never skied there. What happened?"

"My parents and grandparents skied twice a year together, everywhere from Aspen to Zermatt to Chamonix-Mont-Blanc. You know the old saw—never ski the last run? Well, my grandparents did." He paused, swallowed. "A young snowboarder ignored the signs, passed out of bounds above them and fell, and caused an avalanche that sent them both flying over a low cliff. Neither of them made it. I'm thankful my parents had already gone back to the lodge or they'd have been killed too."

"I'm so sorry."

He nodded, the old bittersweet memories blurred, but still moving. "Thank you." Odd, but he rarely spoke about his grandparents' death, particularly to someone he'd just met. Yet he'd spit it out to her.

Elizabeth put her hand on his arm. "What a wonderful life they had."

"Yes, they did. Granddad was a big-time corporate lawyer and grandmother was in technical services at the CIA in Langley until they both decided to take early retirement and have some fun." He let the rest of it pour out of his mouth. "They'd invited me to Aspen with them that year, but I wasn't able to go. Why? I don't remember, but maybe if I'd been with them, I could have helped them."

She said, "Putting away a sense of guilt can be hard, even when you know what you're feeling makes no logical sense. I know that for a fact because I feel the same way about my brother, Tommy, always wondering if I could do something else to help him, which I've come to realize I can't. So I'm left with being an enabler. What happened to the snowboarder?"

"His name is Billy Hodgkins—he was sixteen at the time. My dad told me he went to work in his dad's grocery store in Germantown, Maryland."

"Now there's a load of guilt you wouldn't want to carry, and I'll wager Billy Hodgkins will for the rest of his life."

Rome sure hoped so, but he didn't say it out loud.

Elizabeth got out of the car and stood looking at the house and grounds, breathed in the sweet early-morning air, the rich smell of recently mowed grass from the neighbor's yard. Was that the scent of night jasmine billowing over a tall wooden fence? She turned to him. "It's so different from my house in London. I can't wait to see the inside. And the setting, it's perfect."

He'd always thought so, worked to make it look better and better each year. Was she just being polite? "I've done a lot of work on the house myself, modernizing, making it mine, I guess you could say. If you like, I'll show you the three bathrooms I updated, all marble counters, even towel warmers. The master even has a steam shower."

"Towel warmers? I haven't seen one of those since I once stayed at the Savoy."

He walked her through the two more bedrooms with en suite bathrooms and led her to the master bedroom, his favorite room in the house, its walls a rich cream, filled with glossy dark mahogany furniture he'd found at an estate sale in Virginia and refinished himself. He'd kept his grandparents' two long side-by-side mirrors, but replaced their paintings with watercolors of mountains and lakes.

She said, looking around her, "What a wonderful room, stylish and comfortable. It invites you to sit in that large reading chair with the William Morris reading lamp over your shoulder. And that immense bed—I can imagine taking a run and diving in after a long day, and sinking in, all warm and cozy. I really like the duvet and the lovely shade of gray. I see you made the bed."

"Surprises me sometimes too. From my youngest years, my grandmother told me if I didn't make my bed every day an unexpected guest would show up, see it, and think I'd been raised by wolves. Ah, my cell phone." He slipped it into his pants pocket.

Elizabeth laughed. She spotted a photograph on the chest of

drawers, a family grouping with everyone in ski clothes, at the top of a ski run surrounded by white snow-covered mountains. "Your grandparents and parents, and in the middle that's you, what, maybe ten?"

Rome nodded. "I don't remember how old I was when another skier took that photo. I do remember we were at the Lost Boy run at Aspen, still my favorite run. My mom gave it to me when I turned twenty-one."

"A lovely memory." When she'd first met this tough-looking FBI agent, seen his opinion of her clear on his face, she'd dismissed him as a typical American macho tosser, full of himself, maybe a sexist. What was she to think now?

Elizabeth followed him to the end of the hall, to a large, empty, light-flooded corner room. Rome said, "I'm still thinking about what to do with this room. Well, I bought some art, but that's it so far."

She walked to the middle of the large rectangular room and looked around. "This is like my workroom at home, where I paint. Look at how beautifully the light glistens off the pale gold walls, and the dark gold accent wall sets it all off."

She painted? Yesterday he'd have guessed she spent her days going to fancy teas, shopping endlessly, and dancing in the evenings with the right people at the right places. Painted what? He watched her wander around the room now, touch her long thin fingers to the frame of a watercolor of an ancient sailing ship. She said, "I've always admired watercolors but found what I produced didn't speak to me—or to anyone, for that matter—so I've stayed with acrylics, a perfect medium for me."

He wondered if she'd had any success, but since her daddy was a bloody earl, it probably didn't matter to her. "What do you paint?"

"I guess you could call me mainly a neo-impressionist.

Before this started, I was painting a portrait of my mother for her birthday. She was twenty-two in the photo I'm basing it on, and newly married to my father."

"Do you show your work in a gallery?"

"Yes, in Belgravia."

So she wasn't a dilettante. Interesting. "That's the snooty part of London, right?"

She cocked an eyebrow at him. "Snooty enough." She stopped at the large windows looking over his well-manicured front yard, unframed by curtains or blinds.

Rome realized he'd been throwing enough stereotypical assumptions at her to drown her in. He cleared his throat. "Sherlock is lobbying to make this a music room, with a Steinway. She's quite a pianist, could have been a concert pianist, but she opted instead for the FBI."

A concert pianist? She'd seen the Steinway in the Savich living room, but hadn't asked about who played it. She grinned at him. "Nah. Not a music room. I vote for a gym where you could work up a sweat—weights, benches, mats, elliptical, maybe a boxing bag."

"I keep forgetting you've been indoctrinated by Hurley."

She looked startled, nodded. "You're right. Three months ago such a thing would have never occurred to me." She wondered how much of Hurley would go back with her to London, if she survived.

Rome looked down at his Apple Watch. "I guess we'd best continue on if we're going to get to Hurley's camp in good time. You sure you still want to go?"

"Of course. He'll want to hear all about what's happened. You've never met him, have you?"

He cocked his head at her, still wondering why she wanted to make the trip, but all he said was, "No, but I've heard tall tales over beers with other agents. I'll enjoy meeting him."

It took them close to an hour to get clear of the always-snarled Washington traffic and pull onto I-95. Rome said, "You really think that room should be a gym?"

"Good question. Since I did sweat my eyebrows off with Hurley, so maybe it's a part of who I am now."

"Nah, you're an aristocrat, you don't do sweat, it's not in your blue blood. Why doesn't your father get your brother into rehab?"

"Jumping around from subject to subject, is that something that works with criminals?"

"Probably not."

"Yes, we've all tried countless times with Tommy, but finally last year my father had enough, he disowned him. He does provide him a monthly allowance, but Tommy's always short. I admit I add money to the pot when it's time to pay Carlos, his drug dealer. When my father dies, Tommy will still be the next Earl of Camden, my father can't do anything about it, primogeniture and all that. Now, when anyone speaks of him to my father, even me, he stiffens, gets cold and silent. I have a feeling my mother also supplements, but neither of us ever talks about it."

"Since you live in London, you're Tommy's main caregiver, right?"

"Yes. As I said, I guess I had to admit to being his main, front-and-center enabler." She sighed, but said nothing more.

"So stop it. Get him into rehab, whether he wants it or not."

"Been there, done that, as you guys say, countless times." She turned to look out the window at the line of cars beside them on the highway. "They're going to come, aren't they?"

"They might." He glanced at her, saw she had tensed up. "If they do find you, we'll be ready."

She nodded, tried to relax, but couldn't. She said, "What happened, it's always in the back of my mind, ready to take me by the throat. The hatred I felt pouring off them when they were in my bedroom. The man who straddled me—his knife raised, ready to come down." She drew a deep breath, reached for calm with the square breathing Hurley had taught her. "Sorry, you don't want to hear that again. Hey, why did your parents name you Roman?"

He shot her a big grin. "I was born in Rome on their honeymoon."

Chapter Twenty-three

Titus Hitch Wilderness
Sweet Onion River
THURSDAY MORNING

Autumn sat with her back against a willow tree, her legs stretched out and her ankles crossed, chewing on a blade of grass. Tash sat beside her on a blanket, a paper lunch bag between them. The June sun was bright overhead, and a cool breeze carried the scent of the Sweet Onion River, not six feet away.

Tash was picking at the beginning of a hole in the knee of his jeans. "Uncle Rebel is really worried about Dad, but he doesn't want me to know it. I didn't tell him I eavesdropped and heard everything they said to him."

Autumn knew all about how to eavesdrop and not get caught. "Well done. Like I told you, when you're a kid, it's the only way you can ever find out what's really happening. I heard my mom and dad talking about your dad last night when they thought I was playing with Big Louie and Mackie. Everyone in Titusville knows those FBI agents were in town last night because they stopped at Willie's BBQ after they left your uncle Rebel. Willie told my dad one of the agents, a really big guy with a big mouth, was asking around about Rebel. Everyone likes Rebel, so no one had anything to say to him."

Tash nodded. "Autumn, please tell me the truth. Do you think my father is a crook? Do your parents think my father stole all that money?"

It didn't occur to her to lie to him, even though Tash was only eight years old. Dillon was right, Tash was really smart, he knew what was what. "My mom said since your father's the president and founder of the Navarro Investment Fund he could probably do whatever he wanted, including robbing his clients. But she wondered why he'd do that."

"But you know he didn't, don't you, Autumn? He didn't!"

"No, I don't think he did, Tash."

"Do you know when the agents asked Uncle Rebel about Sasha, he called her a trophy wife. What does it mean, Autumn?"

"I think it's like winning an Oscar. You want everyone to envy you for winning a prize they didn't. Sasha's younger than your father and beautiful, so your father married her to show off to all his friends."

Tash frowned at his scuffed dirty sneaker. "That sounds stupid. My mama wasn't a trophy wife, was she, Autumn?"

"From what you've told me your dad really loved your mom. But maybe he loves Sasha too."

Tash plucked his own blade of grass and started chewing on it. "I told you Sasha doesn't like me. When she talks to me, she always sounds fake, her smile is too, but most of the time she ignores me."

"You don't need her, Tash. I like you, and your uncle and your dad love you. Why should she have to like you too? You're not her kid. Maybe she doesn't like kids."

Tash chewed harder on his blade of grass. "I heard her tell Dad he should send me to a boarding school. I saw brochures to this school in Connecticut on my father's desk at home." He leaned over, picked up his bottle of iced tea, and took a swig. "Dad changed after Mama died. He didn't laugh anymore, at least not much. I remember seeing him crying the first Christmas. He was putting a present for me under the tree. I never said anything, just went back to bed and cried too."

"You both really missed her, Tash."

"Dad played baseball growing up and he wanted me to learn too, but he even stopped throwing balls with me after she died. He was real quiet, stayed at the office later and later. He always used to come and tuck me in at night and read me stories. He does that only sometimes now. Then after that car accident that didn't happen and after I told him about singing to Mom when she opened her eyes and spoke to me, I think he was worried I was sick in the head. When we ate together I saw him watching me, but he never said what he was thinking out loud."

Oh, boy, that sounded tough. Autumn didn't doubt it was exactly the truth from his little boy's point of view. She knew everything would change for her, too, if something happened to her mom. She didn't want to think about it. Autumn closed her hand over Tash's and squeezed hard. "I wish I'd known your mama, she sounds really nice, a lot like my mama. Tash, it sounds to me like your dad just lost his way a little. But he'll come back all the way, and in the meantime, you've got me and your uncle Rebel." She opened her paper bag, dug around, and came up with half a bagel. She pinched off a bite, dipped it into the nearly empty cup of cream cheese, and stuffed it into his mouth, then smeared another piece and ate it herself.

They sat in silence looking out over the Sweet Onion River, narrow at this spot, with rocks across it Ethan's grandfather had lugged there.

Tash said, "Did your folks ever think you were sick, Autumn? Did they ever think you were a freak?"

"Everything was different for me, Tash, because my dad was gifted too. When I was little, lots younger than you, my dad was in jail, and he'd call me with his mind every single day and we'd talk. He didn't think I was weird at all."

"You talked with your minds?"

"That's right. I realize now my mom must have been scared out of her mind I was nuts, but she never let on. Then when Dad died we took his ashes back to his family—the Backmans, in a place called Bricker's Bowl in Georgia." She shrugged, tried to act like it was old news and who cared, though it still scared her to remember them. "That's when Mama realized I really was gifted, and they were too."

"You have lots of friends. Do you ever want to tell them or show them what you can do?"

Autumn nodded. "Sure, but I know I can't. My parents are always reminding me the other kids wouldn't understand, even my good friends. Someday, they say, when I'm an adult, then maybe I'll want to tell someone I care for, but for now, only you know, Tash—well, you and your uncle."

"It's sort of like Superman or Wonder Woman, right? They have to hide who they really are."

She laughed. "We're not from Krypton, we're just kids who are lucky we can do some special things. But we'll always have to be careful, Tash."

"Don't you get lonely? I mean, you can do really special things but you can't talk about it, can't even tell your friends."

"Sometimes. But I have my parents, and they're always telling me that if something bothers me, I can tell them. And for now, you have me to do the same for you. How about we practice again right now?" She grabbed her backpack and turned her back to him. "Tell me what I'm holding in my hand."

Tash scrunched up his eyes and concentrated. "The potato chip bag."

"You saw me pick that up, didn't you?"

"Maybe."

"Tell me what I'm thinking about."

Tash didn't say anything for the longest time. "I don't know, Autumn. I can't see it."

Autumn leaned back against the willow tree and eyed him. "Then let me show you."

A moment later, Tash nearly burst, he was so excited. "You're thinking of a name—Felicity. I heard the name, Autumn, I heard it!"

"That's exactly right, Tash. Felicity is the name I suggested to Dillon for their baby. I wonder what we'll be able to do tomorrow, or next week? Let's go for a swim and have some fun." Autumn jumped to her feet and quickly stripped to her swimsuit, but she didn't beat Tash. She raced after him toward the Sweet Onion River.

Chapter Twenty-four

Hurley Janklov's Training Camp
Claxson, rural Maryland

Hurley walked over to stand in front of the group of eight trainees who'd arrived the day after Elizabeth left. There was instant silence. "Listen up, people, this is Elizabeth Palmer, who trained for three months here with me and is now the meanest Brit on the planet. Elizabeth, come take a look at this new bunch of rookies, tell them what I expect from them."

Elizabeth had no idea Hurley was going to put her on the spot. What to say to these people? Elizabeth walked over to stand with him in front of the five men and three women, all dressed in comfortable dark gray joggers and black sweatshirts with *HJ Survival Training* stenciled in big letters across their chests. They'd come, as she had, to become fit and strong and learn the skills to help them survive in a dangerous confrontation. Most of them, she knew from Hurley, had already been assigned by their international corporations to work in places where being attacked on the street was a real possibility. Their course would last three weeks, a combination of classroom and grueling physical training, including shooting, defensive driving, and much more. Most of them were in their thirties and forties, and all looked already reasonably fit. They were staring at her, the tall blond in tight black jeans, tucked-in white shirt, and black low-heeled boots standing next to Hurley, wondering, she imagined, exactly who and what she was.

She cleared her throat, smiled. "I learned soon enough to do exactly what Hurley told me to do the second he told me to do it, or I'd be down on a mat doing twenty push-ups." She paused. "At the beginning, I could only do one. I was calling myself all sorts of names, Hurley didn't have to. Now I can do thirty, no sweat. Let me say all of you look to be in better shape than I was when I arrived here. I promise you if you work hard you'll have the confidence and the instincts to face just about any situation without freezing up. And that's the real survival key I learned here: never panic, don't stop to weigh and assess and second-guess yourself—act quickly, go all in.

"Your companies made a wise decision to send you here. You'll think Hurley's a dictator and you'll want to kill him before you make it through, but then you'll thank your stars when it's over because you'll realize Hurley's the best. What he's teaching you might save your life, if it ever comes to that.

"Some days you'll want to quit or just lie down and die, and others, you'll be sure you can take down aliens. It doesn't matter to Hurley how much you struggle, how many times you can't do something; he'll never stop expecting you to work until you drop, which you will do many times. I remember leaving him at the end of the day for my love-hate sessions with the ice baths, then with James, the sports-massage therapist who'll work your bodies back into shape so you can go do it all over the next day." She paused, looked at the group, saw alarm, excitement, and many questions. She said, smiling, "There is a big payoff—one evening a week, you'll get to go into Claxson for pizza at Angelo's." She shot a mad grin at Hurley. "Trust me on this: when you survive Hurley, you'll know to your heels you can survive most anything, even your spouses. By the way, Hurley didn't pay me to say that. I paid him—a bundle."

Elizabeth gave Hurley a bow and stepped back to stand

beside Rome. She heard low voices from the small group but couldn't make out what they said.

She whispered, "I hope I didn't scare them off."

He whispered back, "You gave them a goal, to learn to survive, to win, and that's what it's all about."

They remained to watch Hurley put the group through their morning exercises, wincing occasionally at the groans and curses. Elizabeth said, "I never told you about Angelique. She's French and gorgeous and Hurley's wife. She doesn't take grief from him, goes toe-to-toe, and you should see Hurley with their three little boys—I swear they could wear him out. They're a great family. Since I was here for three months and obviously didn't know anyone, I spent evenings with them. Angelique was endlessly kind to me, even taught me how to fishbone-braid my hair. She always praised my progress even when I looked so pathetic and exhausted one of the kids could have pushed me over." She paused. "The boys, they always came and hugged me before they went to bed."

Rome looked at her thick braid. "This is a fishbone?"

"It is. Not bad, right?"

He studied the intricate braid. "Nope, it isn't bad at all."

"On my last evening, Angelique cooked an amazing farewell dinner for me, and I asked Hurley whether I should stay here in the States or go home or move to Timbuktu. He told me only I would be able to answer that when I'd been here in the States awhile—on the outside—and seen what would happen. He told me to trust myself and I'd make the right decision."

Then Elizabeth gave Rome a fat smile, and a red light flashed in his mind. "Today ought to be fun too. Maybe you and Hurley can get in the ring together."

He merely arched a brow at her. Rome looked out over the large multipurpose space—a meeting area, state-of-the-art gym, and boxing ring, surrounded by a small indoor track. He'd seen the beginning of Hurley's extraordinary security when Elizabeth had told him to turn off the small country road and they came to a gate. He'd seen cameras turn toward them and focus. And the gate cameras were only the beginning. There were alarms and more cameras throughout the compound. The compound itself wasn't that huge; it didn't have to be because Hurley kept attendance down to eight people at most. But it had everything from a gun range and steam and massage rooms to dorms and a dining room with its own chef whipping up endless calories. Hurley's own home, all glass and wood, was set on a small rise. Rome had seen two gardeners working to keep the grounds immaculate. Elizabeth had told him Hurley started building the house when he was only twenty-two and added on every year, refining it and adding new outbuildings.

When Hurley and Rome had met, there'd been an instant assessment on both sides. Sure, Rome had seen a photo of Hurley, but it hadn't captured the powerful presence of the actual man. He was wearing an ancient, tight-fitting gray muscle shirt cut off at the shoulders that showed his impressive upper body and outlined his six-pack abs. He wore loose pants like his students, old black sneakers on his long feet. His eyes were dark, his teeth whiter than white against his ebony skin. His face was rough-hewn and his head was shaved. As he walked in front of his eight students, he used his hands to make a point, always assessing their form, pointing out their weaknesses. He was light and graceful on his feet for a man his size.

Rome said to Elizabeth, "I know the companies pay a small fortune for the three weeks their people spend with Hurley, but it's well worth it if their training could prevent another kidnapping. I remember sitting through the films of situational survival Hurley filmed at Quantico—how to escape from the trunk of a car, how to hide in a tree's foliage, how to survive in a swamp or a rainforest, how to take cover in a dust storm. I bet this group will watch some of those same films, depending on where they'll be sent." Rome eyed her. "You spent three months with him, not three weeks. I'll bet your training wasn't all that different from mine at Quantico, since Hurley developed a lot of it."

"Different enough for me to kick your butt, Foxe."

His brow shot up again. "You think so?"

Before she could mouth off, they heard a small boy's voice from outside the gym door, whispering, "Papa's teaching beginners, Major, stay still and watch. Look, there's Elizabeth."

"That's Jean-Pierre. Major's a big black Lab."

"Hurley's nodding to you, probably wants you to demonstrate something. Go ahead. I want to check this out." Rome slipped out the open door to see a small boy about Sean's age, talking earnestly to the black Lab, running his small hands down his back as he talked to him. He saw a tall woman with a head of thick black curls down to her shoulders dressed in jeans and a sweatshirt walk toward them from Hurley's house, her eyes set on the little boy. Elizabeth was right. She was gorgeous.

"Uh-oh, Major, Mom doesn't want us here." The boy ran to her, Major racing beside him.

Rome grinned when the woman hugged the boy to her side, took his hand, and led him back to the big house. She said something to the boy, and they both turned and waved to him.

Rome walked back into the gym and stood next to Elizabeth. She was tucking in her shirt. They continued to watch Hurley work his clients until their clothes were sweat soaked and several were flopped on their backs trying to breathe. He couldn't imagine Elizabeth going one-on-one with him for three months, with all his attention, all his focus, on her. It must have cost a fortune, but then, she was the daughter of an aristocrat and probably never had to pay for a thing in her pampered life, not to mention taking up with a monster—his thought died in its tracks when she said, "Oh, how I feel for them. So many days I couldn't get up, all my muscles simply dead, but for me, it was worth every penny." She laughed. "My banker was horrified when I cleaned out my entire savings."

He was an idiot. She was amazing. She'd survived three attempts on her life, and she'd faced her situation head-on. No more thinking in stereotypes, even if she did talk like English royalty. And she could fishbone-braid her hair. Fact was, he was beginning to like her.

Late that afternoon, when some of the eight recruits were in their first session with an ice bath, Rome and Hurley sat around the desk in his techno-wonder office. Hurley said, "I've spoken to Dillon Savich. He filled me in on what's been going on in London since Elizabeth left here and went into the Hoover. I'm very pleased he and Sherlock have her staying with them. More protection for her." He paused a moment, searched Rome's face. "You've only known her for a day, but you're aware of what she did to save herself before she came to me. Now, her skills match her fast brain. What do you think of her?"

Rome said slowly, "I have to admit when I first met her I wondered if I should call her Your Highness and bow, and from what I'd been told about her, I believed she was a spoiled aristo-crat stupid enough to sleep with an assassin." He paused. "Then I heard what she did in London, how she cut ties, looked you up, and came to you. Only a day with her and I'm impressed. I think she's—solid. The time she spent with you gave her skills and confidence." He shook his head. "Still, that accent of hers makes you wonder whether to bow."

Hurley grinned. "I know what you mean. Did you know she told me why she'd taken Samir Basara as a lover? Did she tell you?"

Rome nodded. "Yes, she spit it right out. It all had to do with her love-hate relationship with her dad. I heard you said she's a brick."

Hurley grinned, showing very white teeth. "When she

arrived here I wasn't at all sure I could help her, much less make that much of an impact, but by the end of the first week, let me say she'd already made a greater impact on me. And after three months? She never gave up, no matter what I demanded of her, even when she could barely move. She even learned how to curse in American. Yeah, she's a brick."

Rome said, "Can you tell me any weaknesses I should watch out for?"

"Good question. When she first arrived she was so scared I could smell the fear on her. That's never good. But that changed, and it worries me. She's maybe overconfident now, maybe too sure of herself, like a lot of fresh recruits who haven't seen real combat. Sometimes she almost seems to be hoping they'll come for her again."

In the living room, Elizabeth and Angelique both had half an eye on the three boys playing softball outside. Angelique said in her lilting French-accented English, "Hurley is seldom wrong about people. He likes your FBI agent, and you know that means a lot." She patted Elizabeth's arm. "And the boys were so excited to meet an actual FBI special agent. He's good with them, and it's sincere. You said he's not married?"

"Don't give me that look, Angelique." Elizabeth was smiling as she watched Eric whack a ball and send it off into the maple trees. One of his brothers ran after it. "He has a wonderful home in Washington. He's rehabbing it himself." She jumped to her feet and started pacing. "The truth is, I just want all this to be over, Angelique, over and done so I can go home and live my life again."

Angelique watched her long-legged stride. She radiated vitality and confidence, so different from when she'd first arrived. She said slowly, "I wonder what normal will mean to you when this is all over. You've changed, Elizabeth. You see people more clearly. To me, you seem ready to take on the world. Hurley is very proud of you. And so am I."

Elizabeth blinked. "Thank you, but you, Angelique, you and Hurley, you're the amazing ones."

Angelique rose, raised her hand. "I see the men are through with their talk. I smell cinnamon, so that means the rolls are ready to eat."

Elizabeth nodded. "I must speak to Hurley for a moment." She passed Rome, who was sniffing the air and heading toward the wonderful smell. "I'll be right there," she said to him, and stopped Hurley. "A few minutes?"

He eyed her, tilting his head in that way of his, and waved her back into his office.

Elizabeth closed the door. Once she was seated in front of his desk, Hurley said, "Rome agrees with me you're better off here than in London. Both he and Savich believe the terrorists, if that's what they are, would be waiting for their chance at you there. Savich had an interesting question: Do they want to kill you or kidnap you?"

Elizabeth said, "He asked me that too. But their hatred, Hurley, I felt it, tasted it, and one of them had the knife raised to sink into my heart. What good is a dead kidnap victim?"

Hurley raised a big callused hand. "I know you believe that, and Savich could be wrong, but one thing I know for sure. If they try for you again, Elizabeth, it will all become clear."

Elizabeth's heart beat in slow deep strokes. She drew a deep breath.

He arched a thick dark brow. "I see. You have something else to say. Come on, spit it out."

She did. "Will you lend me a gun, Hurley? I know it's madly illegal, but I'm scared. Ever since they attacked me in my bedroom and I nearly died, I've been scared. I hate feeling helpless. Please, Hurley. You said you'd teach me to protect myself, but how can I when you know they will have guns and all I could do is give them a kick in the chest? I'd be dead by the time that happened. Dillon and Sherlock wouldn't give me a gun, and you know Rome won't. What good is all my training if I don't have one?"

Hurley started to shake his head, reconsidered. He said slowly, "This is why you came back so soon, isn't it? I'll bet you convinced Agent Foxe it was a great idea for him to meet me, discuss his ideas about protecting you, keeping you safe. You already know you can never be completely safe unless he takes you to a safe house or into a cave. But you came to talk me into giving you a gun. I'll bet my Sunday socks he knows you're keeping something from him."

She shook her head. "No, no, really, I did want you two to meet, wanted to know what you thought of him. And there's no way Rome knows what I'm asking you. I can be very subtle, Hurley."

"My best advice to you, Elizabeth, is to trust Agent Foxe and Agent Savich. I've studied Foxe all day, watched how he dealt with my students, how he dealt with you. He respects your abilities and I know he's well trained. He'll use that to deal with any trouble that comes."

She touched his arm. "He isn't Superman, Hurley, he's only one person, well trained or not, just as I am. The difference between us? His Glock. You're my only hope. I already asked Dillon and Sherlock. I could buy a knife, but what good would that do me? Please, Hurley."

He saw fear in her eyes, fear he hadn't seen since her first days with him. He understood. Without another word, he unlocked the big gun cabinet behind his desk, perused the score of handguns neatly slotted in it, next to the AK-47 and the Browning long gun, old, graceful, and deadly. He pulled out a small pistol, racked the slide, handed it butt first to her. "It's a Ruger sub-compact chambered in .380 ACP rounds, only thirteen ounces loaded. It'll fit in your jacket pocket or clipped to your waistband or belt or an ankle holster. Here's a waist clip if you want to use it."

Her own weapon, at last. "It's so small."

"Not good for distance, but you know that. It's a last-ditch weapon."

She clipped the holster to her belt, slipped in the Ruger. She hugged him. "Thank you, Hurley. You know you can trust I'll be careful with it, you trained me."

"Don't let Agent Foxe see it or he might throw you in a D.C. jail. And then come back for me. I don't want to leave Angelique running the camp; she'd do a better job, and then where would I be?"

"Even jail would be better than feeling helpless. You could be right about Angelique, she's got serious moves, as you Yanks say. You ready for one of her cinnamon buns?"

Chapter Twenty-five

On the road to Savich's house
Washington, D.C.
THURSDAY EVENING

By the time Elizabeth and Rome said their goodbyes and started back to Georgetown, the daylight was vague and shadowy, not quite yet swallowed into darkness. It was only when they were inside the Beltway that Rome spotted a large black SUV three cars behind them. In the next block, it moved up to two cars behind them. Were they waiting for full-on darkness to make their move? There would soon be fewer people on the road, but they were in Washington now, the traffic still fairly thick. What were they planning? To gun them down in a drive-by? Rome shot a sideways look at Elizabeth, saw she was staring out the window at nothing in particular, deep in thought.

He said, his voice matter of fact, "Don't look back, but we're being followed."

Elizabeth said calmly, "The SUV? Yes, I saw them. Hurley taught me to practice spotting a tail, as you call it. How could they have found me so quickly? I've only been here in Washington two days." She heard fear seeping into her voice and wanted to kick herself. She drew three slow, deep breaths. She had a gun, she could use it. She could kick the crap out of anyone, if given the chance.

Rome took a right turn, wound through a neighborhood of apartments, then another right. The SUV stayed two cars back. He saw two people in it, but couldn't make out their faces.

He whipped the Range Rover into another right turn. Rome kept his voice easy, as if they were on their way to the beach. "It means there's a leak in London and someone followed us to Hurley's camp. That's right, keep an eye on them in the side mirror."

A leak? In Deputy Director Eiserly's section at MI5? How could that be? Not important at the moment. She looked at the SUV behind them.

"Can you describe them?"

Time to prove she was competent, time to test her mettle, time to be ready for anything. Her voice was sharp and crisp. "All I can see are two people in ball caps and sunglasses." She paused, added, "Hurley taught me defensive driving. If you'd like to stop, get your gun ready, we could trade places."

The blonde with the fishbone braid, not to mention the aristocratic voice, she wanted to drive? He didn't laugh, because he wasn't stupid. She was probably very good after three months with Hurley. He shot a look at her. "Sorry, we can't stop." He saw a green light ahead turn yellow, waited until it was on the edge of red, and peeled off into a fast left turn. The SUV behind them got stuck behind a small Fiat that had stopped at the light. In the next instant, the SUV jumped the sidewalk, knocked down a row of mailboxes, flattened an urn of flowers, and bounced back down onto the street behind them.

Rome grinned. He hadn't been in a car chase since the academy, a wild ride he'd managed to win. "Looks like they're finished pretending. Hang on, Elizabeth."

Elizabeth's heart pounded in her chest, but she was more excited than scared. She felt the Ruger snug in her jacket pocket. "Should I call the police, or Dillon? Where are we going?"

"To the old warehouse district near Union Market. Less traffic there, more room to maneuver. There's no time to call, this is going to go down right now. You okay?"

"I trained for this, Rome. Remember?"

Rome grinned at her, whipped the Range Rover left, and headed toward smaller, less-traveled streets, the SUV fishtailing behind them. He took a fast right off Brentwood toward the warehouse district, whipped left again into an open loading zone.

Elizabeth shouted, "They're still coming, thirty yards behind us." She didn't take out her Ruger, saving it for a closer target. She grabbed the chicken stick, gripped it tight. *Focus, focus, this is what you trained for.* She kept her voice precise. "The driver still has dark glasses and a cap on, so I can't say much about him, but the passenger isn't wearing sunglasses now. He looks forty, dark skinned, can't tell about his eyes. Rome, he's got an assault rifle. He's getting ready to fire."

Rome jerked his Glock from his waist clip, tossed it to Elizabeth. "There's one in the chamber."

The man with the assault rifle came halfway out of his open window and fired nonstop. The Range Rover's passenger-side mirror exploded and flew off, but Elizabeth fired back until the magazine was empty. Rome switched on his high beams to blind the driver and jerked the wheel hard left.

"My jacket pocket!"

She pulled another magazine from his pocket, ejected the empty one, shoved the new one into the Glock. They were closer now, maybe twenty feet, the man on the passenger side still leaning out the window, firing at them again. Elizabeth pulled back, calmed, recited Hurley's words to her—*slow and easy.* She reared up, sighted, and fired three times, the sound deafening. The third bullet hit him. His weapon flew out of his hands out the window and cracked against the asphalt. She jerked her head back inside. "I shot the bloody tosser, Rome! Now what?"

The SUV went another thirty yards, regrouping, Elizabeth knew, then turned back. Rome once again did a 180 and floored it, directly back into the path of the oncoming SUV. Faster and faster. She knew they were going to crash head-on unless one of the vehicles turned away.

They were nearly in the SUV's grille when the driver jerked his wheel hard left, his tires squealing as the SUV tilted onto its two right wheels. Before it could crash back down, Rome smashed into its right rear panel, trying to roll it over, but it spun and crashed back down on its wheels. They heard a shout, saw blood splattered across the cracked windshield. The driver hit the gas and roared back toward Brentwood Street.

"Take the wheel! Give me my Glock!"

She slapped the Glock into his right hand and grabbed the steering wheel. Rome twisted, leaned out the window, and fired. The back left tire exploded as the SUV screeched out of the warehouse lot, its steel rim sparking madly.

Rome floored the Range Rover, but it limped forward only a few feet before it coughed and went silent. He cursed, pulled out his cell, and hit a number. "Savich, they came after Elizabeth on our way to you. We're not hurt, but we think both shooters are wounded. They're driving a black 2019 Cadillac SUV, white Virginia plate UNR-5396. I shot out a tire, so they can't go far before they have to dump it. We're at the warehouse loading area off Brentwood. My engine gave out and we're stuck here. I'll text you our GPS."

He listened, punched off, and slipped his cell back into his jacket pocket. Elizabeth was nearly bouncing up and down from a massive adrenaline spike. Her hair had come loose and tangled around her face. Rome took her arms to settle her. "Look at me, Elizabeth. You did really well, you hit one of the shooters, maybe the driver too. Now take deep breaths."

She didn't want any deep breaths, she wanted to fly. She preened. *Yes, she had, and he hadn't even seen the Ruger.* She looked at Rome, the calm bastard, as if this near-death experience was old hat to him, something he did once a week and enjoyed. She wanted to kick him.

"They can't run on a rim for very long," he said. "They'll have to dump the SUV. Savich will notify Captain Ben Raven at Metro police. We'll see if they spot the SUV, not that it would matter. I'm sure it was stolen. Let me see if I can get the car running."

He jumped out of the Range Rover and popped the hood. Smoke billowed out into his face. The radiator was smashed where he'd hit the SUV, for all the world like a metal fist had punched it. He wondered what the FBI would have to say about repairs.

Rome climbed back into the driver's seat and smacked his fist against the steering wheel. "I hate we ended on a low note."

Out came her stiff BBC voice, with a bit of a snarky overlay. "Is that what you call what happened? A frigging low note? Are you mad? We—no, I—shot both men and you drove like a maniac, nearly sent them flying top over arse. A low note? And tell me just how you had the time to see the number plate? Much less know the year the bloody SUV was built?"

He grinned. "So Hurley didn't teach you how to pay attention? Maybe he should add that to his curriculum."

She muttered a curse he couldn't make out and punched him in the shoulder. "Everything happened so fast. You did that amazing one-eighty, drove straight at them, freaked them out, then you smashed into them and shot the tire—" Her voice fell off a cliff. She realized she was babbling. She didn't recall ever babbling before.

He studied her face. She still looked pumped, ready to run a hundred-yard dash. "You enjoyed that, did you?"

She stared at him. She felt the weirdest mix of feelings—

elation and terror and determination. She said finally, "Upon reflection, and since I don't feel like throwing up any longer, I'm inclined to say I did enjoy it. How much longer until my heart stops trying to burst out of my chest?"

"An hour or two, then you'll want to sleep for a year. But not yet. We're going to have police cars and FBI agents all over us in a minute. They'll have questions and I'll have a report to write. I hope Savich and Sherlock will feed us again. I'm starving. Maybe a fully loaded pizza from Dizzy Dan's. Or three."

Not a minute later the first police car pulled into the warehouse lot. The officer looked at the Range Rover, then back at them. Rome pulled out his creds, handed them to him. The officer grinned. "Looks like you had yourselves some fun here, agent. Too bad about the damage to your Range Rover. I know, don't say it—you should see the other guy."

Chapter Twenty-six

Tash liked his bedroom. Uncle Rebel had bought stuff for him before he'd arrived—books, a telescope, and an Xbox, which he liked but had hardly used, too much else to do. This nice cool night he settled in and tried once again to reach Autumn with his mind, as he did every night. He pictured her face, concentrated, but he couldn't see her. Maybe it was like a telephone and her line was busy, or maybe she was asleep, or maybe his mind just wasn't strong enough and never would be. But he'd keep trying.

Tash felt the cool night air coming through the open window. He loved being in the mountains, where you didn't roast as much in the summer as you did in Philadelphia. He thought of his father and the familiar fear swamped him. What was he doing, planning? He had to be scared, right? With everyone thinking he was a big-time thief, a criminal, and everyone looking for him. But he wasn't a crook, he just wasn't. His dad was smart and good and he'd loved Tash and Tash's mama, they'd been what was really important to him. Well, and his company. Everything was perfect until Mama had died and everything changed. Where was his dad now?

Tash was still thinking about his dad when he finally fell asleep and fell into a strange dream. It was weird. For the first time in his life Tash knew he was dreaming, but it didn't matter, he saw his father sitting on a bench inside a weird-looking building filled with strange statues and shapes and columns that looked like they had eyes sticking out of them and a ceiling so high he could barely make it out. His dad was staring at long glass windows of all different colors, beautiful, so bright. His brow was furrowed, like he was thinking hard, and he looked sad.

"Dad."

His dad looked up and blinked, but then he sort of shook his head and stared off at one of the windows again.

"Dad."

His dad didn't look up this time, he looked down at his favorite sneakers, sneakers Tash recognized. Tash called out to him a third time, but yet again, he didn't hear him. Suddenly the awful blackness he'd dreamt about before burst through the light-filled windows like a huge wave and began to swallow up the walls of the creepy building, and it was heading straight for his father.

Tash screamed, "Dad! Watch out! Run!"

Tash jerked awake on a yell, his heart pounding, sweating and shivering. He was crazy afraid. He didn't know what to do. He tried to get hold of himself—it was a stupid dream, that's what it was, wasn't it? Still, Tash sat frozen, his heart in his throat, chills raising goose bumps on his arms. He wished his mom was there with him and not in heaven with God. She'd hug him and kiss his forehead and maybe sing to him, and his father would come in and hug them against him and sing with his mama. But his mama wouldn't ever be with him again. Was his father gone now, too, trapped in that strange place? Would that horrible black wave swallow him? What could he do?

Tash jumped out of bed and ran down the hall to Uncle Rebel's bedroom. The door was open. He didn't wait, didn't think, just ran to the big bed, pulled back the covers, and crawled in.

"Tash? What's wrong? Did you have a nightmare?" Uncle Rebel's voice sounded sort of scratchy, like he'd been really deep asleep.

Tash managed to stutter, "I-I saw my dad and he was in this really weird place like where aliens live and this horrible black wave was coming through the bright windows, coming right at him. I knew it was going to swallow him whole. Uncle Rebel, what if it wasn't just another dream? Maybe I was seeing what's going to happen to him. What if that black wave kills him before we can do anything? We've got to stop it, Uncle Rebel."

"Shush now, Tash. You had a nightmare, a doozy. Come here."

Rebel gathered him in, felt Tash burrow even closer. He was cold, shaking. Rebel ran his hands up and down his back, heard him hiccup against his neck. He recognized the scent of his new soap, advertised to smell like a fresh meadow. His dreaming about his dad being in danger in a strange place made sense, given all that had happened. Rebel said, his voice easy, "It's okay, Tash. You're safe with me. Breathe slowly, that's right. Let the dream fade. Now, tell me about this place where you saw your dad and this black wave coming at him."

Tash gave a final hiccup, whispered, "It wasn't like a regular building, even though it had walls and windows. It was really big. There were colored windows—"

"Stained glass?"

"Yes, but not like the ones in St. Paul's in Philadelphia Mama really liked. There were columns everywhere—and colors, red and yellow and green, and statues that looked like they were from the Planet Zod. Uncle Rebel, I saw Dad, I really saw him.

He was sitting all alone on this weird bench and there were a lot of them—"

"Pews, like in a church?"

"Yes, they looked normal, like regular chairs, but everything else was really crazy looking. H-he didn't know that black wave was coming toward him. It's going to hurt him, Uncle Rebel. And he doesn't know!"

Rebel felt him trembling, squeezed him. He whispered, "It's okay, Tash. That sounds really scary, but it was only a nightmare, all right? Just a really bad, vivid nightmare." He hugged him close, kissed his forehead. *He thought he'd really seen his dad? He believed he'd seen something that hadn't happened yet? And it was going to happen to Archer?*

Rebel's logical brain fought the idea. The dream wasn't realistic, it was fantastic, a science fiction setting from a child's imagination. Where could Archer be that looked anything like that? He'd been thinking all day about what Joanna had told him. They believed both Tash and Autumn were psychic, gifted. She and Ethan believed what the kids said they could do, they indeed could, including Tash being prescient. What if the building where he'd seen his father wasn't real, woven out of a child's nightmare images, but the threat to Archer was? Was that possible? He began rubbing Tash's back in light circles. He remembered Joanna's words: *Just be yourself with Tash.*

Rebel said quietly, "I spoke to Autumn's mom today. I meant to talk with you about my visit with her earlier, but then the FBI agents came. She told me that what you said about being gifted is true, that Autumn is too. I didn't want to believe her, and to be honest, I'm still not sure. Give me time, Tash, give me time." What to say to an eight-year-old kid about logic? "This building you described, I don't know of such a place. Tell me more about it."

"I've never seen anything like it either, but it was real, Uncle Rebel, I know it was real. How could I dream something I saw so clearly and it's not really real? And I saw Dad. And he was there."

"Okay. Then it's up to me to find this place that has pews like a church and looks like science fiction."

"So you don't think I'm crazy anymore?"

"I never thought you were crazy, Tash. I'll make you a deal. You can tell me anything and I promise I'll listen."

"Good. That's good. You'll find this place, I know you will. It's real."

"Yes, I will." But what if there wasn't any such place on this planet? Rebel felt Tash's small hand slowly relax against his chest. He said nothing, lay still, listening to Tash's breathing even out into sleep. He stayed awake a long time, wondering, doubting, and listening to Tash breathe, feeling his heartbeat.

Where are you, Archer?

Chapter Twenty-seven

Rome picked Elizabeth up at Savich's house and drove to the Hoover Building through insane morning traffic. He saw no sign they were being followed.

He said, "How are you feeling this morning? Any bruises, sore places, pulled muscles?"

"A bit sore here and there, nothing aspirin couldn't handle. How about you?"

He shot her a grin. "Nothing a shot of whiskey couldn't handle. How'd you sleep? Any nightmares?"

"Not a one, but I'll tell you, Rome, I fell asleep in your Range Rover driving full-tilt toward their SUV front and center in my brain. It was so bloody real, but then I was out like the proverbial log until Sean let Astro lick my face, but not to get up and feed them—they both wanted to snuggle for a while. And that was nice, even though Astro kept licking my face. Any nightmares for you? Or are you too macho?"

Rome said, "Nah, no nightmares. I slept okay, thanks to that finger of whiskey I drank down before I went to bed." He put on his blinker, smoothly passed a Tesla. "Here's an update on the two guys out to do bad things to us last evening: I checked an hour ago and none of the local ERs, clinics, physician's offices, or pharmacies have reported a man paying them a visit with a gunshot wound. The SUV is still missing. As for the guy's rifle that went flying out the window, it was an SR-47. We'll know soon about fingerprints and DNA."

"Do you think the man I shot could be dead?"

"It's possible. If not, it's likely his partner patched him up. He could have been wounded himself."

She chewed this over, looked around the interior of Rome's rented Rubicon, patted the dashboard. "This one looks tough." She gave him a smug look. "It's named after the trail in California, right?"

"Yes, that's right. I figured the weight and the power wouldn't hurt. How'd you know about the Rubicon name?"

"Hurley was talking about it. He was considering buying one. How did you get it so fast?"

He only smiled. "I know the dispatcher. She took care of me last night. As for my Range Rover, it's in the shop. And yes, I know the owner. He can replace the radiator right away, no problem, but the body work, that'll take a while. Savich told me he'll put in the paperwork to the powers that be at the Bureau."

Elizabeth shook her head. "Well, that's the same everywhere, isn't it?"

She saw he was checking his rearview mirror. He looked distracted, as if something else was on his mind. When he stopped for a red light near the Hoover Building she said, "There's something you're not telling me, isn't there? You and Dillon and Sherlock—you're planning something. Come on, Rome, spit it out or I might have to hurt you."

"Maybe. Just wait, Palmer, all will be revealed."

Once they had parked in the Hoover garage, Rome went down on his haunches and ran his fingers under the front left fender. He was whistling Bon Jovi's "Livin' on a Prayer."

"What are you doing?"

"I noticed I was being followed again when I drove home in the Rubicon last night, even though they had to see you weren't with me, and I wondered why. I left the car in my driveway last night to see if they might plant something. And there it was this morning, a tracker—ah, look at this bad boy." He held up a small black disc, about two inches in diameter. "Now they know exactly where we are."

"And that's what you want?"

"Yep. We're hoping to use it against them."

"But—"

"Patience, Palmer, patience."

She came down beside him. "It doesn't look like the tracker Hurley showed me. This one's bigger and more obvious."

"The ones out of CIA tech services are no bigger than a thumbnail, and just as thin. I bet Hurley will get his hands on one in a year or so."

"So they came and put a tracker on your car, but they didn't break into your house and try to kill you?"

"They don't want me, Elizabeth, they want you. What they did last night, attacking an FBI agent on American soil, surprised all of us. They must want you very badly. They're worried we'll respond by hiding you away where no one can find you." He tossed the tracker from one hand to the other.

"Come on, Rome. What are you guys planning?"

He nodded to himself. "All right. We figure we can use this thing against them, Elizabeth, if you're willing to take the risk. We can keep their tracker attached to the car, and we're hoping they'll come after you again."

Elizabeth looked over at three agents exiting their cars and headed for the elevators. She waited until they were out of hearing. "I already told everyone who'd listen I was perfectly ready to be bait, to be the tethered goat. Let them track us, let them take another chance at me. I assume the next time you guys will have me covered."

"Yes, of course." Rome studied her face a moment. "You're sure? You're that confident we can keep you safe?"

"I'm sure."

"Okay, then." Rome went down on his haunches again and stuck the magnetic GPS tracker back under the fender. He rose, wiped his hands off on his pants. "Let's get upstairs and talk through this."

The CAU was already buzzing when Rome and Elizabeth walked in. There was a knot of agents talking to a man and a woman she'd never seen before. They looked ready for war in jeans and light jackets, Heckler & Koch MP5s draped over their shoulders, Glock 19s and six-inch commando knives clipped at their waists, tough black boots on their feet. Rome said to Elizabeth, "These two are from the Washington field office SWAT team. Agent Bea Lyons, and the hulk here is Agent Royce King, call him Buzz. They're both tough as nails, experienced veterans, even though they're both eating Shirley's sugar cookies."

They each shook her hand, eyed her. Agent Bea Lyons had salt-and-pepper hair cut short to a sharp point at her jaw, beautiful dark eyes, and a firm grip. "We were told you spent three months with Hurley, by yourself, and you survived. Well done. Hurley trained Royce and me back in the day. I bet if you tried you could take down Royce here. It would do him good. His mouth is bigger than he is."

King shook her hand. "You can call me Royce. I don't like Buzz, but no one pays any attention to me except Lyons here, and that's because she worships me." He wiggled his dark eyebrows. "It's embarrassing."

"Yeah, that's what I do, moron." She clipped his muscular arm with her fist and took another sugar cookie.

Elizabeth laughed. "Royce it is." He was tall, with a poster-square jaw, and buff as a lifeguard even though he had to be in his mid-forties. He'd probably demolish her in a minute in the ring. Elizabeth realized Agent Royce King couldn't seem to look away from her mouth, but it wasn't about kissing her. He was watching her talk. Funny how fascinated some Americans were with her accent. She grinned at him. "I suppose we could give it a try in the ring when this is over. Hurley did teach me Krav Maga."

King looked surprised, then nodded solemnly. "Sure, we can have a go, though I don't put much truck in Krav Maga, having never had a reason to consider it. Tell you what, Ms. Palmer, let me read up on what it's all about"—he flexed his biceps—"and that's all I'll need. We'll have ourselves a competition, but only if you promise to keep talking."

Savich and Sherlock had stayed back with Rome, watching them. Sherlock said, "They like her. She's as pumped as they are. Rome, you did emphasize to Elizabeth there's a chance every-thing could go south, that trying this is entirely up to her?"

"It's exactly what she wants," Rome said. "None of the at-tacks on her have been very well planned, more spur of the moment—we do this and they try that. I don't think they'll be any more careful today if they come for her. Again, no time to plan. I sure hope I'm right."

An hour later, Rome drove the Rubicon out of the Hoover garage, Elizabeth beside him, Bea Lyons and Buzz King pressed down on the floor of the rear seat behind them. It was only ten o'clock in the morning, but heating up fast. Another scorcher day.

King called out, "Elizabeth, if they're trying to kidnap you for ransom, your family must own half of London to make all this worthwhile."

Elizabeth said, "Alas, my family doesn't own half of London, and you're right, it doesn't make sense. But I'm told terrorists don't give up on revenge."

Rome stayed quiet as she told them what had happened in London, listened to Lyons and King disagree about what they might do next. Neither of them thought they'd attack her this morning, but Rome's gut was telling him they would.

He said, "We're going to head north toward Baltimore on state and county roads, not I-95, to make us an easier target. These goons don't care about civilian casualties, but we do. We'll head toward some of those narrow two-laners that wind through the farm country with a minimal amount of traffic. I'm betting that's when they'll come at us, if they do. Hey, guys, how are you feeling back there?"

Agent King called out, "Me, I'm too old for this crap, Foxe. Lyons looks all stretched out and comfy over there, but I'm wedged into the floor, my knees in my nose. I know you didn't want to rely on a tail car, but I don't have to like it."

Agent Lyons said, "Stop your whining, Royce. I'm old too, and I've got to hug the freaking H&Ks. They're not all soft and cuddly like you are."

King snorted out a laugh.

Rome said, "Elizabeth, keep sharp. It's only you and me, Buzz and Lyons have to stay down. If you see anyone hanging back, holler."

"There are lots of cars, weaving in and out, like a deck of cards getting shuffled."

Rome peeled off the frontage road when he could onto a two-lane country road winding east. It took them past white oaks dotting the landscape to green fenced pastures high with grass on both sides of the road, and more dairy cattle than he'd want to count. There was no traffic at all for minutes at a time. He slowed down, looking to see if a car had followed him at a distance, but there was no one.

King called out, "Elizabeth, if you're bored and want to talk out loud again—you can say anything, doesn't matter—I just want to hear you talk. Hey, I might let you beat me at Krav Maga."

Elizabeth appreciated his trying to distract her, but it was hard enough to breathe in and out, she was so scared and, strangely, excited. *Let them do something, let us win, let it all be over.* Rome's long gun was at her feet, but he'd told her she was to touch it only in an extreme emergency. She hadn't taken the small Ruger Hurley had given her to the Hoover Building, they would have found it at the door, and she could see Rome with his hand out to take it. Ah, but it was snug in the glove compartment, ready if she needed it.

The country road wound through hills and more pastures, past one-lane side roads that led through the pastures and cows toward distant farmhouses. Rome saw a car behind them now with four people in it, two of them kids in the back seat glued to their cell phones.

Suddenly there was a whirring sound overhead. Elizabeth leaned out the window and looked up. "It's a helicopter, Rome, coming over that hill toward us, maybe a hundred feet up."

Rome felt his adrenaline spike. "Guys, we were all wrong. This time they have a plan. Of all the things I expected, it wasn't that they'd come at us in a helicopter. We need to get away from that car behind us, they're civilians, including kids. There's a secondary road coming up, one lane, probably with potholes the size of cow patties, so brace yourselves."

Rome floored the Rubicon to pull away from the car behind them, leaned hard into a right turn onto a weathered asphalt one-lane road, and dodged the potholes. He saw a farmhouse, more cows, but no sign of people anywhere. He called out, "The helicopter's turned, he's following us."

The noise was deafening, scattering the cows beneath it.

Rome said, "The helicopter isn't like any I've ever seen before. Three rotors, looks ancient. It's slewing left and right, looks clumsy, like the pilot's having trouble controlling it. A man's leaning out the open passenger side, holding what looks like an AK-47. He's going to use it. Get ready, guys. Elizabeth, stay down."

Chapter Twenty-eight

Bea rose up fast, then back down. "It looks like an old Sikorsky. Real old, from back in the forties."

Elizabeth's knuckles were white on the chicken stick. Rome was looking calm, the idiot.

The Sikorsky made a low pass over the Rubicon, incredibly loud. It did a slow, clumsy turn, shuddering, and jerked forward again, directly at them. The man on the passenger side leaned farther out the open side of the helicopter and fired. Bullets struck the windshield, shattered it.

Rome jerked the steering wheel to the left, yelled out as he straightened the Rubicon again, "Get down in the well, Elizabeth, now! Guys, get ready."

She wanted to yell she had the long gun at her feet and she should pick it up and fire. But she listened to him, as she'd promised, made herself into a ball, and stuffed herself into the front well of the Rubicon. She saw Rome had cuts on his face, blood welling to the surface and running in rivulets down his cheeks. Another spray of bullets struck the side of the Rubicon, pinged into the rear panels. One of them hit a back window, shattering glass on Lyons and King.

The helicopter flew past them and turned back again, lower now, not more than twenty feet above them, shuddering even louder.

Rome jerked the Rubicon to a stop, shouted, "Now!"

Lyons and King pushed open the rear doors and rose as one, opened fire with their MP-5s, Bea at the helicopter pilot and Royce at the shooter.

King shouted, "Got him!"

Elizabeth leaned up to see the shooter grab his neck, blood spurting through his fingers. He screamed as he fell out of the open door of the helicopter, the AK-47 clutched to his chest until he landed at the edge of the cow pasture and the AK-47 cartwheeled away. A dozen cows mooed loudly, and the herd, as one, moved away faster, toward the far fence.

Neither agent stopped shooting, both concentrating now at the fuselage and the pilot. The noise was horrific. Suddenly smoke billowed up and the pilot pulled straight up, the three rotor blades whipping the air. He made a clumsy turn south.

Bea and Royce shoved in new magazines and kept firing. Enough of this! Elizabeth had trained like a maniac for three months with the biggest badass in the known universe and she was supposed to stay hidden like a helpless wuss? No way. She pulled herself back onto the seat, grabbed up the long gun at her feet, leaned out the window, and fired at the helicopter pilot.

The Sikorsky dipped and twisted, and they could see the pilot desperately trying to right it, to gain control, but it was no good. It started to fall, the engine sputtering. The rotors sheared off the top of an ancient white oak and the helicopter flipped. They heard a long thin scream as it plowed into the ground and exploded. A cow stood apart from her brethren some forty yards away and stopped chewing its cud, watching the helicopter burn.

Rome ran to the burning helicopter and pulled the pilot out and away from the fuselage as Lyons and King ran to the man sprawled on his back in the pasture. Elizabeth knew both men were dead; they had to be. No way the pilot could have survived the crash. She moved closer even though she didn't want to.

She knew she had to. She was a part of this; she was the reason the two men were dead. She looked down at them—both were young and looked Middle Eastern. They carried no ID.

She stood silently off to the side, out of the way, as Rome called Savich, told him what had happened, and emailed photos of the dead men and the Sikorsky.

Hurley had trained her to shoot. Even though she'd seen what happened to targets when bullets ripped into them, it was nothing like this. The impact of seeing violent deaths was something she hadn't imagined—the twisted bodies, and so much blood. Hurley had also presented her with dozens of possible attack scenarios, but they'd been abstract. Reality was something else entirely She swallowed, swallowed again. She wouldn't vomit, she wouldn't. She watched Bea pull out a handkerchief and dab the cuts on Rome's face. "Not bad, Rome, I don't think you'll need stitches. No glass I can see and nothing near your eyes, but when we get back I'll check you with a magnifying glass." She trotted over to Elizabeth, studied her a moment, her white face, her dilated eyes. She took Elizabeth's hand and rubbed it, soothing her, calming her. She said matter-of-factly, "You did good. That's right, take some light shallow breaths, you'll be fine. Now, I see some glass in your hair, but I don't see any cuts. As for Royce, if he's bleeding anywhere, he deserves it."

And Elizabeth laughed. It was shaky, but still a laugh.

Rome stared down at the two young men. "I wish at least one of them had survived. Elizabeth might have recognized their voices, if they were the same two who attacked her in London. I hope DNA will tell us." He'd wanted to check her out, but saw Bea had her well in hand. He knew all the training in the world couldn't prepare you for the real thing. He drew a deep breath. That had been a close one. Without Bea and Buzz they might have succeeded.

Royce said, "If they're local talent, we should be able to

identify them, unless it's new imported talent not on the watch lists."

Rome walked around the smoldering Sikorsky. "I wonder where they got hold of this relic."

Bea brought Elizabeth to stand beside her. Bea studied the Sikorsky's markings. "It goes back to my grandfather's day. I doubt these guys found it stashed in a military hanger."

Rome said, "I'm thinking a museum or private collection."

Royce said, "There can't be all that many of them around. I bet whoever let them fly this prized baby will be royally pissed."

Bea said, "He'll know soon enough when these two don't return. By the time we find him, he'll know we're coming."

Elizabeth looked away from the two dead men on the ground a dozen feet away from her. Her heart wasn't pounding as hard, her insides were calming down. She hadn't thrown up. She didn't doubt they'd find the owners if Bea was right about the helicopter. She felt a spurt of hope. Maybe it would all be over soon. She listened to the three agents talk and didn't move until she heard sirens in the distance.

Several CAU agents were gathered around the conference room table studying the array of photos Rome, Lyons, and King had taken of the burning Sikorsky and comparing them to a series of old photos on a laptop next to them.

Savich punched off his cell and clicked on one of the photos on the laptop. "Dr. Killigan says it's this one, the YR-4A, the original prototype. Only three of them were built before they improved them, to keep the blades rotating in a stable plane and stop the control stick from shaking like a jackhammer. After Dr. Igor Sikorsky demonstrated his namesake in 1940, the Army Air Force, the Coast Guard, and the Royal Air Force ordered a hundred thirty-one of the updated model. One of these updated Sikorskys is on display at the Smithsonian. Killigan doesn't know what became of the three originals, but like us, he believes they're likely in the possession of collectors, if they survived."

Ollie Hamish, Savich's number two, said, "Seems to me the collector has to be complicit. How else could they have gotten hold of it? I can't imagine they could steal it. And the pilot had to have some training. You don't fly one of these old machines on spec."

Agent Ruth Noble said, "But instruction had to be minimal, because they planned this so quickly. From what you said, Rome, the pilot had a lot of trouble controlling it."

Sherlock said, "An old helicopter like this one can't have been housed far from here. And if the collector is the mastermind, he took a huge risk, knowing the Sikorsky could be traced back to him if something went wrong, which it did."

Savich said, "Well, he obviously didn't think you guys would shoot it down. And from what you've said, the man seemed to be shooting at you, Rome, not Elizabeth. Which makes it seem they've been out to take her all along. If that's true, then it seems Elizabeth is very important to them."

Elizabeth pictured the two men who'd died, remembered their cheeks and chins were bone white compared to the rest of their faces, as if they'd just shaved off beards. If Dillon was right and they really didn't want her dead, then why indeed did someone want her so badly? She said, "Me? You think I could be important enough to someone to keep trying to take me?"

But did she believe it? Could she believe it? She remembered so clearly the one with the knife ready to slice up her face, remembered the hatred. Nothing made sense.

"We'll find out, I promise you," Savich said.

"How long do you think we can keep this quiet, Dillon?" Sherlock asked.

"There were no bystanders with cell phones, so who knows? Our team is out there, loading the parts onto a flatbed truck to haul it to Andrews. Would one of them talk?"

Ruth said, "It is a fascinating story, so we probably won't keep it quiet for long."

Savich's phone pinged a text from his laptop. "MAX found the three Sikorskys. One of them is housed near Langley, not five miles from CIA headquarters. The owner is Ammar Aboud, a wealthy Syrian, part of Syrian president Bashar al-Assad's inner circle. Aboud's family is big in shipping and banking. Aboud handles most of his family's foreign business dealings. I'll bet he's here, in the U.S." He shot a look at Elizabeth, who was standing next to Sherlock, nearly vibrating with excitement.

Sherlock said, "A wealthy Syrian? Whatever would a wealthy Syrian want with Elizabeth? What can it mean?"

Rome rubbed his hands together. "Let's visit Mr. Ammar Aboud and break the news to him his prized antique helicopter is scrap metal on a flatbed. I doubt he cares about the two men."

Elizabeth said, "I wonder if he'll give something away when he sees me."

Chapter Twenty-nine

John Eiserly's agent Khaled Aziz closed his brolly when he stepped under the awning of Dever's Café and gave it a good shake. Dever's was an old coffee shop near Parliament favored by the more liberal members of the House of Commons. He looked inside the large glass window and spotted Imam Ali Ahmad Said sitting alone in a corner booth. He walked into the always crowded café toward him, a smile on his face. He didn't know what the young imam wanted because he hadn't told him when he'd called him the previous evening. Ali Ahmad Said had said only that he should come have coffee with him. Khaled's mind raced as he walked toward the imam, his palms sweating. Had the imam asked to see him to tell him he'd been found out? Probably not, or he'd either be lying dead in a filthy alley or floating in the Thames.

The imam waved him to the seat across from him. A young man dressed in Dever's signature red and black wove his way through the tables and took Khaled's order of tea. Khaled waited respectfully for the young imam to speak. Khaled saw no anger in his eyes, no hint of why he'd wanted to see him here, of all places. Could it be the imam had asked to meet him because he'd finally noticed him, heard good things about him? Well, why not? For the past six months, Khaled had been an ardent worshipper, always respectful and admiring, speaking only when spoken to. At the mosque, Ali wore his traditional loose white robe, the jalabiya, and his feet were always bare for public prayer because it would be disrespectful to pray with something on that had a taint, like the sole of a shoe. But today, at Dever's, Ali was a fashion plate—Savile Row black slacks and jacket, white silk shirt, alligator loafers and no socks on his narrow feet. His beard was neatly trimmed, his hair finely barbered.

Ali said in his quiet public-school voice, "Khaled, my friend, thank you for meeting me here. Dever's is one of my favorite cafés in London." Khaled knew that, of course; he knew just about everything about Imam Ali Ahmad Said from the dossier Mr. Eiserly had provided him.

"I've never been here before. It's quite impressive."

Ali nodded toward the window. "It is always raining in London, so very different from Syria. Have you adapted to it?"

Khaled followed his gaze to a relentless drizzle that had turned London gray. He said, "My parents brought me to England as a small boy, so I have few memories of Aleppo, only of feeling a warm sun on my face and seeing beautiful mountains. I grew up near York, and it rains as much in Yorkshire as it does here. Do you know I heard this café has been here for nearly two hundred years? It's difficult to imagine how they stayed dry in London in those days."

Ali smiled. "Yes, imagine walking through all that mud and filth. It's difficult to comprehend. When it rains my father grumbles and curses, says he wants to go home to Ar Raqqah. My mother, who adores Harvey Nicks, merely nods her head, knowing his complaints will pass."

As Ali continued to speak of the mundane, Khaled felt his tension ease. Ali was either an excellent actor, or he had no idea Khaled was an officer with MI5.

After Khaled was served, he put one teaspoon of sugar in his cup and sipped his tea. He sighed in pleasure.

Ali said, "Khaled, I have a favor I wish to ask of you."

Khaled's heart kicked up. "Of course, Imam." He set down his teacup and bowed his head in diffident silence.

Ali sipped his favored bitter coffee, set down his cup, and said in his deep, compelling voice, "The mosque's accountant, Rehan al-Albiri, wishes to retire. I have made inquiries and learned you have an excellent reputation at Culver and Beck. I ask you to consider working with Rehan until you are familiar with his accounting system and then assume his duties. You will have assistants to do your bidding, so for the most part, only your professional oversight is needed. You will not have to leave your position at Culver and Beck, which, I know, is very rewarding financially. You will be well rewarded financially by the mosque as well." He paused, took another drink of coffee, said slowly, "I'm told you believe in the old ways and that your Arabic is fluent."

So the imam had verified the legend created for him by Eiserly's people at JTAC, and it had held, or Khaled wouldn't be sitting here. JTAC suspected the aged accountant Rehan al-Albiri had for many years been presiding over two vastly different sets of books, only one submitted to HMRC, the other recording the real sources of the mosque's funding and outgoing sums to support jihadist groups. Khaled doubted he'd be trusted with seeing the real books anytime soon, if at all, but there was a chance he could find them once he took Rehan al-Albiri's place. Did one of his promised assistants know all about the second books? Rehan had been an intimate of the former imam for many years, and he was a wily old fox. MI5 could never find direct evidence against him, so Rehan still walked in the sunlight, when there was sunlight in London.

Khaled let only excitement show on his usually austere face. He raised shining dark eyes to the imam. "It would be my honor, Imam. I thank you for your confidence in me. If you wish, I will resign immediately from my firm."

Ali waved a graceful hand. "No, no, there is no reason for you to leave your position." He took a final drink of his coffee, stood, and came around to shake Khaled's hand. Khaled quickly rose to stand with him. "Welcome, my brother. It will take some time for Rehan to show you his system, a bit different I suspect from the one you use in your English firm."

Ali straightened his beautiful jacket, picked up his brolly from the seat, and suddenly looked mildly embarrassed. "Ah—I have one other favor to ask. I would like you to meet my parents, and my younger sister, Adara." To Khaled's astonishment, Imam Ali Ahmad Said fumbled with his brolly and didn't quite meet his eyes. "Adara has, ah, seen you at the mosque and particularly wishes to meet you. I know, perhaps you believe her forward, but my parents have indulged her, allowed her to participate in Western ways, as they do themselves, even encouraged her education. She took a first at Oxford, reading Middle East studies. Would you consent to dine with us this evening?"

Khaled remembered seeing the imam's sister standing beside the imam's dark green Bentley in front of the mosque, waiting for her brother, a pretty young woman dressed in tight jeans and a cashmere sweater, her black hair falling in long waves around her face. Their eyes had met briefly and she'd smiled and given him a little wave. He'd smiled back. Her wanting to meet him was a surprise, and he had to admit to a bit of male pleasure. He was certain Eiserly would tell him meeting Adara could be useful. "It would be my honor, Imam. With regards to my new position, shall I come to the mosque to meet Rehan?"

"Yes, that is what he would prefer. You may phone to set up a convenient time for both of you."

When he was alone again on the street, Khaled sent an encrypted text to Deputy Director Eiserly. *Six months of worship and reverence and finally we have a payoff. The imam has asked me to assume Rehan al-Albiri's duties. Only the official books, of course, but it is a start. The imam has even invited me to dinner this evening, unexpected and quite an honor. He said his sister Adara wishes to meet me. I'll make contact again when I've learned more.*

Chapter Thirty

Autumn hiked to Locksley Manor, her special cave in the Titus Hitch Wilderness. She moved the brush away from the cave entrance and crawled in, careful not to squish her bag of potato chips. Once she was through the narrow opening, the cave roof soared to ten feet above her. It was her thinking place, her sanctuary. She carefully pulled brush over the opening until she knew from long practice her cave was once again invisible.

She sank down on the blanket she'd first spread on the floor of the cave when she was seven, frayed now, still as comforting now as it was then. She opened her bag of potato chips and set her bottle of water beside her. She pulled her iPhone out of her hoodie pocket, leaned back against the limestone wall, and stretched out her legs. She scrolled to the photos she'd downloaded of Carla Cartwright, COO of Archer Navarro's investment fund, the woman whose name Tash's dad had texted to Rebel. She'd looked it up—COO really meant second-in-command, the person who ran all the day-to-day operations.

She'd found a photo on Archer's Facebook of Carla standing beside Archer, both grinning madly, taken over four years ago, when she and Archer had set up the Navarro Investment Fund.

Autumn studied Carla Cartwright's face. She wasn't beautiful like Autumn's mom; Cartwright's features were too strong, her chin too aggressive. But her eyes were smart, Autumn could see that, and met the camera straight on. Her dark hair was cut in a bob sharply angled along her jawline. She had pale skin, black hair, blue eyes—Black Irish, she knew that was called, so somewhere along the line, Cartwright must have had Irish ancestors. She scrolled to another photo, this one recent and full length. Cartwright looked elegant and fit. Autumn had read in a Wikipedia article she was thirty-eight, five years older than Autumn's mom, a graduate of the Wharton School of Business. She had an economics degree from Brown. She'd dealt with IPOs—initial public offerings—it said, until she'd hooked up with Archer Navarro. She looked vibrant in the photo, happy, very pleased with herself and her world.

Autumn scrolled through photos of her at the office and events, wearing beautifully fitted business suits in different colors in the daytime and long expensive gowns on formal occasions, where she was surrounded by men wearing tuxedos. There was a photo of Cartwright in leggings and sneakers, running past Betsy Ross's house on Arch Street in Philadelphia. It looked staged because there were no tourists in sight. Another showed Tash and his mom, Celia, and dad outside of Luigi's Pizza, Carla standing behind Tash, mugging for the camera. Tash looked maybe four years old. He was standing between his parents, each of them holding one of his hands. His mom was beautiful, with soft, nearly white-blond hair and the bluest of eyes. They looked like a happy family. Archer Navarro was beaming with pleasure. She remembered the Archer Navarro who'd hired her to shepherd his son for the summer. He didn't look much like the man in the picture. He'd seemed stiff and formal, smiling only when he'd looked at his new wife, Sasha.

Autumn sat back. She didn't want to think about how his or

Tash's lives had changed so completely after Celia died. It was too scary, all the bad things that could happen to people, like cancer or meeting the Backmans.

She shook away the thought and scrolled to a photo of Cartwright wearing a tight, formal emerald-green gown. She looked like an off-with-your-head sort of queen. Okay, enough pictures, time to get on with it.

Autumn punched off her cell, ate one last potato chip, and closed her eyes. She relaxed her hands, palms up, on the blanket. She grounded herself, cleared all the stray thoughts from her mind, and pictured Carla Cartwright's strong vivid face, her smart eyes, her dark hair in a bob.

She concentrated, but she saw only the pictures she'd looked at, not Carla herself. She tried over and over, but it was no use.

Autumn cussed one of the bad words she'd heard from Oscar at the grocery store when he splatted a carton of milk on the floor, but it didn't help.

She concentrated on Tash instead, saw him immediately, sitting cross-legged in Rebel's study, its low lights casting shadows on the walls behind him. He was listening to his uncle reading the novel he'd just sent off to his editor in New York. Autumn heard Rebel's deep voice filled with menace meant to make you shiver. *The strange shapes began to stretch out, taller and taller until they reached the ceiling. They twisted in on themselves, turned inside out, and one of them moved toward him. It was holding something long and blurry that slowly took form. It was an ax. Jamie recognized it from his uncle Elliott's workshop.*

Tash suddenly looked toward her, cocked his head in question. He saw her. He actually saw her. Good. He blinked, smiled really big. It was the first time he'd seen her. She winked at him, mouthed later, and left him there with Rebel, who hadn't noticed a thing.

Autumn checked her watch, wadded up the potato chip

bag, drank the rest of the bottled water, and stuffed them both in her backpack. It was time to get home to help Ethan and her mom feed the critters and make dinner. She decided she'd give all of them big hugs because you never knew when something bad might happen.

Chapter Thirty-one

Rome goosed up his speed to keep close to Savich's Porsche in front of him once he'd turned off the highway toward Aboud's horse farm in rural Virginia. Sherlock was summarizing more information about Ammar Aboud. "Our Mr. Ammar Aboud is an American citizen, born in Boston. Word has it the family wanted him to have dual citizenship because he was expected to conduct business internationally, which he has. His family wealth is two generations old and took a bigger step up when his father married his mother, an heiress to an immense shipping fortune. His father owns hotels, industrial plants making airplane parts, and a chain of banks Ammar will control when Aboud senior retires. Ammar Aboud himself, a widower with one son killed in the Syrian conflict, remarried another Sunni heiress some eighteen years ago and has three children.

"He's a horse racing fanatic, spends a good deal of time here in the United States at his horse farm. He has a collection of World War II fighter planes hangared in Damascus, owns and flies a Gulfstream, the big one, a G5. He's also a gambler, and he rarely loses. He's been here for the past three months; his wife and children are in Damascus. He bought the Sikorsky twelve years ago from a United Arab Emirates sheik, had it hangared here on his property. We're coming up to his property now."

Rome turned off the two-lane country road and followed the Porsche through open white gates. Pastures and paddocks bordered white-painted stables and outbuildings stretched out in the distance. They drove past grazing horses twitching their tails, their healthy coats glistening in the bright late-afternoon sun. The smooth-topped drive was lined with oak and maple trees and curved into a circle in front of a pillared colonial house adorned with flower boxes painted a soft light green and bulging with summer flowers. The house looked freshly painted, a glistening white, like the barns. It looked like a painting.

A stout older woman of indeterminate age dressed in a gray suit and low heels opened the front door and regarded them with no particular interest.

"How may I help you?" she asked in a soft southern accent.

Savich introduced himself, Sherlock, and Rome, but said nothing about Elizabeth, standing behind Rome. They all pulled out their creds. "We would like to speak with Mr. Aboud."

"I'm very sorry, Agents, but Mr. Aboud is quite busy at the moment. I was told he wasn't to be disturbed. I am Mrs. Maynard, his housekeeper. Perhaps I could help you with something?"

Sherlock gave Mrs. Maynard a sunny smile. "Please tell Mr. Aboud this visit concerns his Sikorsky helicopter. Trust me, Mrs. Maynard, Mr. Aboud will want to know what we have to tell him."

The woman cocked her head to the side and considered. "Very well. I will ask if Mr. Aboud wishes to see you. Please come in and sit down in the living room, just to your right."

She ushered the four of them into a long narrow room beautifully furnished with early-American antiques, its walls painted a pale green and covered with American paintings.

Elizabeth recognized several John Singer Sargent landscapes. Mrs. Maynard left them without another word.

Two minutes later, she was back. "Please come with me. Mr. Aboud will see you."

They followed her down a long hallway with a glossy wide-oak-plank floor. The cream walls were lined with stylized American portraits of grim-faced bearded men and stoic tight-lipped women.

In front of the double doors at the end of the long hallway stood a tall man, his arms crossed over his chest, his dark eyes narrowed as he watched their faces. He was well muscled and bald, a stereotypical bodyguard. Mrs. Maynard nodded at him and he moved to the side. She opened the doors, stepped inside. "Mr. Aboud, here are Agents Savich, Sherlock, Foxe, and a guest."

They walked into a large square room strikingly different from the rest of the house. It was a study in stark minimalism— cold gray walls, ultramodern desk and sofa, all glass and chrome, four modern scoop chairs, and a thick, stark white rug. Was the rest of his house simply for show for his rich neighbors? To show them he was like them with his display of valuable American antiques? There was a saving grace—a very large framed picture of one of the pastures with a dozen horses grazing in thick summer grass.

The bodyguard followed them into the large office and stood in a corner, his back against the wall. Rome saw the outline of a pistol beneath his black jacket.

Savich said easily, "Mr. Aboud, I'm FBI Special Agent Savich." He introduced Sherlock and Rome, pausing as Elizabeth stepped from behind Rome. "This is Lady Elizabeth Palmer."

Time seemed to stop. Aboud stared at Elizabeth, finally said, "Ah, Lady Elizabeth. It is a pleasure to meet you, and I must admit, a surprise. I never would have expected you to be here in the U.S. and visiting me in the company of three FBI agents. Of course, I have heard of you."

The photos of Aboud that Savich had brought up on his phone to show her didn't begin to capture his aura of power. He was lean, clean shaven, with thick salt-and-pepper hair, his face long and thin. Despite his bespoke Western clothes and his air of elegant sophistication, he looked to Elizabeth like a modern-day Genghis Khan, with his flat dark eyes and thin knife of a mouth, a man used to getting exactly what he wanted and willing to do anything he needed to get it. She didn't sense any limits in him. "How could you have heard of me, Mr. Aboud?"

He searched her face. "You were not aware your grandfather and mine were friends?"

She said slowly, "I was very young when my grandfather died, Mr. Aboud. My father never mentioned you or your grandfather to me."

"Both your grandfather and mine were acquainted with Winston Churchill. It is a pity no one told you."

Elizabeth wanted to know how this could be, but Savich said, "Mr. Aboud, do you know Lady Elizabeth's father?"

"The Earl of Camden? No, I have not yet had the pleasure."

Savich nodded toward the bodyguard. "I must say I find it unusual you have an armed bodyguard. I had no idea a horse farm in the hills of Virginia was such a dangerous place."

Aboud came around his glass-and-chrome desk and held out a large square hand. "I am in the midst of sensitive negotiations with others who do not wish me to succeed. Please give me your credentials."

After he'd closely studied each of their creds, he handed them back to Savich. He was silent, studying Savich, and Sherlock thought it looked like he was measuring Dillon for a coffin. She wanted to punch him.

Aboud's voice was low and deep, betraying a bit of an Arabic accent with an overlay of British public school. "I recognize you,

Agent Savich, and you as well, Agent Sherlock—ah, America's heroine, are you not?" He gave her a winning smile, but Sherlock was well aware of the sneer underlying his words. Because she was pregnant? Because he thought she, a woman, shouldn't be in a position of authority? Or because she'd killed Basara, a killer, but still a Muslim? She saw Aboud glance at Rome, size him up as he had Dillon.

Aboud's voice became crisp, commanding. "My time is limited, Agents. Mrs. Maynard said you had news of my Sikorsky helicopter. You must know I reported it stolen to our local law enforcement last night. It is very valuable, as I'm sure you must also know. I hope you are here to tell me you've recovered it and caught the thieves responsible?"

Savich said easily, "Unfortunately, your Sikorsky crashed and burned today in southern Maryland. The passenger was killed. The pilot, however, survived. We haven't identified him yet. If you would provide his name, it would be helpful."

Aboud gave a credible start, closed his eyes a moment. He said, "That is very distressing, and yet you have the ill-breeding to insult me by insisting I know this pilot's name, doubtless one of the men who stole my precious helicopter? If I knew who it was who stole my Sikorsky, I would have told the police. I will tell you I was very fond of the Sikorsky. It was my hope to keep it safe and pass it on to my eldest son. And you say it was destroyed? How? Tell me what happened."

Rome said, "Your Sikorsky was shot down earlier today in southern Maryland, as Agent Savich said. The two men in the helicopter were trying to kill Lady Elizabeth Palmer, or possibly kidnap her. FBI special agents shot it down. We are hopeful the pilot recovers enough to tell us what he knows."

Aboud stared at Elizabeth. "Someone tried to take you for ransom, Lady Elizabeth? Here in the United States? I find that perplexing and highly unlikely. I know your father is wealthy, but surely not wealthy enough to tempt someone to steal a valuable antique helicopter to try to kidnap his daughter. How can that be? And why are you even in the U.S. in the company of FBI agents? Why are they protecting you? I can make no sense of any of this."

Sherlock said, "Needless to say, Mr. Aboud, the pilot is under close guard at Washington Memorial. We were informed he survived his surgery and soon will be able to tell us why this happened, and who paid them to do it. You are saying, Mr. Aboud, you don't know why anyone would do this?"

"Of course I have no idea why anyone would try something so absurdly dangerous. Hearing my Sikorsky was used in an attempt to kidnap Lady Elizabeth astounds me. I cannot comprehend such a thing." He looked briefly at Sherlock's thickened waist, a flash of distaste on his thin face. "Why would you expect me to know? I have no animus toward Lady Elizabeth, why would I? I will say it again. My Sikorsky was stolen yesterday from the hangar here on my property. And before you ask, the county sheriff has examined the hangar and could find no evidence of who the thieves were. As you said, the pilot may be able to tell you."

Savich said, "Mr. Aboud, you have a bodyguard here, in your house. Do you also have guards outside, on the grounds, at the hangar?"

"I do, but alas, last night when my helicopter was stolen, Musa was in bed, he'd taken ill." Aboud's eyes went to Elizabeth again.

She said, "I don't understand why anyone would want to kidnap me either, Mr. Aboud. There have been other attempts as well."

Aboud held up a graceful hand showing beautifully kept nails. "Ah, but I do understand why you might believe me responsible, since the Sikorsky belongs to me. Let me be very clear so that you may understand fully. If I wanted to kill you,

Lady Elizabeth, you would already be dead. If I wanted you taken, you'd be bound and gagged and at my mercy. But I do not. Now, since you've made it obvious to me you are not here to assist local law enforcement, I ask that you leave. Musa will show you out."

Musa moved toward them, his eyes on Savich.

Chapter Thirty-two

At the last moment, Musa stepped toward Elizabeth and wrapped his hand around her wrist. Before she could respond, Rome grabbed his fingers, bent them backward hard until the big man gasped and went down on his knees. Rome said in a pleasant voice, "Call off your dog, Mr. Aboud, or I'll break his fingers and he'll be no good to you."

Aboud gave a command in Arabic.

Musa nodded. Rome released his fingers and watched him slowly stand, his eyes never leaving Rome's face. He said in a low vicious voice, "*Sa'aqtuluk.*"

Aboud said something sharp in Arabic to Musa, then changed to English. "He only wished to escort Lady Elizabeth from the room, Agent. Perhaps he was a bit clumsy, but no matter. Agent, you have managed to upset Musa. Were I you, I would take him seriously. He was trained by my father's body-guard, Ibrahim, a great fighter, and he has a long memory. He will not fall for your trick a second time."

Rome said, "*Yumkinuh almuhawila.*"

Aboud's dark eyebrow went up. "*He can try?* You speak Arabic. How is this?"

"I visited Damascus as a boy. I learned enough to know he threatened to kill me."

Elizabeth stared at him.

Rome watched Musa rub his fingers, hatred cold and hard in his flat dark eyes. Rome looked away from him to Aboud. "I'll have another surprise for him if he lays his hand on Elizabeth again, and that one he might not survive."

Aboud said, "Allow me to apologize. Musa should not have touched Lady Elizabeth. But no one appreciates such threats, Agent. It is a pity you think us adversaries. Lady Elizabeth's family and mine have a long history. I have nothing but respect for her family." He smiled at her. "I am very pleased you survived the attempted bombing of St. Paul's last year. A terrible thing. I wish you luck in finding the people responsible for all this misery.

"Musa, if you will please show these people out. Do not touch anyone."

Sherlock said over her shoulder, "Mr. Aboud, since your Sikorsky was used in a violent attack on Lady Elizabeth, federal agents will be back with a warrant. I do recommend you put a leash on your bodyguard here. If he attempts violence or obstructs them in any way, he will be arrested."

Silence followed them out of Aboud's office.

Musa said nothing as he walked them back to the front of the house, all the while flexing his sore fingers. He opened the front door and waited there until they passed by him into a brilliant sunset and soft evening air. They heard a dog bark and a horse nicker as the door closed quietly behind them.

Sherlock said as they approached the Porsche, her voice pitched low, "I planted a bug against a leg of Aboud's desk."

Elizabeth stared at her in amazement. "I didn't see you do that."

Savich grinned at her. "You were looking at Rome and the bodyguard. Well done, sweetheart."

Sherlock said, "I don't think Aboud believed us about the pilot surviving the crash. But it was worth a try, Dillon, to see how he'd react." She opened an app on her cell phone, punched in her password. "Let's see if Aboud has anything to say to his bodyguard." They didn't hear Aboud's or Musa's voice; they heard movement and another voice so quiet Sherlock had to turn up the volume. They could make out only a few words, *planted*, and *desk*, nothing more. Then came a low buzzing noise, and silence.

Sherlock said, "That's it, no more. Did anyone hear if it was a man or a woman speaking?"

Rome and Elizabeth shook their heads. Savich said, "We'll have tech enhance it, see if we can get any more."

Elizabeth said, "I remember now there was a mirror. Could it have been two-way?"

Sherlock sighed. "Yes, maybe, or a video camera tucked away we didn't see. Don't look so down in the mouth, Elizabeth, it would have been an incredible piece of luck if the bug had caught Aboud giving himself away. We'll find out at some point who the person was watching us."

On the trip back to Washington, Sherlock joined Savich in the Porsche and Elizabeth rode with Rome. When he turned onto the country road fronting Aboud's property, Savich said, "Why would a rich Syrian want so badly to take Elizabeth that he'd risk exposure and a priceless antique Sikorsky?"

Sherlock leaned her head back against the headrest. "It can't be only about money. All this frantic effort to take her—for what gain? What could Aboud want so badly? Maybe it goes back to Samir Basara or to the old imam, Hädi ibn Mirza, and the belief she somehow betrayed them. Maybe Aboud somehow connects to them?"

Savich said, "I can't believe you remember the old imam's name. If there is a connection, MAX will find it."

Sherlock sighed. "I'll never forget that name. I do know this, though. If Aboud or someone else behind this is motivated enough, they're not going to stop until Elizabeth's in the trunk of a car. And that isn't going to happen, ever."

Savich looked over and saw Sherlock was lightly rubbing her stomach. He laid his hand on her thigh.

"How's our kid?"

"Beauregard is just fine, jumping around a bit, but radiating well-being."

Savich said easily, "If she's a little girl, what do you think of calling her Felicity? Felicity Sarah Savich?"

Sherlock cocked her head to one side, whispered the name a couple of times. "Felicity. That's quite lovely. But Dillon, he's a boy, I just feel it, even though we didn't let the doctor tell us. Yep, he's going to be Beau, you'll see."

Chapter Thirty-three

Home of the Said family
Knightsbridge, London
FRIDAY EVENING

Khaled loved the insane energy of Knightsbridge, its unending snarled traffic and never-ending construction, its scores of people from every country imaginable on their way to shop or to work. He visited the Victoria and Albert Museum at least twice a year to see the changing exhibits, enjoyed buying a treat in the immense food hall at Harrods and strolling past the small businesses with Arabic signs and Arabic women, some dressed in Western clothes, others, usually the older women, in burkas.

He directed the taxi through the manic traffic to a street he'd walked before, to a dignified old red-brick house with magnificent grounds set behind a wrought-iron fence with ivy spilling over the scrollwork—Imam Ali Ahmad Said's family home. A dark green Bentley Flying Spur and a white Mercedes 550 were parked in the driveway.

He knew the imam's mother often used the Flying Spur, with a turbaned young man as her driver, and always carried a brolly even when the sun was high. Unlike her daughter, Adara, she dressed traditionally, wore a silk burka during Ramadan. Her husband, the imam's father, Mr. Said, owned high-end car dealerships and a travel bureau. His family had long-standing ties to the family of Bashar al-Assad, the president of Syria since 2000, but he was known as something of a bon vivant in London, very unlike his son, who'd chosen to be an imam. Khaled imagined it was Mr. Said who'd allowed Ali's younger sister, Adara, to fly free, adopt Western ways, and attend university. He knew from Eiserly and the imam that she'd flirted with a radical Islamic group while she was at Oxford and enjoyed her share of lovers both at Oxford and here in London. She also drank alcohol, forbidden in the Muslim faith, but not when she was dining with her parents. She'd lived at home since she'd come down from Oxford.

Khaled knocked on the large black front door.

The door opened immediately and there stood Adara, wearing a fitted soft gray knit dress, her rich curling black hair falling wild and sexy to her shoulders, wearing five-inch heels on her narrow feet that brought her to his height. He saw her toenails were painted vivid red. She was smiling at him, showing beautiful white teeth, satisfaction in her smile.

"Do come in, Mr. Aziz. I am Adara Said. You may call me Adara."

"Thank you. Please, call me Khaled."

She laid a soft hand on his arm and said in beautiful public-school English, "Come to the living room. We will have a vodka gimlet, it's my favorite. I trust you are not so devout you will refuse. That would severely curtail my plans for you."

Khaled shook his head.

"Good. We shall sin a bit, then, since my parents had to leave London today and my brother has been called away on an emergency. He sends his regrets. Come."

Khaled walked across the beautiful black-and-white-tiled entrance hall, past paintings and vases of flowers, and into a large rectangular living room with high ceilings and a magnificent Carrara marble fireplace. The furnishings were mostly burgundy leather, oversized, comfortable. He pulled up short.

There were three men seated on two sofas facing each other, all of them Arabs in Western dress, studying him.

Something is wrong. Khaled felt his bowels twist.

Adara said gaily, "You believe yourself clever, do you not, Khaled? My brother believes so, but he's not stupid. He would never be so negligent as to accept you at face value. He's made inquiries. You certainly don't look like an accountant." She shook her head at him, wagged a finger. "Let me introduce you to my comrades. They want very much to speak to you."

Chapter Thirty-four

Khaled looked at the set faces. He didn't want to die at twenty-eight years old with a knife in his ribs. Like the other under-cover officers at JTAC, he knew the risks, knew if his cover was blown he might be killed, but somehow he hadn't really accepted it as a real possibility. He imagined most of the other undercover officers hadn't either, believed being killed in the line of duty was no more than theoretically possible. When you're young, you feel immortal. Until you aren't.

He stood in the lovely Said living room and knew his death might very well be near. He looked from the imam's beautiful sister, still smiling at him, to the three men lounging at their ease, two of them smoking, all of them still staring at him intently. Two of them were his age and wore slacks and dark sweaters. The older man was dressed like a successful business-man from the City, in a black suit, white shirt, and thin purple tie. He was clean-shaven, unlike the younger men, who wore clipped beards. They were looking at Khaled like they might cut off his head and post the video on the internet.

He got himself together as his training kicked in. He stared back at them with an expression he hoped appeared calm and a touch arrogant. He nodded at Adara, pressed the inside seam of his jacket pocket to turn on his recorder. He said, his voice amused, "Comrades? Is that the same as what the English would call her mates?"

The older man rose and stepped forward. He said in a polished public-school voice, "Yes, we are Adara's mates, Mr. Aziz, but understand, we share much more than that. We share more than an allegiance to, say, a soccer team or to drinking pints together at a pub. We share a common cause, a cause to which we are loyal." He shot a look at Adara. "We are brothers and sisters, and we do not tolerate anyone who betrays that cause."

Khaled said slowly, his voice utterly serious, "I've never had the opportunity to be part of such a group. I've never been in the military or any group that faced danger, or shared a profound belief in a cause. I will admit I've felt that was a kind of lack in me. I suppose I started attending the South London Mosque because I was searching for something more meaningful than arranging the profits of rich Englishmen." He paused, looked embarrassed. "Forgive me, my beliefs or lack of them cannot interest you." He searched each of the three faces. "I do not understand why you wish to speak to me."

One of the young men with eyes as dark as a starless night said, "Who are you, Mr. Aziz? Really?"

There'd been no introductions, but they knew his name. Khaled smiled. "I am Khaled Aziz from Aleppo, Syria. My parents moved here when I was very young. They have since returned to Syria."

The older man said, "You said you're searching for something meaningful."

"It's difficult for me to explain, but I will try. When Imam Ali Ahmad Said asked me to see to the books at the mosque after Rehan al-Albiri retires, I was pleased because it seemed Imam had come to trust me, was willing to bring me closer to him, perhaps allow me to be part of something more important than myself."

The men were silent. Khaled turned to Adara. "You said the imam has found nothing damning in my life. But he doesn't know of my foray into gambling at the Balfour Club on Han-over Street?" He stopped, waited, a half-smile on his mouth. He hoped he hadn't gone overboard.

Adara said, "Ali did not discover your foray into baccarat, but Yusuf did." She nodded at the older man. "Yusuf finds out most everything about anyone who could be important to us."

The older man, Yusuf—was that his real name?—studied him a moment. Was he considering pulling a knife out of his pocket and stabbing Khaled in the neck?

Yusuf nodded to the two younger men and each gave Khaled his first name.

Yusuf said, "You wonder perhaps that a woman is part of our brotherhood. You must accept that she is or we will say goodbye to you."

"I will admit to being surprised by most everything I've heard this evening," Khaled said, and again smiled. "But having met Adara even briefly, I doubt she would have it any other way. I hope my being here means she approves of me."

Adara patted his arm. "We shall see. We would like you to join us for dinner at the Carousel Club for more discussion. I trust you like French cuisine and a fine wine?"

Three hours later, once back in his flat, Khaled went into his kitchen, made coffee, twisted the left leg of his kitchen table a quarter turn, and pulled out his burner mobile. He plugged the recorder into the USB port and sent his recording to John Eiserly. Then he texted his impressions:

A lot of polished rhetoric, but nothing damning or specific was said, either at the Said house or at the Carousel club. You'll hear some probing questions and I trust I responded believably.

Yusuf seems to be in charge. He is by far the oldest of the four and smart, I think, very smart. I imagine he could have nodded and either of the young men would have stuck a knife in my gut. Or perhaps it is Adara who is in charge. She was treated with great respect, deferred to. The two young men were acolytes, men you would think would be talking of sports and their love of Guinness. I will await further contact, I hope from Adara Said.

Chapter Thirty-five

Rebel and Tash greeted Autumn and her parents at his front door. Tash was nearly bouncing, he was so excited they'd come; he was talking a mile a minute. "Uncle Rebel made paella, his mom's recipe, and it's filled with all kinds of fish and shells and tomatoes—"

Rebel laughed. "Tash was my cheering section. I just hope it's edible," he said, and waved them into the living room. Joanna had never been in Rebel's house, and she looked around her, admired the high ceilings, the beautiful woodwork, and the art on the pale yellow walls. She said, "I've wanted to see your house, Rebel, after Autumn described it to me. Ethan told me you and the architect worked together on it. It's beautiful."

Rebel thanked her and gave Ethan Merriweather a beer, Joanna a white wine, and Autumn and Tash iced tea, with lots of lemon.

Tash said, "Uncle Rebel sent off his book to New York and he said now he can breathe for a while. He read me parts of the book and it's really scary. I nearly jumped a mile when the hero got a net thrown over him and he was pulled up and he was hanging from a tree branch, and there were snakes and—"

"As I said, my cheering section," Rebel said, and hugged Tash against his side.

The doorbell rang. Rebel excused himself and walked to the front door.

The two FBI agents stood outside, holding up their creds to him, their faces grim.

Briggs stepped forward. "You're under arrest, Mr. Navarro, for wire fraud and conspiracy."

Before he knew what was happening, Briggs had whirled him around and the other one, Morales, had fastened zip ties to his wrists.

Morales said, regret and disappointment in her voice, "We'll be asking Child Protective Services to send someone over to take your nephew, Tash, into foster care."

Ethan Merriweather pulled his badge from his shirt pocket. "I'm Sheriff Ethan Merriweather. Please show me your warrant and your credentials," and he stuck out his hand.

Briggs said, "Stay out of this, Sheriff. This is a federal matter."

"I would like to see your warrant and your credentials," Ethan repeated, his hand still out.

"Don't move, boyo," Briggs said to Rebel. He and Morales handed Ethan their credentials and Morales pulled out a warrant from her coat pocket. Ethan read it over. "You're arresting Mr. Navarro on charges he was involved in the theft from the Navarro Investment Fund?"

"That's right. As you see, Sheriff, everything is in order. We're taking Mr. Navarro to Philadelphia, where he'll be questioned."

Morales said, "Mr. Navarro, I suggest you contact your lawyer and have him or her meet us at the Federal Building on Abbott Street."

"Uncle Rebel!" Task flung himself at Rebel, wrapped his arms around his waist. He yelled at the agents, "You can't take him anywhere! He didn't do anything. Let him go!"

Rebel wished his hands weren't zip-tied behind him and he

could hug Tash, but he couldn't. "Listen, Tash, it'll be all right. We'll get this straightened out before you know it."

Joanna said quickly, "Tash will come home with us, Agents. If they have any questions, have Child Protective Services contact Sheriff Merriweather. Rebel, do you have a lawyer?"

Rebel shook his head. "Not a criminal lawyer, no. I don't think my literary attorney would be of much use."

Ethan said, "I know an excellent criminal attorney in Philadelphia. He'll meet you at the Federal Building. In the meantime, Rebel, don't say anything to anyone. Do not answer any questions. From this moment on, all you do is listen. All right?"

"Yes, I understand." Rebel knelt down in front of Tash, who was hugging him fiercely. "Listen, Tash, you'll go and stay with Autumn. This is some sort of mistake. I'll be back soon, I promise."

Briggs snorted, pulled Rebel to his feet. "Let's go."

Morales said to Joanna, "I'm not going to call Child Protective Services. I can see Tash will be in good hands." She looked down at Tash, his tears running down his face. She shook her head as they left, pushing Rebel ahead of them.

Chapter Thirty-six

Savich house
Georgetown
FRIDAY EVENING

Dillon!

Savich heard Autumn shout his name loud and clear, clearly panicked.

Just a moment, sweetheart. He put down his fork and said to the table at large, "Excuse me a moment. I'll be right back," and he left his dining room, Elizabeth and Rome staring after him.

Sherlock said easily, "He must have just thought of something important and has to make a call," and bit into her BBQ pork spare rib. "What were you saying, Rome?"

Savich leaned against the hallway wall, concentrated, and saw Autumn sitting cross-legged on her bed, her face drawn and pale. *What happened, Autumn?*

We were all at Rebel's house to eat his paella when FBI agents came and took him away. They're taking him to Philadelphia. Dad called Rafael Jordan, one of the best lawyers anywhere, he said. Dad went to school with him. He also told Rebel not to say a single word. Dillon, can you do something?

What are the agents' names?

They're the same two agents who came to his house last time— Morales and Briggs. She's nice; he's mean, a bully. They told Rebel they were arresting him—she slowed a moment, making sure she got it exactly right—*for wire fraud and conspiracy. They think he helped Archer steal money from the Navarro Investment Fund.*

I didn't expect this to happen, Autumn. I can't imagine what they found to arrest him. I'll make another call to the SAC of the Philadelphia field office and get back to you. Listen to me, they'll keep him safe, so don't worry. Where's Tash?

He's staying with us. Mom said she'd deal with anyone who tried to take him away from us.

And she will, Autumn. Try to convince Tash everything will be okay. He needs to hear it from you. I'm counting on you. Can you do that?

He saw her straighten her shoulders, draw a deep breath, and nod at him, complete trust in her eyes. *Yes, I will. Tash is in the guest room. He knows I'm calling you. He's really scared, but I'll go right now and tell him what you said.*

I'll call you as soon as I know what they've found that implicates Rebel.

A money trail, Savich thought as Autumn's face faded away. He prayed Rebel Navarro wasn't really in league with his brother. He stayed in the hall, called Special Agent Claire Gregson, the SAC of the Philadelphia field office, on his cell.

"Claire, Dillon Savich here. I'm sorry to disturb you on a Friday night, but I need to talk to you again about the Navarro case."

Four minutes later, Savich walked back into the dining room, gave Sherlock a brief nod, and said, "Rome, you were going to tell us how you came to speak Arabic."

Sherlock grinned. "And shocked the crap out of Aboud and his bodyguard Musa."

It was obvious to Rome that how he came to speak Arabic was the last thing on Savich's mind, but it was obvious, too, Savich didn't want to talk about whatever had pulled him away, so Rome waved a hand holding a chewed BBQ rib and said,

"You know my dad runs the detectives out of the nineteenth precinct in New York, but his younger brother, my uncle Leo, took a different route. He's in the diplomatic corps. When I was a kid, my uncle did a two-year stint in Damascus on the American ambassador's staff. I spent the summer with my three cousins and we roamed the streets and alleys in the city. We learned how to bargain and how to fight, no holds barred. By the end of my stay, I was pretty fluent in kid street talk. My uncle was appalled whenever he heard his sons and me speaking Arabic, since his spoken Arabic was of a much higher order. I don't speak much Arabic anymore, no opportunity. The CIA did come calling, but I wanted the FBI, always. To be honest, what I said to Musa—the words just came out."

Elizabeth said on a sigh, "I wish I could have spoken Italian as a kid. I could have let loose at Luigi at Marvello's Pizza when he cheated on the pepperoni."

There was laugher, then Elizabeth said, "Dillon, I don't mean to pry—well, maybe I do. Before you left the room, you looked sort of strange, like you were listening to someone—as if someone tapped you on the shoulder."

Savich swallowed a bite of Sherlock's honey corn bread and said easily, "I remembered I'd promised to check in with the Philadelphia field office about another case. And so I did before I forgot. Again."

Elizabeth cocked her head at him. No way could she imagine Dillon forgetting anything. "Did you solve the case?"

"Let's just say I learned some information I need the Philadelphia field office to act on."

Rome wondered what that information was, since he knew of no case from the CAU involving the Philadelphia field office, but it was obvious Savich had closed the door.

Sherlock picked up the conversation. "Getting back to Aboud, we haven't heard back yet about the federal warrant. It's already too late in the day to send out the forensics team to Aboud's horse farm. It doesn't matter, they've already had time to cover up what they can. Still, a team will go over in the morning, examine the hangar, question his employees, see whether the helicopter could possibly have been stolen without inside help and direction. Dillon assigned two agents to do a deeper dive into Aboud's background and affiliations, here and in London, any possible connection to the players John Eiserly is considering."

Savich said, "We need to find the key to his motive. But you know, I doubt he was behind the attacks on you in London, Elizabeth. I'm thinking someone pulled him in after they found out you're here in Washington, and that someone has leverage over him. To use his prized Sikorsky? I can't imagine him doing that willingly. And that smacks of another spur-of-the-moment decision."

Sherlock said, "Maybe it was the voice we heard on the recording. Maybe that person is calling the shots."

Savich said, "We'll find out how Aboud fits into all this, Elizabeth. I spoke to John and he's got a lot of irons in the fire too. He'll shuffle Ammar Aboud into the mix, see if he can't find connections."

"I sure hope one of those irons heats up soon."

Rome patted her arm. "We're good, sometimes miracle workers, and you've only been with us a couple of days. Give us another day, okay? Now, tell us about what your parents are saying."

"That's a good question. I hadn't told my parents I was coming to the FBI in Washington after my time with Hurley, didn't really tell them much of anything. I thought it would be safer for them."

Sherlock said, "So that means anyone watching them, maybe even following them to hear if they said anything about you, didn't know you were here."

Elizabeth brightened. "That's true. But after Dillon told John I was here, I told them we were all working together and that you were keeping me safe. But I haven't mentioned to them that we were attacked in the warehouse parking lot, or by the Sikorsky. What good would it have done except to scare them?"

Elizabeth looked around the table. "I did want to ask my dad whether he's dealt with Aboud, but I decided not to."

Savich said, "That's fine. If he has any connection to Aboud we'll find it, and if something leads us to your father, we'll talk with him then."

He picked up a corn on the cob. He studied her face a moment, then said, "I don't think what's been happening to you has anything to do with kidnapping you for ransom, Elizabeth. I think you're the queen in this game, not your father."

Chapter Thirty-seven

After a more-than-three-hour drive from Titusville to Phil-adelphia with one bathroom stop, Morales pulled the black Suburban into the underground garage of the stark monolithic Federal Building on Abbott Street. During the long drive, Briggs had never let up trying to get Rebel to talk to him. *We charged you because we know already you conspired with your brother. You're in communication with him, on a burner, right? You might as well admit it and tell us where he is and that way you won't spend the next fifty years in a federal penitentiary.*

He went on and on, impatient and loud, until Rebel won-dered if he'd lose his voice. Morales interrupted him at times, kept her voice sympathetic. *Mr. Navarro, I know you think you shouldn't talk to us, but Agent Briggs is right. If you lawyer up, try to conceal your involvement, and don't cooperate, your chance to stay out of prison will be gone, and what would happen to Tash? I know Archer is your brother, but it's over for him in any case. You have to help yourself and Tash, you have to help us close this case. We'll do all we can for you.*

Rebel was angry at first, found it hard to believe the FBI actually had a warrant for his arrest. *Wire fraud and conspiracy?*

What could they possibly have to implicate him? He kept his mouth shut as Ethan had told him to, except to ask once what evidence they had to arrest him in the first place. They didn't tell him, only said he'd find out during his interview, if he cooperated.

He didn't want to admit to fear, so he'd focused on his anger again at being made to feel so helpless, so impotent. Was that how Archer felt? By the time they arrived, he felt numb.

At least Morales had removed the zip ties binding his wrists together on the long ride to Philadelphia, instead using a single loop to fasten his right wrist to the handle of the back door. When Briggs pulled him out of the back seat, he zip-tied his arms behind his back again. Were they afraid he'd try to deck them and make a run for it?

The garage was eerily quiet, and their footsteps echoed loudly in the huge space, nearly empty this time of night. Briggs and Morales, each holding one of Rebel's arms, opened the garage door to the stairwell and walked him up to the lobby. He saw only one custodian there, buffing the huge expanse of its marble floor. A security guard patted Rebel down and sent him through the X-ray, Briggs and Morales behind him.

Briggs pushed him toward a bank of elevators. When the elevator doors opened on the fifth floor, Briggs shoved him out onto a large square landing covered with industrial dark-gray carpeting toward an older man sitting on a high stool munching on a sandwich with one hand, working a crossword with the other. He was wearing a green federal marshal's uniform.

Briggs said, "Finish off the tuna sandwich, Tip. This one gets a holding cell for a while. When SAC Gregson arrives, I'll call you to bring him down."

Tip shoved the last of his sandwich in his mouth, wiped his hand, frowned down at his crossword puzzle, sighed, and took a step toward Rebel. Briggs held up his hand when his cell phone rang. He listened. "Yes, I understand, we'll be there. No, not a word."

He punched off. "The SAC just arrived, and guess what? Little rich boy here got himself a hotshot lawyer, Rafael Jordan. They're coming up together. How'd you manage that?"

Rebel felt hope; Ethan had come through. He remained silent.

Morales said, "So the sheriff did know a lawyer here in town. Imagine, Rafael Jordan. That's some elevated legal company your small-town sheriff keeps."

Briggs gave Rebel a disgusted look. "Hard to believe he knows a big kahuna like Jordan. Not a problem with all his brother's money, right? Hey, Tip, I guess you don't get to toss this boy into a holding cell. He gets the royal treatment instead—the conference room."

Tip gave a rheumy laugh. "I'll live in hope, Lou," and went back to his crossword.

Briggs grabbed Rebel's arm. "Let's go, Navarro."

The special agent in charge was here already? The top dog? And his lawyer was a hotshot? Rebel wondered yet again what the FBI thought showed his guilt when they didn't have anything a couple of days ago.

Briggs marched Rebel through another door into a large room with low-walled cubicles, hardly manned on Friday evening, with only a few agents scattered around in it speaking on their cell phones and typing on their laptops. Offices lined two walls, and another held huge TV screens. Only one of them was turned on, showing real-time surveillance outside what looked like an abandoned warehouse. Rebel thought he'd hate sitting all day in one of those cubicles in that big soulless room.

There was a pause in the big room as one by one the agents looked at him, the perp with his hands zip-tied behind his back.

One agent in his shirtsleeves said to another agent near him, loud enough so Rebel could hear him, "That's Rebel Navarro. I wonder if they'll let him write his novels in jail?"

Morales and Briggs walked Rebel into a good-sized conference room painted a flat institutional green, with no-nonsense industrial blinds drawn down over a single large window. It held a long table with twelve chairs around it. There were more TV screens on two walls, and one was mirrored, probably two-way. Rebel had imagined dismal, airless rooms like this one. He'd written some gruesome scenes in them. How was it possible his life could change so abruptly that he was actually about to be questioned in one?

Briggs shoved him into a surprisingly comfortable chair. "Your big-bucks lawyer won't help you, Navarro. You're so guilty I can smell it on you."

A man's deep voice, smooth as glass, came from the doorway. "Remove the zip ties now, Agent, if you please."

Briggs hesitated until an older woman stepped into the room behind the man. It was his SAC, Claire Gregson. She said in a cool, crisp voice with a hint of the spurs, "Agent Briggs, remove the zip ties, please."

Briggs cut them off.

Gregson introduced herself to Rebel and said, "Agent Morales, Agent Briggs, thank you for bringing Mr. Navarro to Philadelphia. You may leave now. Go home and enjoy what's left of your Friday night. I'll call you if you're needed. Mr. Navarro, I'll give you a few minutes to get acquainted with Mr. Jordan and confer with him." She followed Briggs and Morales out of the conference room.

Rebel rubbed his hands together to get the feeling back. He slowly stood and faced his attorney. Rafael Jordan looked to be in his late thirties, about Ethan's age. He was tall, on the thin side, his onyx-black hair cut close to his scalp, his skin polished ebony. The pale gray pinstripe suit he wore shouted bespoke, no doubt there. What really struck Rebel were his eyes—dark, nearly black behind his dark-rimmed glasses, and sharp with intelligence. He seemed completely relaxed, a man in charge of his world.

Rafael Jordan stuck out his hand. "Ethan called me, told me you were so innocent it was embarrassing. He said he had no idea what the FBI could possibly think they'd discovered since their visit to your house in Titusville Wednesday. He told me everything he knew, which wasn't much, from his point of view. I doubt the two agents told you much either. Now, please tell me you didn't answer any of their questions on your long drive here?"

Rebel said, "No, Ethan told me not to say a word. Let me say, Mr. Jordan, I'm innocent. So is my brother."

Rebel saw Jordan was assessing him, as Rebel had assessed him. What did his newly minted lawyer see? A man who looked to be at the end of his tether, which he indeed was? Did every one of his clients claim they were innocent? Rebel didn't really want to know.

Jordan said, "I've had a couple of hours to review what's been made public about the Navarro Investment Fund investigation. Unless you tell me otherwise, I will assume you know no more about it than that. You have the right, of course, to refuse to answer any of their questions tonight even with me present. However, if you decide to answer a question, if I raise my hand, you shut up immediately. All right?"

"Yes, I understand, and I will. I know you don't know me from Adam, you have no idea if I'm a saint or a sinner, but let me say it again. I've done nothing wrong. I want to get this over with, get home to my nephew, Tash, if I can, like I promised. But I can't imagine not answering questions. I have zero to hide."

"Very well, but again, I'm here if any of their questions are inappropriate or put you in jeopardy."

Gregson opened the door again, looked from one to the other. "Would you like more time?"

Rebel shook his head. "No, we're ready. I told your agents when they first came to my house on Wednesday what I knew. I have no reason not to tell you again, the whole story as I know it, if that is what you wish."

Jordan narrowed his eyes. "Agent Gregson, may I see the arrest warrant?"

She pulled it from a file of papers she was carrying and handed it to him.

Rebel said, "May I have a glass of water?" What he really wanted was a dram of Glenfiddich.

"Certainly." Gregson rose, walked to the credenza along the wall and opened a door showing a small cooler. She pulled out a bottle of water. "Mr. Jordan, would you like something?"

"No, thank you. Maybe later."

She said something about the warm weather to Rafael Jordan as she handed him a plastic bottle of water. Then she sat across from the two of them.

Rebel accepted it gratefully, drank, set the bottle down on the table. He studied the special agent in charge while she pulled out a binder from her briefcase. She looked a bit over fifty. Her short dark hair had a hint of curl and a dash of gray. She wore black pants, a dark green blouse, and a black jacket. This woman might look as mellow as his aunt Lucy, but Rebel imagined she was as tough as the local plumber's Rottweiler and wouldn't take crap from anybody.

Jordan said, "As I told Mr. Navarro, I'm here tonight because I got a call from a good friend of mine, Sheriff Ethan Merriweather of Titusville, Virginia. Ethan told me two of your agents came to Rebel Navarro's house while his family was there having dinner. Sheriff Merriweather assured me Rebel Navarro is being falsely accused and asked me to represent him." Jordan eyed Gregson a moment, turned to Rebel, and smiled. "Let me say first of all that I am pleased he called because both my wife and I read your books, Mr. Navarro. She thinks your name, Rebel, is romantic."

Rebel realized Jordan had made this small detour because he'd seen Rebel was tense as a bow. He wanted to relax him. To his surprise, he smiled back. "Romantic? My blasted name got me into more fights than I care to remember when I was a kid."

The corners of Gregson's mouth kicked up, just a bit. It changed her face, lit it up, made her seem less formidable. So Jordan had wanted to put her at ease as well. She said, "Before we begin, let me say, Mr. Navarro, you appear to have friends in unexpected places. Special Agent Dillon Savich called me from Washington tonight. He wondered what we'd discovered between his phone call to me yesterday morning and our bringing you in this evening. I assured him critical evidence had just come into our hands, but declined to give him the details." She paused a beat. "He did say one of our agents appeared to have taken a dislike to you—Special Agent Briggs. If Agent Briggs was out of line, do let me apologize. He can be impassioned and sometimes he does cross the line." Her voice was very smooth, without a hint of emotion.

Rebel nodded. "I'll say this for Agent Briggs. He didn't give up trying to get me to confess. He made me promises, then threats, all the way from Titusville."

"But they had read you your rights, hadn't they?"

Rebel nodded. "Another first-time experience. May I, with the approval of Mr. Jordan, simply tell you what's happened in the past couple of weeks, tell you what I know?"

Gregson looked over at Jordan.

Jordan said, "Agent Gregson, this is what Mr. Navarro would prefer and yes, I agree. You can ask your questions afterward.

In turn, I trust we'll find out why you arrested him so suddenly and dragged him here to the Philadelphia field office on this fine Friday night. Can we agree on that, Agent Gregson?"

She studied Rebel's face, trying to understand what the catch was, didn't see one staring her in the face, and slowly nodded. "One of the reasons we arrested him is we believed he might be a flight risk like his brother, but we'll get to that. All right, we can see how his story goes, but if I wish to, I'll interrupt him. And we'll start the recording. Any objections, Mr. Jordan?"

"None."

"And you, Mr. Navarro?"

"No."

Gregson recorded the time, the place, and the people present. "First, let me read you your rights again, Mr. Navarro, for the record."

After she asked him if he understood his rights and he dutifully said yes for the recording, Gregson continued. "Mr. Navarro, please don't bother to lie to us. It would be a waste of our time and not in your interest, not to mention exhausting."

Rebel nodded. "I lied my way out of a lot of sticky situations when I was a teenager, Ms. Gregson, but not now. No, not now."

Chapter Thirty-eight

Rebel sat forward in his chair, clasped his hands on the table. "In mid-June my brother, his wife, and his son, Tash, came for a visit to Titusville. I quickly learned my brother's purpose was to ask me to keep his eight-year-old with me for the summer. He and his new wife had planned a honeymoon in Europe, and he thought spending the summer with me would be good for Tash, plus it was his honeymoon. Of course, I agreed. I welcomed the opportunity to get to know my nephew better. Then my brother and his wife flew off to Paris the next day. He called every day and spoke to both me and his son. Then, when the embezzlement news broke, he no longer called. My only communications with him since have been these text messages you've doubtless read since I showed them to your agents Wednesday evening." When Gregson shook her head, Rebel pulled out his cell phone and showed both Jordan and Gregson his brother's texts and his replies. Rebel waited for them to read the texts, then said, "Which brings us to this evening, when Agents Morales and Briggs came to my door again, only this time they had an arrest warrant for wire fraud and conspiracy. They read me my rights and drove me here to Philadelphia."

When Rebel stopped talking, Jordan sat back in his chair, crossed his arms over his chest. He said to Gregson in his deep voice, "Obviously something changed between Mr. Navarro's first interview with your people on Wednesday and tonight.

Please tell us why you suddenly issued an arrest warrant for Mr. Navarro and hauled him here."

Gregson said in a crisp, no-nonsense voice, "Let me say I can see you're probably an excellent writer, Mr. Navarro. Your accounting of what's happened was quite believable, complete with your supporting text messages. However, you are not as competent a criminal. Today our forensic accountants uncovered exactly where more than two hundred million dollars in your brother's investment fund disappeared to. It was wired over time, supposedly as an investment, to a company in the Caymans which existed in little more than name only, and those transfers were made on your brother's workstation, using his passcodes. This Cayman company was only a conduit. The money was quickly wired out of that account to destinations far harder to trace, including cryptocurrency. It's not clear how much of it we'll be able to recover, since as of yet we haven't been able to locate end-point banks.

"The initial account in the Caymans was opened by a shell company owned by an LLC. This account was opened months ago by you, Mr. Rebel Navarro."

Rebel stared at her, slowly shook his head. "I know nothing of any shell company or LLC in the Caymans, nothing. I know what a shell company is, in theory, but I don't know how that works, except what I've gleaned from novels or TV. Why do you think I opened this account and set up the LLC?"

"It's very straightforward. We have your signature on the documents."

Rebel said slowly, "I don't see how that's possible. I've never even been to the Caymans, you can check my passport, so how could I have signed anything there?"

"You didn't need to be there—as you certainly know. You filled out the necessary forms and sent them in by registered mail."

Jordan held up a hand. "Agent Gregson, let me see if I've

got this straight. You think the Navarro brothers conspired together to steal over two hundred million dollars from the investment fund?"

"That's correct, Mr. Jordan. It took our task force some time to get those records subpoenaed from the Cayman banks and from their government registries, but now that we have them, lo and behold, there was Rebel Navarro's name and signature all over them."

She opened her file again, pulled out a sheet of paper, and slid it over to Rebel. "Is this your signature, Mr. Navarro?"

Rebel felt outside himself, as if someone else was studying the signature on a page filled with legalese, a page he'd never seen. He looked at the scrawl, admittedly very like his, on the last page of a legal document, and raised his eyes to look at her. "This can't be my signature. I've never seen these documents." He was pleased he sounded so calm.

Gregson slid a sheet of blank paper over to him. "Would you please sign your name for me right now so we can compare them?"

Rebel looked over at Jordan, who nodded, handed him a Mont Blanc from his suit pocket. "Mr. Navarro, go ahead and sign your name, say, six times. Isn't that what you were going to ask him to do, Agent Gregson?"

"Six times would be good," Gregson agreed, and watched Rebel closely.

When he finished, Jordan picked up the paper, studied the signatures Rebel had written, and handed the paper to Agent Gregson. She compared the scrawled signatures to the one on the documents. She looked up. "They all look the same to me. Do you agree, Mr. Jordan?"

Jordan said, "Of course they do. I would expect them to, since Mr. Navarro's signature is illegible, and that makes it easy to copy." He picked up the pen and signed Rebel's name himself, pushed the paper back to Gregson. "Pretty close, don't you think? And that's without practice. He writes his name like my brother, a physician, on his prescription pads."

Gregson said, a touch of defensiveness in her voice, "It may not be enough to convince a jury, but our investigation has begun. If your client's hands have been anywhere near the money disbursed from that account, you know we'll find it."

Jordan shook his head. "It seems to me this is an elaborate ruse on someone's part, naturally the guilty party's part, to show collusion between the two brothers. By implicating my client, it goes a long way to prove Archer Navarro must be behind the embezzlement." He sat back, crossed his arms over his chest again. "I've seen setups like this before, but I have to say it's unusual to run into a frame using an actual signature that can't be proved to be legitimate, and expect to sell it."

Gregson said, "Mr. Jordan, it's far more likely your client did indeed sign that document. I had him arrested and brought here to give him a last chance to cooperate with us, help us recover the money, and tell us where his brother is hiding, and, of course, what their plan is. Of course I also brought him here so he couldn't leave the country."

Rebel said, "Agent Gregson, I did not sign this document, nor did my brother steal from his own company. As for my leaving the country, you know my nephew is staying with me. You also know he has no other family. I would never leave him, nor would I drag him along to parts unknown." He paused a moment. "Please try to understand. My brother was getting his life back together after the death of his wife two years ago. His company was thriving and he'd just remarried. He was finally happy. He's not a Madoff or Bankman-Fried. There was simply no reason for him to steal all that money from his own clients. My brother is proud of his company, proud he built it himself. Many of his clients have become personal friends. Never would he steal from them. He's been set up just as I have. It has to be someone else who works at his investment fund who's behind this. You read in that text he pointed to his COO, Carla Cartwright."

Gregson said, "We've interviewed everyone at the Navarro Investment Fund who holds a position high enough to make this theft even a remote possibility, including Ms. Cartwright. We found her to be straightforward and helpful, though she is distraught over what your brother—and you, sir—appear to have done. She was forced to agree the transfers were made from your brother's workstation, using his passcodes, and only when he was in the building. So, not a single red flag in Ms. Cartwright's direction. It was your brother, no other possibility."

Rebel said, "I know Cartwright's been with him since he started up the company. He's often told me how smart she is, how much he depended on her, particularly after Celia—his wife—died, and how excellent she was at tech. He trusted her and she knew it. Wouldn't that indicate she could find the means and opportunity?"

Gregson said, "Here's the bottom line, Mr. Navarro. No one at your brother's fund had access to his passcodes, and as I said, Ms. Cartwright had to agree, although she didn't want to. She wanted to protect your brother. And still, even after we verified this was indeed true, she still didn't want to believe her friend, her boss, would do this. Like you, she believed strongly it had to be someone else, not Archer, never Archer. As I said, she was forced to admit only he could have accessed those accounts. Let me point out Ms. Cartwright didn't run to Europe, your brother did."

Rebel said, "My brother simply went on his honeymoon to Europe with his wife and was in Paris when the missing funds were discovered. I know my brother. I can only imagine how frantic he is, how disbelieving that anyone would think him responsible for this crime. I also imagine he doesn't know what to do. Stay in Europe, hidden, until you discovered the real criminals? Myself? I would have come back and raised hell, but it wasn't my decision." He paused, added, "My brother is one of the smartest people I know, a genius with people. I would never accept he would do something so stupid as to use codes only he knew. Talk about painting an X on his back." Rebel sat forward. "Agent Gregson, please believe me when I tell you my brother is very logical, very realistic. He's also got plenty of money, no reason to steal more—to ruin his company and make himself a fugitive. Somehow, someone got hold of those passcodes."

Gregson sat back, crossed her arms over her chest. "Greed is rampant in the land, Mr. Navarro. I've learned no matter how much money an individual has, many simply want more and more. As for your brother, he was astute enough to leave the country before his crime was exposed, astute enough to know if he stayed here he'd be indicted very quickly and possibly not even granted bail. I think it's far more likely he's elected to enjoy the rest of his life drinking mai tais on a beautiful island somewhere with no extradition treaty with us." She paused a moment, leaned toward him. "And you planned to join him, didn't you? Bring his son with you."

Rebel said automatically, "My brother doesn't drink mai tais."

Jordan laughed. "Well, that deflates your imaginative tale, Agent Gregson. Now, let's be realistic, apply some actual logic. You must know by now your agents jumped the gun. They arrested Mr. Navarro in his own home on a Friday night and drove with him over three hours here to Philadelphia. They tried to railroad him, threatened him, tried to coerce a confession with no attorney present. At the very least they hoped he'd break down and tell them where his brother is. If Sheriff Ethan Merriweather hadn't called me, what was your plan? Throw him in jail and wait for him to call a literary attorney or a lawyer in the area with little experience?

"This is a superb screwup, Agent Gregson. Now, it's time for you to release Mr. Navarro on his own recognizance until such time as you actually have some definitive proof he was involved in this, which I really doubt exists. Otherwise, I'll call Judge Hobbs and explain what you've done and be granted his immediate release and you, a reprimand."

Agent Gregson slowly rose. She didn't look happy. "I'm not swayed by your threats, Mr. Jordan, but what makes me pause is that Agent Dillon Savich appears to agree with you. If Mr. Navarro wears a tracking ankle bracelet, I will let him return to Titusville for now to be with his nephew. And I want Mr. Navarro's passport."

Rafael Jordan handed her his card. "Fine, I'll arrange it. Call me if you wish to speak to Mr. Navarro again, no more night visits with cuffs and threats for three hours. In the meantime, I suggest you look into how someone managed to get hold of Mr. Archer Navarro's passcodes."

As they were walking out of the conference room and through the huge office, Rebel saw Briggs standing against a cubicle, a cup of coffee in his hand. He looked at Rebel like he wanted to punch him.

Rebel gave Briggs a little finger wave.

On the elevator ride back to the lobby, Jordan said, "Gregson was hoping her agents would get a confession out of you, and that's the reason for your incarceration with them for three hours. But you held firm. Now, I know about Agent Dillon Savich. He has a rep for not rushing to judgment. I don't know how he became involved with this, do you?"

Rebel knew, of course. Autumn. He shook his head. No way was he going to bring her into this mess.

Now Jordan said, "Well, however he became involved, be grateful. He also has a reputation of being a bulldog, never stops until he has the truth."

That's what Autumn said. Rebel said to Jordan, "I think this whole plan was set into motion months ago. And I was involved to make it seem even more obvious my brother planned it and now it's a family deal."

They walked into the dim-lit federal garage. Jordan said, "I know you believe your brother is innocent. But the sticking point is the secret passcodes. Those passcodes are the keys to the kingdom. I suppose it's possible they could have been hacked. If hackers can get into the U.S. Navy's computers, why not your brother's?"

Rebel said, "My brother bragged they were hack-proof. You heard me tell Gregson that Archer's COO, Carla Cartwright, is a tech whiz, better than Archer was, he told me. So how good is she? If Archer suspects her, that means she somehow got the codes out of him. I wonder if he even knows."

Jordan stopped by a black Mercedes sedan. "Is your brother a careless man?"

Rebel said slowly, "Sometimes in his personal life, maybe, but not with his business. He'd never be careless in his business. It was his baby, his greatest pride."

"Get in, Rebel—may I call you Rebel? Call me Rafael. Being in the trenches on a Friday night tends to make last names rather superfluous."

Rebel nodded. "Rafael. Yes, I'm Rebel."

"I'm taking you to my home, where you can pick up my son's car to drive back to Titusville. He's grounded for a month. I caught him on Snapchat drinking shooters at a party. He's seventeen."

Rebel had to smile. "Guess he underestimated his old man."

"I hope Elliott will continue to do so until he's a fully grown adult with a fully grown functioning brain, though that's never guaranteed, is it? Here is my card. Mail me a retainer for ten thousand dollars."

Rebel nodded. He thought of Tash, wondered what he'd be

like at seventeen. If he drank and got caught, would his father ground him? Would he?

Rebel didn't drive Elliott Jordan's bright red Camaro back to Titusville that night; he drove it to the Burberry Hotel in Ardmore on the Main Line.

He had plans.

Chapter Thirty-nine

Elizabeth's eyes flew open. Her breath was heaving with terror, sweat soaking her sleep shirt. Without thinking, she pulled the small key from her pajama pocket, opened the bedside table lock, and jerked open the pouch that held the bullets for the small Ruger Hurley had given her. She stopped cold. *Get a grip, it was a nightmare, only a nightmare. No one's outside the bloody window ready to smash the glass, leap through, and kill you.*

There was no threat, only a nightmare, nothing more than a pisser of a nightmare. Elizabeth fell back against her pillow and forced herself to take slow, deep breaths.

A dream so clear about being in her bedroom that night, terrified, pinned down on her back and fighting for her life. This time, she'd felt the whoosh of hot air when the knife came down. So real. She had to keep reminding herself it hadn't come down, the man had thrown it into Benny's chest instead, nearly killing him.

—hold the bitch down! I'm going to cut up that pretty face!

The vicious words echoed clearly in her mind, as clearly as the moment the man said them, like he was high on drugs he was so excited. And yes, there'd been a slight accent, like

Basara's, but had she heard his voice before? Was that even possible?

She didn't think, she jumped out of bed and ran to the Saviches' bedroom, raised her fist to knock, then realized it was early, far too early. She pulled back her hand and leaned against the hallway wall trying to get hold of herself. That voice. When she'd finally calmed, her heart rate nearly back to normal, she realized she'd heard that voice only that one day and night in England, and in her dreams.

Chapter Forty

Khaled's apartment
Wyverly Mews, London
SATURDAY

Khaled's mobile sounded out the James Bond theme "Diamonds Are Forever."

Adara.

He took a last bite of his scrambled eggs, drew a deep breath. "Good morning, Adara. Did you sleep well last night?"

Her musical laugh played a glissando on his nerves.

"Perhaps I was lonely, Khaled. Did you think of me after we parted company last night?"

"If I'd known where your bedroom is I might have tried to sneak in."

"Maybe I'd have let you. So tell me, what did you think of my friends?"

"I found the two younger men more or less like me, and then there was Yusuf."

"Yusuf is a master of impressions. He can appear to be whoever he wishes to be, only with a higher IQ. But he's not important at the moment." Her voice dropped low, as if to whisper a secret. "Did my brother tell you I was interested in you?"

"I believe he did mention that, yes. I believe he was embarrassed about it."

Again, her laugh punched right in his crotch. "Since Ali became the imam of the South London Mosque he's having a more difficult time accepting I am not a traditional Muslim woman, like most of his worshippers' poor wives, and never have been for that matter. It's only now he seems to care about it. I have assured him I will continue to do what I wish, but I will be discreet. His only opinion that really matters to me is he thinks highly of you. It's obvious he trusts you or he wouldn't have offered you Rehan's job when the old man retires." She dropped her voice again, ready to share a confidence. "I've seen you at the mosque. When he told me you were an accountant, I did not wish to believe it. How ghastly and boring. Ah, but you showed me last night you are more than that, Khaled. You search for something beyond what the imam has offered you, beyond what this accounting position gives you."

What was this all about? He said easily, "All of us are more than our words, Adara. Words are easy, only actions speak truly."

She appeared to think about that, then, "Did I surprise you when you came to the house last night?"

"I thought I might be killed."

That sexy laugh. "I enjoy drama, it's true. I wanted to see your reaction. Would you draw a gun? Would you run? But no, you reacted well—in control, honest, but careful with your words since you didn't know who or what we were. You did not disappoint me. Nor, I will add, did you disappoint Yusuf. The others, I don't really care about their opinions. They are too young and untried. What did you think of me, Khaled?"

"I thought—no, I think you are fierce and beautiful."

"Ah," she said, and nothing else. Was she thinking about whether to take him as a lover, or of recruiting him? She and her friends hadn't held back that they were political fanatics who wanted to see most everything he held dear destroyed. But they hadn't been sure of him enough to tell him more. Had they killed? Had she killed? Khaled said, "What are you wearing, Adara?"

He heard her suck in her breath and smiled because he'd taken her off guard. She said then, her voice low, seductive, "Would you like to see what I'm wearing?"

"Yes."

"Open your front door."

Khaled felt a bolt of lust so great he nearly ran from his kitchen down the narrow hallway to the small entrance hall. He had no idea what she was playing at. He had to get a grip, he had to stay in control. He drew a deep breath, opened the door.

Adara gave him a slow smile that nearly brought him to his knees. She was wearing tight black leather pants and a black leather jacket with a black rolled neck, a motorcycle helmet tucked under her arm. Her beautiful hair was loose around her face. She stepped into his flat, turned, closed and locked the door behind her.

"I like surprises, don't you, Khaled?"

"I can't argue with this one. You were standing outside my door, waiting for the right moment?"

"I'd say rather I was waiting for you to convince me of your interest. Since I live at home, I cannot do as I wish. My mother's bedroom is only fifteen feet down the hall and she has the hearing of a bat. And don't forget I promised my brother I would be the soul of discretion. So, I came here, to get the lay of the land, as it were."

"As you know from last night, I have no mother here. You are very welcome."

She laid her motorcycle helmet on the small table next to a letter holder and a small vase of tulips, two days past their prime. She did a small spin, laughed, and threw her arms around his neck. She whispered against his cheek, "Isn't it marvelous? We're all alone, we can do exactly as we please." She kissed him, wet and deep. Every rational thought fell out of his brain. She was beautiful, she was soft and warm and eager, and it had been so long, he'd been so focused on his job. He picked her up in his arms and nearly ran down the short hallway to his bedroom. They stripped off each other's clothes and he jerked back the dark blue quilt to lay her onto her back. He lowered himself over her, all of her against all of him, and thought he'd explode.

But there were things a man didn't forget, and though he was trembling on the edge, he was thorough. He gave her pleasure first, reveled in her moans, then nearly fainted with his own release.

He fell onto his back beside her, his heart pounding, and wondered how it was his neighbor hadn't heard them and banged on the wall. He felt boneless, his brain scattered. He felt the bright morning sun beat against his face through the open window blinds. He pulled her close, and she rested her face on his shoulder, her breath warm against his flesh. He savored the feel of her, though he knew in a corner of his mind if she somehow found out who he was, she'd stick a knife in his heart without hesitation and very likely without a single regret. That thought brought him a bit of clarity, but only for a moment. He wanted her again. He came over her, leaned down and kissed her ear, her cheek, her eyes, and whispered against her mouth, "I am incredibly thankful today is Saturday." He let her push him onto his back and do as she wished, and what she did was splendid.

When they finished again, he smiled up at her and lightly ran his palm down her flank. "You are amazing."

So beautiful she was, her thick black hair tousled, her eyes closed, her lashes thick and black. She slowly opened her eyes and smiled at him. "And you too are amazing, Khaled.

I wondered if I would be disappointed, but I was hopeful because I liked the cut of your jib. I love that saying. When I said it to my mother, she just stared at me like I'd cursed because she had no idea what it means." She raised her hand and stroked his morning scruff. "I dislike the full beards so many Muslim men insist on wearing in London, as if to flaunt their differentness."

"That's something I've never thought of, but perhaps you're right."

Adara came up on her elbow over him. "Do you remember last year when St. Paul's nearly blew up?"

His brain snapped back to awareness. Be honest, don't overdo. "Everyone remembers. It was terrifying, horrendous. So many people would have been crushed if MI5 hadn't spotted the terrorist in time."

"Now that depends on your point of view, don't you think? Some at the mosque vowed jihad when Samir Basara was betrayed and murdered in cold blood by that American agent."

"No doubt some true believers would swear he was, but I remember it turned out he was only a well-paid assassin. And no Muslim would admire such a man."

"An assassin? I'd say rather Samir Basara was a pragmatist. I see no conflict in attacking injustice and making oneself richer in the process."

He said, "I understand fighting for what one considers justice, but confusing the issue by being paid to kill while wreaking havoc on hundreds of innocents?"

"Ah, but they were all white-skinned English. Would you consider them innocent victims?" As she spoke, Adara laid her hand on his belly, and since he was young and he wasn't dead, he responded. She leaned down, licked his neck, and said against his wet skin, "At Oxford, my friends and I did just as we pleased, said whatever we pleased. No one cared. The professors encouraged the students to explore their beliefs, whether religious or revolutionary, no matter how outrageous.

There were the Communists, a motley, crass lot, and the fervent Muslims who were always probing, searching out those of us they could bring into their fold. The professors seemed to think we were radicals because our views and our brains weren't fully formed. Why not let the children pay with their ideas until they became reasoning adults?" Her voice turned vicious. "I've never seen such a bunch of fools."

Then suddenly she laughed, kissed him all over his face, and rolled away from him. "Like most people, I've always wanted to decide what it is I want in my own life, Khaled, a concept many Muslim women can't seem to comprehend, even here in England. They have no power, obey their husbands completely, and accept their lives. Do you think that's right and just?"

Khaled streaked his fingers through her hair, smoothing it. "Perhaps it is right for many, Adara, but I know it isn't right for you. I'm searching myself for what it is I really want. That's why I've become so involved at the mosque. Your brother has helped me start to understand what it is I truly believe, and what those beliefs might demand of me."

She appeared thoughtful. "Ali told me you were smart. You attended Cambridge and excelled." She paused again. "So I hope you will understand. I've wanted nothing more than to get past all the endless rhetoric of my elders and search out for myself what I want to believe, what I need to believe and how I wish to live my life. We will speak of this again, but not now. You've exhausted me." She kissed him on the cheek, rolled away from him, and fell asleep as easily as a child.

Khaled listened to her even breathing, leaned over her, and studied her face. She looked so innocent, her skin smooth and soft with youth and health. Had she come to him simply because she wanted him? Or perhaps to satisfy her curiosity about him? Or to test him? He doubted she did anything without a reason. She'd appeared pleased with him, so it had been a test. Had he passed?

Khaled dozed off, awakened when he heard her moving about. He opened his eyes to see her naked, smiling down at him, her bra in her hand. "Must you go?"

"Yes, I must." He propped himself on pillows and watched her dress. She leaned down, kissed him, smoothed his hair. She straightened over him. "I didn't tell you—Samir Basara and Yusuf were friends. Yusuf vowed revenge. I wonder if he will ever manage it."

Khaled said nothing. He pulled on a tatty robe his mom had given him years before and walked with her to the front door. She kissed him once again, said, "Don't call me, I will call you," and was gone. He listened to her retreating footsteps.

Khaled locked the door and walked to the kitchen. He tipped up the kitchen table, twisted the table leg, and pulled out his burner mobile. He sent another text to John Eiserly telling him he had bedded Adara Said, or rather, she'd bedded him, and that he'd scheduled a meeting with Rohan al-Albiri, the imam's accountant, on Monday. He slid the burner mobile back into the empty slot and twisted the leg closed again.

Chapter Forty-one

Rome's house
Wilton Place, Washington, D.C.
SATURDAY MORNING

Special Agent Roman Foxe jerked awake, sat straight up in bed, and shouted to the ceiling, "The class ring!" He grabbed his cell from the charger on the nightstand and started to punch in Savich's cell, then looked at the bedside clock. It was only 7:00 A.M., too early to call on a Saturday morning. Sherlock was probably still asleep. He wasn't about to wake her up. He remembered a pregnant friend telling him with a bun in the oven, you needed more sleep than a cat.

He fluffed up the pillow, leaned back, closed his eyes, and thought about his call to Mrs. Ballou—now Mrs. Cynthia Hendricks and a grandmother of four—to notify her as gently as he could that her first husband's remains had been discovered after more than forty-five years.

She'd said in an emotionless voice, "Wilson was murdered, wasn't he?"

"Yes, ma'am. Agent Ballou was shot through the back of the head and buried near the Calmett River outside Bensonville, Virginia."

In the same emotionless voice she'd said, "I assume you

people no longer believe I killed him, that I shot him in the head and buried him myself?"

"No, ma'am. It looked like a professional hit." He wasn't about to tell her Ballou had been tortured, bones broken, his skull fractured.

"I told the FBI I knew to my gut Wilson was involved with criminals, that he probably betrayed one of them, but no one believed me. Well, at last it's over and done with. Send what's left of him to me and I'll see to burying him."

"You were right, Mrs. Hendricks, about his involvement with criminals."

"Of course I was right. I lived with him ten years, I knew what he was. He always thought he could handle anything, with his la-di-da FBI training. It was a game to him, going off the range, outwitting the people he was supposed to arrest. Well, he was wrong, wasn't he?"

"Yes, this time he was."

"I don't suppose you'd like to apologize for making my life hell for six months? Even though it's been over forty-five years, a nice groveling apology would still be nice to hear."

Given what he'd read in those old files, he couldn't blame her for that dose of snark. He'd said in a formal voice, "I would like to apologize for all the FBI agents who disbelieved you in 1978, Mrs. Hendricks. I checked the evidence locker, and we did recover his wedding ring. We also found a safe-deposit key in his shoe. Did you know he had one, at what bank?"

"Thank you. About the key, I have no idea, Agent Foxe."

"We've finished examining the wedding ring. I'll send it to you."

"Thank you, Agent Foxe. I know you aren't to blame for all the torment—your parents probably hadn't even met yet when Wilson was killed. I'll put the wedding ring in with his class ring. Perhaps his son will wish to have them, although I doubt it.

His father was never around much and so he wasn't important in his young life."

Rome hadn't paid any attention to what she'd said about the class ring, just hung up, glad that chore was over. But now, her words had popped back to him in his dream, flashing neon.

Ballou's class ring hadn't been with the remains, only his wedding ring rattling around on his skeleton's finger. After the safe-deposit key was discovered in his shoe along with the long number scrawled on a torn slip of paper, his wedding ring was tested and examined six ways to Sunday.

But what of Ballou's class ring? Some men's class rings were splashy, large enough for a jeweler to make an enclosure in their crown to store a keepsake. Ballou might have used the class ring to store another number—a longitude to match the latitude he'd hidden in the heel of his shoe. It was possible—not likely, but possible. He tried to calm himself. The odds were, Ballou's class ring was only a class ring, nothing more. But maybe—

Rome reached again for his cell, thought better of it. It was still early, too early to call Mrs. Hendricks to ask her to let him examine the class ring. And why should she? He'd have to come up with a good reason the FBI wanted to examine the ring after forty-five years. Somehow, he'd have to win her over.

He nearly jumped out of his skin when his cell blasted out a turkey squawk, a sound guaranteed to wake him from the deepest sleep. He saw the name, answered immediately, instantly alarmed. "Sherlock? What's wrong? What's going on? Is Elizabeth all right?"

"Yes, Rome, everything is fine. How would you like to come over for breakfast? Dillon is making pancakes, with blueberries dotted on top for Sean."

Blueberry pancakes, one of his favorites. "Bacon?"

Sherlock laughed. "Of course."

Rome said, "And I've got some news for you guys. Give me twenty-five minutes."

When Rome arrived in the Savich kitchen doorway only fifteen minutes later, after a fast shower and little traffic on a Saturday morning, Savich was standing at the stove flipping pancakes, while Sherlock set an extra place for him. Savich said something that made her laugh as she pulled warmed syrup out of the microwave. Elizabeth was measuring Sean against the back-door frame, marking his height with a blue marker that hung from it on a string. The back door was open to a lovely morning breeze coming through the screen. Astro saw bacon in Sherlock's hand and leaped a good three feet, yipping madly.

Sherlock, laughing at Astro, saw him. "Rome! You made good time. Come in and pour yourself a cup of coffee. You can sit down next to Elizabeth when she's through measuring our five-year-old giant. I promise Dillon's coffee is always perfect. And wait 'til you taste his pancakes, though in all honesty, I think mine are better."

Elizabeth grinned over at him and said, "Maybe not a giant, but Sean is going to be as tall as you are, Dillon, maybe taller." She gave Sean a tap on the shoulder. "He's already taller than most of the weeds in my back garden."

Rome walked to the table, pulled out a chair, and sat down. "Weeds? I thought your highness lived in one of those fancy crescent deals in the very best part of London where weeds are banned."

"I got special dispensation," she said without pause. "And yes, I do have a small garden." She passed a stick of crispy bacon to him. Astro looked like he might leap for it, so Rome only ate half and gave Astro the rest. He leaned back in his chair and sighed. "There has to be bacon in heaven."

Savich, the vegetarian, gave him a raised eyebrow. "I hope you're hungry, Rome. I tripled the recipe."

Silence reigned for five minutes once everyone was seated

around the table and the pancakes were served. When Sherlock saw they were all slowing down, she said, "Elizabeth, tell Rome about your dream."

Elizabeth poured more syrup on her last bite of pancake, chewed, and swallowed. "I dreamed again about the two men who attacked me that night in London. The first couple of times, the nightmares scared me to death, but over time, I've gotten more used to them. They're always a little different. This time I could actually see the flash of the knife as the man straddling me screamed, 'Hold the bitch down! I'm going to cut up that pretty face!' I heard excitement, pleasure in his voice."

Rome said, "Was it a young voice, Elizabeth?"

His matter-of-fact tone pulled her back from the terror of the dream, focused her mind. "Yes, I'd say early to mid-twenties."

"Remembering it now, do you believe he wanted to disfigure you, out of spite, hatred, whatever—or kill you?"

"Well, since he wanted to carve up my face, for whatever reason, I know in my gut he wanted to kill me. And he was happy about it."

Sherlock said, "That sounds personal, really personal."

"It does indeed," Savich said. "Your attackers weren't simply hired, Elizabeth, they were a part of it. How that fits in with Aboud remains to be seen. Rome, you told Sherlock you have news for us?"

"Well, to be honest, it's more a hunch, but a good one," and Rome told them about his own dream and his call to Mrs. Cynthia Hendricks, once the widow of Wilson Ballou. "She was still pissed at the FBI for hounding her in 1978. I apologized, told her we would be sending Wilson Ballou's wedding ring back to her." He stopped, gave them a grin. "When I told her that, she said she'd put his wedding ring together with his class ring and give them to Ballou's son."

He looked around the table at the blank faces. "The class ring. It wasn't with the skeleton, and when Ballou's house was searched in 1978, there was no mention of finding it. I'm hoping the class ring can lead us to whatever it was that Ballou stole, whatever it was that got him killed. It's possible the longitude we're missing might be scratched onto it, or hidden inside it. And Mrs. Hendricks has it. Elizabeth, I'd like to go in person and ask Mrs. Hendricks if she'll let me examine it. If she agrees, I'd like you to drive with me to Baskin Ridge to see it. It's only about an hour and a half away, and there's nothing here in Washington for us to deal with. What do you say?"

Sean said around a mouthful of pancake, "I think Mom and I should go with you to visit Mrs. Hendricks, Uncle Rome. Everyone loves Mom, and maybe the lady will give us all some cookies."

Chapter Forty-two

Cynthia Hendricks's home
Baskin Ridge, Delaware
SATURDAY

With the promise his mom would make him cookies at home, Sean agreed to let Rome and Elizabeth drive to see Mrs. Hendricks without him. After what Rome hoped had been an apologetic and self-deprecating phone call, she'd reluctantly agreed. Rome pulled into a driveway, parked beside a Ford Escape. It was a lovely ranch-style home with a yard full of flowering bushes, oaks, and maples. Hanging from a thick oak branch was a much-used tire on a thick rope. The lawn was freshly mowed and in the summer heat the smell was amazing.

When Mrs. Cynthia Hendricks opened the door to Rome and Elizabeth, his first thought was that she didn't look like the grandmother he was expecting. In a photo he'd seen of her taken in her early thirties in 1978, she was very pretty—small and blond, her pale blue eyes frightened and defiant. She was still small, barely came to Rome's shoulder, but now, her once frightened and defiant eyes were hard and knowing. Life had made her a person who hadn't taken crap from anyone in a very long time. She was wearing white pants and a white blouse, her hair pulled back in a ponytail, flip-flops on her feet. He smiled at her. "Mrs. Hendricks?"

She looked Rome up and down. "Of course, I'm Mrs. Hendricks. So you're Special Agent Roman Foxe, and I do indeed see you weren't even on the planet when those idiot agents gnawed at me like dogs with a bone back in '78. I'll never forget those snotty-nosed agents with their shiny black shoes, acting like I was guilty as sin when they had no proof of anything." She took a deep breath. Rome knew she'd been waiting to get that bile out of her system; he couldn't blame her.

"For whatever reason you said you wanted to look at Wilson's class ring. Well, come in, come in. I've got some coffee brewed and ready. My husband, Alex, is down at the lumberyard. He and one of our sons run it. And you," she added, looking finally at Elizabeth, "you don't look like an agent. Who are you, his girlfriend?"

"No, ma'am, I'm Palmer, his bodyguard. He's very important and the FBI doesn't want anything to happen to him."

Mrs. Hendricks gave Elizabeth the eye and sort of smiled, but it fell off her face when she remembered her mad. "Not a likely story, but you're clever, I'll give you that. Whoever you are, Palmer, come along, both of you."

She seated them in her living room, photographs of her family and grandchildren on every surface and gorgeous handmade afghans tossed over chairs and the single big sofa. Rome said, "Let me tell you again how very sorry I am that you had to go through such a painful experience with the FBI in 1978."

She snorted and pointed to the coffee, sugar, and cream on the tray. "Alex says it was because Wilson was one of their own and they were royally pissed he betrayed them. Help yourselves." Rome poured himself and Elizabeth a cup, sat back, and took a drink. It was deep and rich and had quite a kick. He said, "You have a lovely house, Mrs. Hendricks."

"Yes, thank you, I know. Enough playing nice, Agent Foxe. And you, Palmer, who are you really, besides his bodyguard?"

"I am Palmer, first name Elizabeth. I'm not his girlfriend

or with the FBI, but I'm involved in another case and he asked me to accompany him. My job is to make sure he's polite and thorough."

"You're English. A lovely accent, I've always thought. Do you know Colin Firth?"

"Sorry, no, ma'am. He's quite too important for the likes of me."

"You sound hoity-toity enough. Of course, you could be lying again, and I have to admit, you do it very well." Mrs. Hendricks took a small drink of her fierce coffee, then handed Rome a small box from the side table beside her chair. "All right, Agent Foxe, here's Wilson's class ring from Alabama. I can't imagine why you want to see it. It's been stored away in that box for over forty-five years." Mrs. Hendricks sat back in her chair, her legs so short her feet barely touched the floor, and watched both of them with an eagle eye.

Rome's heart kicked up. He slowly lifted the class ring out of the box and wiped it gently on his sleeve. It was thick and heavy and large, with *University of Alabama* etched around its perimeter. There was a red stone at the center with a raised *A* on it, not a ruby, but pretty. As Rome slowly examined the ring, Elizabeth turned to Mrs. Hendricks. "Agent Foxe told me you have three grandchildren. Are these their photos?"

"Yes, they are." Mrs. Hendricks picked up a framed photo from the side table beside her. "These are Chloe and Timothy and Judson from last Christmas. The man standing behind them is Wilson's son, Avery. He's smart as a whip, announced when he was fifteen he wanted to be an FBI agent, like his dad. You can imagine I nipped that in the bud after Wilson went missing, and after how the FBI treated me. He's a criminal attorney now, and he's successful. Well, maybe that's not so strange."

Elizabeth shot a quick look at Rome, saw he was turning the ring every which way, prodding and pressing. "They're handsome kids, Mrs. Hendricks. I have only one younger brother, Tommy's his name. He lives in London." *What to say about Tommy? That he's a drug addict and I left him in London over three months ago and pray he's all right?* She tried to think of something simple and positive to say without lying, ended up with, "He really enjoys music, jazz specifically."

"Nasty, no rhyme or reason," Mrs. Hendricks said. "Jazz, not your brother."

Rome continued running his fingers over the ring. He'd nearly given up when he felt a small strip of metal give way at the side of the red center stone. The stone lifted. For a moment, he simply stared at it. There was a folded bit of paper in the small space behind it. He looked over at Mrs. Hendricks, saw she was lifting a framed photograph of a smiling preteen girl and handing it to Elizabeth. He quickly slipped the small bit of paper into his pocket, then pressed the red stone down and it clicked into place.

He waited, listening. "You see how very pretty she is. My husband says she's the image of me at that age, and I laugh, since he didn't know me when I was thirteen." Elizabeth asked her more questions, said complimentary things about every one of her children and grandchildren, all of them old enough to be parents themselves.

Rome finally cleared his throat and stood. "Mrs. Hendricks, thank you for showing me Mr. Ballou's class ring. You've been very helpful."

Mrs. Hendricks scooted forward in the chair until her feet were firmly on the rug and stood up. "You won't tell me why you wanted to see Wilson's class ring?"

Rome smiled. "The ring wasn't mentioned in the reports from 1978. I only wanted to be thorough." He nodded to Elizabeth.

Obviously, Mrs. Hendricks wanted to question him more, but Elizabeth was fast. She walked to Mrs. Hendricks and shook her hand. "Thank you for the coffee, ma'am. I enjoyed spending time with you. Your children and grandchildren are amazing. No wonder you're so proud. And yes, I'll bet your husband is right, she does look like you when you were her age."

Mrs. Hendricks smiled at Elizabeth, shot Rome a look that said it all quite clearly—*You're as big an idiot as those agents back in 1978. All that nonsense about Wilson's stupid class ring? And like those morons, you won't tell me a thing.*

As soon as they were in Rome's car again, Elizabeth said, "There was a compartment in that bloody ring, wasn't there, Rome? What was in it? Come on, out with it."

"A piece of paper. Let's drive well out of sight of Mrs. Hendricks and we'll look together."

Rome pulled over to the curb in the next block under the shade of an oak older than his grandparents. He took a deep breath and pulled the small folded slip of paper from his pants pocket. Elizabeth crowded in, nearly on top of him, she was leaning so close.

"Ease back, Palmer—a good bodyguard's name. You did good with Mrs. Hendricks."

"Thank you."

"Okay, let's see what we've got here." His fingers were clumsy he was so excited. Slowly, he unfolded the yellowed paper, so small there was barely room for the tiny handwritten markings. He looked at Elizabeth and gave her a blazing smile. "It's a precise longitude, and I know it passes through northern Virginia, like the latitude we found in Ballou's shoe. I think we know where to find whatever it was he was killed for."

And she leaned forward and threw her arms around him. "You did it, Rome. They might make you director for this. You'll be the youngest director of the FBI ever. You'll see. Let's go find it right now. I'm thinking diamonds? No, maybe bearer bonds. This is so exciting."

At that moment, Rome wasn't thinking about what they might find and what it could mean, he was aware only of

Elizabeth, her warm breath on his cheek, pressed against him. She was laughing, happy, her blue eyes warm and excited.

She kissed him on the mouth.

His well-ordered world toppled over. He didn't want to, it was the last thing he wanted to do, but he forced himself to pull back from her. It hurt to put that space between them.

"I—I can't do this, Elizabeth, it's against the rules."

"What rules?"

"What I meant to say is I'm on the job as an FBI special agent who's supposed to be guarding you, keeping you safe, not kissing you. I'd willingly give up my prized Roger Maris baseball card to do more than kiss you, but I can't."

She gave him the lopsided grin he realized was unique to her and she kissed him again, sank into him.

It was a bad idea, really bad, but it felt so good he didn't stop. He put his arms around her, pulled her to him over the center console.

Elizabeth pressed against him, even with the console digging into her stomach. She felt his hands over her back, tangling in her braid, caressing her neck. Her life was crazy, uncertain, terrifying, but nothing mattered in this moment; only he did, Roman Foxe. She knew in her soul life had sent her this man. If he didn't know that yet, he would.

Chapter Forty-three

Rebel parked seventeen-year-old Elliott Jordan's beautifully re-stored 1975 Camaro across the street from a gem of a cottage in Ardmore, a rich suburb of Philadelphia built along an old Penn-sylvania railroad line. What the pristine white cottage, with its deep-set porch lacked in sheer size and the ponderous elegance of its affluent neighbors, it made up for in grace and charm. High Italian cypress trees filled the yard, circled in front of the bow windows.

He'd parked across the street under a large oak and watched Carla Cartwright come out of her house wearing workout clothes, carrying a gym bag. He'd seen photos of her, but he'd never met her. She looked quite fit, her dark hair pulled back in a ponytail, her skin very white. He couldn't see her eyes behind her sunglasses, but he knew they were blue. He decided not to approach her, he'd wait. He watched her pull her late-model Toyota Corolla out of her garage and pull out onto the road. He followed her at a discreet distance. He wasn't surprised when she pulled into the Five Points Gym three miles away.

He drove to a small café nearby, had a cup of coffee, read the

Wall Street Journal on his phone, then drove back to her house to wait for her.

Close to an hour later Carla Cartwright pulled back into her circular driveway. He watched her stride to the front door, unlock it, and walk into her house.

He waited a moment, drove into her driveway, stopped behind the Corolla. He drew a deep breath as he walked to the dark-blue-painted front door. He felt calm and centered and ready. He'd been scared when the FBI took him into custody, and when Gregson had turned on her recorder and read him his Miranda rights again, but he wasn't now. He knew what he was going to say. He gave the griffin-head knocker a sharp rap and waited. He heard light footsteps, then a woman's voice. "Who is it?"

"Rebel Navarro, Archer's brother. May I speak to you, Ms. Cartwright?"

The front door opened and Rebel faced the woman he believed had framed both him and his brother. She'd obviously worked out hard, her face still shiny with sweat. He hadn't expected her to be so tall, only an inch or so shorter than he was. She looked younger than her thirty-six years with her fair complexion and razor-sharp cheekbones. She wasn't beautiful, but she was striking.

She froze an instant, but then she smiled, stepped back. "Yes, of course I recognize you. It strange we've never met before. Please call me Carla. Come in, come in."

He shook her hand. "And I'm Rebel."

She stepped back, waved him in. "Have you heard from Arch? Did he send you?"

"No, sorry, I don't know where he is. Have you heard from my brother?"

"Well, yes, some texts at first, then nothing. It's such a pleasure to meet you, Rebel. Arch speaks of you so often. Is Tash all right?"

"Yes, Tash is fine. He'll be staying with me until this mess is cleared up and Archer is home, which will be soon since he's innocent."

She said, no change in expression, "Perhaps the FBI will uncover something to exonerate him. It's been chaos at the firm, the FBI everywhere, everyone being questioned about Arch, the forensic accountants all over the computers, the client records, access."

He said from behind her, "Arch?"

She turned, smiled. "I've never called him anything else since the evening I met him at the Spark and Clyde Bar on Clark Street in Philadelphia six years ago." The smile fell off her face. She laid her hand on his arm. "I'm so very sorry, Rebel, very sorry indeed for what's happened."

"For what's happened? So you think Archer stole that money from his own firm, his own clients?"

She gave him an ineffably sad look. "I must be honest. I don't know what else I can think. Everything the FBI has found points to him, no way around it. Come this way, we'll go into the living room."

She led him through a distinctive harlequin-patterned black-and-white entry hall and through an arch into a small parlor, its walls a light cream with one vivid red accent wall, dramatic and fitting. The art covering the walls was starkly modern, and he wondered why she'd juxtaposed the bizarre slashes of red and black with the good antiques. He really liked the Victorian love seat covered in a rich red velvet and the three high-backed chairs in brocade.

She waved him toward the love seat but didn't sit herself; rather, she stood with her shoulders against the mantelpiece. Rebel said, "From what my brother has told me over the years, I know you two were close. It was my feeling there was trust between you."

"Yes, that is true."

"Then how can you possibly believe he'd steal from his own company?"

"Of course I don't want to believe it, but this is what I know and what I must accept. Archer and Sasha had just left on their honeymoon to Paris. We were finishing a routine review when the examiners found a large investment among our offshore holdings that had been slowly drained over months, from an account owned by a business that turned out to have a legitimate address and profits. I'd been left in charge, of course, and they asked me to explain it, but I couldn't. I didn't know about any of it. It turns out the transfers into and out of that account were made using Arch's passcodes, and the FBI told me the passcodes were from his own workstation, and the missing two hundred million dollars was transferred out over time, even into some cryptocurrency."

He nodded. "Yes, that's what I was told. Still, it doesn't make sense. Knowing Archer as I do, as you do, it's impossible."

"Look, Rebel. I'm sorry, but it had to be Arch. There was simply no one else who had access to his passcodes, not even me, and I hate it." She dashed away a tear. "There's no other explanation. Believe me, I've thought and thought." She struck a fist against her open palm. "I hate this, hate it, but I have to accept Arch has destroyed everything we built, he's broken faith with me, all of us at the firm, and all our clients, many of them his personal friends, with all the charities, the pension funds, the foundations that put their trust in us. I keep asking myself how he could have done such a thing, how he could be so different from the man I believed he was. If the fund goes under, and it's likely it will, no one will hire me again, or any of our top people. And your brother did this to us."

She pushed off the mantelpiece and began pacing. She swiped her palm over her eyes again, smearing her mascara. "I told myself there'd be no more tears, no more wishing I had a gun to shoot him. Look, I've been the one fielding the calls from all our investors, since of course they can't reach Arch. Over and over I've begged them all to keep faith with us. I try to explain the inexplicable, tell them there's ongoing investigation about where their money went. The FBI Financial Crimes Team has frozen the piddling money that's left. I hope I can keep things afloat, but if I'm honest with myself there's little chance now. I'm very afraid they'll put us into receivership, start bankruptcy proceedings."

She shook her head and gave a bitter laugh. "Who am I kidding? Even if I could possibly turn things around, Arch is the one with the magic touch, the talent to bring in clients and keep them happy. He could talk the fillings right out of your mouth, my mother would say. She gave him two million dollars to invest for her, and it's gone now. And yes, I replaced it." She smacked her hand into her fist, anger radiating off her. "Let me ask you this, Rebel. If your brother is so innocent, why did he run? Why won't he come home?"

Rebel said, "All I know is he went on his honeymoon, was in Paris when this broke. Maybe Sasha talked him into running. Maybe he's afraid he'd be railroaded if he comes home, maybe Sasha too. Could be they'll believe she was in on it with him."

"Sasha? That poor little cow? She worships him, but understand—she has no say in anything. I think she'd lie and cheat for him, do anything to keep him safe and with her. But if he did come back, I have no doubt she'd trail after him like a dutiful little hausfrau, no hesitation."

"You don't like Sasha? Didn't she once work for you?"

"Yes, I liked her. Fact is, she's a bit dim, but a good worker, just not good enough."

Rebel said, "Archer's passcodes. He once told me it was a foolproof system. Do you agree?"

"Yes, random passcode generators, two-step authentication, access limited to a defined workstation, and only Arch had those passcodes, no one else. They were accessed from his own workstation." She shook her head. "I remember Arch challenged hackers in a tweet to try to break into our workstations, offered a ten-thousand-dollar reward, but none of them could do it.

"I remember asking Arch once if Celia knew how to access his passcodes, and he laughed. She could care less, he said."

Rebel sat forward, clasped his hands between his knees. "If I'm to believe my brother did this, I have to understand why. My brother was very proud of his investment fund; you more than anyone know that. It was his creation, his baby. He made it successful, so please tell me, why do you think he would destroy his own company when he knew only he could be blamed for it?"

She picked up a photo off the mantel, stared at it a moment, and said, her voice defeated, "I've asked myself that question so many times and I've never found an answer. Maybe it goes back to Celia's illness. Her death nearly destroyed him, Rebel. He became quiet, withdrawn, depressed. It seemed to me he'd lost all joy in life, no matter how hard his friends tried to rally him, no matter how I tried to help him. Of course, there was Tash, but from what I saw he pulled away from Tash as well. He pulled away from all of us. It was tragic and I was scared to death for him."

Rebel said, "But Archer got over his depression when he married Sasha. He seemed happy when I saw him before he and Sasha left for Europe, before this entire mess blew up. You really haven't answered my question. Why would Archer destroy his own creation? He didn't need more money."

Carla fanned her hands. "As close as I thought we were, I wasn't in his brain. Maybe Sasha wasn't enough for him, maybe he was bored and wanted a new challenge. Maybe he wanted to see if he could get away with it. I was one of his best friends, I thought I knew him almost as well as Celia did, and I still don't know."

Time to bring the hammer down. Rebel said, "The reason I'm in Philadelphia is that the FBI arrested me last night and brought me here to their field office. They said their forensic accountants found my name linked to the account in the Caymans where that missing money was sent."

She stared at him, said nothing.

"Let me be perfectly clear. Archer would never do that to me, and of course I know of no account in the Caymans, so that means whoever set up Archer over these past months decided to forge my name on an official bank document—as an extra nail in the coffin to implicate Archer even further." He paused, then said, "The FBI almost believed it, until they uncovered some flaws."

Carla slid her tongue over her bottom lips, stared at him. "There were flaws?"

He smiled as he rose. "Enough for them to release me after they talked with me and my lawyer, and examined the evidence closely. Whoever tried to implicate me to make it seem my brother and I were both involved made a mistake by faking my signature. They ended up agreeing someone was trying to set both of us up." He said slowly, "Do you know what? Archer believes it was you, and I agree with him. You stole the two hundred million dollars. But, Carla, you made a big mistake when you decided to implicate me."

He shook his head at her. "My brother described you as brilliant, but the signature you planted came across as an amateur move. You should have left well enough alone."

She jerked her arm off the mantelpiece, stepped toward him, and yelled in his face, "How dare you! I wouldn't do that! The fund was my life too! I'm devastated by what's happened. Forge your signature? That's absurd."

Rebel wagged his finger at her. "Amateur, as I said. You should have practiced copying it a bit longer. The FBI is going to dig deeper now, not simply accept my brother is guilty. Expect a visit from them, Carla. I do believe they've got you in their crosshairs."

For a moment he thought she'd strike him, but she pulled up short. No more screaming at him, now her voice was low and vicious. "I don't have to put up with this. What you're accusing me of is ridiculous! I've never done an amateur job in my life! It's all on your damned brother. He's ruined his own life, and now you're trying to ruin mine to save his hide! Get out, now!"

"Soon now, I can feel it—my brother will be coming home a free man."

"I told you to get out! I did nothing wrong, nothing. None of this is on me, whatever you say. It's all on your brother."

A cell phone buzzed. It was Carla's. She pulled it out of her pocket, looked down, frowned. She strode from the living room. Rebel slowly followed her. At the front door, she whirled around. "You bastard, the FBI will never believe any of your crap. I don't ever want to see you again."

"Well, maybe at your trial," Rebel said. He gave her a salute, walked out the front door, and closed it quietly behind him.

He was smiling as he climbed into Elliott Jordan's Camaro. All in all, a good morning's work.

He was aware Carla Cartwright was watching him from her living room window as he drove away. He smiled in the rearview, flipped off the recorder he'd had running on his cell phone.

He'd already called Ethan earlier to tell him he was ready to come home, asked him to pick him up at Rafael Jordan's house. He couldn't wait to return his teenager's hot rod; he wanted no more people staring at him. He was going to give a copy of the recording to Rafael. He imagined Rafael wouldn't be pleased with his going off the range and facing down Carla Cartwright, but Rebel knew he'd listen to their conversation and act accordingly. Of course she hadn't admitted to anything, he hadn't expected her to, but she'd nearly exploded when he'd said his forged signature was an amateur job. She'd think the FBI would be looking at her closely now. Maybe she'd make another mistake, try to cover something else up they'd probably never have found.

Chapter Forty-four

It was pitch black, the rain coming down as it could only in London, a gash in the sky Millicent's mother used to say. She kissed her son's cheek, slid into the Bentley parked near the elevator while Tommy opened the door and held an umbrella over her head.

He leaned in, kissed her cheek. "Be careful, Mum, it's a nasty night."

"You know I'm always careful. Just an angry rain god, nothing I can't manage," she said.

"Ring me when you're safe at home."

"Of course." She drove away from the elegant, prestigious building, the Corinthian, built in the 1920s, its flats high ceilinged and spacious, modernized yet again six years before. She'd rented Tommy a lovely end flat on the sixth floor. He deserved it, because he was clean now and ready to lead the life he was meant to lead before he became an addict. Millicent drove into London at least twice a week to see him since he still couldn't come home; his father didn't allow it. She knew Elizabeth had given him money before she'd left England so unexpectedly, but Millicent still supplemented his allowance.

She hadn't discussed it with her husband, nor did she tell him where she went when she was driving to London. She knew he was well aware she was visiting Tommy, but he'd never said a word to her about it. It was easier that way.

Millicent leaned forward to see better past the frantically moving windscreen wipers. Admittedly, the downpour was bad, but as she'd told Tommy, nothing she couldn't handle.

She was so proud of him. She knew she'd never forget the day her heart had swelled with relief and surprise when he announced he was clean, sober, and proud of it. She wondered if it was his sister nearly being murdered that had helped him finally straighten out his life. She'd moved him into his new apartment four days later.

Millicent was only halfway down the block when the robust Bentley heater started gushing out warm air. The rain grew heavier and the windscreen wipers automatically adjusted.

She wasn't aware of the dark van driving slowly half a block behind her, all her thoughts concentrated on the road ahead. And on her son. She realized she was only about ten minutes from Elizabeth's house in Belgravia, at the end of the beautiful crescent at Eaton Square. She visited every Friday to ensure everything was still in good working order, often stopped to look at the portrait her daughter was painting of her, nearly finished by the time she'd left. Had she really looked as young and vibrant and deliriously happy as Elizabeth had portrayed her from long-ago photographs? She couldn't remember.

The relentless rain sheeted down. Even the warm air from the heater felt a bit damp. Finally, Millicent turned onto the M25 motorway, then from the M25 to the A23, always a lift since it meant she'd be home in under forty-five minutes even with the blasted endless rain.

She thought of her husband—Sebastian, such a romantic name, she'd always thought—how he'd charmed her, seduced her. She'd been wildly in love within days of their meeting at the French ambassador's party, a charming Frenchman with bad teeth whose name she couldn't remember.

The windscreen wipers struggled to give her sufficient visibility as she continued south. There were few cars on the motorway even for a Saturday night because of the rotten weather.

Millicent turned on the music system and began singing along with Adele's "Hello." She had a small voice, but it was true, and she knew all the words. The windscreen wipers seemed to slap away the rain in rhythm with her singing.

She and Adele sang three more songs as Millicent drove through Burgess Hill and its tangle of roads, some modern and asphalt, some cobblestone. She knew them like the backs of her hands, like old friends. Rain ran in rivulets on the pavements.

Five kilometers later she drove through the small village of Baggley-Cliff, its one main street empty, its shops dark, hunkered down against the fierce rain. No wonder, it was close to midnight, later than she usually drove through. She and Tommy had eaten pizza and spoken of so many things and so she'd stayed and stayed. She saw one dim light in Mrs. Gilray's bar, with only two cars parked in front.

Just beyond Baggley-Cliff, she turned the Bentley onto a two-lane country road. She was nearly home, only another kilometer.

She slowed, turned onto a short, paved drive, and stopped in front of elaborate iron gates with a giant *D* scrolled across the top that had been there for three centuries. Her home stood on a small rise in the distance, past an ancient drive lined on both sides with lime and ash trees, a few oaks sprinkled in over the centuries. When she'd first come to Darlington Hall as a new bride, she'd felt it welcoming her, and that had never stopped. The Hall was part of her, and she loved it as much as her husband. Lights shone from the large windows like beacons. Benbett, the Palmer butler for thirty years, always left those lights on for her until she was safely home. Would Sebastian be up, waiting for her? Probably not. She doubted he was even there. Millicent sighed, stopped the Bentley, and pressed the gate button on her key fob.

The mammoth old gates slowly began to open inward.

Before she could drive through, something struck the Bentley hard from behind, pushing its rear to the side, throwing her against the door. She froze, too shocked to move, but only for a moment. She jerked open her seat belt and looked back, terrified.

Two people dressed in black jumped out of a van behind her and ran toward her, carrying what looked like a cudgel. Where had they come from? Why hadn't she seen them? How could this be happening? She remembered the distress alarm, smashed the small button. An earth-shattering screech came from inside the Bentley and out into the night. Millicent heard dogs barking in the distance. Her dogs, and they were probably racing toward her. Who were these people?

A man, his masked face blurred in the heavy rain, slammed something against her driver's-side window. The alarm continued to screech, and the estate dogs were still madly barking, closer now. Would someone hear the alarm? Would the alarm sound in the police station as it was supposed to? It had never been tested. It was a hammer the man was slamming against her window, cracks from its blows webbing the glass. Another man was slamming a hammer against the right rear window.

All she heard was the beating hammers swung over and over by the men dressed in black, no faces, just black masks, and the sound of the alarm, until a police car's distinctive siren sounded in the distance. The hammering stopped; the men whirled around, raced back to the van, and threw themselves into the back. Another man, the driver, backed up and screeched away before the side doors had even slammed shut.

For what seemed like an eternity to Millicent, there was only the sound of the rain striking loud as bullets against the Bentley's roof, the continuous screech of the alarm, and the barking of the dogs now swarming around the car.

Millicent opened her door and jumped out, heedless of the heavy rain drenching her, and tried to calm the three bulldogs, all barking ferociously, a protective wall around her. She fumbled with the distress alarm, pressed the button again, and the screeching abruptly went silent. She patted the dogs' heads again and again, telling them they were brave and she loved them.

A police car slammed to a stop behind the Bentley. She yelled to the two constables that three men in a dark van had tried to kidnap her, and she waved frantically down the road. No wasted time—the police car backed up and chased after the van, its siren again blaring into the night.

Two more police cars arrived, their sirens blaring loud enough to wake the dead. One of the officers held an umbrella over her head while another tried to start up the Bentley. The grand old lady started right up. The police cars followed the Bentley through the gates, down the drive to the Hall. Millicent finally felt her heart slow. Who on earth were those men, and did they really want to kidnap her? It seemed insane to her.

Through the rain she saw Seth McComber, in charge of the home wood and the Darlington guard dogs for over twenty years, trotting back to the Hall with the dogs, using his gnarled walking stick. Everything seemed so normal, but it wasn't. Millicent felt suddenly exhausted, adrenaline crashing, she supposed, and she wanted to cry, something she hadn't done in a very long time. The terror of those men hammering on the Bentley windows was still loud in her mind.

What would have happened if the alarm hadn't sounded in the police station?

She hoped Sebastian was home. She pictured his face, his arms around her telling her it would be all right. She willed him to be there, for her. She needed him, needed him very badly.

Chapter Forty-five

When Savich's cell blasted out the Blues Brothers' "Gimme Some Lovin'," he was dreaming he and Sherlock and Sean were standing at the top of the Lost Boy run at Vail, the sun glistening off the acres of new snow in front of them. Sherlock was hugely pregnant, singing at the top of her lungs and waving around her ski poles, but it didn't seem to matter to anyone.

He jerked awake, saw it was nearly 1:00 A.M. As always with a late call, his heart pounded, aware someone he loved could be in danger, or worse.

"Savich."

"Hello, Savich, John Eiserly here. Sorry to call you so late, but I knew you'd want to hear this immediately. There was an attack on Elizabeth's mother, Lady Millicent, tonight at the very gates of her home near Brighton, Darlington Hall. They were out to kidnap her, not murder her, or they could have simply shot her through the car windows, but they tried to bludgeon their way in. She'd been visiting her son, Tommy Palmer, Elizabeth's brother, in London, and three masked men evidently followed her home.

"Luckily, her Bentley was equipped with a distress alarm

connected to Darlington Hall and local police emergency, and constables arrived very quickly. She was shaken, of course, but uninjured. The weather was—still is—filthy, so she didn't see much, only the two men, both in black clothes and masks, and a driver in the dark van. The attack was unexpected and vicious."

Eiserly let out a well-bred curse. "I don't know what's happening here, Savich, but it seems whoever failed to take Elizabeth using the Sikorsky helicopter decided they'd have better luck going after her mother. None of us saw this coming."

Savich said, "If whoever is behind this wants revenge, they could have simply killed Elizabeth's mother."

"But they didn't. Oh, yes, I did confirm Aboud and Samir Basara knew each other, but not well."

"They'd have to have been blood brothers for Aboud to feel strongly enough about him to go after Elizabeth with his helicopter."

Eiserly said, "Remember Sherlock said the attempts on Elizabeth could be about something else entirely? I suppose it's possible Bashar al-Assad, the president of Syria, could have an interest. He badly wants British sanctions lifted now the civil war is nearly over. Aboud's family and Assad's have long-standing ties, and the Aboud family's import-export businesses in Syria have been badly hurt by the sanctions. I do know Lord Camden, Elizabeth's father, was a member of the Foreign Office group that decided the sanctions we imposed, but the final decision wasn't his by any means. Perhaps he could help get the sanctions lifted, but I doubt it.

"And someone you can't identify was at Aboud's horse farm in Virginia? It makes my head hurt, Savich. Please call me after you've spoken to Elizabeth. Again, sorry to wake you, but as you know, His Majesty's Government never sleeps. Love to Sherlock."

Savich punched off and turned to Sherlock, who was up on her elbow listening intently.

Sherlock said, "Should we wake her up and tell her now?"

"If we did, she'd be on the phone making reservations for the first flight to London. Let's wait until morning."

Sherlock said on a yawn, "Do you think Aboud believes Elizabeth's father really has enough juice to get the sanctions lifted? I'm with John—it gives me a headache, Dillon. Let's tuck it in."

She added in a sleep-slurred voice, "Whatever this is about, Aboud's not the key to all this."

But then what was it about? "Sleep now, sweetheart. We won't figure it out unless we get some sleep."

Sherlock didn't answer him, she was down for the count, her breath slow and steady against his neck, a soft curl brushing his cheek. Savich gently pulled her closer, felt the baby move against his side, and something else—contentment. He smiled. He couldn't wait to meet his little girl, and Felicity was an excellent name.

Chapter Forty-six

Rebel Navarro house
Titusville, Virginia
SATURDAY NIGHT

Rebel was home in bed, Tash sleeping beside him, his hand on Rebel's arm. Tash hadn't wanted to sleep alone after Morales and Briggs had hauled Rebel away Friday night; actually, he hadn't wanted to let Rebel out of his sight. Rebel understood. Tash had been terrified he'd lose him, just as he'd lost his father. When Ethan pulled his Range Rover into the Merriweather driveway that afternoon, Tash had shouted and run toward them into Rebel's arms, hugged him as tight as he could. They'd held each other until Rebel promised him he was home to stay, and he prayed that was true. He still had his ankle monitor, which meant the FBI knew he'd gone to see Carla Cartwright that morning. But he'd gotten no calls, no threats from Gregson or Morales or Briggs, no black SUVs roaring into his driveway there to arrest him again.

It was the middle of the night and the house was quiet. A quarter moon shined through the window and the air was cool, a slight breeze stirring the curtains. It was a perfect summer night and he was in his own house and his own bed, but he couldn't sleep. He thought again about his talk with Cartwright.

Had he spooked her enough to make another mistake? Was forging his signature the first?

When he'd given a copy of the recording he'd made to Rafael Jordan, Jordan hadn't yelled at him for pulling that stunt. Rather, he'd looked thoughtful, shaken Rebel's hand, and told him to take care of his nephew, he'd be in touch.

Rebel drew several deep breaths and closed his eyes, tried to find calm. He remembered his brother's face when he'd hugged Sasha in his kitchen here in Titusville, the hunger he'd seen in Archer's eyes when he looked at her, and why not? He knew Archer didn't feel the all-consuming love for her he'd felt for Celia, but Sasha was young and beautiful and smart, and she acted like she worshipped him. He remembered he'd prayed Sasha would give him another chance at a happy, full life. And then this mess had happened. He doubted it was Archer's idea to hide, wondered if he'd agreed to stay for Sasha.

Before he fell asleep, Rebel felt Tash's hand move, clutch at his arm. Was he having another nightmare? Should he wake him? He didn't, he fell asleep.

Tash was dreaming about his father again, sitting in that strange building with people milling around him, gawking and oohing and aahing as they stared at the weird statues and columns and all those bright-colored windows, huge windows that went on forever. His dad's shoulders hunched forward, his head bowed. Tash knew he felt alone. And he was scared.

His father stood, made his way through the crowd of people, and walked out of the huge building. He stopped under a bright morning sun and stared back at it. Tash saw strange, huge towers that speared into the sky and fat columns that looked like they had holes in them. It was like a fantasy out of one of his video games set on an alien world. He saw Sasha walking through the crowd toward his dad. She slid her arm around his back, and he leaned down and kissed her. He heard his father say against Sasha's cheek, *I wish I could make this all go away, Sasha.*

Tash jerked awake.

"Uncle Rebel?"

Rebel woke from a dreamless sleep in an instant. "Tash? What's wrong? Did you have a nightmare?" He glanced at his Apple Watch in its charger, saw it was four in the morning.

Rebel pulled him close, heard Tash whisper against his shoulder, "I saw Dad again, in that weird place. There were so many people, but I knew h-he felt really alone. He just kept staring in front of him, not really seeing anything. Then he went outside and stood looking up at all the really tall columns and towers—it looked like a huge church, but really strange. And then Sasha was there and they hugged and held hands, and I heard my dad say *I wish I could make this all go away, Sasha*. And then I woke up, an-and I could still hear his voice in my mind."

Rebel pulled Tash closer, said slowly, "You thought it was a church, Tash? A weird-looking church? Really big?"

"Yes. And when Dad went outside I saw the sun and it was morning and it was already hot."

A strange-looking church? Could it be possible?

Rebel leaned over, pulled his iPhone off its charger, typed in three words, and stared at the series of photos. He showed them to Tash. "Is this the church you saw?"

"Yes, yes! That's it. How did you know?"

"I finally realized your description sounded like Gaudí's masterpiece. It's a huge basilica in Barcelona, Spain, called La Sagrada Família, The Sacred Family. Gaudí designed it way back in 1883, and work continues on it today. It's morning now in Barcelona, like in your dream, and the summers are hot there. Have you ever seen pictures of it before?"

"No, Uncle Rebel, I've only seen it in the dreams. I've seen Dad there every time."

Rebel kept Tash close and leaned back against his pillow. He said aloud, "Maybe your dad is staying near the basilica, maybe within walking distance."

"I never saw a car," Tash said, his voice slurred. Rebel said nothing more. He heard Tash's breathing even into sleep.

What Tash had told him was hard to accept, much less understand. He could either keep fighting it, or he could do what he could to find out if Tash's dream was real. What to do? His brother had decided he didn't want to be found, not yet. Shouldn't that be his decision? If Rebel told the FBI where Tash had seen him in a dream, they'd either laugh and suggest a shrink or they'd call the Spanish police to arrest him. What to do?

Tash suddenly jerked upward. "Uncle Rebel, Dad's in danger, and it's coming closer, and he doesn't know it. I know it means something really bad is going to happen to him really soon." Tash began crying, heartbreaking kid tears. "We have to help him. Please, Uncle Rebel, we have to help him."

Rebel said slowly, "Then we will, I promise, but it's the middle of the night, Tash. In the morning I'll speak with Ethan. You know Agent Savich in Washington is a good friend of theirs, and he's already helped me. He thinks both your dad and I are innocent. He'll do everything he can to help your dad and keep him safe. I know it's hard, but you have to go to sleep again, both of us do, all right?" Rebel realized in that moment he had no choice. He had to believe this danger Tash saw coming toward his dad was real. What to do?

Tash swiped away his tears, tried to settle again. While Uncle Rebel spoke to Autumn's dad, he'd tell her and then Autumn could tell Agent Savich herself. Tash knew there wasn't much time left, the really bad was coming, and it was close.

Chapter Forty-seven

Barcelona, Spain
SUNDAY

Archer Navarro walked up the narrow pathway to the small bungalow with a red-tiled roof that he'd rented with Sasha under an assumed name, with the cash he'd managed to access in Paris before they'd run. He and Sasha had settled in among the other bungalows for rent in the quiet neighborhood, a half mile from Gaudí's Basilica de la Sagrada Família. He spent a lot of time in the basilica and in a nearby internet café, scouring all the news sources for any mention of the Navarro Investment Fund investigation. It was hard to keep at it, because there wasn't anything new to report, but he had to; it was the only way he had to follow what was happening in Philadelphia. He and Sasha had pulled the SIM cards out of their cell phones so they couldn't be tracked, but he was still afraid, given top-notch technology, that if he called anyone at the firm, or texted Rebel or Tash again, he'd be found and arrested, and then he'd be of no use to anyone, not to Tash or to Sasha.

The FBI said no comment because it was an ongoing investigation. Were they looking at anyone else, or was he the only one with the bull's-eye on his chest? He imagined cops everywhere were on the lookout for him. What about Carla? No, he was the prime suspect. He'd read speculation in the financial columns about whether she could keep the fund operating, or whether it would end in receivership. He was being compared to Madoff, arrogant and indifferent.

He spent hours walking through La Sagrada Família, mostly to distract himself, but still he felt alone even with the thousands of tourists visiting daily. Like them, he marveled that a structure so unique and bizarre and moving actually existed. He tried to lose himself in the crowds, always alert for anyone staring at him, listened to the drone of the English tour guides until he thought he could lead a group tour himself. He studied the incredible stained-glass windows, memorized the patterns, marveled at the colors, mostly to escape for a little while. But always in the back of his mind was Tash, how he missed him, how he prayed he was all right. He thought of Celia, dead over two years now, but still in his thoughts every day. What would she think he should do? But he knew. Celia would tell him to go back and fight. He was innocent.

It was Sasha's reaction to his returning to Philadelphia that had persuaded him to come to Barcelona. She'd panicked, been on the verge of falling apart. She said she couldn't face seeing him hauled away, and what about Tash? How could she take care of him herself, with all the paparazzi and the press and the scammers who'd be harassing them? She begged him to stay with her and hope that in the meantime the authorities would find out who it was who really did this. Sasha was as much a victim of what had happened as he and Tash, as much as everyone who'd depended on the fund and on him, whose financial lives had taken a nosedive. She was still on an emotional cliff. He knew he had to protect Sasha now, until she was ready to face what would have to come.

But during the long starlit nights lying in a chaise longue in the yard, or in the bungalow with Sasha, he could think of nothing else but the mess he'd left behind in Philadelphia and all the people who'd put their trust in him and cursed him now. Was he still in Barcelona for Sasha's sake, or because he was a coward?

He walked to the bungalow's front door, past the yards of tangled roses threaded through the once white fence. It was a lovely Sunday night, not so hot now since the sun had nearly set. The yard always smelled of sweet oranges, and their scent wafted into the bungalow through the open windows. He breathed in their scent and held it. A little thing, but it gave him a moment's pleasure.

He walked into the small living room and saw Sasha sitting on the old green leather sofa, reading. She was always reading, usually a murder mystery. Her delicate bare feet were propped up on an old coffee table, a glass of fruity sangria at her elbow. She was wearing her white capri pants and a snug white top that showed off her perfect young body. They'd been married only six months, so little time to know happiness again before the world had fallen on their heads. Only Sasha could distract him, but never for long. He felt a familiar pang of guilt for leaving her alone so much.

She looked up, smiled at him, put her novel down, and patted the seat beside her. "You were at the basilica again?"

He nodded, sat down beside her, sinking deep. He leaned over, kissed her ear. "It was more crowded than usual, so many summer visitors. I can't blame them. Gaudí's mind, his vision, always captures me too. Whenever I'm there I spot yet another shape I hadn't seen before. I wonder if Gaudí lived now whether he'd ever find the money to bring that incredible fantasy to life."

Sasha took a small sip of her sangria and said, her voice thoughtful, "Maybe not on this extraordinary scale. I imagine if he did live today, he'd produce something very different, but whatever it would be, it would be as fantastical and as moving. I'm glad it's here for you."

Archer marveled at how Sasha seemed to see to the heart

of his feelings. She'd accepted his claim of innocence without question. He hated what this mess was doing to her, hated that she was afraid. He dreaded her pleas to him when he talked about going home.

"Turn your back to me, Archer, and let me give you a neck rub. Your shoulders are in your ears."

Her strong fingers began to knead his shoulders and neck. It felt incredible. He had to try again, he had to. "We should go home soon, Sasha. Our staying here doesn't make it more likely I'll be cleared, but less likely, each day. At least if I was there, I could tell them the truth, correct any mistaken notions they have, take a lie detector test, and surely that would have to mean something. I would make sure my lawyer would protect you until I'm freed. And Tash. I know he'll be fine with Rebel until this is all over."

Her hands stopped moving. He heard her draw in her breath. He turned to look into her exquisite face, framed by blond curling hair, so unlike Celia's pale blond hair, gone down the shower drain in gobs after the chemo started. He remembered Celia laughing as she modeled a curly blond wig for him. He saw her bone-white face, so thin at the end, her beautiful eyes half-open in death, saw Tash pressed against her side, sobbing. He remembered how in the last moment of her life she'd said Tash's name and told him she loved him. Tash had said he'd sung to her with his mind, a lullaby she'd sung to him when he was younger. Archer had wanted to believe him, wanted to think he'd shared that last moment with Celia, but he couldn't. Still, it was always there in the back of his mind, always a question. Now it didn't seem to matter much.

She finally answered him. He supposed he'd expected tears, more pleas to stay put, to wait, but she said, "I know how hard this is for you, Archer. I know you want to go home and the only reason you're staying is for me. You know I'm scared, scared for both of us. I don't know how I could stand seeing you dragged

away from me in handcuffs. Please, just a few more days together before we go. I promise to stop being a coward and a
wuss. You and I, we're an unbeatable team. Maybe something
will happen, maybe the FBI will figure it out." She pressed her
cheek against him, kissed him.

"All right, a few more days. Thank you, Sasha." He sighed.
"Of course it's all about the damned passcodes. I'm the only
one who has them, the only one who could strip money out of
the accounts. So it only makes sense they'd believe me guilty.
Only me. But somehow, someone managed it, and maybe you
don't want to hear this, but I'm convinced that someone had to
be Carla. I've always told you I admired her skills, and I realize
now, somehow, some way, she got hold of my passcodes. I can
see her setting this all up, timing it perfectly to be discovered
just after we left the country." He laughed. "What we wanted
to be a magical honeymoon the FBI saw as a criminal running,
a sure sign of my guilt. And all the while—well, enough of that,
I'm talking myself in circles." He looked at Sasha, prayed no one
suspected she was his accomplice. He touched his forehead to
hers. "No matter what happens to me, sweetheart, I'll make
sure you'll be all right."

She kissed his cheek, laid her hand on his forearm. "I know
you've always been close to Carla, Archer, always believed
her to be your closest friend, your ally. You were the one who
brought in the clients, and she managed the tech side. The truth
is I didn't want to believe she'd betray you, but now I realize
she probably did, she's the only one who could. I can actually
see her doing it, gloating, preening at how smart she is. I guess
it's time I told you the truth. I'll say it straight out. I never liked
Carla, particularly when she was my boss. She was demanding,
impatient, cutting—a stone-cold bitch to me. She was all honey
coating to you, but to everyone else she was mean spirited. I was
happy when I finally managed to slither out of being her assistant and head over to accounting, because otherwise, I would

have quit. You were always so nice, not only to me, but to everyone. And then you and I became we.

"Now, how can I help you prove you're innocent?"

He felt a load of guilt lift off his head. He hadn't realized Sasha disliked Carla. Did she now really believe he was innocent? Would she really go with him soon? He could see Tash again, toss a football with him. "I'm not sure what either of us can do, Sasha, but I do know I can't do it from here. A few days, then."

She looked out the living room window to the small garden with its wildly blooming roses and orange trees, looked back at him and laid her palm against his cheek, and nodded. "We've talked about this before, and I agree, you know that. I don't know how Carla pulled it off, but let's try this. I'll make a list of those in the firm I think could be helping her. You make a list and we'll compare them."

He hugged her close. She whispered against his neck, "You're a man who's honest to his bones. I'll never forget that, ever again."

He stroked her smooth cheek. "I don't know what I would have done these past weeks without you." He picked up her sangria and took a deep drink, gave her a blazing smile. "When we go back, Sasha, with you by my side, together I know we can do anything."

Chapter Forty-eight

Darlington Hall
Country home of the Earl of Camden
Near Brighton, England
SUNDAY EVENING

When Rome drove their rented Vauxhall Corsa through the massive gates of Darlington Hall, Elizabeth was surprised she saw the huge edifice in the distance with different eyes. Even though she'd been raised here, knew every inch of the grand mansion like the back of her hand and every tree in the home woods, after only three months in the States, the huge Palladian mansion, home to generations of Palmers, suddenly looked like a relic from the past, frozen in time. The closest the modern world intruded was five kilometers away, the Davy Clink Pub, built in the 1860s.

Rome stopped the car, stared. "If I put my feet up in there, drank a beer, and asked to watch football, would I be hauled off to the Old Bailey?"

She grinned at him. "Buck up, Rome. My parents enjoy all the modern comforts of home, including a telly and a fridge. They might try to impress you, though—a Yank—and offer you the full aristocratic experience, replete with a one-hundred-and-fifty-year-old brandy after dinner in a gold snifter, of course." She nodded toward the huge windows set behind the white columns along the façade. "See those tall central Palladian windows flanked by narrow ones on each side? I used to draw on the glass. Drove them crazy."

"Do I say my lord and my lady?"

"Sir and ma'am will do, since you're a barbarian and aren't expected to know any better."

Whenever Elizabeth walked into the immense black-and-white-tiled entranceway of Darlington Hall with its soaring ceiling and huge chandelier, only belatedly electrified, she felt she should be wearing a corset and a dozen petticoats beneath a velvet gown that weighed a couple of stone. Benbett, the Palmer butler since before she was born, was there to greet them when she and Rome walked in through the giant double doors. He gave her a deep bow and stoically accepted her enthusiastic hug.

He said to the strapping young man standing off to his left, "Jeffrey, see to Lady Elizabeth's luggage. And the gentleman's."

Benbett's grand old voice sounded wonderful, and she couldn't help it, she grinned shamelessly and hugged his stiff self again. She turned in a circle, looking up at the scores of large oil paintings that covered the pale cream walls as well as those marching up the wall of the huge staircase, all paintings she'd studied and copied since she was a child. With Benbett all stiff and formal, regarding her with indulgence now, surrounded by the gilt and glamour of ages past, she felt a familiar stirring, a recognition in the deepest part of her—she finally felt like she was home again.

"Benbett, this is Special Agent Roman Foxe from the FBI in the States. He's here to keep me safe."

Benbett gave him a short bow and a slight smile. "Special Agent Foxe, welcome to Darlington Hall. Allow me on behalf of all the staff to thank you for protecting Lady Elizabeth."

Elizabeth's mother came running out of the drawing room, calling her name. Elizabeth met her in the hallway, hugged her close, kissed her cheek. She pulled back, studied her mother's beloved face, saw shadows under her eyes, but saw too the beautiful smile. "It's so wonderful to see you! Do you promise me you are all right? Mom, I'm so sorry this happened to you, it's all my fault, I'm so sorry."

Lady Millicent took in her daughter's face, so much like hers when she'd been Elizabeth's age. "Yes, love, I'm just fine today. Your fault? Don't be foolish, or I'll have to deny you your biscuit and send you to bed early without your tea. Yes, it was frightening and such a shock, when those horrible men tried to kidnap me right at our gate, but it's over now and I'm fine."

Millicent hugged her again. "You came so quickly. Thank you, darling, thank you. It has seemed so long, these three months you were away with that Hurley Janklov fellow learning how to defend yourself. I understand, I really do. I wanted you to be safe, and you didn't want to be helpless. But now you're back, and I'm so proud of you. And I see you brought along this handsome young man who's been looking after you."

Elizabeth introduced Rome, watched her mother study him, then the smile and the handshake, all so discreet and proper she wanted to laugh. Then she looked over her mother's head and saw her father standing tall and straight in the doorway of the formal drawing room, looking the perfect aristocrat as always, his arms crossed over his chest, wearing a bespoke gray suit, a lovely pale gray silk shirt, and a dark blue tie. He smiled at her, the special smile he'd reserved for her since she was a child. She took a running start and jumped into his arms, wrapped her legs around his waist. He whirled her around just as he had when she'd been seven years old. She breathed in the woodsy outdoor scent of his cologne, which she remembered from her earliest years.

He kissed her ear, set her down, kept her hands in his. "My beautiful girl, I heard what your mother said to you, and she's right in every way. We are proud of you, and you are in no way to blame for anything. Looking at you is like seeing Millicent again so many years ago. I'm not sure you should have come, but I'm very glad you did." He touched his forehead to hers. "We'll get through this nonsense, all of us together."

"Dad, they went after Mother because they knew they couldn't get to me, not with Rome and the FBI guarding me."

Sebastian looked behind her to Rome, tall, fit, too good looking surely for a federal agent. He met Rome's eyes, saw intelligence and depth. This man was not only tough and trained, he was a thinker, and that was good. "So you are Special Agent Foxe, as I believe you FBI agents are styled. You're the fellow who's been looking after my daughter since she finished with Janklov. I assume you are armed?"

Rome wondered if he should bow and was relieved when Elizabeth's father extended his hand. He said, "That's right, sir, I was granted that privilege by Mr. Eiserly of MI5. And both of you are right to be proud of her." He looked at her mother, then back to her father, deepened his voice. "I didn't know her before, but now, I can tell you she can be quite fierce, something of an English Amazon." Rome watched her father take in his words, very aware he'd been studied and weighed, to good account, he hoped. He felt the pull of the man, the charisma bred into his bones. Elizabeth's mother was still so happy to see her daughter she was nearly dancing. He agreed with her father, his wife seemed the picture of what Elizabeth might look like in twenty-five years. Elizabeth had her father's height, but her features carried her mother's stamp—blond hair, blue eyes, and a lovely English complexion.

Millicent led them into the formal drawing room usually used only when they were entertaining. "Please, Special Agent Foxe, do sit down. I'll ring for tea. Well, no need, Benbett is nearby, he always knows exactly what is needed before I do."

Rome felt like he'd been plunked down in Downton Abbey, dozens of paintings on the walls, so much incredible woodwork, fat cherubs staring down at him from the ceiling. He and Elizabeth sat side by side on an elegant pale blue velvet sofa that looked as old as the Pilgrims. He gazed out the eighteen-foot windows that framed distant tree-covered hills and valleys dotted with small lakes. The water looked nearly violet in the dying light. To his jet-lagged eyes, it all looked barely real, like an impressionist painting. Yard upon yard of gold brocade was looped back beside the windows to let in the last of the late afternoon light. He wondered how much they weighed, and how many hands it required to take them down when they needed cleaning. He was grateful when Lady Millicent placed a cup of black coffee, not tea, in his hands. He tasted it, found it weak, the taste strange to his American palate, and discreetly set the saucer on an end table next to a century-old Tiffany lamp.

Besides tea and coffee, there was a pile of pastries still warm from the oven. Rome gladly accepted a slice of some sort of heavy yellow cake with raspberries, obviously made in the Downton Abbey kitchen.

It took only a slight nod from his lordship for Benbett to pour Rome a finger of whiskey in a Baccarat crystal glass. How did he know? It didn't matter, Rome was grateful. He took a sip and realized he was drinking a whiskey probably as old as the Declaration of Independence.

Sebastian said, "We have some time to relax and chat before dining, say in half an hour?" He smiled at his wife, picked up her white hand, squeezed it. Elizabeth blinked. Had her leaving, and his wife being nearly taken from him, changed him? Or had it happened slowly, and she hadn't realized it before she'd left? Her father said with obvious pride, "First off, let me say your mother knew what to do. She pressed that distress button immediately. The sound of it made me rise straight out of my chair in the study, it was so loud. The police were here in a short time, scared the culprits off. If they'd been any closer the dogs would have taken them down. It's a pity they weren't caught."

Millicent said, "It was thanks to your brother, Elizabeth. Tommy insisted we install the distress button in the Bentley. He was worried for me after what happened to you, and with you out of the country, he said he didn't want to take any chances with me."

At her mother's open mention of Tommy's name, Elizabeth shot a look at her father. His expression remained remote. He shrugged. "Your mother assures me Tommy is not presently using cocaine, that he's been clean for over three months. She visits him a few times a week, and that is how, Deputy Director Eiserly told us, the men who attacked her knew where she'd be. It was only a matter of following her discreetly back to Darlington Hall. It was a filthy night and that helped them."

Was this really true? Tommy hadn't used for three months? Had it taken her leaving England to make Tommy realize his life was in the crapper and he had to change it? It was a depressing thought. She prayed it was true. She wondered if her father was considering bringing Tommy back into the family, but now wasn't the time to ask him.

Benbett ushered them into the small family dining room with a beautiful walnut table with twelve exquisite chairs set around it. Millicent whispered to Rome that Cook had made her specialty, French onion soup. When a bowl was set in front of him he breathed in, tasted, and wished he could skip the rest of the meal and eat, say, six more bowls. When he finished, Benbett was at his elbow with another bowl of the amazing soup.

Over the stuffed pork and asparagus, Sebastian said, "I spoke twice today, before you arrived, with Mr. Eiserly of JTAC about what all this might mean, who might be responsible, and why. Well, at least about what he suspects, since there's been so little time to investigate what happened last night. He believes, and your mother and I agree with him, the two attempts on your life you've told us of near Washington were no doubt planned by that man Ammar Aboud, but whatever his reasons, they originated here in England, no question, now that Millicent has been attacked as well. Mr. Eiserly told me Aboud's many holdings in Syria have suffered under the sanctions and possibly his motive is to force me to get them removed, which isn't at all realistic. Aboud isn't stupid. He must know mine was far from the only hand involved in setting the sanctions, that I can hardly simply revoke them myself. Eiserly agreed."

He paused. "The question we face is who here in England is working with Aboud, perhaps directing him, and why."

Rome set down his fork. "Sir, I must be blunt. The attempts on Elizabeth in the United States as well as the ones here in England—they didn't seem to want to take her, like Lady Millicent, but to kill her. If she was meant to be killed, we must look elsewhere for a motive for Ammar Aboud's involvement, because with her death, there would be no leverage. Eiserly no doubt told you the FBI did a complete search of Aboud's office, his house, his stables. Nothing was found. There's been endless discussion about whether Aboud's involvement was out of revenge for Samir Basara's death. Mr. Eiserly looked into connections and found evidence Ammar Aboud and Samir Basara were acquainted, but bosom friends? Apparently not. More than that we don't know yet."

Elizabeth sat listening quietly. It was still hard for her to accept someone wanted her dead so badly. Beyond that, her brain was fogged with jet lag. She was exhausted and imagined Rome was as well.

It was ten o'clock before she and Rome said good night to her parents and Elizabeth escorted Rome up the magnificent central staircase to a large bedroom with elaborate molding and wallpapered with Dutch country scenes. He eyed the antique four-poster bed and armoire that looked centuries old.

"Rome, Benbett told me Cranford hung your clothes in the armoire. Your folding clothes are in the drawers."

He drew her into his arms, kissed her nose. "That's all well and good, but where is the chamber pot and the copper tub?" He could picture it, a tub set in front of the Carrara marble fireplace a century before, filled with hot water hauled up by maids from the kitchen.

She laughed. "I remember my great-aunt Agatha showing me her hand-painted eighteenth-century chamber pot collection. They were works of art. I used to set my dolls in them. I think Mother has them stashed in one of the upstairs bedrooms. We're all modern now. Come, have a look at the bathroom."

The large, pale-blue-tiled en suite bathroom was thoroughly modernized, with a lovely large shower and a mile of marble counter. Impressive, but he preferred his own. There wasn't a towel warmer.

She leaned up, gave him a quick kiss on the mouth, and stepped back before he could grab her. "I'm so glad Mr. Maitland and Mr. Eiserly agreed to your coming with me, Rome. All the discussions at dinner, they're swirling around in my head like a black cloud. I'm nearly dead on my feet."

"Going over the same ground with different people can be useful, new ideas can surface, but now, like you, I don't have a working brain. When my head hits the pillow, I think I'll be out in no time too." He kissed her again, wished she could stay with him, but it wasn't possible here under her parents' gigantic roof. "What happens tomorrow morning? Will a maid wake me up with a lovely hand-painted bed tray? Or Benbett to guide me to breakfast? Or Cranford? Who is Cranford, by the way?"

"No maids, no trays, sorry. Cranford is my father's valet. He will see to you while you're here, but tomorrow morning we're both going to be allowed to sleep as long as we like. I'll help you find breakfast. You can buzz for Cranford to button your shirt for you, maybe lace your sneakers or iron your boxers if you wish. But be warned, Cranford, like Benbett, is quite the snob, so he might turn up his nose at looking after an American." She paused, looked him up and down. "On the other hand, he might enjoy dressing your buff young self with your six-pack abs, as you Yanks call them. I imagine Cranford would faint if he saw Hurley's chest without a shirt on. He'd believe him a different species. I do think my parents like you, by the way. Well, you're still an oddity to them, but an accepted one since they know now you saved their precious daughter's life more than once. We'll have to see if they still approve of you in the light of day." She laughed, touched his arm. "Good dreams, Rome."

Rome stood in the doorway and watched her walk away down the wide corridor with an ancient Persian carpet running down its length and niches set into its walls holding busts— were they long-ago earls or Greek philosophers? He'd been told he was in the family wing. That sounded to Rome like the White House.

Rome stripped to his boxers, looked at his buff self in the long bathroom mirror, and laughed. He brushed his teeth and fell into a featherbed that enveloped him like a cloud.

Chapter Forty-nine

Savich looked up from his tablet to see Sherlock coming out of the bathroom wearing a blue T-shirt and sleep boxers, the shirt tighter this week over her growing stomach. He said, "Come here, sweetheart, let Dr. Savich take care of your shoulders."

She walked over to him to get her back massaged. "Keep that up and you'll have a slave."

"I like the sound of that. I was reading a long email from Rome. He said he's eating off eighteenth-century plates at the Palmer country estate, Darlington Hall, and sleeping on a mattress so soft maybe it was once a cloud, which made sense to him because the bed was set so high he nearly had to jump to get into it. He said His Lordship, the tenth earl of Camden, seems to have accepted him, if only because he's there to keep his daughter safe. The countess, Lady Millicent, looks like an older Elizabeth and is 'jolly' charming. It's clear to Rome whoever followed Lady Millicent home was out to kidnap her, not to kill her, or they could have simply shot her on the spot."

Sherlock sighed. "And we have to ask yet again—what's the point? What do these people want? How does Aboud fit in?"

"I emailed Rome to keep his ears open and meet all the

players. He's smart, intuitive, I'm thinking he might see something we can't from three thousand miles away." He continued to knead while he kissed her ear. "And I've been working with MAX trying to find Archer Navarro in Barcelona. He's being real careful, his phone turned off, no car rentals, his passport and credit cards unused since Paris. I called Alejandro Perez at Interpol, and he's agreed to monitor the traffic cams and the CCTVs near the Sagrada Família, but there's been nothing yet. I've asked if they do locate him, they do not act, but notify me.

"What really worries me is Tash thinks time is running out to find him, that there's real danger coming his dad's way. From what Autumn told me about Tash's gifts, I believe it. Without involving Agent Gregson or Mr. Maitland, there's little else I can do."

"I could go to Barcelona myself. I could take Ruth with me."

Savich shook his head, laid his palm on her belly. "And what about Felicity?"

"You meant to say Beau, didn't you? Beau would be fine. I'm as good to go as ever, only a little thick around the middle. I could practice my Spanish while I'm there."

Savich considered this as he worked a knot out of her shoulder. "If Archer Navarro is spotted and if they can discover where he's hiding, then I'll consider it."

Chapter Fifty

Khaled raised his face to a bright sun and a warm June breeze on his way to Dever's Café. It was a day to celebrate in London—not even a hint of rain, blue sky, even a couple of clouds lazing about overhead. He'd received a text from Imam Ali Ahmad Said asking to meet him there for lunch, not a hint what he wanted. He'd prayed hard Ali hadn't somehow found out he'd slept with his sister.

Dever's was as busy as usual, mostly with politicians in their lightweight summer suits, huddled together over their steaks and pommes frites, plotting how to raise more taxes from the population.

Khaled wasn't surprised to see Ali seated at the same corner booth on a small dais near the back of the café, where the more elite members of Parliament often jockeyed to hold court, looking out over the lesser members. Ali was perfectly tailored again in a Savile Row suit, light gray today with discreet darker gray pinstripes, a white shirt, and a dark blue tie. He looked like one of the richer members of Parliament, not a holy man. Ali looked up at him, with his fluid, dark eyes that gave the impression they saw everything, and nodded. Khaled gave him a small bow. "Imam."

"No, Khaled, we are not in the mosque. You may call me Ali. Sit down." He motioned to a waiter.

Khaled ordered Fortnum & Mason black tea and Dever's specialty, baked sole and haricot verts. He said, "I thought you would be at dinner Friday night, but neither you nor your parents were there, only Adara and three of her friends."

Ali said with an elegant shrug, "In my family, as in life, the unexpected is the norm. My parents dined with the Algerian ambassador and I was, alas, otherwise occupied with a last-minute invitation. I trust you enjoyed yourself?"

Khaled's tea arrived already steeped. He squeezed in a dollop of lemon and sipped slowly. It was excellent. "Yes, I did. I'm sorry you were called away. I had hoped to see you at your home."

A perfect eyebrow arched upward. "My home? I thought you knew. Then again, why would you? No, I live in Holland Park. I purchased a house there three years ago."

The imam, who had already ordered, took a bite of his sole, savored it. "My sister tells me you and her friends ate at the Carousel Club. I trust you found the food and the company enjoyable?"

"Yes, it was a very nice evening. Adara and her friends were excellent company."

Ali laughed. "She has many friends. I've met those three gentlemen and found them deferential and devout—well, except for Yusuf. He's a mystery I've yet to figure out. The two young men come to our mosque to worship. Where Yusuf worships, I have no idea. And tell me, Khaled, what did you think of my very Westernized sister?"

Khaled swallowed, remembering every detail of their time together on Saturday. He cleared his throat. "She was very gracious. I trust she gave you a positive report?"

"She did. She said she also enjoyed seeing you on Saturday."

Luckily the waiter arrived with his lunch, giving Khaled time to think. Was the imam toying with him? His muscles clenched. Please, Adara couldn't have told him how they'd spent the day.

The imam gracefully ate another bite of sole, and added, "Did you enjoy the tennis tournament?"

Khaled's heart started beating again. He even managed a smile. So that was what Adara had told her brother. Thankfully he'd seen the sports report on the telly and knew what had happened at the Wembley tournament. "No one particularly enjoyed it since a Frenchman won, but I suppose we can't expect the English to win every time."

"Ah, you consider yourself English then, Khaled, not Syrian?"

"I am both, now and until I die. And you, Ali?"

"It is true England provides us with many opportunities few enjoy in Syria. But every day I miss the warmth of the Syrian people and our country's great beauty. I am Syrian, Khaled, now and always, until I die. How can it be otherwise, when the English still reek of colonialism and sanction us for defending ourselves within our own borders against those misguided barbarians? It is unacceptable. Finally, the war is nearly won and the Arab League has welcomed us back after so many years in the cold. And yet the English persist in their sanctions, as if they still rule us."

What was this all about? Khaled's sole tasted dry as cardboard in his mouth. He put aside horrific images of Assad's butchery against his own people, insurrectionists and civilians both. The government had won, but at a terrible cost. He looked up from his green beans. "Of course, Imam, the sanctions should be lifted. I know little of how these policies are decided, but what you have said is doubtless true of the West. Then again, war, devastation, and unfairness have been true of all cultures since the beginning of time."

Ali said nothing, merely arched a brow.

Khaled wondered if he should have given him blanket agreement, but he couldn't, simply couldn't. He continued carefully. "I spoke with Rehan al-Albiri and will meet with him tomorrow, as agreed."

Ali nodded. "Yes, Rehan told me. He is familiar with your career at Culver and Beck, and he's impressed with you. You are very young, Rehan told me, to hold such a high position. It's a testament to your abilities."

Khaled said, "I'm glad he thinks well of me. He's a splendid old man. He warned me his accounting system is quite different from what I use on a daily basis, but it has served the mosque very well for a long time."

"I'm sure you will master it without difficulty," the imam said. "Rehan has agreed to your offer to join us and take over his duties. He will prepare a contract that includes your compensation, which I insist you accept. Ah, yes, forgive me, but I promised him I would ask. Rehan has a grandson who wishes to join your firm and wonders if you would be so kind as to provide a recommendation for him."

Khaled felt immense relief. John Eiserly would speak with the partners at the firm, and all would be well. He said, "I will ask Rehan about his grandson when I meet with him. If I believe his grandson would prosper at Culver and Beck it would be my pleasure to recommend him."

Ali nodded. "Thank you. By the way, did you hear about the attempted kidnapping of the Countess of Camden? Saturday night at the gates of her country home?"

Khaled only cocked his head to the side in question. "Yes, I read about it in the *Evening Standard*. Very odd. Why do you mention it?"

"There were attempts to kidnap her daughter, Elizabeth, some months ago. She was connected to the near bombing of St. Paul's last year, and so to our mosque. Such criminality happens often in England, and yet they continue to blame us."

"The press profits from their speculations, Imam. It is what they do."

Ali nodded to the waiter to remove his plate and looked down at his exquisite Patek Philippe watch. "Ah, it grows late and I must go home and change. I am expected at the mosque. I must be properly attired before I meet the faithful."

With a final nod to Khaled, the imam rose, left cash on the table, and hurried out of the café. Khaled sat unmoving in his chair. He slowly sipped his tea, drummed his fingers on the table. Why had the imam brought up the attempted kidnapping, only to drop it? And Lady Elizabeth's name as well. Did he truly not know who was responsible? Khaled realized he was no longer certain of anything.

Chapter Fifty-one

Darlington Hall
MONDAY

After a very late breakfast, Elizabeth introduced Rome to the rest of the staff and gave him a tour of the Hall. The day was clear and sunny, and Lady Millicent encouraged Elizabeth to show Rome the grounds. Elizabeth gathered the three King Charles spaniels lazing in a spear of sun in the vast drawing room and introduced Cleo, Disraeli, and Gladstone to Rome. He went down on his haunches and reached out a hand for them to sniff. Thirty seconds after they'd all licked his hand, they were prancing around him. He gathered them to him, laughing.

Elizabeth, watching, laughed along with him. "They're my mother's dogs. They quite adore her, and you as well, I see."

They set out for a walk with the dogs through the immaculate gardens, throwing small branches for them to chase and fetch, and then on to a lovely century-old trail, bounded by ancient stones, through the home wood to a small lake with a stone bench beneath a willow tree. The dogs, finally exhausted, sprawled on the bank, eating treats Elizabeth had brought for them.

Rome and Elizabeth sat on the hard bench listening to birdcalls and the squirrels scurrying through the trees. Again,

Rome thought Darlington Hall was a place out of time, enjoyed by the very entitled few over the centuries, but still they'd made it magnificent. They didn't speak about serious things, both tired of going over the same ground, and there was nothing new to say in any case.

Rome asked, "How many workers does it take to tend the gardens and mow the lawns?"

"Now there are only three. Father showed me the old account books once. There were a dozen up until World War I, but after the war of course things began to change, like the establishment of the Inland Revenue Service." She waved her hand around her. "It feels strange to talk about such privilege today. I'm the daughter of an earl, but in reality I'm like everyone else—I worry about my heating system and my refrigerator going haywire." She punched his arm. "Unlike you, I've never been to Damascus or learned Arabic."

Rome didn't say anything. He looked at her laughing mouth, took her in his arms under the willow tree, and kissed her, with Disraeli lying on his foot. Heat, so much heat, kisses deepening, their hands on each other's clothes, when Elizabeth's cell blasted out the sound of a honking duck.

It was Lady Millicent inviting them to join her for lunch.

They touched foreheads, breathing hard, then laughed, the dogs prancing around them.

Lady Millicent sat them down on one of the dark blue velvet sofas in the sun-filled informal family room as lunch was being prepared. It was a more modern room than the formal drawing room, inviting and comfortable, with oversized chairs and books on every surface, ready to be picked up and read and laid down again on any surface, didn't matter. Exquisite throws were scattered over the backs of the sofas, and a dozen pillows added color. Walnut bookshelves lined one wall, bulging with books of all kinds, not lined up neatly but shoved in haphazardly, this way and that, another sign this was a room where you

could put your feet up and relax. A formal portrait of Millicent
was hung over a small marble fireplace, across from another set
of arched Palladian windows, their heavy draperies pulled back
and looped around graceful golden hooks. Cleo, Disraeli, and
Gladstone were sprawled dead to the world in front of them.

Millicent said, "It looks like you've exhausted them, running them all over the grounds with you." Rome walked over to
them, went down on his knees, and gathered the three spaniels
together, stroked their silky ears.

The dogs gave Rome some final licks, but they didn't return
to their places in the sun. They trotted over to Millicent, who
reached into her pocket and pulled out treats for them.

Elizabeth grinned at her mother. "Do you know before
Rome and I went outside with them I automatically put treats
in my pocket for them? Such a longtime habit."

Millicent said, "Benbett does as well. I'm sorry you missed
seeing your father this morning, Elizabeth. He was forced to
leave early for a meeting at the Foreign Office before he went
on to the bank."

"My fault for sleeping so late, Mother. There'll be time to
catch up."

Millicent began to pleat the pale-blue-and-white-checked
throw over her lap. She heard her voice hitch and forced a
smile. "Mr. Eiserly insisted I inform him whenever I plan to
leave Darlington Hall so he can send out two officers to accompany me. That needn't be often, usually only when I drive
to London to visit Tommy. Your father spoke with him twice
yesterday about what happened." Millicent paused, then spit it
out. "I know you and Rome plan to see your brother tomorrow,
and I wanted to prepare you first, without your father present.
I promise you you'll be amazed how much he's changed when
you see him. He's still thin, but he exercises and runs most
days and he looks so much healthier. His eyes are bright and
focused. When he convinced me he really was sober, I moved

him out of the small flat where he lived in Notting Hill into the Corinthian on Carberry Street. His flat is on the end, on the sixth floor. It is certainly better suited to his station. Do you know the Corinthian?"

Elizabeth nodded slowly, taking it all in.

Millicent sat forward and Elizabeth saw she was nearly jumping with nerves. "I'm glad I can speak to you without your father here. I've told him Tommy has changed, that he's clean, no more drugs, not for over three months. This time I'm convinced he'll stay that way. Your father doesn't believe it, and I can't say I blame him after the many times Tommy disappointed him, betrayed his word and his honor, as your father puts it. But after what's happened, after Tommy's distress alarm saved me, I'm hoping he'll change his mind. I'm hoping Tommy can come home where he belongs."

Elizabeth rose, sat down beside her mother, and took her hands in hers. "I'll know if Tommy's clean. If he is and if I'm convinced he is committed to staying clean, I'll help you convince Father."

Millicent threw her arms around Elizabeth. "Thank you, thank you. I don't know what changed, but I know, I simply know in my heart, Tommy really means to stay clean this time." She looked over at Rome, sitting cross-legged on the carpet, the dogs sprawled all over him. "Rome, I know you hear a lot of lies, given what you do. When you meet my son, you'll see him with clear eyes and I hope you'll know if he's sincere, committed."

Rome looked at Elizabeth's mother, saw she wanted desperately to believe her son had changed.

"I'll do my best," he said and hugged a madly licking Disraeli.

Chapter Fifty-two

Navarro Investment Fund headquarters
79 Carlton Street, Philadelphia
MONDAY

Madelaine Willig, Carla Cartwright's executive assistant, tapped lightly on the office door and stuck her head in. "Special Agents Briggs and Morales are here, ma'am. Your meeting with accounting is in fifteen minutes."

"Good. Show them in, please, Maddie."

She rose from behind her desk and straightened her skirt. She'd managed a good rapport with Morales on the phone and hoped to make the most of it.

When they stepped into her office, she said, "Agent Morales, Agent Briggs, thank you so much for coming." She stepped forward, shook their hands. "Please sit down. I am so relieved you're here. What I have to tell you is very disturbing."

Morales and Briggs sat down on the dark gray leather sofa, Cartwright across from them. Morales said, "You told me on the phone Rebel Navarro visited you Saturday morning. He seemed out of control, made wild accusations, and frightened you. You were afraid he would attack you and you grabbed the fireplace poker to defend yourself? Is this correct?"

Carla nodded. "Yes, it was horrible. I was so relieved when he finally left."

Briggs said, "Why didn't you call us immediately instead of waiting until this morning?"

Cartwright shook her head, looked embarrassed. "I should have, I suppose, but I wanted to think about what happened, be sure in my own mind I hadn't overreacted, that Rebel Navarro wasn't just frightened for his brother and needed to blame someone here at the Navarro Fund, and picked me. But I've given it a great deal of thought and I'm sure now I didn't overreact, and that's why I called you. He scared me, Agents. If I hadn't had the poker, I don't know what he would have done. He told me you'd arrested him on Friday because you'd uncovered evidence tying him to the account in the Caymans the money from our fund was wired to. No matter how much I tried to tell him I didn't know anything about that, he claimed he didn't believe me. As I said, he yelled at me, accused me of embezzling the funds myself and framing his brother and him. He was completely out of control." She drew a deep breath. "When I grabbed the poker and kept asking him to leave, he finally mumbled something about making sure I'd regret this and left."

Morales leaned forward. "Do you wish to press charges against Rebel Navarro, Ms. Cartwright?"

She was quiet a moment. "I should, I know it, but no matter what he and Archer have done, I couldn't bring myself to do that. Not only is he Archer's brother, he's taking care of Archer's little boy." She looked like she was going to cry. "From what he said your forensic accounting people found, I have to face the fact both Archer and Rebel planned this. How could it be otherwise? I hate it, just hate it. I always thought Archer was my very best friend. I trusted him completely." She swiped a tear from her cheek.

Morales sat forward, patted her hand. "This is obviously very difficult for you, Ms. Cartwright."

Briggs said, "Can't say I'm surprised at your reaction, Ms.

Cartwright, but I am surprised Rebel Navarro went to your home, confronted you, scared you."

"I don't understand. Your people found proof of his guilt. Why did you release him?"

Morales said, "We really can't talk about that, I'm sure you understand. But we can make certain Mr. Navarro doesn't bother you again."

Briggs rubbed his big hands together. "It's true his lawyer got him released for now. But things are coming together. We'll find Archer Navarro, and then we'll find the money."

"But I don't understand what he hoped to prove. I mean, I do understand he desperately wanted someone to blame, but it sounds like he is as guilty as his brother, so what was he doing coming to my house? Blaming me when he knew it wasn't true?"

Briggs shrugged. "Maybe he wants us to think he's innocent, or maybe he isn't mentally stable. After his behavior to you Saturday, you'd be a good witness to that."

Cartwright slowly nodded. "I suppose you're right. He mentioned a signature your people found on damning documents and he claimed it wasn't his. But how could that be possible?"

Morales said, "Again, forgive us, Ms. Cartwright, but we can't discuss that. But there'll be more evidence. There always is."

Morales rose, and Briggs followed suit. Cartwright slowly got to her feet, tears still sheening her eyes. "It's all so horrible. I always believed Archer—Arch, as I've always called him— and I were joined at the hip. I still can't get my mind around how he could have done this to me, to the firm, both him and his brother. And to that precious little boy, Tash. What will happen to him?"

"That's not for us to decide, ma'am," Morales said. "Is there anything else you'd like to tell us?"

"I suppose not. We're still scrambling here, endless calls from our clients and meetings with the regulators."

Morales said, "I'm pleased you finally called us, Ms. Cartwright. It means a lot. We'll make sure there's no need for you to be alarmed further about Rebel Navarro. Since he's wearing an ankle monitor, we can prove he went to your house. We'll make sure his lawyer knows we'll arrest him if he comes near you again."

Morales's cell buzzed a text. She pulled her cell from her jacket pocket, looked down at it, and smiled at Cartwright. "Our boss texted us that Rebel Navarro's lawyer has a recording Navarro made when he came to see you on Saturday, and he's sending it over to us."

Cartwright said slowly, "A recording? You said he made a recording when he was at my house?"

"That's right. You won't have to testify against him after all, Ms. Cartwright. All you said he did will be on the recording. Good day to you."

Cartwright heard Briggs say, "But why did Navarro's lawyer give us the recording when it damns him?"

Carla watched the two FBI agents leave. She stood in the middle of her office, unmoving, thinking through what this could mean. She didn't want to accept it, but she knew she had to, she had no choice. She had to act, and she had to act now.

Chapter Fifty-three

Locksley Manor, Autumn's cave
Titus Hitch Wilderness
TUESDAY MORNING

Autumn handed Tash half of her croissant, a bit flattened by the two apples in the bag, but who cared?

"It's still warm, kind of," Tash said, and took a big bite. "After that hike getting here to your cave, Autumn, I could eat it raw."

"Big eew!" She laughed, tapped him on the arm. A month, only four weeks, and he now looked as healthy as a stoat, her father had said that morning, and his endurance was improving by the day. She'd bet Tash would never let himself be bullied again. Autumn checked her watch. It was time for them to get down to business. She said slowly as Tash wiped his hands on his jeans, "I told you I spoke with Dillon—Agent Savich—last night. The fact is, Tash, Dillon told me even MAX, Dillon's magic database program, hasn't found your dad yet. He's in Barcelona, but where? I want us to put our heads together, that is, our minds. Let's try to find Sasha. If she's at home, maybe we can see exactly where she and your dad are living. Then I'll call Dillon. Okay now, think about her, Tash, and tell me about her."

"You saw how pretty she is. She can make her voice all

sweet, and she was always patting me, like she really liked me, but I knew she didn't mean it. When she and Dad got married, she treated me, you know, like I was a stray living with them. She gave my dad all her attention."

Autumn didn't hug him or console him, she gave him a purpose. "Finish your croissant and we'll give it a try. Do you have a photo of Sasha on your cell?" Autumn studied her. "You look at her again, then let's both try to see Sasha."

The two kids sat on the worn plaid wool blanket on the sandy cave floor and leaned back against the limestone wall. Autumn took Tash's hand, squeezed it. "We can do this, Tash, together. Now, picture her."

They both closed their eyes, concentrated, and a hazy white cleared slowly and there was Sasha sitting on a sofa, humming as she painted her toenails pink. Her thick blond hair was in a ponytail. Autumn was so excited they'd connected she wanted to shout, but she forced herself to say quietly, "Look how she's dressed, shorts and a thin top. Since they're in Barcelona, it's warm."

Tash said, "Look out the open windows, Autumn. See the backyard?"

"Yes, okay. Lots of flowers, roses mainly, and look, orange trees. I can almost smell the oranges."

Tash said, "I wish Dad was there with her, talking to her, but I don't see or hear anyone else. He's probably back at that crazy church. She's alone."

"Tash, look outside again. See the boy watering the flowers? He's wearing earbuds, and yes, see? He's talking to somebody on his cell."

"I can hear him, but I don't understand. He's not speaking English."

"Again, Barcelona. He's speaking Spanish, but I can't make out much since I've only had a year of Spanish so far in school.

Wait, did he say *festival*? It's gotta be the same word as festival." Autumn concentrated. She could make out the word for girlfriend—*novia*—and *La Sagrada Família*, the basilica in Barcelona where Tash had seen his dad. Then the boy stopped talking, made some kissing noises into his cell, punched off, and got back to work.

Autumn said, "The house looks small, Tash, and see the house next to it outside the window? It's got a red-tiled roof, looks like a little bungalow, and its yard is filled with more orange trees, roses, and bright red bougainvillea. You dad's house seems to fit right in with the neighborhood. He's being careful, staying away from the expensive places. Let's try to see the front of the house."

Tash said, "See the little kid on a bicycle? Wait, Autumn, there's my dad! He's walking toward the house. See? See?"

"Yes, he's wearing khaki pants and a short-sleeve white shirt and sneakers on his feet. He looks so much like Rebel, but he's thinner."

Archer Navarro was walking slowly, shuffling really, his head down, his shoulders slumped. He looked sad, not like a man who'd stolen a gazillion dollars.

"Tash, let's try something. Let's both really concentrate, see if we can actually connect to him."

"What? Do you really think we can actually talk to him? Not just see him? But how, Autumn?"

"In your mind, Tash. Say hello. Be calm and easy, you don't want to scare him to death if he hears you. It's like when you spoke to your mom. You can do it. We can do it together." She felt him squeeze her hand.

Dad? It's me, Tash.

They watched Archer Navarro walk into the house, unaware of them.

"Keep trying, Tash. Squeeze my hand."

He tried again, but Archer Navarro didn't hear him. He took a deep breath in, seemed to be smelling the oranges, and walked over toward Sasha.

"It's no good, Autumn. We can see him, but—" He looked like he wanted to burst into tears.

Autumn pulled him to her side. "It's okay, Tash. We saw him and he looks fine. I'll call Dillon."

Chapter Fifty-four

Adara Said and Khaled sat in the crowded restaurant eating scrambled eggs and muffins. She leaned close. "I love all the noise here, doesn't matter the time of day. No one can hear what anyone else is saying. We could talk about everything you and I did to each other on Saturday and no one would know." She ran her fingers up his thigh, laughed, took a bite of eggs. "Here's my advice to you. Don't recommend Rehan al-Albiri's grandson to your accountancy firm. He's a wanker. It wouldn't take long before everyone would want to kick you out."

Khaled laughed. "And how do I avoid it without making your brother the imam and Rehan al-Albiri want to kick me out?"

She shrugged. "Drop a hint in your boss's ear and let him take the blame."

"Yes, perhaps that would work. That's good." Khaled could tell John Eiserly what Adara had said and let him deal with it.

Adara took a big bite of her muffin, said when she'd swallowed, "I have news, Khaled. That witch Elizabeth Palmer—excuse me, *Lady* Elizabeth—the witch whose mother was nearly kidnapped on Saturday, has flown her broomstick right back into London when she heard about her poor dear mother,

God bless the old bitch. And she's not alone. She's got a body-guard with her, an American FBI agent named Roman Foxe."

Khaled's brain raced, but he forced himself to scoop up his last bite of scrambled eggs, then cocked his head at her. "She's a witch? Why do you dislike her so much? Has she done something to you? I read she's a fine artist."

"Hah. Any child can paint. It's only because she's a bleeding aristocrat that anyone even looks at her crap. Everyone knows she whored for Samir Basara, but no one seems to care."

"If you say so. Do you know her? You've seen her art?"

Adara shrugged. "I know what I know. She's a worthless upper-class leech, lords her lineage over everyone, like they all do. Here, have another muffin."

Khaled backed off. "When I had lunch with your brother. Strange you brought it up, but he spoke of the attempted kidnapping of Lord Camden's wife Friday night and about Lady Elizabeth's troubles as well. You must have had a very bad experience with Elizabeth Palmer for you to hate her so much."

She smiled, thoughtfully chewed on a limp piece of bacon. She said in an offhand voice, "No need for you to know about everything, Khaled. All in good time."

She looked down at her sports watch. "Finish your lunch. We have nearly an hour before you have to be back at your boring job. Let's spend it at your apartment. Maybe I'll share a secret with you."

Khaled clasped her hand in his. "I love secrets, Adara, particularly a woman's."

Chapter Fifty-five

Savich took a drink of his strong black breakfast tea and looked over at Sherlock. She was chewing on a piece of crunchy bacon while Astro yipped at her on his hind legs, his tail waving faster than a metronome. She broke off a piece and snuck it to him. "Sean, I know you saw me, but don't you give him any more. He's had enough and you know it's not good for him."

"My teacher said fried food isn't good for anyone."

Sherlock laid her hand over her heart. "Even fried ice cream?"

Sean looked horrified. "She couldn't have meant that, Mama."

Savich said, "Sean, I hear Gabriella, time for you to gather your stuff and head out to school."

Sean jumped out of his seat and leaned against his mother's belly. He kissed her, kissed his father, yelled out, "Come on, Astro!" and raced out of the kitchen.

They heard Gabriella greet him. "Good morning, my super-hero, and look, Mighty Dog. Ready to go, Sean? Astro and I have big plans after we drop you off." Gabriella stuck her head in the kitchen doorway. "Sherlock, Dillon, good morning!" and she was gone, talking to Sean again. "And when I pick you up from school, I want you to tell me where Kazakhstan is."

They were putting away the dishes, one of Savich's hands rubbing Sherlock's back, when his cell belted out Van Halen's "Hot for Teacher," one of Sherlock's favorites.

"Savich."

"Good morning, Savich, John Eiserly here. I promised Lord Camden I would call you without delay. Let me say he's livid over his wife's near abduction Saturday night, not to say what nearly happened to his daughter, and he demands we work together more closely to find whoever is behind all this, since you Yanks can't seem to do the job alone. Oh, yes, he wanted me to thank you, belatedly, for keeping his daughter safe."

Savich grinned into the phone. "Tell him we're profoundly grateful to have earned his thanks."

"Seriously, Savich, there's a new development. I've kept this from you thus far—a question of operational security—but I've had an undercover officer, Khaled Aziz, in place at the South London Mosque for some time now. He's managed to impress the new imam and met with his younger sister, Adara. In fact, they've been intimate. I want you to listen to the recording Khaled made of their conversation this morning."

Savich heard a young woman's voice.

"*I have news, Khaled. That witch Elizabeth Palmer—excuse me,* Lady *Elizabeth—the witch whose mother was nearly kidnapped on Saturday, flew her broomstick right back into London when she heard about her dear mother. God bless the old bitch. And she's not alone. She's got a bodyguard with her, an FBI agent named Roman Foxe.*"

Eiserly stopped the recording. "Not much else there, nothing actionable. But still, it's a great deal. How does she know so much about Elizabeth Palmer? And Roman Foxe? Where'd she get his name? She clearly hates Elizabeth." He paused, spit it out. "We believe Adara may have been involved in the attack on Lady Millicent, but we have no proof as of yet. Is her brother, the imam, involved?"

Savich said, "Which brings us back to the question of why. All to pressure your government to remove your sanctions from Syria? Think of the sheer complexity of pulling off the kidnapping of a peer's wife or daughter and forcing your government to remove the sanctions. All the moving parts would have to work together seamlessly, and it would depend on a number of people to do exactly as they're told and keep their mouths shut. And if the imam is part of it, is he taking his orders from Aboud?"

John sighed. "Or maybe, Savich, this all does have to do with revenge against Elizabeth and her family for Samir Basara, however tortured that motive might be."

Savich said, "My gut rejects revenge for Basara as a motive."

"I guess mine does too." John laughed. "I must say, it must have shocked Aboud to his heels when you arrived at his house and informed him your people shot down his helicopter and his two men with it."

"He tried to hide it, but he was stunned. And yes, I did enjoy delivering the news to him. However, we can't underestimate him, John. Did I tell you he covered his bases by reporting his helicopter stolen the night before?"

"I bet she's now glad he did."

Savich said, "John, I hope you're planning to bring Rome and Elizabeth in on this, for their own protection."

"Of course, I've arranged to speak with them this afternoon."

Savich dug into a particularly tight muscle in Sherlock's shoulder and she moaned with pleasure. John said, "Dare I inquire what you're doing, Savich?"

Savich laughed, said, "Didn't you rub Mary Ann's back when she was pregnant with Cici?"

"She wouldn't let me go to sleep until I did. Tonight I'll hear my perfect child's golden voice, telling me she's hungry, which means a fresh peach, which, thankfully, any adult hovering over her will provide without hesitation. Then she'll want me to read her *Peter Rabbit*. I'll keep you posted, Savich. Give my best to Sherlock, and my best advice? Do what you can to keep her happy."

"You can count on it." Savich punched off. He said to Sherlock, "You heard everything. Anything to add?"

Sherlock dropped her head so he could knead her neck. "You're always telling everyone in the unit to keep it simple and to remember Occam's Razor—horses, not zebras. So, forget all the serpentine possibilities—who has a nice clean motive? Ah, that feels wonderful."

Savich smiled at her. She was right, answers usually came down to straightforward motives, hidden maybe, but always there, behind the distractions. He started massaging her back again.

Sherlock groaned, whispered, "Keep that up and I'll be your slave."

"I like the sound of that. I'll think about what I want. John said Cici likes *Peter Rabbit*. Do you think Felicity will go for a smart bunny?"

"I did, and I'll bet you did too, but you mean Beau, don't you?"

"We'll see. I'll make you a deal—you make a lemon meringue pie for dessert tomorrow night and I'll play 'Hot for Teacher' and you can salsa. I'll follow it with another massage."

Chapter Fifty-six

Rome decided driving in London was an endurance contest, like driving in New York City, except on the wrong side of the road. Plus there were more tour buses flogging through the snarled traffic, their guides shouting out the stops and their histories on bullhorns. At least today Elizabeth was driving, and it seemed to Rome she enjoyed every honking horn, every near miss as pedestrians trotted out into the chaos. And the bicycles, in and out, between and around cars, like maniacs, never seemed to have a care in the world.

Elizabeth pointed out sights to him as she drove their rented Vauxhall Corsa through the morass and weaved her way expertly through side streets until they reached Eaton Square.

She swung behind a crescent of white houses and parked behind the last one. She led Roman around to the front and said, "Breathe in, Rome. I love this spot, with all the marvelous scents of the summer flowers across the street. And all the trees in the park mute the traffic noise. Even the air smells different here in this one quiet place. Let me show you my house." She paused, gave him a grin. "Yes, it does have a name—Palmer House. I fibbed because I didn't want you to smirk and get snarky."

He shook his head. "Why would I smirk? The U.S. has houses with names too, like Mount Vernon, Monticello, and the White House."

She stopped, smiled up at him. "When we go back, I'd like to see those places."

He said carefully, "You're considering coming back with me to the United States?"

She looked at him, but didn't answer. Rome wanted to grab her, make her tell him, but he let it drop. For the moment.

Palmer House felt more at ease with itself than Darlington Hall. Elizabeth gave him nuggets of its history as she led him through the rooms, the kitchen included. She called out all the faded glory—tatty arms on that chair, rugs so old she was afraid she'd put a hole through them.

Rome stood in the middle of the drawing room and soaked it in. The air fairly pulsed with history. Portraits of eighteenth-century women and men in their white wigs, wearing clothes that looked vastly uncomfortable, a great-great this and a great-great that, and there was the sixth Earl of Camden and would you look at those side whiskers, he could sweep the floor with them. It made him wonder what his great-greats had looked like.

When they stepped out of the dark and silent library and its three walls of built-in bookshelves stuffed with books, she said, "My father knows I love this house, but when he dies Tommy will become the eleventh Earl of Camden, and it will no longer be my house, unless Tommy allows it. He'll also inherit Darlington Hall, its grounds, and whatever income it brings."

"But if Tommy falls off the drug wagon and your father doesn't bring him back into the fold, won't you inherit everything, including Darlington Hall?"

"Nope, that's not how it works in England. It's called primogeniture. The eldest son or male relative usually gets everything and any child unfortunate enough to be female gets only what he allows her. Don't scoff, there's a pretty good reason for it. It's meant to keep property in one family until there are no more sons or male relatives. If my father doesn't reinstate Tommy, he'll still inherit all the entailed property—Darlington Hall and Palmer House—but unless my father changes his mind, he won't get my father's bank or his investments. It would probably come to me. I could, however, sign over a lot of it to Tommy, but I'd have to break my father's will to do it."

"But Tommy would still be the new earl and live in luxury at Darlington Hall?"

She shook her head. "Consider the amount of money it requires for the upkeep and maintenance of Darlington Hall. It's a constant drain. There's always something breaking down, and the repairs are daunting. And paying staff and tradesmen? Another huge ongoing expense. Tommy would have to sell the paintings and furnishings, fire people who've been with the family for decades." She paused a moment. "Well, maybe he could try to find an heiress, but they're not thick on the ground." She drew a breath. "I pray with all my heart he's really changed this time and my father reinstates him, takes him in at the bank, trains him so he could eventually take it over." She sighed. "As for me, I have no worries. My financial future is secure in either case because I can support myself quite nicely, and I don't need all that money. The amount of money we're talking here? Rome, it's more than I could spend in three lifetimes. I know I've been putting off going to see Tommy. I'm so afraid I'll know he's lying to Mother."

Rome said matter-of-factly, "If he isn't lying, he's one of the precious few."

Elizabeth drew herself up. "That's what I have to believe—he's one of the precious few."

She took him upstairs, passed by three closed doors, and stopped in front of the last, slowly opening the door. "My workroom."

Rome walked into a large square room and felt the instant warmth of the bright sunlight that poured in through its floor-to-ceiling windows. It felt like a peaceful sanctuary, a place to feel nourished and safe and creative. A dozen paintings leaned against the pale yellow walls, covered with white cloths. Elizabeth stood silently in the center of the room, watching him. He nodded toward one. "Show me?"

She said nothing, removed the cloth, stepped back.

He knew her paintings were displayed in a gallery in Belgravia, knew she painted what she called neo-impressionism. He supposed he'd expected a blurry scene of boats on a lake or people in a park. What he saw was a drowsy meadow filled with yellow wildflowers, a single chestnut horse grazing, ancient oak trees crowding in around it, all under a cloud-strewn sky. The colors were soft and blurred just the right amount to emphasize the beauty, the wonder. He wanted to step into the painting and lie down amid the flowers, stare up at the sky and dream the afternoon away. He turned slowly and stared at her. "Show me more."

She pulled the white covers from more nature scenes, each of them evocative, drawing you in. Then she uncovered her portraits, again softly blurred, and yet so real you wanted to meet the old man picking a cucumber from a village market stand, or laugh with the young boy splashing in the village pond, chasing ducks.

She drew a deep breath and pulled the soft cloth from the painting on her easel.

Rome stared at a starkly sharp painting of a laughing young woman, her blond hair loose and long, dancing in an unseen breeze, wildly happy. It was Elizabeth's mother.

He stared at what she'd captured in her mother's face. "You can feel her nearly bursting with joy. You want to know her. Her happiness flows over you. It's incredible, Elizabeth."

Elizabeth said quickly, "It's not quite finished; the background needs more work." She paused, added, "I'm going to give it to my father on his birthday so perhaps he'll remember all the feelings he had for my mother then, and stop—" Her voice fell off a cliff.

"His philandering?"

"A very civilized way to say it. It's something I could never understand. My mother is loving and beautiful." She paused, frowned. "But you know, he was different with her yesterday, maybe because he nearly lost her. He sat close to her with his arm around her, careful of her, loving."

Rome said, "I like your mom. I saw you in her twenty-five years from now. I agree with you, your father was clearly afraid for her, focused on protecting her."

Elizabeth nodded. "It was like he didn't want to let her out of his sight, Rome. He—he touched her hair." She covered the painting again, turned on her heel, and walked to the door. "Come," she said over her shoulder, and gently closed the door behind them.

She showed him the master suite last, a mix of antiques from Italy and France covered with ancient crocheted throws, and a touch of the modern, a TV on a dresser table facing the big sleigh bed.

"This is where you were attacked?"

He could see she didn't want to remember that night, much less talk out loud about what happened there. He took her arms in his hands, stared down at her a moment. "Your grandfather thought Roosevelt was valiant. I think you are too, Elizabeth."

"*What?*"

"You heard me. You survived three attacks here in London through your own wits. You found Hurley and stuck with him, made yourself into a force. When you and I were attacked, you fought them with me. And now you've shown me another part of you—your art, and you've made me see you differently once again."

He cupped her face in his hands, leaned down, not very far at all, and kissed her, only a light touch of his mouth. He straightened, sifted his fingers through her hair. "You've made me see how very fine my life could be with you in it."

She swallowed, breathed in his scent, male and soap and a girlie shampoo. For the first time, she saw herself through his eyes. He knew her now, and he thought she was valiant? She said, "But I slept with Samir Basara, an assassin, believed in by jihadists willing to do whatever he told them to do. And why? The truth is I found him fascinating, and like I told you, perhaps just as important, I wanted to stick my father's nose in it because I was so angry at how he was treating my mother. Samir was Algerian, a Muslim, anathema to my father as my lover. But for John Eiserly, I along with hundreds more would have died in St. Paul's last year. Basara knew he was sentencing me to death and he didn't care. He felt as much contempt for me as my father did for him.

"I was careless, Rome, shallow, selfish." She gave him a crooked smile. "I'm not valiant. Rome, I'm not special at all."

He cocked his head at her. "Well, okay, if you insist, but I have to tell you, I think you're an excellent artist."

She sputtered and punched her fist into his belly. "That's all you have to say after I spilled my innards to you?"

He wasn't ready and it hurt. He tried to grab her arms, but Hurley had taught her well. She hooked her foot behind his calf, jerked him off balance, and sent him on his back on the ancient threadbare carpet. He grinned up at her, brought his own leg up, and tapped her behind her knee. She flew forward, and he grabbed her arms when she landed on top of him. He flipped her onto her back, grinned down at her. "Don't try to outsmart the master. You wanted me to agree with you that you acted like a selfish twit? Well, maybe, but that was then and now you're someone else, the person you were always meant to be."

"What does that mean? Let me go, you idiot!"

Time slowed. He looked down at her face. "I mean the person I want to be with for the rest of my life."

She licked her lips, gave him a mad grin. "Well, then. That's better."

Chapter Fifty-seven

Tommy's flat
Carberry Street, near the Thames, London
TUESDAY

Rome found a parking space a half block away from the Corinthian. He looked around as he closed Elizabeth's door. "Some neighborhood. Your mother told you your brother lives in that building? It looks like it belongs on Park Avenue in New York. Elizabeth, stop worrying. You know your brother. You'll know the truth about whether he's still using, maybe even before I will."

Elizabeth felt hopeful and frightened at the same time. They walked past an old gentleman dressed in dark blue and gold who doffed his hat and bowed Elizabeth into an exquisite art deco lobby, all geometric shapes and clean symmetrical lines, except for two large palm trees sitting healthy and proud in art deco square pots. The doorman pointed them to an ancient elevator that clanged them to the sixth floor. They walked down the wide carpeted hallway to the end flat, with a glossy black door and a lion-head knocker.

Elizabeth's heart was pounding as she pressed the bell beside the knocker.

They heard faint voices, then a man's heavy step. The door opened and there stood a fit-looking stranger about her own age, dark skinned, dark eyed, clean shaven. He wore a slouchy gray sweatshirt, black jeans, and high-top sneakers on long narrow feet.

He stared at her a moment, and at Rome, turned his head back into the flat, and said, "I'm late, Tommy, I've got to go. You've got visitors." He turned back to them and said, "Sorry, I was just leaving," squeezed around them, and hurried down the hallway to the elevator.

Tommy came into the entryway. He gave a start, stared, and smiled. "Elizabeth? Is it really you? I hoped you'd come. It's so good to see you." He held out his arms and Elizabeth ran to him, pulled him close and kissed his face, mussed his beautifully cut hair.

"Oh, Tommy, it's so lovely to see you too." She pulled back from him. "And look at you. Goodness, you're the image of Father. All big and handsome." She hugged him again.

Tommy closed his eyes a moment, seemed to breathe her in. He looked up at Rome, cocked his head. "You're the Yank guarding my sister?"

"Yes, that's right," Rome said.

Elizabeth introduced them. "Rome's a special agent with the American FBI. And yes, I suppose he's something like my bodyguard."

Tommy didn't let her go, merely stuck out a hand and shook Rome's. "It's great to meet you. You have my thanks, forever. Imagine, the FBI. Come in, come in."

Elizabeth and Rome followed Tommy down a short hallway paved with lovely parquet into a long, narrow living room with large windows framing the Thames and the London Eye, an exquisite, dramatic view. Boats of all sizes plied the water, from barges to a boat filled with tourists.

Tommy grinned, waved his arms around. "My flat's something, isn't it? Mother picked it out, moved me in. When she visits she loves to sit by the window while we talk, look out over the Thames, and people-watch, I believe you say in the States. Please, sit down."

Tommy Palmer was beautifully dressed in a pale green cashmere sweater and pressed chinos, black alligator shoes on his feet. He looked clean, healthy, his color good, though he was on the thin side. He and Elizabeth shared the same vibrant blue eyes, slightly uptilted like their mother's, but Rome was struck more by how much he resembled his father when he smiled. Before Elizabeth could sit down on his burgundy leather sofa, her brother pulled her close again, squeezed her until she squeaked.

Elizabeth, Rome thought, looked thrilled. She leaned back in the circle of his arms. "You look amazing, Tommy, just perfect."

He kissed the tip of her nose, made her laugh.

Rome said, "We met a man at the front door who nearly ran past us."

Tommy said, "That was a friend of mine, Alberto Albi, goes by Al. His parents are from Marsala, Sicily. He spent his childhood there, claims he still misses baking in the hot Sicilian sun."

A drug dealer? Rome asked, "How did you meet him?"

Tommy sat forward in his chair, clasped his hands between his knees. "Happenstance, really. About a month ago I'd just finished my daily long walk and stood outside the Grenadier, a pub in Wilton Mews, and decided it wasn't too early for a Guinness. Al was at the bar drinking a pint and we got to talking. I ended up telling him I was a recovering addict. He listened, then told me straight up he understood because he'd been through recovery too, and from that beginning we became friends." He shot a look at Rome. "He dresses like an oddball, doesn't he? Actually, Al's a successful game developer. I'm not surprised he had to run. Al's always late. He had a meeting with one of his people."

He suddenly frowned. "How is Mother? Since I'm not welcome at Darlington Hall, I've only been able to speak with her on the phone. I haven't seen her since Saturday night. She's been too shaken up to drive back to London, and I doubt too Father would even consider letting her."

Elizabeth said, "She's still a bit shaken, but all in all, she's pulled through in her usual style. Tommy, the distress alarm you bought for her is what saved her, and believe me, she's reminded Father of that more times than I can count."

Tommy breathed a sigh of relief. "We were lucky with that alarm. I was worried for her after what nearly happened to you, Elizabeth."

She studied him. "Tommy, I see how healthy you are, how focused. Believe me, I didn't know what to expect, but seeing you now—I really believe Father may be close to accepting you've changed for good. Be patient, Tommy. He needs more time. All will work out, you need only continue as you have been."

Tommy shook his head, smiled. "There's little else I can do. Let me get some tea, or something stronger, Agent Foxe?"

"Call me Rome. Tea would be very nice."

He rose. "I'll be right back. I've already made some." They heard him whistling in the kitchen. He was soon back carrying a tray with a pot and teacups, cream and sugar on the side, and a covered plate. "You should try my favorite biscuits, chocolate, of course. They're from the bakery down the street. I'm trying to fatten myself up, not much more to go, maybe a stone."

Tommy passed around the tea and said around a mouthful of biscuit, "Tell me what's been happening in the States, Elizabeth. You left so suddenly, without telling me where you went. I understood, though it was a shock."

"I'm sorry, Tommy. Father thought it was for the best. And I did too, it kept you safe."

"Mother did tell me now about your three-month stay with that defense trainer, Hurley what's his name."

She laughed. "Just remember Hurley."

"I called Mr. Eiserly. He told me you went to Washington and hooked up with the FBI." He paused, shook his head. "I was scared spitless when he told me they found you there and attacked you with a helicopter of all things? Mother and I have talked of little else recently. Has the FBI made any progress, Rome? Mr. Eiserly said there were several possibilities but he wouldn't discuss them with me."

Rome sipped his tea. "Yes, there are several leads we're following about the attacks on your sister. The truth will come out, it usually does. Tommy, your sister has survived so far because she's tough as nails. She insisted on coming back immediately after we heard about the attempt on your mother."

Tommy took her hand, squeezed it. "I wish the authorities would hurry up and figure all this out, Elizabeth. You might still be in danger. I'm so glad you came back. I hope you'll stay home now."

She looked at his strained face. "We'll see." She changed course. "I took Rome to see Palmer House. But this view, Tommy—maybe we could trade places. I'll bet your toilet never plugs up."

Tommy laughed. "When Mother brought me to see this flat for the first time, she told me she'd fallen in love, not with the toilet, but with the view."

"Tommy, believe me when I say you really do look marvelous, and yes, another stone will suit you fine. You simply radiate health and, well, contentment. I promise I'll join Mother's chorus getting Father to reinstate you."

Tommy said, "That really means something since you've seen me at my worst. So thank you, Elizabeth. It means a lot to hear you say it."

Rome set down his teacup and leaned forward, his hands on his knees. "Why did you stop using, Tommy?"

Elizabeth nearly came to his defense, as she usually did for her brother from their earliest years, but she stayed silent.

"The truth? I looked in the mirror one morning, only half out of my mind on cocaine, for a change, and nearly threw up at what I saw. It was a moment of clarity, I guess you could call it. I looked at myself and saw my own death. I called Carlos and told him I was going clean and not to call me. Actually, I begged him not to call me. My mantra from that day on was to survive one day at a time. It took me nearly a month before I felt human."

Rome said, "I know how tough it is to stop cold turkey. It's amazing, really. What are your plans?"

Tommy paused, sighed. "I'm hoping Father contacts me, but I don't blame him for waiting to see. I would do the same if I were he. In the meantime, I'm building myself up, had my first workout with a personal trainer Al found for me. I walk everywhere and think about what I might do if Father doesn't accept I've changed for good. And I'm reading textbooks on economics and banking." He waved toward the pile of books on the coffee table. "So if and when he gives me another chance, I won't be completely ignorant. I do know how many times I've lied to you, Elizabeth, lied to everyone, lied to myself." He laughed. "I saw Carlos last week and he almost didn't recognize me. He didn't even ask me if I wanted coke. He gave me a slap on the shoulder and said, 'Good luck, mate.'"

"That's wonderful, Tommy."

"Enough about me. Tell me about your three months with this Hurley fellow."

Elizabeth did as he asked, answered all his questions about her life with Hurley, told him about the Roosevelt memorial, reminded him how their grandfather had worked with Churchill and met Roosevelt. She told him most everything except for her feelings for Rome. He asked so many questions that finally she threw up her hand. "That's more than enough. I hate to leave you, dearest, but Rome and I have an appointment to see Mr. Eiserly, so we need to go. I'll be back to see you soon." She hugged him close, kissed his cheek. "I'm so proud of you. I can't wait for all of us to sit down together to a magnificent feast at Darlington Hall."

Instead of riding the elevator, they walked the stairs to the ornate lobby, with its wide symmetrical windows. Elizabeth said, "I'm pleased Tommy has a friend. I wish we could have met him, maybe seen Tommy through his eyes, asked him questions about his own recovery." She eyed him. "You haven't said much. It's all right, I know it'll take time for you to come around to trusting my brother. But I'm quite certain he's clean, and he's been clean for what, three months."

Rome said nothing, merely took her arm as they walked into the bright sunlight. They heard the echoes of motorboats and voices from the tourist boats. When they reached the car, Elizabeth gave him a grin. "You need more practice. Just remember the center line is your friend. And if you see my lips moving, that will be praying."

Chapter Fifty-eight

"Ah, Rome?" Elizabeth nearly grabbed the steering wheel when the Vauxhall came a hair width away from smashing a cab's side mirror.

Rome wasn't about to admit it was way too close, no self-respecting man would. He laughed. "Don't have a stroke, you're in safe hands. I think I've got this driving on the left down, except maybe at the intersections."

"Okay, if you say so. Do you know Benbett taught me to drive?"

"The butler taught you to drive?"

"Benbett was a fan of the race car circuit when he was young. He was an amazing teacher. He taught Tommy too."

"My mom taught me. She was a wild woman, still is." With the windows down, the traffic noise was awesome. He said, "Only Manhattan beats this traffic. Much of the time it's faster to walk than take a taxi. Few drive their own cars. But here— didn't you tell me you have to pay to drive in central London? Can't say it seems to have kept anybody away."

"That was the hope way back when, but the government always needs more money, so any excuse will do. But it makes you wonder what it would be like in London if it didn't cost so much to drive here. We're nearly there. See the white building on the corner of Parliament Street? That's the Red Lion Pub. It's the second-oldest pub in London, here for over three hundred years." She gave him a sideways grin. "Older than the United States."

He grinned. "And what's the oldest?"

"Thought you'd fool me, but I've got a brain for trivia—the Seven Stars in Holborn, opened sometime in the seventeenth century. There's a parking garage straight ahead, right down the block."

When they walked out of the garage onto the street again, the sun had disappeared in a darkening sky. Rome knew that meant it would rain any second. "How can the weather change so quickly? We were ready to sunbathe ten minutes ago."

She laughed. "Welcome to England, Rome."

Given its age, Rome expected the Red Lion Pub would be a dark, low-ceilinged room with ancient age-scarred beams smelling of decades of ale, but instead another preconception bit the dust. He walked into a light, airy room with high ornate ceilings and only a discreet smell of Guinness, a light perfume in the air. Elizabeth waved to a man standing beneath a graceful chandelier beside a table for four along the wall.

"There he is, John Eiserly, the deputy director of JTAC. Believe me, he already knows who you are. We'll finally find out why he called us in. I hope he has some news."

To Rome, Eiserly looked very English indeed. He was in his mid-thirties, fair, slender and dapper in his muted dark blue suit and white shirt. They shook hands.

"I've looked forward to meeting you, Agent Foxe. Please be seated. Elizabeth, you're looking well." He drew up, blinked. "And you look like you could take down any malcontent to come after you."

"Thank you. I certainly hope so."

As soon as they sat, a cheese plate and tea appeared. And a fourth plate and cup. Rome would have preferred coffee, black and strong, but after adding some lemon, it was quite good.

John said, "How is your mother coping?"

"She seems all right, given the shock and terror of it all. It will take time."

John raised his cup. "Indeed, a trying experience for her. Agent Foxe, thank you for protecting Elizabeth. Savich told me you saved her life."

Rome said easily, "Actually, Elizabeth helped save herself. She knows how to do that now, sir, as you already know."

"I do want to hear more about your three months with Hurley Janklov."

Elizabeth was tempted to show him her biceps to admire, but the waiter staring at her, for whatever reason, wouldn't understand. "Please tell us you have news, John, news you wanted to deliver in person?"

"Indeed, I do. Ah, here he comes." John gave a wave to a swarthy man about Rome's age striding tall and straight as a sapling toward them. He was tall, good looking, and clean shaven, his black hair forming a near widow's peak, his nose a sharp blade. He dressed like an upper-level businessman.

John said, "I decided we should all meet here rather than at Thames Hall on the off chance someone from the mosque might see Khaled. Elizabeth, Rome, meet a very brave man, our undercover officer at the South London Mosque, Khaled Aziz."

Rome rose, shook his hand. "It's a pleasure, Mr. Aziz."

Elizabeth cocked her head. "Mr. Aziz." There was a clear question in her voice. He offered his hand and she shook it.

John looked around and lowered his voice, though conversation in the pub was at crowd level. "Of course you're wondering what Khaled has to do with your situation. As I said, he's been undercover at the South London Mosque for the past six months working to gain the trust of the new imam, Ali Ahmad Said, and more recently, the trust of his younger sister, Adara Said. I will let Khaled tell you why I brought you here, what it is Adara said to him at lunch today." He nodded to Khaled.

Khaled said, "I suppose I should tell you first off that Adara Said and I have gotten very close quite quickly. I can do better than tell you." Khaled pulled a small recorder from his pocket and pressed play.

They heard a young woman say with great excitement, *I have news, Khaled. That witch Elizabeth Palmer—excuse me, Lady Elizabeth—the witch whose mother was nearly kidnapped on Saturday, flew her broomstick right back into London when she heard about her dear mother. God bless the old bitch. And she's not alone. She's got a bodyguard with her, an FBI agent named Roman Foxe.*

Khaled stopped the recording when a waiter passed by and slipped the recorder back in his pocket. "That's the essence of it. Adara wasn't any more specific, didn't tell me why she hates you or how she knows you are here with Agent Foxe. But I think we'll know very soon now, and I think it's likely she and the men she calls her comrades might be responsible for the attacks on you and on your mother. I fear she may be planning to kill you."

Elizabeth was shaking her head back and forth. "But why? I don't even know this woman. Why does she hate me so much? It makes no sense."

Rome took Elizabeth's fisted hand in his and lightly stroked her fingers. "Khaled, you have no idea why they're doing this? Why they want her dead?"

"No. I know I can't push. But soon I believe she'll tell me. We don't know yet if her brother, the imam, is involved. Mr. Eiserly has photos of Adara for you. Study them, and be careful. I'll contact John again when I learn more. Now I must go."

Khaled dabbed his napkin on his mouth and rose. "A pleasure to meet you both. Please stay safe, Lady Elizabeth." He strode toward the café door, his umbrella already unfurled when he reached it.

There was silence at the table. John finished off his tea, set his cup neatly in its saucer, and rose. "And I am expected back at Thames Hall. A pity, I'd have enjoyed a pint and hearing stories about this Hurley Janklov, Elizabeth." He reached into his pocket, pulled out a thumb drive, and gave it to her. "This is everything we know about Adara Said and her known associates. We've made great strides in determining why you and your mother were targeted. Be patient, it's coming together. Special Agent Foxe, it was a pleasure to meet you. Keep our girl safe."

He nodded to them and left. Like Khaled, his umbrella was ready for the elements before he reached the door.

Elizabeth stared at the tea leaves at the bottom of the cup. She touched Rome's arm. "Please don't tell Mother anything about this yet, all right? She'd lock me in my room and bar the windows." She frowned. "Adara Said. I'd never considered a woman would be involved." She gave Rome a twisted smile. "If I'm a witch, I would wish for a magic wand to send Adara Said and her compatriots, whoever they are, to a gulag in Siberia."

Chapter Fifty-nine

That afternoon, Archer nearly fell over with shock when his fat, hard-nosed landlady, Señora Capilli, knocked on his front door and handed him her cell phone, told him he had a call. It was Rebel and an FBI agent, Dillon Savich, and they told him they knew where he was and were going to bring him home. How had they found him? Rebel said it was Autumn and Tash, then Rebel had spoken with Agent Savich, and he'd explain it all when Archer was home again. They believed he was innocent, and they would help him prove it. Rebel told him how he'd been arrested and how everything had started to unravel when Carla Cartwright had lied to the FBI about him. They'd called her in for questioning. Soon now, soon, and he'd be free and clear. And the biggest news? Two agents were already on their way to pick him and Sasha up in Barcelona, and they would be arriving first thing in the morning.

After Archer had returned Mrs. Capilli's cell phone, he yelled Sasha's name, grabbed her up, and whirled her around in his arms. "That was Rebel. They know I'm innocent! We're going home tomorrow morning, early!"

He didn't get the reaction he'd expected. Sasha didn't believe this FBI agent, not for a minute; it was a lie to get him back and throw him in prison, and they'd talked his brother into helping them. They argued for hours, but Archer refused to budge. He knew there were no guarantees, but it didn't matter. He wanted to go back, no matter the possible bad consequences. He told her about Carla being brought in to be interviewed by the FBI. Still, Sasha had argued.

He reminded her she'd said she wanted to go back with him, they'd face everything together, but she insisted they were lying to him and now she didn't want to go, not until he was sure.

Archer had to believe Sasha would come around. She had before, she would again. He'd even tried to explain he wanted desperately to see Tash again, to hug him tight, breathe in his kid smell, promise him he'd never leave him again, but still, no go.

Now it was late, middle-of-the-night late, and Archer, unable to sleep, began to pack. As he was folding a shirt to put into his suitcase on the bed, he wondered what exactly Rebel had meant about Tash and Autumn helping find him in Barcelona, but of course he already had a good idea what Rebel meant, he'd known for some time what Tash could do. And Autumn too? When he saw Tash he would tell him he should have believed him from the start. He was sorry, but he'd listen now. Tash could tell him everything.

Archer looked down at his watch, shook his head at himself, still disbelieving he was wide awake and packing in the freaking middle of the night. He was nearly all packed and ready to go, Sasha too, after angrily throwing her clothes into her suitcases. She hadn't slept either, her angry breathing in his ear. He heard the shower turn on, pictured Sasha stepping into the narrow stall, pictured her lathering her beautiful body, something he always enjoyed doing himself. He had to believe she'd be happy with his decision once they were home again and he was cleared. They could begin their lives again.

He looked down at Sasha's four suitcases, three of them

closed and bulging because she'd been too upset to fold her clothes neatly. The last one, a carry-on that held her cosmetics, was still open, and he wondered yet again how she'd been so willing to go home with him in a few days, just a few more days, yet now, when everything looked positive, she no longer wanted to go. It made no sense.

He looked around their bedroom, saw nothing else to pack. He heard the faint sound of a cell phone buzzing. A text? It wasn't his cell phone; his burner was in his coat pocket. It wasn't Sasha's burner phone either; he saw it on the dresser getting a final charge. The sound seemed to have come from one of Sasha's suitcases on the floor at the foot of the bed. He pulled it up on the bed and opened it, carefully lifted away the beautiful lingerie he'd bought her in Paris. Wrapped in two bras at the bottom of the suitcase was a cell phone. He stared at it, baffled. Why would Sasha have another burner cell phone? Why was it hidden? Why didn't he know about it? He picked it up, looked down at a text: *Archer's suicide not an option now. Meet you in Marrakesh. GO.*

Archer stared numbly at those few words. At first he didn't understand. Then he saw the text was from Carla, and in an instant he knew what the words meant, understood everything, and his world fell apart. Sasha had been planning to—what? Poison him? And make it look like he'd killed himself because of what he'd done, because he was guilty? He couldn't breathe until his pain flipped to rage at her betrayal, and rage at himself for being so stupid. His hands trembling, Archer scrolled through a dozen more texts going back to the middle of June, when they'd first arrived in Paris, all of them from Carla, upbeat and smug, encouraging Sasha to keep him happy and hidden until it was time. The two most recent texts read: *Miscalculated, called in by the FBI, but will figure it out.* And just that morning: *May have to move up timeline, keep you posted.*

He looked down at his wedding ring. *Celia, I've been a great fool.*

Archer heard her say from behind him, "Well, this changes things."

He started to turn when something struck the back of his head and he was down.

Chapter Sixty

Barcelona

Sherlock looked down at her phone, saw the location she'd pin-dropped was just ahead. She pressed the button to roll down her window and leaned out to feel the warm night air on her face. She said, "There's the bungalow on the right, Ruth, just as Autumn and Tash described it."

Ruth cut her lights and turned off the Corsa's engine in front of a small, pale yellow house with a red-tiled roof and a small garden filled with flowers and orange trees. "They've left a light on," Ruth said. "Guess they couldn't sleep. They're probably already packed, waiting with their luggage by the door. I'm glad we're earlier than we thought. I'd just as soon be on our way to the airport before the traffic gets nasty."

They walked quietly to the front door and knocked. No answer. Sherlock called out, "Mr. Navarro?" and knocked again. She looked at Ruth, put her finger to her lips. "Something's wrong." Sherlock pulled out a credit card, went down on her knees, and slipped it between the door and the doorframe. The lock clicked open as she'd hoped.

They stepped quietly into a small, dimly lit living room, saw a low-wattage light coming from the bedroom. They didn't hear any voices, but they heard someone moving about.

What was going on? What had happened here? Sherlock had no intention of rushing in. She eased around the bedroom door and looked into the bedroom. Archer Navarro was lying on the floor between the bed and the window, unconscious, his wrists and ankles wrapped with duct tape. And there was Sasha, ready to climb out a window with a carry-on bag in her hand.

Sherlock said, "Going somewhere, Sasha?"

Sasha was fast. She leaped back, ran to Archer, grabbed a steak knife she'd left beside him, and stuck the tip against his neck.

Both Ruth and Sherlock had their Glocks at the ready.

"Even if you shoot me, I can still stick this knife in his neck. Are you two the FBI agents? Two women? And one of you pregnant? What are you doing here in the middle of the night? You're not supposed to be here until the morning."

And like Archer, Ruth and Sherlock understood. Sherlock said, "I'm Agent Sherlock and this is Agent Noble, and we're here to take you and your husband back to Philadelphia, and yes, we're women, and yes, I'm pregnant. So what? As it turned out, our boss, Mr. Maitland, arranged for a ride for us on a CIA G5, and unexpected tailwinds got us here a lot sooner than we'd planned."

Ruth said, "Looks like you don't want to come back with us, Sasha. At least you didn't kill him." She cocked a brow. "Wherever did you find duct tape in Barcelona?"

"Shut up! Now, I'm going to leave and you two aren't going to stop me. Do you hear me? You try, and I swear I'll shove this steak knife into his neck."

Sherlock realized Sasha Navarro was panicked. She had to calm her to keep her from doing something crazy, like murder her husband. "Sasha, listen to me. I know you're afraid, you're feeling things have spiraled out of control, but listen to me, we can work this out. First you have to get that knife away from

Archer's neck. You don't want to hurt him. Come, let's talk this over."

Sasha screamed, "I wouldn't believe a word out of your mouth! Now, you two bitches will listen to me. Throw your guns on the bed. Toward me, now! Or I'll skewer him!"

So much for calm and reason. Sherlock saw Sasha's hand was shaking. Not good. Did she really think she could still run? Maybe they should let her run it if meant saving Archer Navarro's life.

Ruth said, "We can't do that, Sasha. If we give up our weapons we'll be drummed out of the FBI. Didn't you know that?"

"Wh-what? That's ridiculous! Stay back, do you hear me?"

They saw a drop of blood on the knife tip and held perfectly still.

Sasha's voice was low now, scary low. "Move back to the wall—slowly, and sit on the floor, next to the dresser. Lay your precious guns beside you."

Ruth and Sherlock eased down on the faded green carpet, leaned back against the wall, and set their Glocks down close enough to be within grabbing distance.

Sherlock studied the young woman in her tight jeans and white shirt, boots on her feet. Her hair was still wet, pulled back in a ponytail, her face clear of makeup. She was scared, nearly out of control, didn't know what to do, and the really bad thing was she was an amateur, and that made her all the more unpredictable and dangerous.

Sasha said, her voice petulant, like a child's, "You weren't supposed to be here for hours."

Sherlock said, "As I said, our plane got us here much earlier. You were trying to escape, Sasha, not kill your husband."

"No! I wouldn't have—I really was going to leave! You saw me, nearly out the window. There was no point in killing him."

Ruth said, "And then what? Meet Carla Cartwright on a

lovely island with all that embezzled money and spend the day on the beach?"

"I told you to shut up. You don't know anything. I'm not going to let you ruin things now, no, not now."

Archer Navarro groaned.

Sasha looked down at him, and Ruth grabbed for her Glock. Sasha screamed, "Stop, or he's dead! Push that gun away from you." She dug in the knife, and more blood welled. "Why did you have to wake up, Archer?"

Archer groaned again and raised his head, his eyes dulled with pain. He looked up at Sasha, then over at Ruth and Sherlock, met Sherlock's eyes. She saw grief in his, and immense anger. He whispered to them, "I'm sorry."

Sasha shoved the knife harder against his neck. "Be quiet, Archer. I'm so tired of listening to you talk, talk, talk." She looked from him to the agents and back again. "Now you're going to help me get out of this."

Archer jerked and pulled on the duct tape, but it didn't give. He craned his neck to look up at her. "At least you didn't kill me before Carla texted you not to. It was too late, wasn't it, too late to feed me poison because no one would believe you now, what with Carla in trouble and the FBI coming. That was your plan, wasn't it, Sasha? Easy and bloodless."

Sherlock said, "That sounds right. What were you going to feed him, Sasha? Oxycodone? Fentanyl? And you'd tell the police your poor husband had been so depressed, he couldn't stand the humiliation and the guilt. Quite a plan, but it's over now. Come on, put down the knife. You can tell us all about Carla, about how she sucked you into this, and tell us how to get the money back. I'm sure the prosecutor will make a deal with you if you tell us."

Archer craned his neck to look up at Sasha again. "You and Carla planned this for a long time, didn't you, Sasha? Whose idea was it?"

"Why don't you just keep guessing?"

Ruth said, "Of course it had to be you, Sasha, to access Mr. Navarro's passcodes, give them to Carla to empty the accounts."

Archer said in a surprisingly emotionless voice, "This is all on me. I trusted you, Sasha. You never asked me about the codes and I never used them around you. So, what did you do? Drug me? Hide a video camera in my office? And Carla broke the encryption on my flash drive? I know she could, she's that good."

Sasha gave him a full-bodied sneer. "It wasn't difficult, Archer. It would have been over by now if not for your blasted brother. But I can still get out of here." Sasha threw the roll of duct tape over to Ruth. "You will duct-tape the pregnant one's hands and ankles."

Ruth said, "But once I get her all trussed up, how can she duct-tape me?"

"I'll tell you what to do after that. Do it now!"

Archer heard her voice shaking. He said slowly, "I thought it was Carla, even though we'd built the company together. But not you, Sasha, I never would have suspected you. I guess there's no bigger mark than a grieving man, especially for a beautiful young woman who pretends to adore him."

"This wasn't about you, Archer. You were only a tool. And by the by, you were really quite tolerable, for the most part."

Archer looked over at Ruth taping Sherlock's ankles, saw her pull a small gun from Sherlock's ankle holster. But how to get it into Sherlock's hand? Archer jerked his neck away from the knife, shoved his feet against the bed, and slammed his shoulder against Sasha.

"No!" Sasha jumped back. She looked mad, out of control. She raised the knife over Archer's chest. Ruth grabbed her Glock and fired, a clean shot in Sasha's right arm. Sasha screamed and the knife went flying. Sherlock grabbed the knife and sawed through the duct tape while Ruth bent over Sasha. "Listen to me, little girl, press your hand as hard as you can against the wound. Come on, do it, or you'll bleed to death. Don't you dare cry, press!"

But Sasha was rocking back and forth, crying. Now free, Sherlock grabbed one of Sasha's tops and wrapped it tight around Sasha's arm and pressed Sasha's hand to the cloth. "Get yourself together. Press and keep pressing, hard. We'll get you help."

Ruth cut the duct tape from Archer's ankles and wrists with Sasha's knife and helped him to his feet. He rubbed feeling back into his hands, stomped his feet. He didn't look down at his wife, but at Ruth and Sherlock. "Thank you both."

He turned finally to look at his wife, still crying, tears seeping beneath her closed eyes, pressing the pink shirt he'd bought for her in Paris to her arm. He picked up the knife she'd stuck against his neck, looked at his blood on the tip, tossed it on the bed. He looked down at her again, said in a dispassionate voice, "I loved you, and I believed in my heart you loved me, as you well know. You saved me from the grinding depression I felt after Celia died, made me look forward rather than backward to what I'd lost. Your timing was perfect—my seduction, our marriage, and the honeymoon, when the time was right to see me blamed for what you and Carla had done.

"I see now Tash wasn't happy, and I ignored it, because I needed you so much. I'll never forgive myself for that. I'm going to make it up to him. If not for my son and that wonderful little girl Autumn and my brother—" He swallowed.

Sherlock said, "It's over now, Mr. Navarro. We'll take Sasha to a doctor, get her patched up enough to fly, and get you both back to Philadelphia."

Sasha turned to Sherlock, stared at her with hate-filled eyes. "If you hadn't come so damn early, I would have gotten away."

"Didn't work out for you, did it, Sasha?"

Chapter Sixty-one

Darlington Hall
WEDNESDAY MORNING

Elizabeth ate one of Mrs. Gamble's famous walnut muffins, warm from the oven, while she listened to her father and mother speaking low to each other. Since they'd come, they no longer sat at each end of the table, the whole table apart, but really a continent apart. Rome sat beside her, seemingly busy with a plate of scrambled eggs and bacon, but knowing him as she did, she didn't doubt he heard everything, was aware of even Benbett and Cook speaking over by the dome-covered trays on the eighteenth-century sideboard.

The earl took a sip of coffee, set his cup in its exquisite saucer, and said to her, "Elizabeth, your mother started visiting Tommy soon after you left, and I raised no objections, though I knew almost certainly he would disappoint her yet again. It's now over three months and I accept from both you and your mother that he's clean. I cannot forget Tommy helped us by providing you the alarm to install in the Bentley for your mother and connected to the police station." The earl paused, drew a deep breath. "I've given Tommy's situation a great deal of thought, of course, and now both of you have agreed, I am willing to meet with him. If he is remorseful, and he stays free of drugs long enough to convince me, I will consider asking him to start work with us at the bank. A newcomer's position, of course, at the very bottom rung of the ladder, but I hope he would welcome it. Perhaps in time, he might prove he deserves more of his inheritance." He looked to his right, to Millicent's face, now brimming with hope. "But I must be certain in my own mind, all right, Millicent?"

Millicent hugged her husband. To Elizabeth's pleasure, he pulled her close and softly kissed her hair.

Chapter Sixty-two

Even with the wipers going full power, rain bulleted against the windshield, blurring the world outside their rented car, but Elizabeth didn't mind. She was ebullient, so enthusiastic and happy she couldn't stop talking. "Rome, it's been so long, I guess I wouldn't allow myself to believe it would ever happen, Father agreeing to meet with Tommy and giving him another chance. There's hope now, nothing certain, but hope. I'm so looking forward to seeing him, telling him the good news. Mother told me she wouldn't call him, she'd let me tell him." She ran her fingers over Rome's raincoat, swallowed. He turned to look at her, saw tears sheening her eyes. "At breakfast, Rome, did you see how Father was sitting next to my mom? How he hugged her? Do you think perhaps they—Rome, watch out for that dog! Okay, he made it across the road."

"I promise I saw it all. Now I've got to focus, Elizabeth. I can barely see the road, and where is that freaking center line? My lifeline? When we left the Hall it was only sprinkling, but now look at it—raining so hard it's like the sky's split open.

He strained to see a road sign. "Okay, only another two kilo-meters and we'll be in Baggley-Cliff. I remember this stretch—

lots of curves and side roads. I'll try not to land in one of those ditches and drown us."

He had an instant to react when a large white van roared out of a side road and T-boned the Vauxhall's passenger side. Elizabeth yelled as the airbags exploded. Rome couldn't see, but he held on to the steering wheel and fought to keep the car from being pushed sideways into a ditch filled with water. He managed to pull them back onto the road. He shoved the airbag out of the way and yelled, "Elizabeth, are you all right?"

"Yes! What happened? That van—"

Over the pounding rain they heard the van doors open and slam shut. Rome grabbed his SIG out of his waist clip. "Down, Elizabeth!"

Elizabeth's voice was amazingly calm. "I nicked one of Father's handguns, Rome. Here they come, four of them—let's get the bastards."

He saw she had a 9 mm Glock. Well, of course she did. "Keep your head down, I'm going around the back of the car."

Bullets clanged against the passenger side of the car and shattered the window. Elizabeth shook off shards of glass and flattened herself in the well, then rose up and fired off most of her magazine. She heard a yell.

Rome slithered out the driver's-side door and elbow-crawled to the rear of the car. He could make out the white van through the deluge and four people walking toward them, with their faces covered. One was firing an H&K MP5, thirty-two rounds, the sound of it deafening, only slightly muted by the heavy rain. The others had handguns, and they were firing at Elizabeth. He rose up and fired at the man closest to him, hit him in the shoulder. The hit spun the man around. He screamed and fell, but then he rolled, came up on his knees, raised his handgun toward Rome. Before he could fire, Rome shot him in the chest. He collapsed onto his back on the road.

The others turned their fire on him, just as he'd hoped. He flattened himself behind the back tire an instant before a bullet struck the ground beside him. A dozen bullets ripped into the side of the car; another struck the tire, which hissed out air. He leaned out, fired back, fear and rage hot in his belly, until his magazine was empty. He slammed in his only other magazine and fired again, but he knew that soon, once it was empty, it wouldn't matter what he did. When Elizabeth was out of ammunition, they'd simply walk up and shoot both of them. He'd failed.

No, not just yet. Rome crawled to the back of the car again and reared up. Through the thick rain, he saw to his astonishment one of the men step behind the other two and shoot them both in the backs of their legs. They yelled and collapsed to their knees, their weapons clattering to the wet pavement.

"You bastard!" It was a woman's voice.

The man picked up the H&K, pulled the black hood off his head. It was Khaled Aziz.

He yelled, "Stay down, both of you, or I'll finish it. Put pressure on those wounds so you don't bleed to death."

Rome ran to the bullet-ridden passenger door, jerked it open. "Elizabeth?"

She was lying in the well. She gave him a maniacal grin, her Glock still in one hand, her other hand pressed against her neck. "Rome, don't worry, it's—just a flesh wound."

He saw blood snaking through her fingers and nearly lost it. He tore off his coat and shirt, pressed his shirt against her neck, lifted it only for a moment. "Okay, you're going to be okay, it's through and through, only a long gash through your skin." He closed his eyes for a moment. An inch inward and she would have bled to death.

She said, "That man who shot them, it was Khaled. What's he doing?"

"He's checking the two he shot in the backs of their legs."

Khaled came running up, pulled a cell phone from his jacket pocket, and gave his name and location, all in a calm voice, as if he did it every day. He punched off his cell, gave both of them the once-over. "We'll have help momentarily. Elizabeth, your neck—how bad?"

Khaled bent over to examine Elizabeth's wound when another bullet struck the car door, where Khaled's head had been an instant before. Rome whirled around and fired once, twice.

The woman yelled out, "No! Yusuf!"

Khaled and Rome ran to stand over him, lying flat on his back, the rain splashing on his black-hooded face, mixing with his blood, rivulets of red snaking off his body onto the pavement. He wasn't moving.

The woman was yelling curses at them. Was it Adara Said?

Khaled said in an emotionless voice, "I really didn't want him dead, Adara. He should have listened to me and stayed down."

She cursed again, her voice choking with rage and pain. Khaled walked over to her, went down on his haunches, took off his belt, and wrapped it around her leg. "Pull this belt tight or you'll bleed to death."

"I'll kill you, you bastard. He'll kill you."

Rome said, "Who is that, Adara? Your brother, the imam?"

She pulled the belt tight around her bleeding leg, still cursing. Khaled pulled off her black hood. Rome stared down at a young woman, her hair sodden and flattened to her head, the rain mixing with the tears on her very pretty face.

Khaled leaned close. "It's over, Adara. Who's going to kill me?"

She spit up at him, hissed, "Go to hell," and turned her face away.

"Stay down, Adara. Help is coming." Khaled said nothing more to her, walked with Rome back to the car, where Elizabeth sat against the bullet-ridden seat, her eyes closed, her hand pressed against her neck.

Khaled said, "I was an idiot not to check Yusuf for another weapon. I could have gotten you killed, Lady Elizabeth. Thank you for putting him down, Rome." He frowned. "But you know, I liked him. A pity the choices he made."

Rome said matter-of-factly, "I wish I hadn't killed him, because he might have told us who's behind all this. You have no idea, Khaled?"

Khaled shook his head.

Elizbeth leaned against the torn-up seat, stared out at the carnage, two dead men and Adara Said, her hand pressed against the back of her leg. It had happened so quickly. Life and death, decided in seconds.

Rome leaned in, checked her wound again. He closed his eyes a moment, then kissed her forehead. "Hang in there, kiddo."

"My plan exactly, Special Agent." Elizabeth didn't feel any pain, only a relentless chill. She saw two cars had stopped on the country road, waiting to pass. No doubt the police had gotten calls from both of them. No one got out to help or to ask what happened. She couldn't blame them. Through the blur of rain, she saw a man's face through his windscreen, snapping photos on his mobile. She pressed Rome's shirt harder against her neck, watched Rome and Khaled motion the cars to pass slowly through.

Chapter Sixty-three

Even now, as Rome sat beside Elizabeth in the Darlington Hall drawing room, pressing one of the earl's handkerchiefs lightly against her neck, the same thoughts careened again and again through his brain. If the bullet had struck her neck an inch inward, she'd have bled to death; he couldn't have saved her. And yet again, Rome shook his head. She'd be fine. She Would Be Fine. Adara Said was on her way to the hospital, Yusuf and the other man, whose name Rome didn't know yet, had been picked up in a coroner's wagon headed for the morgue. Still, even now it was over, the familiar fear broiled in his belly, and with it rage, rock-solid rage. Who was the "he" the woman Adara had yelled about?

The earl paced, his eyes never leaving his daughter. He'd canceled his planned meeting with the Home Secretary when his daughter had arrived home wounded. He said again, "We should have you transported to St. George's Hospital, Elizabeth. You must let us take you."

"Father, you've seen the wound," Elizabeth said for at least the third time. "It's only a gash, a small, shallow little gash. The last thing I want to do is drive off to hospital. We rushed back home rather than call you so you could see for yourself I'm fine.

Dr. Benton-Johns will be here in a few minutes, and he will agree with me."

Millicent managed a watery laugh. She stroked Elizabeth's fingers. "You're very brave, my darling."

Elizabeth sighed. "I didn't do much of anything helpful, just got myself shot. No, maybe I did hit one of them, but it didn't bring him down. I'm sorry, Rome."

Millicent swallowed. "If Dr. Benton-Johns believes you should go to hospital, you will go?"

"Let's wait and see, Mother. I'm quite comfortable on this sofa, and I promise not to move." Her neck was burning, but she could easily bear it, maybe because the aspirin Rome had given her was finally kicking in. Rome lifted the handkerchief he'd been pressing against her wound. "No more bleeding. And you're not as pale as you were. How's the pain?"

She poked him in the arm. "Get off your worry horse, all is good."

He wondered if he could trust her to tell the truth about the pain with her parents there. He'd wanted to carry her into the Hall, but Elizabeth hadn't let him, insisted she was ambulatory, thank you very much. "Everyone's coming. I don't want to scare them to death." Benbett was hovering soon enough, directing them unnecessarily toward the drawing room, but Rome let him do it, knew he had to feel like he was doing something to help. Even the cook arrived, flapping her apron.

He said again to her parents, "I don't believe she'll need stitches. I think sterilizing the wound and Steri-Strips will be enough."

She started to turn her head to face him, winced. "Mom, Dad, please, I'm not going to die. Dad, loosen your jaw and talk to me. I heard you speaking to Mr. Eiserly. What did he have to say?"

"Only that the van was stolen. He'll come back to me when he has more information." He didn't look happy.

Elizabeth gave him a grin. "Thank you for kissing off the Home Secretary to stay with me. What did Lord Corinth have to say about that impertinence? I mean, I wasn't dead, after all."

Benbett came back into the drawing room carrying a silver tray. "What you need, my lady, is another cup of tea. I brewed it myself. And Cook has added some sugar biscuits, as her ladyship suggested."

Rome smiled. Tea seemed to be the Brits' restorative for every condition, be it hysteria or a bullet wound. But he didn't leave her side. Touching her, hearing her talk, calmed him.

Benbett announced, "And finally—Dr. Benton-Johns is here, my lady."

Dr. Benton-Johns, a spry seventy-five, came striding into the drawing room. She turned her head slightly to see him, regretted it. Her mother noticed her grimace and covered her hand.

"Hello, Dr. Benton-Johns," Elizabeth said. "A pleasure to see you again. I will give you a dozen of Cook's sticky buns if you pronounce me good to go."

"Do not wish to go to the hospital, do we? All right, so we have a bullet wound, I'm told. Let me cast a sapient eye at your neck and make my pronouncement. Are the sticky buns fresh out of the oven?"

"Yes, sir. Lots of pecans on top."

Elizabeth remembered she'd always loved to hear him talk. His expressions were quite unexpected. She held her teacup between her palms and savored its warmth as Dr. Benton-Johns examined and cleaned the wound with alcohol, well aware everyone's eyes were on his every move. He reassured them all as he worked, aware the young man next to him—an FBI agent!—was eyeing him as if he'd shoot him if he hurt her. He lightly rubbed on an antibiotic cream, pulled the flesh together with Steri-Strips, flattened a small bandage over the strips, gave her a tetanus shot, and held out two bottles of pills. "Your neck will cause you only a modicum of discomfort over the next few days, provided you take two aspirin every four hours. You have a bit of tea left; take one of those antibiotic pills and two aspirin now. They will make all neck unpleasantness de-materialize in short order. No driving and keep your head still for a day and a half." He patted her head, rose, and smiled down at the lovely too-pale young woman he'd known since she was born. "I didn't bring a lolly for you, sorry. No hospital needed. Where are my sticky buns?"

Before he left, Elizabeth knew Benbett would tenderly place the sticky buns on a beautiful Meissen plate, covered to keep them warm, and put it into Dr. Benton-Johns's hands.

He nodded to the earl and countess but addressed Rome. "Since you are in law enforcement, I will assume Lady Eliza-beth's gunshot wound has been reported to the authorities?"

"Yes, and she's given them a statement."

"Then I need take no further action. Benbett, I daresay it's time for another cup of tea for our young lady, perhaps with a touch of his lordship's fine Oporto brandy. Now, if you don't feel tip-top in a couple of days, go to hospital. You will wish to consult with a cosmetic surgeon in any case to reduce the chance of scarring. Now I'm off. Mrs. Hudson is in labor as we speak. Thank you all for this unexpectedly exciting day, more for me, I daresay, than for you." He left the drawing room, with Benbett at his side, carrying the sticky buns.

Elizabeth was soon sipping hot tea, this time laced with brandy, and chewing on a sticky bun of her own, wondering which of her mother's Hermès scarves would hide the bandage on her neck. She closed her eyes a moment against the voices talking around her. She had so many questions for Khaled, the undercover agent, and for Mr. Eiserly. Most of all, she wanted to face down Adara Said, maybe put her hands around her neck and shake her a bit.

She heard Rome say, "I don't think the rental company is going to like what happened to their Vauxhall Corsa."

Her father said in his firm, crisp voice, "After they hear the news about the shootout, they'll be talking about it endlessly."

Millicent said, "Speaking of wounded vehicles, my poor Bentley Flying Spur will be repaired by Tuesday. Perhaps we should buy a more stately Bentley, like a Mulsanne. What do you think, Sebastian?"

Elizabeth stared at her father when he laughed. So handsome he was, even more so now he no longer looked scared and angry. He stroked his chin. "Or perhaps a Porsche, Milly—you could outrun all those unsavory malcontents."

Elizabeth slowly sat up, bringing everyone's attention back to her. "Rome, I want to go to St. George's after all. Not about my neck—I want to see Adara Said. I imagine John Eiserly and Khaled Aziz might be there. I'm hoping they at last know who is behind all this misery."

Rome wanted to order her not to move a finger, maybe take a nap, but he understood. He looked at that stubborn jaw, the determination. "All right, we'll go. Sir, ma'am, please don't worry, she gives me one frown and I'll bring her right home."

It obviously wasn't all right with her parents, but Millicent helped her daughter rise and pulled her against her for a hug. "I know neither your father nor I can dissuade you. But my dearest daughter, if you ever scare me like this again, I will deny you your favorite lemon biscuits until Christmas."

Elizabeth laughed. "May I borrow a scarf, Mother? Cover the bandage so a doctor doesn't grab me?"

The earl ran a fingertip over her eyebrows, kissed her cheek. "We love you very much, Elizabeth. I hope you'll have more luck with Mr. Eiserly than I. He said Adara Said isn't saying anything."

In a few minutes Millicent was adjusting a lovely Hermès

scarf around her daughter's neck to cover the bandage while Rome was in his bedroom reloading two magazines. He wasn't taking any chances.

The earl gave Rome the key fob to his Range Rover. Elizabeth and her parents stood near the front door, Benbett beside them, while Rome fetched the Range Rover from the garage. Elizabeth kissed her parents and slid into the car. Rome said to her, "If anything hinky happens, this time I'm going to get the neck wound, all right?"

"I think you'd look dashing in an Hermès scarf."

He put the Range Rover in gear and headed to the road. "I think it's about time we got this done."

Chapter Sixty-four

MI5 officer Theodore Bryer rose from his chair outside Adara Said's hospital room when he saw Mr. Eiserly, flanked by Lady Elizabeth Palmer and a tall dark-haired man he'd never seen before, coming his way.

He stepped forward, eyebrow raised. "Sir. Lady Elizabeth. You're the American FBI agent?"

"Yes. Rome Foxe." The two men shook hands.

"Lady Elizabeth, may I say I'm pleased you're all right. Sir, there are photos and videos of the aftermath of the attack all over the internet. The hospital switchboard is overwhelmed with questions from the media."

Eiserly nodded. "I'd be astonished if it weren't."

"Sir, the nurses are talking, too. Ms. Said is refusing to see her parents, and her father has already complained to the media, claiming his child was fired upon by hoodlums and threatening to call the Home Secretary."

Eiserly only nodded. He said to Rome and Elizabeth, "Officer Bryer placed a voice-activated recorder under Ms. Said's bed before she was brought in after a series of tests. We'll be able to hear and record whatever is said. It's quite legal, hospital is considered a public place. She doesn't know yet, but I've agreed to allow her imam brother up to see her before she's taken to surgery to repair her left leg. Perhaps we'll learn whether he was working with her. Is she lucid, Officer Bryer?"

"They've given her morphine for her pain, and the nurse told me she's awake."

Rome said, "Have you heard Ms. Said say anything since she was brought back to her room?"

"She answered questions the nurse asked her, that's all."

Eiserly looked at the scarf around Elizabeth's neck. "Khaled assured me your wound is minor. He was impressed with both of you."

Rome said, "Without him, we wouldn't be here breathing. My rental car is scrap metal, enough bullet holes for a war zone."

"A pity we don't have the other two alive, but perhaps Ms. Said will tell us what we need to know. We've already identified the older man who was with her as a Yusuf Ibrahim. We were familiar with him, suspected him for some time of plotting to skirt our Syrian sanctions for the benefit of his family's businesses, but something like this? A surprise. His flat is being searched as we speak. We should know soon who the other man was."

A nurse walked out of Adara's room. "You can see her now. I've given her more morphine for her pain, but she's perfectly lucid. You will have only about twenty minutes alone with her before she goes to surgery."

Eiserly said to Officer Bryer, "If any reporter happens to sneak up here, give him a good cosh if you like."

"Yes, sir!"

The three of them walked into a room with two beds, one of them empty. In the other lay Adara Said, on her back, her eyes closed, two hospital pillows under her head, her left leg slightly elevated and wrapped in bandages. Elizabeth thought she was beautiful, her thick black hair dry now and curling wildly around her face.

Elizabeth had asked John if she could speak to Adara first and he'd agreed. At his nod, Elizabeth stepped forward. She said quietly, "Ms. Said."

Adara's eyes opened slowly, focused on Elizabeth. She gave her a bitter smile. "You're like a cat, so many lives. I know I shot you, I saw you fall back, but here you are, up and about again, standing over me while I'm here flat on my back."

Elizabeth lightly touched her neck. "I understand your thigh is fractured."

Adara's expression remained impassive, as if she knew she'd run the race and lost. "They told me it's shattered, actually. They told me they will have to put a long rod through it. I'll be scarred and walk with a limp, perhaps for the rest of my life."

"Aren't you more worried you will spend the rest of your life in an English prison?"

Adara said nothing.

"Why do you want to kill me? I don't even know you. You even reached out to the United States, didn't you? To Ammar Aboud, a friend of your family's. Come, Adara, tell me why."

"Perhaps before you finally die, I'll tell you. I would have told you that night in your bedroom, if I'd only had a little more time."

Elizabeth said, "But you didn't; you and your partner failed. Now you're not going to have another chance. Adara, tell me who this 'he' is who wants me dead so badly. You can't possibly think whoever 'he' is will come forward, say one word in your defense, do you? He'll sit back and watch you declared guilty and hauled away to prison. Are you going to let him do that? Who is he, Adara?"

"Such a stupid cow you are." Adara turned her face away.

Rome stepped up beside Elizabeth. "Would you prefer to talk with Khaled Aziz?"

She slowly turned her face back to them. They saw a flash of rage, then it was gone, extinguished, as if she knew exactly what would happen to her now and she no longer cared. "That scum, that lying traitor? I was stupid, I trusted him too quickly. I hope he dies along with you."

Eiserly stepped close, studied her face a moment. "If you tell us who you were working with, the crown will be open to reducing your sentence."

She smiled, actually smiled at him. "You pink-faced English pig, do you think I'd be stupid enough to believe a word out of your mouth? As for you, Lady Elizabeth, you've already proved yourself nothing more than a lying whore." She looked away again, grimaced because she'd moved her leg.

What did that mean? Elizabeth stepped closer to the bed. "Adara, why did you call me a whore?"

Adara's fists bunched, but she said nothing, kept her eyes closed.

Elizabeth leaned over her. "Does it have to do with Samir Basara?"

Adara opened her eyes, looked toward Rome standing at the end of the bed. "You're younger than poor Samir, so does she now whore for you? Does she spread her white English legs for you so you'll protect her? Just as she did for Samir, for the jewelry he gave her, not that she kept it, she sold it. And I know why. Samir didn't care. He enjoyed using her. He didn't care a flick if she got buried under tons of rubble at St. Paul's. Go away."

Chapter Sixty-five

St. George's Hospital

John Eiserly, Rome, and Elizabeth were drinking tea in a small doctor-patient conference room on the third floor of St. George's Hospital, the door closed to mute the harried voices in the hallway outside. Elizabeth lightly rubbed her fingertips over her neck but dropped her hand when she saw Rome was watching her, worry clear on his face. She shook her head, smiled at him.

Eiserly's mobile gave a little beep. He pressed an app and listened. "Ah, here we are. The imam has arrived in time to visit his sister."

The imam's deep voice came through clear, rough with anger. "MI5 told me everything you've done and all but accused me of ordering you to kill this woman I don't even know. Why in the world did you do this, Adara? Try to murder an English aristocrat and an American FBI agent? They said even Ammar Aboud is involved? And Yusuf is dead! He's dead! Who are these people to you? What is this all about?" His voice grew fainter, then stronger as he paced back toward her bed.

Adara said, "It has nothing to do with you, Ali. If that's all you have to say to me, go away."

He said, his voice louder, his anger clear, "Ah, I see. My sister on trial for attempting cold-blooded murder has nothing to do with me. Our family's reputation will soon be destroyed, I will be destroyed, and it has nothing to do with me? If I strangled you right here, right now, few would blame me, least of all our parents." His breathing became harsher as his anger grew at her silence. "What is wrong with you, Adara? You're smart, you took a first at Oxford, you had everything a woman could want! Why would you do something as insane as this to me, to our family?"

Adara breathed slowly, in and out. She said only, "I was betrayed."

"Women who live like you, doing just as you please, are easily betrayed! Allah help me, I didn't think you were such a fool."

"You were betrayed too, brother."

That drew him up. "By whom? Who betrayed me, except you?"

"Khaled Aziz. Didn't the MI5 officers tell you? I trusted him because you'd vetted him. He's an undercover agent with MI5 at your precious mosque. And you trusted him. If I'm a fool, you're a greater one. He was there to bring you down."

There was harsh breathing and shocked silence. The imam said finally, his voice defensive, "The officers who questioned me didn't mention Khaled. Very well, so Aziz betrayed both of us. I did come to trust him, but only because Rehan praised him. But how could he have hurt us? There was little for him to find, except for you, it seems. Rehan never would have allowed him near the second set of books he'd kept for years."

Adara laughed. "Your conceit has always amused me, Ali. Of course you would have given him all the responsibility. You know it, I know it. He was that good, I admit it. I'm pleased you're going to lose it, along with everything else."

His voice was bitter, disdainful. "And you? You will be an old woman with no teeth before you are ever released from prison. You will have no family, no friends." His voice was quiet now, as if he was whispering in her ear. "At least tell me why you wanted to kill Elizabeth Palmer. Why should it matter to you if I know? The officers told me she'd only returned to England because of the attempted kidnapping of her mother." He paused. "Wait, you were responsible for that, too, weren't you? The countess, the wife of Sebastian, Lord Camden, a bloody earl! Have you gone completely insane? Embroiled yourself in some sort of twisted jihad? What?"

Adara remained silent.

The imam spoke to her in Arabic, harsh words that sounded like curses, before he switched back to English. "Our father can't save you from this. Even if he wanted to, he couldn't. I imagine he will bow his head and say you are only a woman, too easily swayed to betray her family. He will secure you the best team of barristers in England because he must, but they will not be able to save you. Do you think our parents will come and visit you in prison? That I will come?

"The media will crucify you, crucify our parents and the mosque, call into question the loyalty of every Muslim in England. You have plunged us into a nightmare, Adara, an endless, bloody nightmare."

When Adara finally spoke, her voice was thick with pain, but still defiant. "Unlike you, Ali, I acted. You were too busy enjoying your wealth and position, pontificating about the plight of our people, but too much of a coward to act yourself. You should have been urging the faithful in your precious mosque to join us to create havoc in this benighted country. Unlike you, I'm not a coward."

The imam was silent for a moment, and then his voice was more measured. "You know as well as I do this has nothing to do with jihad. Why Elizabeth Palmer? What is she to you?"

Adara's voice held only indifference. "I have no reason to tell you anything."

He sighed, said in a quiet voice, "I must know what this is about, so our father and I can know how best to proceed."

Contempt was thick in her voice. "I'm not telling you anything. Can you not figure it all out yourself, since you, Ali, are such an intelligent man, so committed to your faith, so honorable, so holy? You were given everything, our father and mother worshipped you, bragged about you incessantly. I've heard them recite that drivel so many times over the years I wanted to throw up. I always knew I was smarter than you, but nothing was given to me, I had to make my own way." She gave an ugly laugh. "Yes, I failed, but at least I tried. There's nothing more to say, brother mine. You want to know what this is all about? If you're so smart, Ali, why don't you figure it out?"

They heard the imam's breathing, deep and angry, but he said nothing more. They heard his footsteps retreating toward the door, heard him open it and close it behind him.

John Eiserly closed the app on his mobile. He sighed. "Amazing, this hatred for her brother. It's a pity she said hardly anything else."

Rome said, "John, there is another matter that concerns me. Revenge. Do you fear for Khaled Aziz's life?"

"Khaled will soon be on his way to Scotland to join a local mosque in Edinburgh. He'll be safe." He took Elizabeth's hands in his. "I'm sorry, Elizabeth. It seems clear the imam wasn't involved in the attempts on your life. We still don't know who brought Adara into this. As for either of these two, I doubt they'll speak to us again."

Elizabeth squeezed Eiserly's hand. "Thank you, John, for having Khaled in place. Rome and I have been talking, and now we must go."

John said, "You know something. Where are you going?"

Rome and Elizabeth walked out of the conference room without answering him.

Chapter Sixty-six

London

WEDNESDAY AFTERNOON

Elizabeth's fist knocked on the beautiful black-lacquered door. She felt Rome's hand on her shoulder.

It was all so simple, inadvertently out of Adara Said's mouth at the hospital, yet Elizabeth still nurtured the hope it was somehow a mistake. They were wrong, had to be wrong; there was another explanation. The thought it could be true hollowed her out, shattered her heart. Her neck began to throb and she welcomed it.

Tommy opened the door, stared at her. He gave a joyous shout, grabbed her and pulled her against him. "You're all right! Mother called me and told me what happened, that a bullet actually grazed your neck. I could hardly believe it, but now you're here with me, and safe." He kissed her cheek, pulled her closer. The sound of his voice, the feel of his arms around her felt so familiar and comforting, his scent the same she'd known for so many years.

He eased her back. "Sorry, I'm forgetting you're wounded. Mother said she'd covered it with one of her scarves. Yes, very stylish. Does it hurt? Are you all right, really?"

"Yes, yes, I'm fine."

Tommy looked her up and down. "Mother told me you were attacked close to Darlington Hall, like she was when they tried to kidnap her. What are the police doing? And MI5? Do they have any idea who's behind this insanity? I'm sorry, Elizabeth, of course you've already been answering all their questions. And you're hurt. Please come in and sit down, both of you, rest.

"Rome, I'm so thankful you were with my sister and protected her. Come in, both of you. I have some more biscuits from the bakery and some tea."

Rome looked around. "Where's your friend Al?"

"Al? He's in and out, but I haven't seen him today."

When Tommy went out to the kitchen, Rome and Elizabeth walked over to the wide window in the sitting room with its full-on view of the Thames and the London Eye. The rain had finally lightened to a sluggish drizzle. A sliver of sun was trying to fight its way through the clouds. A few brave riverboats had come out on the water carrying hardy visitors on their decks, their black brollies lined up like a funeral cortege. A tour guide was speaking into a megaphone, but the sound didn't penetrate the thick glass.

Tommy was back within a couple of minutes carrying a loaded tray. Rome and Elizabeth sat on his beautiful brocade sofa and Tommy poured them tea, offered them biscuits on a napkin. He sat opposite them, his hands clasped between his knees.

"Rome, again, I want to thank you again for watching over my sister, here and in the United States."

Rome said easily, "I can't take the credit for saving Elizabeth in the attack this morning. It all goes to an MI5 undercover officer, Khaled Aziz, a very brave man. He saved both of us, as I'm sure your mother told you. Without him we wouldn't have stood a chance."

"I hope I can meet him and shake his hand." He gave a boyish grin so like his father's, a grin she'd seen on his face since he was a toddler and she his big sister, always looking out for him. "Hey, maybe you should get a distress alarm yourself."

She forced the words out. "Your timing with that distress alarm was amazing, Tommy. What happened to Mother certainly brought me back here fast. You must have known I'd come."

He cocked his head at her, smiled, but said nothing.

Elizabeth sat forward, reached for his graceful hands, long fingered with buffed nails, like their father's. "Tommy, I have some things to say to you, things I obviously didn't say enough to you over the years." She drew a deep breath, looked into his eyes. "I loved you from the moment Mother birthed you. I held you in my arms in the hospital, snuggled you, rocked you when you cried. Of course, Father was so very happy. You were his long-awaited son. Looking back, I've come to realize I encouraged you to think you were the prince of the kingdom. I spoiled you just as our parents did. All of us gave you too much, never corrected you. We always made excuses for anything sketchy you did, even if it was obvious what you did was malicious. And then you went up to Oxford and you came back hooked on drugs."

Tommy cocked his head at her. "Why are you saying all this, Elizabeth?"

"Because I enabled your drug habit for years and I want you to know I'm sorry. My only thought was to keep you safe if I couldn't talk you into another rehabilitation program. And I knew if I didn't give you money, you'd owe it to dangerous street people, and to be honest I was terrified you might become a criminal if you were desperate enough for money to buy your cocaine.

"I should have continued to push you into rehab, but I didn't. I should have cut off your money, but I didn't. I loved you and

I kept making excuses for you. I convinced myself you'd stop taking drugs when you realized you weren't really living your life, you were existing, and only for your drugs.

"Every time you went to rehab, I tried to convince Father this time would be different, you'd change, but it never lasted. When he wanted to disinherit you, both Mother and I begged him not to, to wait, please wait, he'd see, you would change. But Father finally had enough." She felt tears sting her eyes. "I'm sorry, Tommy, I'm so very sorry for my part in what happened to you."

Tommy was shaking his head. "Stop blaming yourself, Elizabeth. I've always thought of you as my guardian angel, so please don't feel guilty for my own decisions. When you left, Carlos told me you'd given him enough money not only for my drug supply but for my expenses.

"Then Mother came to see me and for the first time we talked, really talked. I realized she and Father were terrified of what had happened here in London to you and they were afraid of what could still happen to you. She didn't think it would stop because you'd left. And who was behind it all? She cried, Elizabeth, and I sat there, high, unable to do anything, for you or for myself. After she left, tear tracks on her cheeks, it was then I really saw myself, saw what I was, and I knew if I didn't change, I wouldn't be good for you, for anyone. I would die.

"I stopped that day. I refused to see Mother for weeks. You know all about what withdrawal is like for me, you've seen me go through it in rehab. Honestly, at the beginning I thought I'd rather die, and I wanted cocaine so badly I would have robbed the king himself, but I didn't, I stuck to it. And now it's over." He gave her his grin again. "You're here and you're safe, both you and Mother, and you both say Father just might be coming around to welcoming me back in the fold, might be ready to trust me, finally." He paused, cocked his head. "I know you're supporting me. Let me swear to you, I will never go back to cocaine."

Elizabeth said slowly, her eyes on his face, "No, I don't believe you'll ever do drugs again." She paused, swallowed. "Tommy, when did you stop taking cocaine?"

He shrugged. "I told you, I made up my mind a few days after you left. Why?"

She didn't know how she got the words out, but she did. "I wonder about that now, Tommy. I wonder when it was exactly Mother told you I was in Maryland at Hurley Janklov's camp, because I know you'd talked the information out of her. You also knew when I drove to Washington to ask the FBI for their help."

"Yes, of course I knew. Mother saw how frightened I was for you. That can't surprise you. I wanted to help, I was desperate to help. Why do you bring this up? Why is that important?"

Even as he spoke, Elizabeth saw it in his eyes, eyes so much like hers—a flash of knowledge, of guilt. And contempt? She felt hope crumble.

Rome pulled out his phone, scrolled through photos, handed his phone to Tommy. "Do you know this young woman?"

Tommy studied the photo, slowly shook his head. "It looks like she's on a hospital bed. Who is she?"

Rome's voice was calm, calm as death. "You're quite the actor, Tommy, but let's cut to the chase. No more lies, no more playacting. This young woman is lying in St. George's Hospital. And you know very well she is Adara Said, the only one of Elizabeth's attackers who survived today.

"You knew you couldn't ask your drug dealer Carlos to help you find people to kill Elizabeth. He liked her, probably had a crush on her. So where to go? And then you remembered the last imam was involved in Samir Basara's plot to blow up St. Paul's with your sister in it. Surely there were other jihadists there who would want to make a statement, kill an aristocrat, and make money as well. And if they failed, the mosque would take the blame, not you. I imagine you chanced to meet Adara there. She was young, beautiful, newly graduated from Oxford, smart as a whip, and the daughter of wealthy Syrians, above reproach. You didn't approach the imam, no, you approached her and you had a plan.

"You made sure she found out fast just who and what you were—the son of the Earl of Camden—and of course her interest in you grew. You became lovers, didn't you? It couldn't have taken Adara long to realize if she played her cards right she might eventually become a countess, with control of more money than even her parents had, money she could do with as she pleased.

"I can see you luring her in, reinforcing her dreams, even driving her past Darlington Hall, describing its history to her, describing all the valuable furnishings and centuries-old artwork. I bet you whined to her it should all be yours, didn't you? But as things stood, you wouldn't get any money, it would all be your selfish sister's, a bitch who didn't care about anyone but herself, even slept with a Muslim, Samir Basara, to make fun of her family, your own sister, worth nothing at all, the only impediment to your happiness, to gain what was rightfully all yours. I'll bet you promised you'd marry her if she arranged to get rid of this hated sister once and for all."

Tommy grabbed Elizabeth's hands, enclosed them in his. "Elizabeth, you can't believe such a thing. It's all a story, made up, why, I don't know. But you must believe me, nothing he said is true. I'm your brother, I love you, I would protect you with my life. I don't know this woman. You can't believe this man, you hardly know him. He wants you and your money for himself."

Elizabeth slowly pulled her hand away from her brother's. Her voice was emotionless. "We showed Adara's photo to your doorman, Clyde Bettin, when we came in. Of course Clyde is loyal, but with the encouragement of a gratuity, he told us he'd seen you with Adara going out the delivery entrance several times a week since you moved in. He admitted he wondered why you seemed to be hiding her. He told us he saw the two of you laughing and kissing outside a café just down the street one afternoon. He said you broke apart when you saw him, and he appreciated the ten-pound note you palmed him later that day."

Rome said, "Maybe it'll make you feel better to know Adara didn't give you up when she was questioned at St. George's, but it turned out she didn't need to. You see, she let out something she couldn't have known unless you told her. Something that should have been so insignificant, really, but wasn't in this case. Only you, Tommy, only you knew Samir Basara gave Elizabeth the jewelry she sold to keep you in drugs and to keep you safe. Adara knew that, Tommy, because you told her."

Tommy jumped to his feet and began pacing in front of them, back and forth. "Yes, all right, yes, I did know her. I met her through a friend, through Al, but I didn't think Mother and Father would approve of my dating a Muslim, not after your fiasco with Samir Basara, Elizabeth, so we decided to keep out of sight for a while. Yes, she did want me to marry her, but whatever she did, I had no part in it. That's the truth. You can't believe this, Elizabeth, you must believe me, you must."

Rome spoke over him in a calm, steady cadence. "At first, like Elizabeth, I didn't want to believe her own brother would want to murder her. I know how much she's always loved you, protected you, provided for you. Even when we arrived, we weren't sure. There had to be an explanation. But the fact is you not only wanted to be reinstated so you'd inherit your share of your family fortune, that wasn't enough for you. You wanted your sister's inheritance as well. You wanted it all. So did Adara."

They heard the front door open. Al's voice called out, "Tommy, we've got trouble. Come here!"

Chapter Sixty-seven

Rome slowly rose, turned to see Al come striding into the living room. He slipped his Glock out of its waist clip, hugged it to his leg. He said, "Come in and sit down, Al. Why don't you tell us your real name? You're no more Sicilian than I am."

He stopped in his tracks, his eyes flying to Tommy's face. Tommy said, "His name is Jalal. He's a friend of Adara's and, I thought, of mine."

Jalal was silent for a long moment, studied their faces.

Rome said, "You need a better tailor, Jalal. I can see your gun." He raised his Glock. "Reach your left hand into your jacket and pull out your weapon. Carefully place it on the floor."

Jalal didn't say a word. His eyes never left Rome's face. He slowly pulled a Beretta out of its shoulder holster, laid it on the floor, and straightened.

Elizabeth said slowly, "Do you know, Jalal, I've had nightmares about that night you attacked me many times over the past three months. I heard your voice over and over again. And then I heard it again, when we chanced to meet you here yesterday, but it didn't register. Then just now? Yes, I recognize you, loud and clear. Who else was with you that night? Adara? But you were the one who held me down and wanted to cut my face. You were the one who threw your knife into Officer Bewley's chest." She looked back at her brother, who was standing motionless.

Rome said, "You left so quickly when we came yesterday because you were afraid Elizabeth might remember your voice."

Elizabeth looked at Jalal's fisted hand, at the ring on his middle finger. "That first time, the afternoon at Eaton Square, I was carrying a bag of groceries, alone, and you thought it was a perfect opportunity to run me down. I know it was you driving that day, too, Jalal. You're wearing the same ring. I remember it well."

Jalal looked down at the ring his grandfather had placed on his finger at thirteen, the ring that proclaimed he was a man. Bile and rage mixed in his throat.

Rome said, "You failed, and then Elizabeth left England. I have to admit I'm impressed with your commitment, though not with your competence. I imagine it was Adara who contacted the people in Washington who tried yet again, once Elizabeth left Hurley Janklov's compound."

Tommy said, "Listen, Elizabeth, I know that sounds bad, but if this man and his friends tried to harm you, it's on them, not me."

Rome never looked away from Jalal as he said, "Tell us, Tommy, did you and Adara discuss killing your father, perhaps a year or two after you were married?"

Tommy shook his fist in Rome's face. "How dare you, you bastard, you bloody American! Your accusations are absurd. Don't listen to him, Elizabeth. Adara, whatever she did, she did it alone, without my knowledge or consent. You have to believe me."

Jalal finally spoke, yelling at him, "You fool, shut up!"

"I'm not a fool! Elizabeth, I know nothing about what these people did, and Adara—it must have been her idea. She wanted to marry me, have all the inheritance. It was my fault. I thought Adara loved me. I wouldn't have married her, ever; she's not of our class. She's not English. This is all on her. You must believe me, I would never agree to killing you. Never. You took care of me for years. I always knew how much you loved me. I've always looked up to you. You know that."

Elizabeth felt tears sting her eyes, swallowed. She said quietly, "It's over, Tommy. We're going to call Mr. Eiserly. They'll come and arrest you both. You've broken my heart, Tommy, our parents' hearts."

Tommy straightened, and suddenly, he laughed, right in her face. "I suppose I was spoiled, a proper little shite. And yes, I did make the wrong sort of friends at Oxford, dear sister. But my friends didn't get me hooked on cocaine. I did that myself, and I reveled in it. I couldn't stop, didn't ever want to stop."

He laughed again. "But there you were, Elizabeth, always there, always ready to take care of me. You didn't think I knew you took gifts from that hired assassin Samir Basara, pawned them to ensure I had drugs, but Carlos knew, and he told me. He meant to impress me with how good you were to me."

Elizabeth said quietly, "You didn't have to try to kill me, Tommy. I think Father would have come around eventually, now that you're clean. You would have had almost all of it, the title, Darlington Hall, Palmer House. I always wanted you to have what should be yours, always, Tommy."

Rome said, "But that wasn't enough, Elizabeth, it never was. Tommy wanted it all. He wanted your inheritance too, and he was willing to kill you for it. I imagine he'll continue to blame Adara for everything, even from his prison cell. At least it's doubtful he can go back on cocaine in prison."

Tommy shook his head back and forth, looked at each of them. "How could you let this man, this stranger, convince you I'm guilty, Elizabeth? It was Adara, all of it. She used me, manipulated me to get what she wanted. I'm your bloody brother, dammit! Your brother."

"Yes, Tommy, I know exactly who and what you are now."

His eyes narrowed on her face. He laughed. "Look at you, all sad, tears in your eyes. All an act. You've always resented me, haven't you? You kept me in cocaine for years, and why? You knew I'd be the next Earl of Camden, knew Father would beggar me and you'd get it all. But that wasn't enough, you wanted control over me, didn't you? While you, the upstanding daughter, showed our parents you were the only child they could trust, the only one worthy of their love. And you managed that, didn't you?"

"Tommy, please stop this. It's over, all of it." She looked over at Jalal. "I didn't want to believe any of it before we came here, but now? It's all so clear, right down to Jalal's ring."

Jalal said, "It's useless to keep trying, Tommy, you might as well give it up. Imagine, she made out my ring even in that downpour. As for you, Tommy, you sound like a tosser and quite tedious. You want the truth? Adara wanted me near you to be sure you didn't slide back into your precious cocaine. But you weren't about to backslide. You knew exactly what you wanted, and you used us all to get it. Your death, Lady Elizabeth, would have filled his pockets to brimming." He slipped a small Ruger from the sleeve of his jacket into his hand and pointed it at her. "I'm close enough, Mr. FBI Agent, only six feet away. Don't even consider trying to shoot me. Trust me, at this distance I'll shoot her face off. Drop your Glock now."

Rome knew what his training required, but without hesitation, he dropped his Glock to the beautiful Turkish carpet at his feet.

Jalal said, "Well, Tommy, you assured us no one would ever suspect you, the grateful little brother, so brave to stop his addiction without anyone's help. But they figured it out, didn't they? And now Adara will go to prison. My fiery Adara, who hated all things English, wanted to be an English aristocrat maybe more than she wanted your fortune. But most of all, she wanted to prove to her parents she was better than her brother, the imam. She would be the Countess of Camden." Jalal laughed. "She had dreams of what she'd do with your money. Maybe she would have killed you—after, of course, you or she, or both of you, dispensed with your parents."

Tommy said easily, "Of course she wanted it all, we both did. She would have made a splendid countess. With her beauty and charm she'd have been the toast of London. Sure, there'd have been talk, just as there was when my whore of a sister here parted her legs for Samir Basara. She would have reveled in it. And her brother, the imam? He would no longer be able to look down on her as he does every woman, pat her on the head like a good little dog when she said something clever."

Jalal said, "He's a man, of course he'd consider her less than he is. As for you, I tried to talk her out of coming here so often, and so did Yusuf, but she only laughed, told us no one would ever consider Elizabeth's precious brother was involved. And you laughed as well. I admit I was amazed you were able to stop using cocaine, but you wanted your sister's money even more than she did."

He looked at Elizabeth. "Do you know, I trusted Khaled Aziz because Adara did. I would have been with them if only I hadn't had to be at my job." He paused, looked at each one of them. "So, Tommy, what do we do with these two? If they know, perhaps Eiserly knows as well. Perhaps he even knows they are here."

Tommy said, "It's possible. You and I will be all right if you do exactly what I say. We cannot kill them here, so call a couple of your firebrand friends, take these two somewhere. Make it so they're never found."

Jalal gave a short laugh. "I don't have any friends left. They're all dead, because of you. I do promise this, though: before I leave England, I will kill that traitor, Khaled. For Adara. You never deserved her." He studied Elizabeth's face. "Killing these two will relieve only some of my pain."

Tommy said quietly, "You called me tedious, you think I'm arrogant. Well, it was your people who were incompetent, you included, Jalal. You can't pretend otherwise. You tried three times to kill her, but you failed. And you can't put the blame for that on that undercover officer. Those first three attempts were on you alone."

He shot Elizabeth a look. "I will grieve with my parents when we're all told of Elizabeth's disappearance. And his. They will lean on me in their grief, and I will comfort them. No one need ever know." Tommy stopped, studied Jalal's set face. "You must know someone happy to rid the world of two infidels for a great deal of money, you medieval fanatics always do. Come, give me the little gun while you make the calls. Then you can leave with them, and we'll never need to see each other again."

Jalal said, shaking his head, "I don't think so, Viscount. I will kill these two, for Adara. But you first, you pathetic shite." He swung the Ruger toward Tommy and shot him in the heart. He looked dispassionately down at Tommy. "I always thought you were pathetic—selfish and greedy to your miserable soul." He looked back at Elizabeth and Rome. "I'll leave this benighted city. Sorry, but the three of you will kill each other."

As he reached down to grab his Beretta off the floor, Elizabeth jumped forward, kicked her foot into his chin. He grunted, reeled but tried to grab his gun. Rome pulled his knife from its sheath around his ankle so fast it was a blur and sent it straight into Jalal's neck. Jalal fired as he went down. The bullet went into the large window, spiderwebbing the glass. Jalal stared at Rome disbelievingly as he lifted his hand, lightly touched the handle of the knife in his neck, and fell to the floor.

Elizabeth dropped to her knees beside her brother, pulled him up in her arms, rocked him. "Tommy, no, no, please—"

Tommy opened his eyes, already filming with death, and gave her a twisted smile. "Adara called you a worthless whore. I defended you, at first." His head fell to the side. Elizabeth bent over him and wept.

Chapter Sixty-eight

Savich sat at his ease across the conference table from Carla Cartwright and her lawyer after introductions, a cup of tea by his hand. He'd said nothing as SAC Claire Gregson Mirandized Cartwright and turned on the recorder, reciting the names of those present and the date. Reggie Astley, Carla's high-powered Philadelphia criminal lawyer—with ties to the mob, it was said—then spoke in his commanding baritone.

"Agent Gregson, we're here because you threatened my client with arrest this morning on a charge of embezzlement of two hundred million dollars from the Navarro Investment Fund. You have not provided any evidence to prove this ridiculous charge, or even how Ms. Cartwright was able to do such a thing. Let me remind you, Archer Navarro is still hiding somewhere and is obviously the guilty party in this crime. My client assures me there was nothing you could have found in your search of her office and home today since she is innocent of all these charges. We are here as a courtesy, though it was very inconvenient for both of us. I believe it is time for you to tell us why."

Gregson nodded to Astley and said to Carla, "Ms. Cartwright,

I asked you to come back this evening because we have reason to believe you own a prepaid cell phone that hasn't yet been found in our search of your house or office. Where is it?"

Carla Cartwright gave her a blank look. "A prepaid phone? A burner? Why would I own such a thing?"

"We have irrefutable information that you indeed do, Ms. Cartwright."

"Wait, now I remember. I did buy one, some time ago. I got it as a gag gift for a friend which I was unable to give him. Of course I had no need of it and so I probably tossed it. I honestly don't remember."

Astley said, "A perfectly reasonable explanation, Agent Gregson. What are you getting at?"

Gregson said, "And the name of this friend?"

Cartwright shrugged. "Honestly, it was a while ago, I'm not sure. I only remember he was unable to attend the function."

"Asked and answered. Let's move along, Agent Gregson," Astley said.

Gregson said, "The thing is, Ms. Cartwright, Mr. Astley, we obtained a warrant granting us access to cell tower records near your home. We found that a number of texts had been exchanged between a cell phone very close to you and one in Europe, all in the last couple of weeks. Does that help you remember?"

Cartwright cocked her head to one side, touched her long fingers to the beautiful pearls around her throat. She looked the same professional, confident exec, utterly in control, in her stylish black Armani suit with a white silk blouse. She wore her hair in a chignon, as she had yesterday when Gregson had first interviewed her. Her voice stayed smooth and calm. "Why on earth would I text anyone in Europe? You think I texted Archer and Sasha on their honeymoon, after all that's happened? That is nonsense. It was someone else close, in a nearby area."

Astley said, "Agents, you know you can't tie any such communications to my client specifically. Your search of her local cell tower traffic is nothing more than a crude attempt to implicate her. It's Archer Navarro you should be trying to find, his brother you should arrest—again. My client has already told you everything she knows about this debacle. She admitted to you yesterday, after hearing the recording, she overreacted when Rebel Navarro visited her on Saturday, a natural reaction.

"Ms. Cartwright has been nothing but a trusted and loyal employee. It is her employer, a man she believed to be her friend, Archer Navarro, who is hiding somewhere outside the country to avoid arrest. Now, if you have nothing else, we're finished here. Ms. Cartwright was already exhausted trying to deal with everything that's happened at her firm, and now by your attempts to intimidate and implicate her."

Gregson looked down at her watch, then at Savich. He said, "Ms. Cartwright, have you ever been to Barcelona?"

Cartwright froze.

Astley said, "Come on, Agent Savich, why this ridiculous question?"

Savich continued. "Any plans to go to Marrakesh, Ms. Cartwright?"

Astley struck his fist against the tabletop. "Enough! If you have nothing more appropriate to ask, we're leaving."

The conference room door opened, and Sherlock, her hand placed lightly on Sasha's back, walked into the room, Ruth Noble and Archer Navarro behind them. She gave Savich a nod and a smile, passed over Astley, nodded to Gregson, then looked at Carla Cartwright. Cartwright wasn't looking back at her, she was staring at Sasha and at the sling on her arm.

"I'm Special Agent Sherlock. As I'm sure Ms. Cartwright already knows, this is Sasha Navarro, and Special Agent Ruth Noble and Mr. Archer Navarro. I apologize for being a bit late, but we had an emergency to attend to before we could leave

Barcelona. Mrs. Navarro had a bullet wound in her arm and had to be treated."

Carla Cartwright yelled at Archer as she lunged to her feet, "You'll go to prison forever, you thieving bastard! I can't believe you shot her. You're a monster!"

Mr. Astley rose slowly to his feet, obviously confused. "So this is Archer Navarro. I trust you will arrest this man, Agent Gregson. Not only did he flee the country, but agents were dispatched to bring him back. And now it seems he shot his wife?"

Sherlock looked from Sasha to Astley. "Mr. Archer didn't shoot her, I did. No choice. It's very possible she'd have shot us all if she'd had the chance."

"No, no, that's a lie. I only wanted to leave." Sasha cupped her arm and moaned.

Gregson stood. "We will deal with how and why it was necessary to shoot Mrs. Navarro, but we have other matters to attend to first."

Astley was smart and experienced, and knew he'd been set up. They'd come from Barcelona? Agent Savich had known they'd be coming, and so had Gregson. It was all a ploy to keep him and his client here until they arrived. Whatever it was they had come to say, he knew his client was about to be screwed. He cleared his throat loud enough for a jury to hear. "Feel free, Agent Gregson, to interrogate Mr. Navarro until next Tuesday, if you wish, but my client and I are leaving."

Gregson said easily, "If she attempts to leave, Mr. Astley, I will arrest her. Now, everyone sit down."

Sherlock smiled at him. "Please be patient, Mr. Astley. Agent Noble and I will clear up everything very quickly." She looked over at Sasha, who was staring down at her feet, looking for all the world like a teenager busted for drugs, defeated and pale, her hair in a ratty ponytail, a bloodstain on her white blouse. Still, she looked beautiful, like a tragic heroine. Cartwright was looking at Sasha too, trying to get her attention, and Archer was staring at Cartwright. It looked to Sherlock like there was both sadness and absolute fury in his eyes.

On the long flight home from Barcelona, Sherlock had told him everything his brother, Rebel, had done and how his son, Tash, and Autumn Merriweather had helped Savich find him in Barcelona. He'd said nothing and finally fallen asleep from exhaustion. So had Sasha, drugged to the gills on enough pain meds to be out for most of the flight.

Savich studied his wife's tired face. Even her usually bouncing curls looked wilted. He'd finally gotten the unvarnished truth from Ruth and his heart had nearly stopped. What was to have been a simple pickup, nothing dramatic or dangerous, had turned into a life-and-death situation. But he knew nothing was ever easy, and he'd hesitated to send Sherlock and Felicity to Barcelona. But her stubborn chin had gone up, and what could he do? When she'd marched into the conference room and smiled at him, he'd finally calmed. She was fine, Felicity was fine, and because of her and Ruth they were nearing the finish line.

Astley said, "All right, then, Agent Sherlock, Agent Noble. You brought Archer Navarro back. And Mrs. Navarro, wounded. What is it you have to say?"

Sherlock reached into her jacket pocket and pulled out a cell phone. "This is the burner phone Sasha Navarro had with her in Barcelona. Mr. Navarro accidently discovered it when it pinged a text. Let me read you texts going back to when Mr. and Mrs. Navarro landed in Paris on their honeymoon."

Astley, no slouch, immediately said, "Agent Gregson, we don't know whose cell phone that is, and it could very well have been tampered with by Mr. Navarro—"

Sherlock said, "Sir, please bear with me, the phone's owner will become apparent very quickly, as will its authenticity. This is the first text Sasha Navarro sent from the De Gaulle Airport upon their arrival in Paris." She read aloud, *"Here at last. I know*

what to do, don't worry. Archer can't wait to get me in the sack.
Love you. S.

"Here is Ms. Cartwright's reply: *Keep him happy, everything's*
set, I'm pulling the trigger soon. CC."

Astley interrupted her again. "Agent Gregson, this is nonsense, and inadmissible. We don't know—"

Sherlock said smoothly, "Mr. Astley, this text is signed with
your client's initials—CC—others as well." Sherlock stared at
Cartwright a moment. "And you, Ms. Cartwright, sometimes
you called Sasha sweetheart. And that makes it all clear—you
and Mrs. Navarro were more than friends, you were lovers."

There was dead silence around the table. Astley and Cartwright both sat frozen. Sasha moaned again, hugged her arm.

Sherlock continued. "The texts are quite clear, and I will
read all of them if you wish, but for now, let me just say Sasha
Navarro was waiting for Ms. Cartwright to tell her when to
poison her husband with an overdose of narcotics and present
herself as the grieving widow who had no idea what he'd done
until he finally confessed it to her, and no idea of where he'd
hidden the money he'd stolen. He'd killed himself, obviously
out of guilt and the knowledge there was no way he wouldn't
be arrested and disgraced. Ms. Cartwright here was waiting for
the perfect moment to order up his suicide."

Sherlock paused. "But things didn't go as planned. Everything
hit the fan with Rebel Navarro's help, and you texted Sasha to
get out, no way to get away with poisoning her husband now.

"Sasha Navarro assaulted her husband when he found her
phone and read Carla's final text: *Archer's suicide not an option*
now. Meet you in Marrakesh. GO.

"She knocked him unconscious, bound him in duct tape.
When Ruth and I arrived, she put a knife to his throat. Once
we subdued her, she confessed. And these texts clearly imply
the two of you planned the embezzlement months ago, well
before Sasha married Mr. Navarro. Mr. Astley, let me be blunt.

The federal prosecutors are going to lick their chops. Don't you think it's time to get the best deal possible for your client?"

Sasha raised her defeated eyes to Cartwright. "I'm sorry, Carla, I'd almost left when they arrived. He'd found my burner, so what could I do? They found us in Barcelona, I don't know how, but they did. I would have poisoned him, but you told me not to, so that's on you because you said to wait. Why?"

Carla Cartwright said, "Shut up, Sasha. For once in your life, shut up."

Savich said, "Here's the why, Mrs. Navarro. Rebel Navarro made a liar of your partner and she realized it was too late for you to poison him. No one would accept it, since it wouldn't make sense anymore. And that's why she told you to cut and run."

Carla Cartwright suddenly jumped to her feet, waved her fist at Sasha. "If only I hadn't listened to you about implicating Rebel Navarro! I knew then it was risky, and there was no need, but I listened to you, you stupid little twit! You couldn't even manage to hide your phone!"

Carla's lawyer stared at her, silent, stiff. Didn't she realize she'd just locked the door on her cell?

Sasha hugged her arm to her chest as a tear streaked down her soft cheek. Archer imagined the pain meds were finally wearing off, and he realized he didn't care. All he'd been was an easy mark, a man depressed and still grieving his late wife, and here this beautiful young woman appeared to worship him. He felt immeasurably exhausted, emotionally and physically, but at that moment, he saw Tash in his mind's eye, his perfect gifted little boy. He couldn't wait to thank him, to hold him, to breathe him in. He said, "Carla's right. Trying to make my brother look guilty was a good-size blunder. Rebel's the one who beat out the two of you. As for me, my only crime was being fool enough to trust you."

Chapter Sixty-nine

Plattville, Virginia
TWO DAYS LATER

Led by Savich, a group of special agents quietly exited their vehicles, weapons at the ready, their Kevlar vests snug beneath their FBI jackets. They knew from surveillance there were only three people in the house, so no need for a tactical team. Still, Aboud's bodyguard, Musa, was a wild card, very dangerous.

Savich knocked on the door.

The front door opened on Mrs. Maynard, Aboud's housekeeper. She took a quick step back. "What on earth is this about? What are you doing here with all those weapons?"

"We are here for Mr. Aboud," Savich said. He saw Maynard's hand move toward her watch and grabbed her wrist. "No need for an alarm, Mrs. Maynard. Alerting Mr. Aboud wouldn't be a good idea, for you or for him. There's no need for any violence. Give me the watch." But Savich himself unclasped the watch from her wrist, examined it a moment, and slipped it in his jacket pocket.

Savich continued, "Special Agent Lucy McKnight will take you to the living room and ask you some questions. Be honest, and don't forget, lying to a federal agent will send you right to jail. We know the way to Mr. Aboud's office."

They walked down the long hallway, past its display of

American antiques and paintings, to the big double doors. Sherlock didn't knock. She opened the door quickly, and three of the four of them came fast into the room. Ruth Noble stuck her Glock under Musa's chin before he could straighten from his chair beside the door. "That's right, don't move or I will have to shoot you." Ollie Hamish disarmed him and stepped back.

Aboud's hand went to his top desk drawer.

Savich said, "No, Mr. Aboud, don't even think about your weapon."

Suddenly Musa threw his fist under Ruth's Glock and sent it spinning to the floor. Ollie turned his own gun when Ruth quickly grabbed Musa's thumb and bent it back, forcing him to his knees. She stood over him, his thumb still in her hand. "That was rude. Now there will be restraints, and additional charges of messing with a federal officer."

While she was zip-tying Musa's wrists, Savich said, "Mr. Aboud, please press your palms to your desktop."

Ammar Aboud did as he was told. After two beats of silence, he said in a calm voice, "May I inquire why you have invaded my home with armed agents and attacked my bodyguard?"

Savich said, "Here is the answer to your inquiry. You are under arrest for the attempted murder of Elizabeth Palmer." He read Aboud his rights.

Aboud never changed his expression. He observed the agents dispassionately, spoke to them like a king addressing his troublesome subjects. "Is this about Lady Elizabeth again? I will tell you I've heard from a business acquaintance in London that it was her brother, Tommy Palmer, Lord Audley, who was responsible for the attacks on her life. I also heard he was killed."

Sherlock said, "Your information is accurate, sir, as far as it goes. As I think you know, too, others were involved, including Adara Said. You, sir, and her family have known each other for years. In fact, you've known Adara since she was born."

Aboud shrugged. "Of course, I know the Said family. Why would I deny it? Mr. Said and I have done business for years. If Adara Said was involved, it has nothing to do with me. What reason would I have? It's ridiculous. Is this about my Sikorsky again? You know it was stolen, I reported it."

Savich said, "Mr. Aboud, come out from behind your desk and place your hands on top of your head."

Aboud slowly came around his desk, his hands on his head. Savich quickly patted him down. Aboud glanced over at Musa, who was cradling his thumb, looking stoic.

Savich said, "Ollie, check his desk, the top right-hand drawer."

Special Agent Ollie Hamish held up a Smith & Wesson 9 mm pistol. He shook his head. "Are you so stupid you would have actually drawn a weapon on federal officers?"

No answer. Ollie bagged the gun.

Savich said, "We know your helicopter wasn't stolen, Mr. Aboud. You were covering your tracks reporting it stolen on the chance your plan went sideways, which it did. We did lie to you in our initial interview. Neither the pilot nor the shooter survived. The pilot of the Sikorsky has been identified as Ansir Hussein, a veteran of Assad's government forces in Syria. His DNA identified your Sikorsky mechanic, Ali Amin, as his half brother, also a veteran of Assad's government forces until two years ago, when you recruited him and brought him to the U.S.

"He blames you for the death of his half brother Ansir, who'd had no experience flying the Sikorsky, yet you insisted he do it. He gave you up without a whimper. Yet another poorly planned attack."

Aboud said, "May I put my arms down?"

Savich nodded.

Aboud said as he began rubbing his arms, "I understand now. As you know, my Sikorsky was very valuable. I think Ansir and his brother stole it and planned to sell it, after attacking Lady Elizabeth, for whoever it was who paid them. Ali Amin came up with that story to protect himself. You must have offered him immunity, an obvious ploy no jury would believe. If ever this nonsense came to a U.S. court, my lawyers would destroy him."

Sherlock said, "Mr. Aboud, we're well aware killing Lady Elizabeth wasn't your idea, that you didn't wish to be involved, but Adara Said gave you no choice."

Aboud stared at her, slowly shook his head.

"During our first visit here, I planted a bug on the leg of your desk. When we listened to the recording, all we had was a few words before it was destroyed. Our technicians determined it was a woman's voice, a young woman with a British accent. In London, Adara Said was recorded in the hospital after she was shot during the last attempt on Lady Elizabeth's life. It occurred to us it could be the same voice. Acoustic analysis confirmed it was Adara Said we heard. We know she flew into Dulles two days before your Sikorsky was used in the attack on Lady Elizabeth. The GPS in her rented Tesla showed she drove here."

Savich picked it up. "As I said, you didn't choose to try to kill the daughter of a peer of the English realm, but Adara knew something dangerous enough to force you to agree. In our search of your office our agents found papers in a hidden safe. They were written in Arabic. The translation is very clear, Mr. Aboud. You paid Samir Basara a vast sum to murder Admiral Lord Hawley. Basara chose to fulfill your contract by killing him in the bombing of St. Paul's last year. If the bombs had exploded, there would have been well over a hundred deaths and it would have been called a terrorist attack, as Basara wanted his men to believe. No one would have suspected it was done to kill one man, Admiral Lord Hawley.

"It was Admiral Lord Hawley who ordered your son's fighter jet shot down by a British missile fired from a ship stationed in the Mediterranean. He'd strayed too close and was considered an immediate threat. This was your first son, Mr. Aboud, by your first wife.

"When Samir Basara's plan to kill him by bombing St. Paul's failed, you arranged to kill Hawley yourself. You flew to London seven months ago, stayed two days at the Connaught before you flew on to Damascus, the same day Hawley was killed in a supposed hit-and-run auto accident."

Aboud's face was white with rage. "Yes, yes, I was happy to hear Hawley was dead. He was responsible, he killed my son. But you will listen to me—I did not pay Basara to kill him. I did not order him run down in London!"

Savich said, "Your barrister will advise you, sir. We don't know which of your crimes will send you to prison for the rest of your life, and I really don't care. We're done here." Savich nodded to Sherlock and zip-tied Aboud's wrists behind his back. Like Dillon, she didn't know which of his crimes he'd pay for, but it didn't matter. Elizabeth was safe.

Chapter Seventy

Navarro house
Titusville, Virginia
FIVE DAYS LATER

Archer Navarro sat beside Tash in his brother's backyard, his face raised to a cool breeze cutting the afternoon heat. He realized he was happy, and it caught him off guard. He remembered the shock when he found out the two people outside his family he was closest to, the two people he'd trusted and cared about, had betrayed him. Wonder of wonders, the shock didn't feel as sharp today. What was sharp was realizing his life was his own again. Today he was surrounded by his family and by new friends who'd worked to save him. He would owe them forever.

His brother and Ethan Merriweather were manning the grill with beers in their hands, talking about the Eagles' chances this upcoming season. He breathed in the scent of the sizzling steaks and hamburgers, even the light scent of the wrapped corn on the cob on the grill destined for Agent Savich, a man he wanted to be part of his life, now that he had a life again. He heard Sherlock laugh, light as a sweet kiss, as she talked with Sheriff Dix Noble, Agent Ruth Noble's husband.

After his first bite of a fully loaded burger Archer doubted the day could get better, until Tash leaned over him and swiped a potato chip through some bean dip, laughing like a loon at something Autumn said. Archer's arm went around his son and squeezed him, and Tash's smile bloomed up at him, wide and happy. He kept staring at his little boy, tanned and fit, strong, and what a talker he was now. That was thanks to everyone in Titusville, and especially the little girl next to him, Autumn Merriweather. He'd spoken at length with Rebel and with Autumn's parents about the gifts the kids shared, gifts he now embraced. He wondered yet again what would have happened if they hadn't found him in Barcelona. He thought of Celia, thanked her silently for giving him their son, their gifted son. He would take his clues about how to deal with Tash's gifts from the Merriweathers now, and from Agent Savich. They'd told him not to worry, that it would be enough for them to be honest with each other, and for him to love and support Tash as any father would his son. And to believe him.

When they finished apple pie and a gallon of vanilla ice cream, the sun had begun to fall in the blue cloud-strewn sky, giving the mountains a purplish haze. Everyone was still sitting around the table, talking—Sherlock and Ruth, the two agents who'd come to Barcelona to bring him home, and their husbands; Joanna and Ethan Merriweather; and Tash and Autumn, whispering in each other's ears.

It was time. Archer rose, cleared his throat. The conversations fell away as he looked around the table. "I want to thank all of you for believing in me. Without all of you, I might not be here." He looked at his brother. "Rebel, you used your magnificent brain to nail Carla, and you protected Tash, tended to him, loved and supported him. It's easy to see you and Tash have come to love each other—I didn't have to give this much thought. Tash, here's what your uncle and I have decided.

"I will leave you here for the rest of the summer while I try to set the Navarro Investment Fund to rights, woo back some clients if I'm able to. I'm hoping some of them will forgive me for my failure to protect the money they invested with my fund. Even though Carla refused to give the location of the money she and Sasha stole, it's being tracked, and some has already been found and returned.

"By the end of the summer, I hope to be able to cut down on my time at the Philadelphia office and work remotely." He laid his hand on Tash's shoulder, looked down at him. Everyone was waiting, waiting—

"I plan to move here to Titusville, and with Rebel's help, build a house for Tash and me. Tash will have both me and his uncle with him much of the time, and all his new friends, especially you, Autumn. Tash, you will stay here with Rebel when I'm in Philadelphia and attend school here. What do you think?"

Tash jumped to his feet and threw himself against Archer's side, hugged him as hard as he could. Archer leaned down and pressed his face against his son's hair.

Archer looked over his son's head at Rebel. He knew he'd never be able to repay him, but he'd try.

Everyone spoke at once. Autumn beamed pleasure at Tash, her thoughts clear as a shout in his ear. *It's going to be amazing, Tash. Amazing.*

Chapter Seventy-one

Clapper's Ridge, Virginia
THREE WEEKS LATER

On a bright sunny day in August, Rome, Savich, Sherlock, and Elizabeth drove into Clapper's Ridge, a charming small town nestled in a hollow of hills and forests, its cobbled main street lined with clever boutiques and cafés. According to Siri, Clapper's Ridge boasted ten thousand souls and swelled to twenty thousand in the summer. The air was fresh and sweet. At the town's elevation and under its thick trees, it wasn't even August hot.

They wove through thick traffic on Main Street to Bigger Lane. Elizabeth glanced down at her phone and said, "Turn here, Dillon. Serenity Cemetery is up this hill about a quarter mile." She grinned. Dillon already knew that, he'd entered the precise polar coordinates Wilson Ballou had hidden in his shoe and in his class ring into MAX's geocoding tool, and MAX had homed in on three adjacent graves at the Serenity Cemetery, all of them visible from space. It boggled her mind.

They walked up a graveled path toward the graves, all silent now, Rome carrying a shovel. There were no burials today, only the distant sound of a backhoe digging a grave off to their right.

As they walked along beautifully kept rock paths past the graves, Elizabeth put away her mobile and wiped away a tear.

Rome stopped, lightly touched her cheek. "You all right, sweetheart?"

"It's so beautiful here, I can't help it. Look." They stood on a gentle uphill rise and looked at Clapper's Ridge through a veil of thick oak and maple trees. She swallowed. "It reminds me of Tommy's grave at Darlington Hall. Remember how it overlooks a valley, too, with century-old oak trees?" And Elizabeth again saw her mother's face, white and drawn, as if all hope had been sucked out of her, and how her father had pulled her mother close, bowed his head, and whispered to her. So much pain, crippling pain. As they'd spoken quietly to each other, she'd wondered if the tragedy of what had happened had finally brought them together. Elizabeth had stood flanking them along with Rome, Savich, Sherlock, and John Eiserly, and felt deadened with grief and shock—her brother had wanted her dead. How to ever reconcile that? Now, as she looked through the summer leaves, she saw Tommy as a little boy preening when he kicked a soccer ball, high and sure, to their father. It was only when he'd gone up to Oxford that everything changed, or had it really?

Elizabeth's grief still bowed her. And her guilt? Had he come to hate her because she'd given him the money that had kept him in his pit of addiction, dependent on her? Or had it been about her inheritance and her money all along? She didn't know, and now she'd never know. And did it really matter that much now?

She thought of John Eiserly's belief that her mother's attempted kidnapping was a ruse, designed to bring Elizabeth rushing back to England, where she'd be vulnerable again, after Adara's recruiting Aboud had failed in the States. He believed Tommy had arranged for the alarm to be installed in his mother's

Bentley only to make it plausible her mother would escape the kidnapping. And what did that matter now?

As they walked past the hundreds of graves, tears still blurred her eyes. She felt Rome's arm around her. Throughout the days and weeks, he'd stayed close, comforted her, held her in the night when her tears broke through, just as he was doing today. She swiped away her tears, smiled up at him.

She heard Sherlock say, "There it is, the grave of Florence Torrence, Ballou's grandmother."

The grave was a bit sunken, but the grass was thick and green over it, the marker beautifully carved with her name, *Loving Wife and Mother*, and the dates of her birth and death. Another time, another life, with its own happiness and grief, like every life. Like Tommy's short life.

Elizabeth lightly laid her hand on Rome's arm as they looked down at the grave, and felt a spurt of excitement. "If you hadn't been such a bulldog, Rome, and woke up thinking Wilson Ballou's class ring might be the key, what Wilson Ballou hid here all those years ago would have stayed hidden in his grandmother-in-law's grave forever. I'm still betting it's uncut diamonds, ten million pounds' worth."

"Nope," Sherlock said. She patted her stomach. "Beau and I discussed this, and he thinks it's bearer bonds."

Savich said, "Are you sure it wasn't Felicity?"

She shook her head, gave him a smile. "Nope, it was Beau, loud and clear."

Elizabeth could only laugh at the ongoing joke between Dillon and Sherlock about the sex of their child. Bets were running high in the CAU, most going with Sherlock, the reasoning being she was the one doing the heavy lifting. She should know. Elizabeth was one of the few who believed Savich, since he always seemed to know things no one else did.

Rome and Savich took turns digging. They didn't have to

dig far before the shovel struck metal. Rome went down on his hands and knees and swiped away the soil. He pulled out a small metal box bound with duct tape and grinned maniacally. He cut through the duct tape and paused, looked at everyone. "Sherlock, you told us what Beau thinks. Elizabeth, what do you think?"

"A long-lost Shakespeare manuscript with handwritten notes in the margins about stage directions and costumes. That would be priceless. On the other hand, it could be diamonds, lots of diamonds."

"Okay, I'm with you. Diamonds. We're all in, five bucks, right? Savich, do you want to do the honors?"

Savich said, "Since you're the only reason we're here, Rome, have at it."

Rome slowly pulled the box open. He peeled away a bundle of thick cloth and a layer of soft black wool covering a waterproof plastic bag. Inside it was a layer of bubble wrap he couldn't see through. He carefully removed the wrap and saw a small, flat walnut box.

Rome slid the hasp aside, lifted the wooden lid. He pulled away a folded sheet of paper and looked down at a very old single red stamp.

Sherlock studied the strange stamp. "Well, look at that. No five bucks for any of us."

Rome opened the sheet of paper and read aloud, *"Avery, if you hear this note was found, it means things didn't go as I planned and I've no doubt died. This is my legacy to you. I wish I'd been a better father to you. Your dad."*

Savich took a picture of the stamp, texted it to the CAU for MAX's help. Three minutes later, he read, "It's the only surviving British Guiana one-cent magenta stamp from 1856. It was stolen in 1978 from the Ellison Tussey collection." He looked at them and smiled. "It's valued today at nearly ten million dollars. Either Wilson Ballou stole the stamp from the Tussey collection himself or, more likely, he stole it from someone he was investigating and they killed him for it. I hope Mr. Ellison Tussey is still alive. He or his heirs are in for a surprise." He looked at the note again and shook his head at the endless vagaries of life.

Chapter Seventy-two

Special Agent Ollie Hamish raised his champagne glass. "Here's to Rome and Elizabeth. May she speak with a sexy English accent for the rest of their lives."

"Hear, hear."

Rome laughed. "If our kids speak with her accent, I'll have to teach them how not to get the crap beat out of them at school."

Special Agent Lucy McKnight asked, "But how is that going to work? Will Elizabeth move here or will you guys live in England? Elizabeth's an artist, so she's portable, right?"

Elizabeth said, "It's true I'm portable, but I want to be close to my parents since so much has happened, too much." She shook her head, smiled. "Dillon, tell everyone what you've done."

Savich said, "Actually, it's John Eiserly and James Maitland who've made this happen. They've come to an agreement, a sort of Proserpine arrangement, Mr. Maitland called it. Rome will stay with us for six months, and then he and Elizabeth will move to London, and he'll work as an officer at JTAC, under John Eiserly, for his six months. It's a good deal for John since Rome has worked in counterterrorism. He'll also serve as our liaison. John is trying to be stingy, but we're not letting him. Knowing Mr. Maitland, he'll see the Brits loosen their purse strings."

Shirley, the CAU secretary, finished her sip of champagne and eyed Rome and Elizabeth. "Are you getting married here or in England?"

Elizabeth said, "Both. Because of the death of my brother, our ceremony will be private. Then we'll have another ceremony here with Rome's extended family and all our friends. I don't wish to be indelicate, but we do expect lots of wedding presents."

Rome hugged her, raised his champagne. "I'll drink to that. And yes, Hurley and his family will be coming as well."

Ruth Noble said, "Wowza! That's quite an engagement ring you're wearing. Just look at the ornate filigree and that single large elliptic diamond."

Elizabeth stuck out her left hand. "It belonged to my great-great-grandmother, Eloise, a celebrated belle of the Belle Époque who married a French marquis. After he died in 1910, Eloise moved back to England and became a leader in the suffragette movement." She pulled out her mobile and scrolled down. "Here she is." They passed Elizabeth's cell around to stare at a grand old lady with white hair piled high on her head and a snap in her bright eyes.

Agent Davis Sullivan said, "You're a lucky man, Rome. Not only don't you have to buy an engagement ring, you get to hear Brit spoken until you cock up your toes."

Laughter. "Hear, hear!"

Elizabeth smiled at the group of people who'd become her American family. She tucked her arm through Rome's, felt his familiar strength and warmth. She thought of the journey she'd taken, ending with a new life. It wouldn't be perfect, no life was, but she knew, together, it would be an adventure.

EPILOGUE

George Washington Memorial Hospital
THREE MONTHS AND ONE WEEK LATER

Felicity Sarah Savich was born on a cold, windy Halloween night at three in the morning.

Just past dawn, Savich gently picked up his daughter from the small crib beside Sherlock's bed and gazed into her blue eyes. She looked steadily back at him, but Savich knew she didn't really see him yet. Sherlock's eyes. He smoothed the curling question-mark knot of red hair that covered her small head and smiled.

Sherlock said, "Felicity—she's perfect, Dillon."

"She is indeed." As Savich rocked her, he wondered how long it would be before Beau Savich came into the world.